Also by Raymond Barnett:

Jade and Fire
Relax, You're Already Home
The Return to Treasure Island
The Death of Mycroft

THE
CHINA
ULTIMATUM

Raymond Barnett

iUniverse, Inc.
Bloomington

The China Ultimatum

Copyright © 2012 Raymond Barnett

iUniverse books may be ordered through booksellers or by contacting:

iUniverse
1663 Liberty Drive
Bloomington, IN 47403
www.iuniverse.com
1-800-Authors (1-800-288-4677)

ISBN: 978-1-4759-2693-4 (sc)
ISBN: 978-1-4759-2694-1 (e)

Printed in the United States of America

iUniverse rev. date: 5/14/2012

to Tam
fellow pilgrim along The Way

At the beginning of this new century, nowhere is the danger for Americans as great as in the Taiwan Strait, where the potential for a war with China, a nuclear-armed great power, could erupt out of miscalculation, misunderstanding or accident.

—Nancy Bernkopf Tucker,
Professor of Diplomatic History,
Georgetown University

The Taiwan issue is the only one with the potential to ignite a war between China and the United States. To the People's Liberation Army (of China), U.S. programs with Taiwan signal fundamental American hostility to the return of China to the status of a great power…We are coming to a point at which we can no longer finesse our differences over Taiwan.

—Ambassador Chas W. Freeman, Jr.,
U.S. Foreign Service (Retired)

mountain

Chapter One

Day One. *The Indian Embassy, Washington D.C.*

Philip Dawson drained his second Dom Perignon as he gazed around the embassy courtyard, wishing that a scotch was available. Carbonated wine was a poor substitute for strong liquor, to his mind. Washington's elite stood easily among the statues and fountains, giving no evidence of misgivings about the champagne or the canapes either, their voices rising above the murmur of cascading water. Many clustered around the television screen in the corner, where the Taiwan shipping tycoon Sung Lee was admitting yet another failed attempt to avert the impending war with China.

Philip's thoughts, though, drifted hundreds of miles away, to New York's Shawangunk mountains. Long stretches of sheer limestone cliffs. Digging your toes into tiny cracks while spread-eagled two hundred feet up the cliff, wondering where the devil you were going from there, as the sharp resiny smell of pines rose from the forests below.

It had been a year since he'd negotiated the Kashmir Accords whose anniversary tonight's reception celebrated. A year since he'd been on any cliff anywhere. He only felt really alive on a climb, yet he'd been fighting State Department bureaucrats in memos for a solid year now, without once feeling the hard slap of hand on rock. How could he have let the capitol's frenzied pace suck him in?

"Philip, dear. You're thinking of your rocks again, aren't you?"

Tiffany Hayes materialized in front of him. Blond, gorgeous, her blue eyes boring into him. She wasn't the Gunks, but at least she had another

1

champagne for him. She was another reason for the year without a climb, and she was damn near worth it. That scotch-tasting party she invited him to shortly after his return from New Delhi had started it all, and it had been quite a ride. He liked her, a lot, but her single-minded devotion to parties and politics just didn't fit him very well. Even if she was the granddaughter of the President of the United States.

He took the champagne and drained it. Tonight was the night to face up to some things, and if scotch wasn't available, expensive champagne would have to do.

"Caught me, Tiff. But no more dreaming. I cleaned out my desk at State this afternoon and I've got something for Talbin in my pocket—I'll give it to him tonight."

Tiffany rolled her exquisitely defined eyes. "Not another resignation letter?"

They both laughed, as Philip looked around for another champagne. "Yep. Except this one will actually get to the man, as soon as I see him tonight. And this weekend I'll be a hundred feet up on the Gunks."

She stared at him, suddenly serious. "You wouldn't."

Quickly her gaze shifted away, to the groups of people who timidly waved to her and Philip, not daring to disturb the capitol's most famous couple, the beautiful blond scion of a political dynasty, and the tall, rising State Department star with the ready smile, easy-going manner, and unruly brown hair.

"Elise! Brandon! So good to see you!" she trilled.

He nodded. "Yes, I would. And after the Gunks, a cross country trip. The Red River Gorge in Kentucky, Sam's Throne in Arkansas, Maple Canyon in Utah, then Yosemite. It'll take most of a year, I'll bet." A lopsided smile lit his broad face below the Roman nose.

"But darling. What about us?" she whispered fiercely, acknowledging the greetings of more couples.

"Oh. Well, I've been meaning to have a talk with you about it," he said, lifting his chin in greeting to a passing State Department colleague.

"Well, it sounds like that little talk's overdue, doesn't it?" she snapped. "Here comes the Ambassador. Try to get your precious rocks out of your head for a few moments, dear."

Philip grinned as the burly figure of Ambassador Ghandi approached through the crowd, his cream Nehru jacket accentuating his tanned handsome face, his silver ring beard surrounding a huge smile as he caught Philip's eye.

"Philip! And Tiffany. So good to see you."

"Ambassador. I do believe you're Philip's favorite at this whole gathering."

The Ambassador's smiled broadened. "Well, he's my favorite. The young man who guided and prodded the Pakistanis and us to an understanding over Kashmir that has lasted one year now."

"Secretary of State Talbin was the driving force, really," Philip asserted. "I just handled the details, kept the tea coming."

"Nonsense, Philip. You were the one who knew us well enough to bring us together, to keep us up all those nights hammering out your compromises. And did I ever tell you how key your climb of the Burudum Cliffs was, before the talks began?"

Philip's eyes lit up. "Oh, really?" he said, draping an arm around Tiffany's shoulders to make sure she heard this.

"None of us had ever thought those cliffs were climbable. Not only did you climb them, but in a time that has not been equaled since. We thought—if this man can climb the Burudum, perhaps he can bring us and the Pakistanis together."

"You're too kind, Mr. Ambassador," Philip said with a grin. "The record still stands only because your countrymen are too smart to try some of the dumb moves I made on that climb. I remember especially the end of the third pitch, where—"

"Didn't Philip stay at your villa before the talks began?" interrupted Tiffany, who had heard of that infamous third pitch of the Burudum more times than she cared to remember.

"He was our honored guest," the Ambassador answered. He put a large arm around Philip's shoulders. "He is, in so many ways, the son my wife and I never had."

Even Tiffany was speechless.

"Much rock-climbing recently, my boy?" he asked quietly.

Philip's grin faded, and he shook his head.

"Careful, my boy. The rocks are your soul. You cannot neglect your soul."

Philip cast a pointed glance at Tiffany and tightened his grip on her shoulders, just as the sound of a yapping dog rose above the din of Washington's elite gossiping.

"Ah. Tiffany's other companion, Daisy, has arrived," said the Ambassador as he stepped back. "And I see John Ravenhurst, your grandfather's close advisor, headed our way, Tiffany. Since I have sometimes wondered in public whether Mr. Ravenhurst isn't more intrigued by war than by peace, I think it's time for me to circulate. Philip, I'll make a speech that will embarrass you when Secretary of State Talbin arrives. Until then."

"I'm gonna need another drink," Philip murmured to Tiffany as the sharp, white face of President Hayes' chief advisor, John Ravenhurst, approached. Miraculously, a waiter with one champagne left on his tray materialized at Philip's elbow, and Philip eagerly snatched it up. He was lifting it to his lips when Tiffany firmly put her arm in his, preventing the drink from reaching its fervently-desired destination.

"He's the second most powerful man in Washington, my dear," she whispered while fashioning a brilliant smile at the approaching figure. "Let's consider that drink a reward if you keep your chit-chat civil, shall we?"

Tiffany extended her other hand in a warm greeting. "John! So good to see you."

Ravenhurst smiled a tight, smug smile as he took her hand and lingered over it. "My dear Tiffany. Sorry to be late. Your grandfather and I have been very, very busy with this Taiwan crisis. War and peace demand complete attention."

"We're so fortunate to have such keen minds as yours..." Tiffany faltered, wondering how to finish her sentence shy of maudlin, when a drumbeat of high-pitched yaps rose above the surrounding sounds. A moment later she was rescued by the arrival of her Yorkshire terrier. She withdrew her hand from Ravenhurst's to take the little dog from her maid, gripping Philip's arm ever more tightly for moral support.

"Oh, here's Daisy! Say hello to Mr. Ravenhurst, Daisy." She held the dog up.

"My favorite presidential granddaughter's favorite companion," Ravenhurst said with a sly glance at Philip. "May I present Miss Daisy with—" He deftly grabbed the champagne from Philip's hand. "With a glass of very tasty champagne."

Daisy lunged toward Ravenhurst's hand and knocked the glass sideways, spilling champagne all over Tiffany's arm, as she shrieked and laughed at the dog's antics.

Shaking his head, Ravenhurst let Daisy avidly slurp the few drops of champagne left in the empty glass. The dog emitted appreciative yaps between slurps, much to the enjoyment of everyone in the vicinity, save Philip.

"You know, John, I was really looking forward to that champagne," Philip said to Ravenhurst in a dangerously calm voice. Tiffany lifted her wet finger to Philip and ran it along his lips. "This will have to hold you, my dear, for now."

Ravenhurst shifted uneasily under Philip's glare. "Sorry about that, Philip. But comic relief is very welcome, when you're wrestling with the demons of war all day."

"China's ultimatum to Taiwan, you mean?" Tiffany said.

Ravenhurst sighed, deeply. "The only place on a very troubled planet where we're one small miscalculation away from a nuclear war. Yes."

"And working against a deadline yet," Philip said, tasting the last sweet bit of Dom Perignon from Tiffany's finger on his lips. It had a nice tang to it, he had to admit. "The President is going to send Secretary of State Talbin as the mediator the Taiwanese requested?"

Ravenhurst shook his head. "Unfortunately, Talbin is needed here, Philip, with Syria threatening to enter Iraq to support the Sunnis, and Iran pledging to enter the fray also. We seem to have wars erupting all around us. Dangerous times. Exciting times."

Daisy began wriggling in Tiffany's arm. When Tiffany couldn't quiet her, she turned and handed the dog back to the maid, who was from Scandinavia and matched Philip's six feet two with about the same height, although proportioned much differently. Philip judged that the dog and the maid about balanced each other out.

"Well, good luck to whoever you send to Taiwan," said Philip. "The poor bastard will have his hands full. Probably Baden, from the East Asia desk?" As he said it, an unaccountable thrill shivered up his spine.

Ravenhurst pursed his lips. "Perhaps. Several names are being bandied about. May I speak to you privately, Philip?"

"What? Why, sure."

"Pardon us, Tiffany," Ravenhurst said, opening his palms. "Duty calls. Good luck with Daisy, there." The dog was yapping excitedly as it tried to wriggle out of the maid's arms now, attracting amused stares all around.

Philip felt a little agitated, himself, as he walked away with Ravenhurst. He shrugged the feeling off. It was just champagne, after all. Still, he felt curiously on edge.

"The President would like to see you, young man. Tonight," Ravenhurst said in a low, dramatic voice. "May I send a White House limo to pick you up, in fifteen minutes?"

Philip stopped in his tracks. What the devil? He had only talked to President Hayes twice in his life, once when he and Talbin triumphantly returned with the Kashmir Accords a year ago, and then last Christmas, with Tiffany at a family gathering. His heart was racing—surely not over what Ravenhurst had said? He focused his mushrooming mind on Ravenhurst.

"Why, of course I'll come. In fifteen minutes? What about?"

"Good. I'll see you there." Ravenhurst glided off.

Philip put his hand on a nearby table to steady himself. Yes. His heart was definitely racing, and he fought an urge to dash around the courtyard. What the hell was going on? His face felt hot, and his right leg began to twitch.

"Philip. Are you all right?" he heard Tiffany say beside him.

Philip laughed a tight, humorless laugh. "I don't know. I feel…like everything's going fast. Excited. Weird."

"Too much champagne, I think," laughed Tiffany, putting her arm in his.

A real laugh now, from Philip, although much too loud. "Not this boy, on only three glasses. What was in that last glass, anyway?"

Tiffany stopped laughing. "Whatever it was, it got poor Daisy in a tither, also. I had to send her home with Katrina, she was making such a nuisance of herself. Are you all right, Philip?" she asked again.

He rubbed his forehead. "I don't know. I've gotta move. You socialize while I walk around. I'm meeting your grandfather in fifteen minutes, and I'd better feel a hell of a lot more focused than I do now."

"Really? Whatever about?"

"Ravenhurst wouldn't say. Probably just a photo op, to get some publicity out of the Kashmir Accord anniversary." He looked around the room. "I gotta move. Keep an eye on me, huh? Don't let me collapse or anything. But if I do, send a St. Bernard with scotch to the rescue. No more champagne."

He moved off a few steps, unsteadily. "And if you see Talbin arrive, come and get me. I've gotta get this letter in his hands before I change my mind."

sea

Chapter Two

Hsiao Lung Bay, the northeast coast of Taiwan. Dawn

Meiling Bei pulled hard on the steering wheel, forcing the red Miata through the last tight curve on the mountain road, then let the wheel slide smoothly through her hands as it straightened out and the car shot onto the coastal road and immediately banked steeply down to the shore. The newspaper on the side seat slid toward the door. She stopped its movement with one hand, and grinned at the hollow feeling in her guts as the car entered the downhill bank, thinking back to the roller coaster half an hour north of Berkeley. With Tom Ling. Back when she was in love and he was alive.

Tires squealing, she turned into the parking lot at the shore and slid to a halt. She sat there, exulting in the rush that came from the melding of eye, mind, and hands forcing her car from Taipei to here in less than an hour. Here. She drank in the waves lapping the sand, the dark bank of clouds offshore to the east, jagged shards of pink breaking through at a dozen spots along the sea horizon. As she sat, she traced the change spreading over her sleek body, the quiet calm replacing the rush. She liked both. She liked being alive.

When she was relaxed, she took the keys from the ignition, her eyes involuntarily straying to the headlines of the newspaper angled on the side seat. Large black characters told of the continuing impasse in the reunification talks, beside a photo of Taiwan's negotiator Sung Lee grimly striding past one of the huge columns of the Sun Yat-sen Memorial. A color map showed the position of Chinese forces massing on the Fujian coast, 112 miles west of here, red arrows pinpointing the 1200 missiles, green the airfields where stealth-shrouded jet fighters sat, awaiting the deadline China had imposed, only nine days away.

Plenty of time for that world, later, she thought. Missiles, bombs, and the Shen clan conglomerate puzzle. But now, she was here. She took off the light jacket over her black bathing suit, and dropped it on the seat, atop the paper. A dozen fluid steps brought her to the ocean, and she stood ankle deep in the water, inhaling the fresh chill air, studying again the shafts of pink breaking through the dark clouds. What brush strokes would she use to build the clouds up like that? Was there some yellow in that pink light? The water slapping against her calves was cold at first, then warm compared to the wind on the wet skin.

Sea gulls flapped past her, their raucous calls smothered by the swooshing of the incoming waves. She shifted to stay balanced as the sand dissolved under her feet with each incoming wave. A soft laugh. The sea playing with her already. For the first time this day she thanked Ma Tsu, goddess of the sea and protector of sailors and women, for the sea and the pleasures it brought her. Her patron goddess, her Ma Tsu, who had guided her through so much in her thirty years.

She moved another dozen steps into the water, then launched herself in a flat dive and with smooth, methodical strokes pulled away from the beach. She swam hard to counter the sudden cold shock of the water, and within a minute was fifty feet out at a twenty foot depth. She turned, and soon was swimming parallel to the beach. Her body pulsed with the familiar sensations: the steady pull then stretch of her arm and leg muscles, the cold bite of the water, the strong sea smell in her nostrils as she lifted her head for air every third stroke, the blue sheen of the water out of the corner of her eyes as she sucked in the air.

She was laughing. At the pleasure of the sensations. At being in the sea. At being young and strong. Alone, yes. But alive. Cavorting with the sea goddess Ma Tsu. The laughter trailed off as she felt the first tug of a riptide, then the strong surge as the massive body of water pushed her away from the shore, spawned by the ever-changing combination of wind, currents, and underwater terrain. The tempo and exertion of her strokes jumped a notch as she reasserted her course parallel to the shore, perpendicular to the rip's push. She swam hard for ten minutes before she escaped the riptide, and was so far out that she couldn't see the shore. That caused a moment of alarm, but she put the dark clouds obscuring the sunrise to her back and swam steadily to the west for another ten minutes, finally sighting cliffs above the shore, then the palm trees along it.

She was exhausted and her arms wooden by the time she studied the near but unfamiliar shore, saw the great roars of spray as the waves broke against rocks there. She scanned the shore right and left. There. To the right, an area with no spray. *Ma Tsu, let it be a safe passage between rocks.* She swam stiffly for it, and let the waves push her into the passageway. She feebly kicked but mainly the incoming wave pushed her in, and her knees banged against rocks. Then she was tossed onto a narrow rocky beach, and deposited roughly on cobble-sized stones as the water receded. She lay there, exhausted.

Another wave came in and crashed over her, rolling her several times on the rocks. She pushed herself up with a groan and crawled on her knees another ten feet away from the water, and with a grunt sat down on the cobbles, facing the sea. Never turn your back on the sea, she thought. *I love you, Ma Tsu. I love your sea. Riptides, even. But you are a stern goddess. Like life. Rich. Beautiful. But demanding respect, and an alert eye.*

She sat there on the cobbles, mind and body numb from her exertions, her bruised knees aching. Tom Ling's face appeared in her mind. They had planned to marry, have a family. The old, deep panic feeling swept over her, the panic of being alone, and of dying barren, with no one to mourn her and carry part of her into the future. She let the tears come, let the nausea well up, the trembling sweep over her. Sobs wracked her body for a minute, then another. Then she took a deep breath, and gave her panic to the universe. Here, the sea was green with a hint of aquamarine, white as it washed ashore. Here, things were as they should be in the world. Ma Tsu would look after her, she reminded herself. Surely. She wearily climbed to her feet and began limping her way south along the shore.

In fifteen minutes she saw her beach, with the tide pool she liked to explore between her and the beach. Two figures bent over in the tide pool, a mother and her daughter, by the looks of them, collecting limpets or the small abalone, probably. The little girl saw her first, and waved as she tugged on her mother's shirt. The mother stood up as she approached, a young woman, pretty, a yellow bucket in her hand. With a start she recognized the mother as Sung Lee's mistress. One of the two. Meiling had seen her at his seaside mansion not far from here, earlier this year when she was doing a story on the shipping tycoon. Back before China had changed everything by imposing the deadline for reunification, and Taiwan's president had tabbed Sung Lee as the wretched man to grapple with the nightmare for them all.

"Hello. You must not be seeing much of Mr. Lee these days," Meiling said as she limped within talking range.

The mother's smile froze and her hand drifted to the black front pack she wore, resting lightly on it. She has a gun in there, Meiling thought with a shock. Of course. Sung Lee's mistress wouldn't just wander the coast without protection. Meiling looked around. No, no bodyguards. A car was parked high up, on the hairpin curve. Probably there. She noticed another car, higher up. Two body guards?

Her eyes returned to the mistress, who was warily staring at her, hand on the front pack. Could she get a story out of this? Taiwan's negotiator wrestling with the demands of the giant China as his young mistress wanders on the seashore with their daughter? She totaled it up. This would be, what? His seventh daughter? She glanced at the girl, who had wandered into a portion of the tide pool with an abundance of coral.

"Be careful!" Meiling called out to the mother. "Your girl. That pool has the little octopus, of the blue rings."

"Syau Loo! Away from there!" the mother said sharply. The girl jerked and scampered away, kicking up small sprays of water which glistened silver in the slanting rays of the growing light.

"Thank you," the woman said, frowning. "I've heard the blue-ringed one is bad."

"But not aggressive, thank goodness. Still…"

"Syau Loo can pester me, she can certainly pester a little octopus."

They both laughed.

"Good hunting," she said to the mother, and waved to the little girl. No, you can't make a story out of 'Life goes on, as Sung Lee tries to ward off the threatening China monster.' She wondered if the Americans would really send a mediator to help with the impasse, as Taiwan's president had requested three days ago.

Meiling limped to the beach. She claimed her clothes from the car, showered under the freshwater nozzle, and changed into her blouse and suit in the beachhouse. As she spread her swimsuit to dry on the back of the car's side seat, she noticed the green light blinking on her message machine. She punched the button as she ran a comb through her damp hair. It was short, and would dry quickly.

"Ah, Miss Bei," an unpleasant voice rattled from the machine. The Managing Editor. "You're usually back from your swim by now," continued the harsh voice. "Someday you're going to drown yourself and cause me the trouble of replacing you. Don't you realize how hard it is to find a decent reporter these days? Well, assuming you are still alive and listening, the Publisher has given me a special message for you. You're off the Shen clan conglomerate investigation. Yes, they are complaining of you and your snooping around. Which makes us worried for your safety. Murder is very much part of old Shen's business plan, and it's hard to replace a good reporter, as I said. The Publisher has another assignment for you. It's about the reunification negotiations. Seems the Americans are in fact going to provide a mediator, although we don't have his name yet. Surprisingly, China has agreed to it. I'll give you more details. Be here at ten. See you then. And don't get yourself drowned, Miss Bei."

mountain

Chapter Three

Washington, D.C. The White House

President Hayes and Ravenhurst were staring at a television as Philip was escorted into the study off the Oval Office. Hitting the mute, the President motioned Philip to one of two pink and white damask chairs fronting his oak desk, which was littered with haphazard stacks of paper.

"Good to see you, Philip. You know John Ravenhurst, I assume." Philip nodded as Ravenhurst took the other chair. Outside the social setting of the Indian Embassy, Ravenhurst looked every bit the former CIA Director he was, a brilliant strategy analyst with nary a single restraining moral scruple. Actually, that didn't bother Philip, certainly not as much as the President's sloppy desk.

"Hello, John," Philip said affably, remembering Tiffany's advice to be civil. Thankfully the agitation and racing heart had passed several minutes ago. He needed a vacation. Which was mercifully about to begin, since he had thrust his resignation letter into Secretary of State Talbin's hand before he had left the Indian Embassy.

Ravenhurst gravely nodded, and fixed Philip in his gaze, his head swinging side to side. Since Philip rather liked snakes, he found Ravenhurst interesting. Dangerous, to be sure. But you just treated him like any deadly reptile. Be wary and keep your distance. Gaboon viper, he thought, as the head oscillated. No, more whip-like. He noted the man's trademark loud tie, overlooked at the reception. Bright red with yellow stars. Coral snake, then. Red and black, good jack. Red and yellow, kill a fellow.

"Philip, you're probably wondering why I wanted to see you," the President resumed as he lowered himself into the chair behind the desk. Philip loved the President's mellow voice. Smooth as blended Scotch, as he'd described it to Tiffany. The President was a big man, with a shock of white hair above his ruddy face. He looked every inch a President, and sounded like one, too.

"Our friends on Taiwan have asked for a mediator to help them deal with communist China's ultimatum for reunification. It's going to be a tough assignment."

Philip wondered what this had to do with him. But it felt bad.

"Taiwan doesn't want to give up the freedom they've flourished under all these years. We can't let the Chinese swallow Taiwan." The big man warmed to the subject, rising from his chair like a whale breaching water, so engrossed he left the remote behind. "Taiwan stands for everything we stand for. Democracy, capitalism, freedom."

Philip cleared his throat. "Sir, all true. But may I ask what it has to do with me?"

The President turned to face Philip. "I want you to be the mediator, Philip. To go to Taiwan and find some way to satisfy China without sacrificing Taiwan's freedom."

Philip usually liked surprises. Not this one, though.

"Uh, sir. I can't do that. I don't know much about China. In fact, I've just resigned my post at State, to pursue some other interests." A wave of desire rippled through him, a lust for the hard, honest slap of rock against his hand that he could sense was about to be stolen from him. He badly needed to get back to his climbing. "So, I'm sorry. But no."

"You majored in Chinese history at Yale, I believe?" he heard Ravenhurst say from his side.

"I concentrated on China and India, both. But everything I know about China is book-learning. I've lived in India. My roommate at Yale was the son of a rajah, and I spent a couple of summers training hawks on his family's estates." He was scrambling, desperate for a solid reason to turn down the assignment.

"Philip, you're our best negotiator," persisted the President. "You showed that in New Delhi a year ago. This is going to be a tough one. We need your skills and experience."

"But that's the point, Mr. President. I know India, knew the issues inside-out last year. Hell, I already knew most of the negotiators on both sides, knew what they liked to drink, what kind of women they liked to sleep with. China? It's been years since I've paid any attention to it."

"We'll give you Baden, from the East Asia desk, plus Baden's specialists. And Talbin says you can have Assistant Secretary Dirk on your team, as well, to add heft to it. They can bring you up to speed."

Again, Ravenhurst from the side. "Your grandfather was a clergyman and a peace-maker, wasn't he? Bringing people together who were in conflict?"

"Yeah, a missionary to China in the thirties, then back home during the civil rights movement."

"China and Taiwan are on the brink of war," Ravenhurst pressed. "Actually, it's brilliant timing on China's part. We thought we were out of Iraq, when the new Sunni regime in Syria threatens to jump in and protect the Iraqi Sunnis. Naturally, that sets off Iran, protecting the Iraqi Shiites. We can't let everything we accomplished in Iraq be jeopardized, can we? Plus the Taliban are about to take over again in Afghanistan—that needs attention—"

Ravenhurst leaned back in his chair, tenting his fingers as he continued. "So maybe we are a bit preoccupied, and stretched a bit thin. We certainly don't have much to help Taiwan with. China knows that. Is trying to exploit it, feeling much too confident since our troubles with the recession of '08 and the ongoing deficit crisis. China's riding much too high, and needs to be taken down a notch. Your job is to devise some reunification formula that keeps Taiwan free and independent, and somehow persuade China to live with it. And to let China know that if they refuse to bend, we'll support Taiwan with the only thing we currently have available—our nuclear arsenal."

Philip sat stock still, his reeling mind suddenly supremely focused. Had Ravenhurst really threatened a nuclear war?

He looked to the President, standing behind his desk.

"Is this true, Mr. President? Nuclear war if we don't get what we want?"

The president stared somberly at Philip, then nodded his head.

Philip exhaled. Goddamn it. I hate old men who bandy war about as a policy option, he thought. Especially nuclear war. Whether it's on the Indian subcontinent or Taiwan. He groaned at the thought of what he was about to put off. He saw himself as a boy climbing the rugged granite cliff outside his hometown in Vermont, his grandfather belaying the ropes.

There was the rub. His grandfather wouldn't let him turn this down. Dead more than a decade, but still with him. Grandpa had given Philip the tools and the passion to help people, to bring them together, just as he had in China and Vermont. This was another chance to make a difference. Just like in New Delhi. He exhaled again, and heard himself say the words.

"Yeah, Mr. President. I'll take it on."

Hayes breathed a sigh of relief. Philip didn't look at Ravenhurst. As the President began to speak, Philip cut him off.

"Let me review my understanding of our position, Mr. President. Me and Baden and Dirk are to come up with some formula that satisfies China's desire for official reunification of Taiwan, but that in fact retains the functional independence of Taiwan. And to let China know that we will not tolerate the use of force against Taiwan in any event, and reserve the right to respond with our nuclear arsenal, if need be."

The President nodded. "Not that Taiwan needs much help from us. Thank God George Bush sold them all those F-16s back in '92. Hell, even Clinton came through, with Stinger ground-to-air missiles, Super Cobra attack helicopters, antisubmarine missiles."

"Plus three Knox-class frigates," Ravenhurst added. "And George W. gave them four Kidd-class destroyers, eight submarines, and a dozen P-3 Orion submarine hunters, then topped if off in 2008 with 30 Apache attack helicopters and over 300 Patriot missiles."

"Obama added a hundred more Patriot missiles and 60 Black Hawk helicopters to round things off," the President concluded. "Plus some minesweepers and Harpoon missiles, and upgrading the F-16s."

"Impressive firepower," commented Philip. "How much of this weaponry, and command structure wielding it, do we need retained by Taiwan?"

"Most or all," the President snapped. His face turned red. "You can't very well be functionally independent if the other fella is armed and you're not."

"And the specific forms of union we're comfortable with?" Philip asked.

The President waved his hand impatiently. "Baden on the Far East desk will let you know where we are on that. And all the other concerns. It's incredibly complex."

"Well, no more complex than in New Delhi last year, I suppose," said Philip.

The President fixed him with a heavy stare. "That's just it, Philip. Huddle with Baden and Dirk and the team. Get all the details in your head. But remember what I said. Functional independence. In every respect. Or there's no deal."

"Well, it won't be easy, sir," observed Philip, shifting uneasily in the chair and staring at the armrest. What was pink and white doing in a President's private office? Tiffany had probably picked it out. "In fact, I'm not sure it can be done."

The President lumbered back to his desk. "We're pinning our hopes on you, Philip. John, see that he has cable and phone access to me twenty-four hours a day. And give the press a release announcing Philip as the requested mediator, immediately. The Communists' deadline for an agreement is the 30th—nine days from today. Baden and Dirk and the rest of the team are scheduled to leave for Taipei on Air Force Two at midnight tonight. I want you to join them—can you manage it?"

Join them? He had planned to be climbing in the Gunks this weekend. It was his life blood. Was he shoving it aside yet again?

"Yeah, I guess I can," he heard himself say. "Midnight, huh? They know I will be heading the team, and will need heavy duty briefing on the current status of things?"

The President looked at Ravenhurst. "Break it to them, John." His gaze swept back to Philip. "There's just as many factions that don't want you to succeed as in New Delhi. Just like there, we can't rule out violence directed at you and your team. Be careful. You'll have the same tight security as in New Delhi."

"Fine, and I'll want Tom Morgan from the CIA for my personal security man. Just like in New Delhi. Without a veto from other echelons on his activities."

"Sorry, security for this is already set up, and it's being run through Homeland Security channels," said Ravenhurst.

"I can't concentrate on negotiations unless I have confidence my back is covered. That means Tom. We go way back, beyond New Delhi, even."

"Sorry, boy," Ravenhurst said crisply.

Philip rose, feeling suddenly lighter and happier. "It's been real nice chatting with you, Mr. President. Hope you find someone to help you out. Have a good evening." He turned and headed for the door, walking quickly.

A moment's hesitation from the President, and a quick glance at Ravenhurst. Then he spoke. "John, get this Morgan from CIA. I want him on the plane tonight, integrated into the rest of security but with autonomy in his decisions. Understand?"

Ravenhurst's head wasn't moving. His jaws clenched.

"Yes, Mr. President."

Philip paused at the door. "Oh, and John. It's true you've got a couple of decades on me. But if you ever call me 'boy' again, I'll forget my upbringing and knock the crap out of you. Even in front of a President." He glared at Ravenhurst, then left the room.

search

Chapter Four

Keelung, northeast of Taipei

Sung Lee clicked off the television and tossed the remote onto his desk with a scowl. His wide forehead above the large, hooked nose was creased with worry lines. He was puzzled, and he didn't like being puzzled. Too often it had led to loss of fortunes. And of lives. Why hadn't the American President chosen Secretary Talbin? The young Dawson was good, and they said he knew something about China, but he didn't have the clout of a Secretary of State.

Lee strode to the window overlooking the docks in Keelung. He was tall, and still reasonably trim and strong, even in his late seventies. It was raining, as it always was in Keelung, especially with fall approaching. He watched the water slap against the window and roll down the glass in long courses. Not that it mattered what the American President did, or who he sent to the negotiations. Sung Lee wasn't used to failure, but even he couldn't force a bridge over so huge a chasm, whether in nine days or ninety.

His eyes focused beyond the window, at the ships in the harbor, blurred by the rain. Nearly all of them his ships, since the others had moved their operations to Kaohsiung. His eyes searched for the dilapidated rowboat, set in a commemorative steel sculpture in front of his main dock. He found it, and smiled, an unusual event for him.

He remembered the bitter smell of the vomit that he regularly scooped out of the little boat, from those drunken men he ferried back to the Fuzhou dock from the brothels in the harbor. His eye swept from that old rowboat in its steel embrace out to his fleet in the harbor. Ma Tsu had indeed blessed him, from that old rowboat to today. In return, he had been a generous patron of the black-faced sea goddess' temples up and down the south China coast and Taiwan.

But at the moment, he didn't feel blessed. He felt worried. He walked back to the desk and punched the preset number for his stevedore on the docks.

"Liu. Start diverting our returning ships. Reroute some to Singapore, some to Kuala Lumpur. And send out the big transports still here, with or without loads. Anywhere, but one by one, no fanfare, no obvious pattern. Leave only the ferries and smaller ships. Finish it up in nine days."

He knew Liu would understand. The man was even older than he was, and had been with him back in Fuzhou, before they brought everything to Taiwan in 1949.

"Yes, Mr. Lee," the stevedore said on the line. "What about your family?"

Lee grunted approvingly. Just like old Liu, to think of his family.

"Make reservations for my wife and the girls to leave, two in five days, two in seven, Lee Taitai last. To Hong Kong. I'll tell them."

Another pause. "Yes, sir. And Hsiao Loo and Hsiao Pang?"

He grunted, and considered it. He had faithfully provided for his two mistresses, and the three daughters they had borne him. Neither one was with child.

"They'll stay," he decided. "Make sure they have plenty of food and provisions. Who are their bodyguards, now?"

"One-eyed Lu and Big Zhou."

He nodded. "Extra supplies and a bonus to them. Extra ammunition, too. It could be chaotic here."

"Yes, sir. And Mr. Lee. Today is the anniversary of your mother's death, sir. I've ordered candles and incense for her tomb. They will be delivered by five o'clock."

"By the gods. Yes. These cursed negotiations have pushed things from my mind. I'll stop by on my way home. My wife and daughters have been contacted?"

"Yes, sir. They will be at the tomb at five o'clock."

"Good. No, make it six. I just heard that the Premier will be dropping by to see me at four, and it could easily go beyond five. I'll meet them at the tomb at six, and we'll light the incense at her altar. We'll also swing by the Ma Tsu Temple on Chengdu street."

He hung up the phone, and considered whether he should move his mother's remains off Taiwan. And then the old question came nagging again: who would light incense for him, when he was dead? He had everything in the world except a son. And a father. Without a son lighting incense at his altar, he was a lost soul, one of the Hungry Ghosts wandering the netherworld untended, uncared for.

But no sense in bringing that up now. His fate was his fate. Should he move his mother's remains off Taiwan? What would it be like in nine days, after the deadline? He had no doubt that China would make good its promise to use force if no agreement were reached. Did that mean missiles and bombs? Would cities and ports be struck, as well as military units? Would Taiwan be turned into a smoking ruin?

Leaning heavily onto the desk on stiff arms, he reviewed the situation yet again. Most of the Kuomintang Nationalists, whether the old party stalwarts or President Ma Ying-jeou's young faction, were ready to make a deal, and they controlled the Legislature and much of the island's wealth. The Democratic People's Party was the sticking point. Even though the DPP had evolved from their radical pro-independence founding principles, they wouldn't accept any formula that denied Taiwan its functional independence in all areas. Ever since their man Chen Shui-bian had captured the Presidency in 2000 and again, narrowly, in 2004, their approval of any formula was vital. They had about half of the people on the island behind them, even though they'd lost the 2008 and 2012 elections to Ma's Kuomintang party. He had tried hard, but he couldn't bridge the gap between the DPP and China.

There were very few things he wanted that he couldn't get. A father whose identity he knew. A son to light incense at his altar when he was dead. And now an agreement to save the island that had made him rich. The things he most desperately desired were out of his reach. Ma Tsu had blessed him in so many ways. Why withhold his deepest wishes? Could she be that cruel?

"Mr. Lee? Mr. Lee?"

His secretary's voice broke the black spell. He punched the intercom.

"What? Yes, Miss Ling?"

"Your youngest daughter is here, Mr. Lee."

He frowned, thinking of his string of appointments today, politicians and business leaders, publishers. Little Jade had been spoiled, of course. But still she shouldn't call on him here. Even if she was getting married in a month, and would have the biggest wedding in Taipei's history. If there still was a Taipei in a month.

The door flew open and Little Jade rushed into the room, looking older than her twenty years, in a silk blouse and wool skirt. She threw her raincoat on the chair by the door as she acknowledged her impropriety, briefly flicking her large eyes downward.

"Father, please don't be angry."

Seeing her, his rugged face nearly softened. "Little Jade, you know—"

"Yes, Father. But I made a promise to your mother."

"Little Jade. I know that today is the anniversary of her death. I've made arrangements to meet you all at her tomb at six this evening."

The girl shook her head, reminding Lee of the way his mother herself had stubbornly shook her head at him. Except her hair had never been as styled as Little Jade's. And of course, he had never known her to laugh, as Little Jade did all the time.

"No, Father. This is something else. Something from her. To give to you."

He scowled at her, puzzled for the second time this morning. This had all the makings of an unlucky day.

"Father. A week before she died, she gave me an envelope."

Lee could believe that. Little Jade had been his mother's favorite.

"And?"

"And made me promise to give the envelope to you, but not until she had been dead ten years." Tears welled up in her eyes. "I cried then, too. But I did what she told me. To hide it from you and Mother for ten years. And now here it is."

She held out her right hand, while she dabbed tears with her left. In the outstretched hand was a red envelope—the lucky color. And in his mother's spidery characters, his own name, on the envelope.

A sense of dread came over him. He didn't want to take the envelope, red or not.

"You open it, Little Jade."

She stared at him, also afraid. Normally, one didn't want much to do with the spirits, even the spirit of a beloved grandmother. But she slowly unfolded the envelope. A photograph was inside, nothing else. She handed it to her father, her hand trembling.

Lee took the photograph. It appeared old, black and white, faded. He turned it right-side-up, and stared down at it. His mother, very young. Smiling, yet. He had never known her to smile. He gasped—she was holding hands, with a man. A man whose blurred face was turning away. The impropriety was shocking. Unless—

Little Jade reached out and turned the photo over in his large hand. On the back, again in his mother's spidery hand, four characters: "Sung's father."

She uttered a little cry, as Lee collapsed into the chair behind the desk. They both stared at the characters, then Lee turned the photograph over. Yes, it was his mother.

"My—my father!" Lee whispered, his voice hoarse and cracking.

"Who—who is he?" Little Jade asked, her voice also strange.

Lee stared at the picture. The man had the high cheekbones of a northerner, and a prominent nose, for a Chinese. Much like Lee himself. His face was almost in profile, as he turned away from the camera. "I have no idea who he is, Little One. But now I have a picture of him, at least. My father!"

He jumped to his feet, and punched the button below the intercom. His secretary scurried quickly into the room.

"Miss Ling. Feed this photo into our scanner. Make—what? Five copies of it." He stalked about the room, still holding the photo, spitting out orders, feeling more alive and sure than he had for weeks.

"Give four of the copies to Little Jade, for the family. Little Jade, you to the Palace Museum photo archives, check Shanghai region material from the 20's and 30's. Daughter Number Three to Hong Kong and then Shanghai newspapers, photo archives of the same region and time. Daughter Number Two shows the photo to old Wang on Fu Jiang street—she lived in Shanghai until the Japanese came. Daughter Number One to the senior professors at the Universities here—at least the mainlanders. All before the deadline in nine days. Understand?"

He stopped. Little Jade nodded, her face flushed.

"Miss Ling, send—no, handcarry—the original to that new young fellow in our Computer Graphics section—the bright one, just graduated from Berkeley—"

"Hsing Foong."

"Yes. Have him digitally enhance the photo, all that stuff he knows. Tell him I'll be at his desk at eight tomorrow morning, to see what clues we can get from it."

Lee looked down at the photo, small and fragile in his gnarled hand.

"The fifth copy to me," Lee said in a voice suddenly quiet. "I will keep it, myself." He gazed down at the old photo, reverently. "No. Make six copies, Miss Ling. We'll put the sixth copy on our family altar, next to my mother's photo there. I will burn incense to my father, tonight. I don't know what his name is, yet, but I have his face." He stopped, his voice cracking. He looked at Little Jade. "Soon I'll have a past. Our ancestral line will be established, little one."

He didn't say it aloud, but he felt it, to his bones. That if he could find a past, it would lead to a future. Somehow, the blurred face from the distant past would save him from wandering forever in that clamoring throng of lost souls, the Hungry Ghosts.

sea

Chapter Five

Taipei, Taiwan

Meiling emerged from the elevators and turned right into the newsroom, walking down the long aisle between the desks with athletic, graceful strides. She wore her hair short and untinted to play down her attractiveness. It didn't work. Her strong, slim body and air of exuberant health still drew stares. The women reporters smiled at her, liking her too much to be jealous. The men either studiously ignored her or leered.

"Good job on the Keelung shipyard troubles, Weikung," she said to a thin young fellow at a work station in the business table. "Just the right blend of color and facts."

Weikung beamed, embarrassed at the attention but pleased by the praise.

"Yeah, pretty soon they'll be giving you a private office, just like Meiling," an older man in the next desk joked, not looking up from his computer screen.

Meiling waited for the laughter to fade, then bent down to Weikung and said in a loud whisper, "Keep practicing your typing, so you won't have to look at your fingers all the time like old Pang there." She flashed a dazzling smile at the older man.

Pang howled in mock outrage, and another wave of laughter rippled across the large room as the Managing Editor got up from his newsroom desk and waved Meiling into his nearby private office.

"Just think how much faster I could produce a newspaper if my reporters joked less and worked more," he complained as he sat. He was a small man, old and perpetually rumpled. "Straight from our honorable Publisher, Miss

Bei. You are to drop everything else you're working on and concentrate on the mediator the Americans just announced—what is his name?" He consulted the computer monitor on his desk. "Dawson. Philip Dawson. The fellow who worked the miracle in New Delhi last year."

He uttered a rasping laugh and looked over at Meiling as he spun the monitor to face her. "He'll Soon discover that miracles are in shorter supply in East Asia."

Meiling pulled her skirt over her knees as she crossed her long legs and settled back into the chair, ignoring the photo on the screen. "What's this nonsense about dropping the Shen Clan conglomerate story?"

A sober look flashed onto the Managing Editor's face. "Forget the conglomerate, Miss Bei. They're furious with you. They claim you burgled your way into their offices to get those files and memos. Did you?"

"Of course. How else was I to get them?"

He raised his eyebrows. "Where did you pick up your expertise in burgling?" "Remember that series I did on Taipei's private investigators?"

"Ah yes. What a great title I chose for that series. 'The Murky World of Taipei's Charlie Chans.'" He stared proudly into the distance.

"Well, the people I interviewed are really good at picking locks. They taught me everything they knew. Real friendly folks, once you get to know them. Rough, but friendly."

"Everyone wants to know our ace reporter. We can't lose you, Miss Bei."

"Now look, we can't just drop it. The material I got shows a huge gap between their reported income and the real income. They're making money on some concealed enterprise, lots of it. It's doubtless illegal, and has got to involve smuggling something in or out of Taiwan in large quantities. Maybe both. Now the way I see it—"

"You don't see it, any more," he interrupted. "Forget the story. It's not worth your life, Miss Bei. Is it?"

She settled back into the chair. He was serious. Was it worth her life? Of course not. But she'd been threatened before, and barged ahead. She was strong and smart, and kept her eyes open wide.

"We're not dropping the story, Miss Bei. We're letting it simmer for a while, work with the authorities to coordinate protection for our reporters, then we'll get back into it. When we're ready to move again, Weikung will be our lead man."

"Managing Editor, Weikung is good, but—"

"I want all your notes on Weikung's computer before lunch." He said it flat, almost angry. "And watch yourself, Miss Bei. They made it pretty clear—if you go further on this, they'll retaliate. You'll be fine, so long as you drop it. Which you will."

It was the first time she'd ever been pulled from a story, and she hated it. Every inch of her rebelled. From the Managing Editor's tone, it was useless to argue with him. She sighed, and put on a defeated face. "All right. So instead of bringing down a crooked conglomerate, you want me to provide celebrity background on the American mediator?"

"Not me. Our Publisher himself is assigning you. And he wants considerably more than background color. I am instructed to tell you that you are to get into the confidences of this Philip Dawson and inform our large readership what his feelings are regarding his mission here. How he plans to pull off this next miracle of his."

She gazed at him for a long moment. "Speaking of miracles, did he tell you how I was supposed to accomplish this singular feat?"

The Managing Editor's wizened face broke into a happy grin. "Yes, he did. I will quote him. 'Have Miss Bei use all her considerable charms to bewitch the American. They love Asian women.'" He beamed as he waited for her reaction.

It was too much, especially after getting yanked off the Shen story. In a flush of anger she lunged from her chair to the edge of his desk and spit out the words clearly.

"Tell the honorable Publisher to go screw himself." She was so angry she didn't even notice the renewed throbbing in her knees.

He drew back, her intensity robbing him of some of the enjoyment at her reaction. But after a moment he laughed, nervously, his face shriveled and comic, like a monkey's. As she stood there, arms crossed and fuming, Meiling wished she had a banana to cram into his gaping mouth. Or better yet, into—

"Now, Miss Bei. You must put up with our Publisher's earthy way of expressing himself," said the man, composed again, although still keeping his distance from her. "Quite seriously, though, we want you to get very close to this Dawson, and give our readers some startling insights into him as a person and how he's going to attempt his impossible assignment."

"Nice touch, Managing Editor. You give me an impossible assignment, to add color to his impossible assignment." She shifted her weight, the pain in her legs finally getting through to her. "See, you're already becoming original and witty, and you've barely begun the assignment. You'll do fine. He doesn't stand a chance."

She uncrossed her arms and sat down, again carefully folding her skirt over her knees. "Right. He's doubtless happily married with six children."

The grin left his face. "Miss Bei. You're already known as a *nyuquanren*, a strong woman. Talented, a painter as well as a journalist. Although a bit strange, what with your morning swims and all. This assignment should intrigue you. Think of it as an opportunity. To make yourself the talk of Taiwan. See what you can do with it."

She sat back into her chair, still angry. The Managing Editor didn't look so much like a monkey when he wasn't grinning. He was just a shriveled old newpaper man, trying to squeeze what he could out of his reporters.

"I'll see what I can do, consistent with the traditional Chinese values of propriety and morals which our honorable publisher is always referring to in his speeches. And I'll need some help—Ping will do."

As she rose and left, he called after her. "And don't forget. All your conglomerate notes to Weikung by lunch."

By the time she reached her own office at the other end of the newsroom, most of her anger was gone. She glanced at her watercolor of her swimming beach, on the wall opposite her desk. That helped. She opened the conglomerate file and scrolled down it for some minutes. She picked up a pencil and wrote down a telephone number on a slip of paper. Then she closed the large file, and opened an e-mail note to Weikung.

"Weikung. Here's the Shen Clan conglomerate file. Watch yourself; they're evidently very angry at me." She attached the file and hit the send button.

She picked up the phone and punched in the number she had written on the paper.

"Hello? Meiling Bei here. I need to talk to you."

A pause, as she listened to the furious whisper on the other end.

"I know, I know. But I just need a few more things from you. It won't take us five minutes. Can you see me today?"

She shook her head at the string of curses from the other end.

"All right. Yes, I know it. Until then."

*   *   *   *   *

Meiling arrived early and sat nervously on a stone bench beside the island pavilion in the north end of New Park. On the other side of the pavilion, forming the east boundary of the park, traffic surged down Kungyuan Road. Her eyes restlessly scanned the green and gold eaves of the pavilion, and kept darting back to the footbridge that led here.

One more session was all she needed. A very short one. Her informant from the conglomerate had told her exactly where the key files were and their passwords. But he hadn't told her what the item was that accounted for the huge unreported income. All she needed was a word, really. One word, then she would heed the Managing Editor's warning and get off the story.

Weikung could take it from there. The conglomerate dealt in lots of products, from textiles to the old man's antique jade. But it was probably something electronic. Computer chips, most likely. Components smuggled in from Hong Kong, perhaps. Assembled here. Then smuggled out, avoiding tariffs and taxes.

Her eyes darted again to the footbridge. She glanced at her watch, and breathed deep. Her heart was racing. It was foolish, of course, to meet the informant again, after the conglomerate's threat. But she refused to leave the story hanging, when all she needed was one last piece of the puzzle. One word, then she could walk away.

Where was he?

She heard tires screeching on Kungyuan Road. A moment later, shouts, quickly followed by screams. More screeching tires. She jumped to her feet, and listened, every muscle taut. More screams. Without thinking, she found herself hurrying across the footbridge, down the pathway paralleling the fence, and out the east entrance to the park. She ran along the sidewalk and shoved her way through the gathering crowd.

A body on the sidewalk. White shirt, brown pants, black shoes. But no head on it, just a bloody stump above the red-splattered shoulders. Then she saw it, a couple of yards toward the fence. Eyes open wide, staring unseeing straight at her. Hair sticking out wildly in all directions. Her stomach tightened up, and nausea gripped her. She put her hand to her mouth. She only needed one word from him, but the stiff white lips wouldn't produce even that. Her other hand went to her stomach, and she stumbled away as the wail of sirens filled the air.

mountain

Chapter Six

Aboard Air Force Two

Philip stared out the window from the work study of the airplane. Below them, large patches of darkness between clusters of lights. He imagined the rocks underlying the dark patches. Sandstone, mostly, here in the east. Where would they be, by now? Kentucky? He pictured the long, winding canyons of the Red River Gorge, the steep, sweeping walls of orange and gold sandstone. Athletic climbing, challenging.

As soon as this Taiwan thing was over—win, lose, or draw—he'd take six months off. Hell, maybe a year. Maybe a lifetime. Nothing but ledges and overhangs and cliffs. Of course, Tiffany wouldn't be interested in an ex-rising star in the D.C. galaxy. He'd miss her. A lot. But it was like the Ambassador had said. You don't neglect your soul.

"Here we are!" came the ever-excited voice of Baden as he staggered into the compartment, his curiously long arms full of briefing folders. What was that condition, that Lincoln had had? Long arms and legs. But accompanied by melancholy, and that certainly wasn't Matt Baden. He headed the Far East desk at State.

On the other hand, there was Sharon Dirk, who followed Baden into the compartment. Tall, lean, ascetic. Alternating between Duke's famous political science department, then some high position at State. Hard to like, but a brilliant analyst. That was the important thing. She'd have the insights, he'd persuade everyone to sign on.

"Give me those folders, Baden," he said. "I've got a lot of catching up to do, and only North America and the Pacific to do it over."

"Oh, come on. You studied China as hard as I did at Yale. You pretend to be a good ol' boy, out of your depth on China, but I know you. You're pretty damn sharp."

"Oh, right. Ask Morgan, back there."

The big Secret Service man flipping through a *People* magazine looked up.

"What's that?"

"Tell Baden here what an intellectual whiz I was in high school, Tom." They had been buddies growing up back in Vermont, pursued separate paths after high school, and only last year at New Delhi had they reunited.

Tom Morgan grunted. "Before or after your mom's death, Phil?"

A brief silence in the room.

"Whatever," Philip said.

"Before, the boy was as average as oatmeal," Morgan said, leaning back and trying unsuccessfully to get comfortable in the chair. "After, when he decided he had to get into Yale and save the world, he was oatmeal that worked awfully hard."

Everyone laughed, even Sharon Dirk.

"See?" Philip said. "Oatmeal. That's me."

"With a lot of sugar in that oatmeal, to hear the secretaries talk," Dirk said dryly. Morgan nodded. "Yeah. There was always that, even in high school."

"For Christ sake, let's get to work," Philip said. "Baden, or Dirk, what do you have for me, here?"

Baden sifted through the green-jacketed briefing folders. "A separate folder for each aspect. Trade. Communications. Legal codes. Taiwan's negotiator, Sung Lee, and his team. Zhu Liang, China's man. History of the negotiations. And so on."

"I get the picture. How do we split up the issues, once we get there?" Philip found the folder on Sung Lee and opened it, glancing between it and the two diplomats.

A hesitation. Baden spoke. "Well, you head the team, Philip. But we'd suggest this. Dirk in charge of one group, that tackles the thorny but resolvable issues. Economics, trade, and legal structures. I head another group, that handles a lot of relatively straight-forward stuff they've already made a start on the past several years. Transportation, communication, cultural exchanges." He hesitated, looking at Dirk.

Dirk's cold face was impassive as she spoke. "That leaves you with the difficult issues, Mr. Dawson."

"Oh, come on. Call me Philip."

"All right. Philip. The really hard issues. Nature of the union. The name that Taiwan gets, as a result. And disposition of the military forces of the two sides. Issues that may not in fact have a resolution. Issues on which there's been no progress—well, since 1949. Every time they take up the questions, it's like it was still Mao and Chiang Kai-shek, still fighting to the bitter end."

An awkward silence.

"You've got folders on those issues?" asked Philip.

Baden's finger indicated the two thickest folders.

"Good. I'll digest them, then I'll want to talk to both of you about it. A lot."

Baden started to gather up the rest of the folders in his arms.

"No. Leave them all here. I'll want to read them, also. You folks get some sleep. We'll start talking in—what? Six hours or so? Bring the rest of the team in here then. I want everyone to know where everyone else is, and where we think we're going."

"Right-o," said Dirk, with a look at Baden. "See you then." She rose to leave.

"Just a minute," Philip said, holding out his hand as he glanced over the last page of the folder on Sung Lee. "What do you make of this fellow, Lee?"

"A tough one to gauge," said Baden, slowly shaking his head. "He's not like us or anyone we're likely to know. Never went to college. Never knew his father. Rose up from the bitterest poverty imaginable."

"He can't be stupid," Philip said thoughtfully.

"Oh, no," Dirk said quickly. "He's smart as a fox. But that's it. Animal smart."

"We really don't know what to make of him," Baden admitted. "Which is why we requested you to head the team, Philip."

Philip looked up quickly. "You, then. Thanks a lot." He wasn't smiling.

Baden's cheerful face turned grim.

Dirk came to his rescue. "If you can get through to Indians and Pakistanis, maybe you can get through to Sung Lee. It's just a hunch. A hope."

Philip tossed the folder onto the table. "So he didn't go to Yale or Duke," he said with a slight smile, putting his feet up on the table. "I need something on him, folks. What's he beholden to? What's important in his life? What crimes has he committed?"

"Oh, he's got lots of skeletons in his closet," Dirk said. "He's run rough-shod over any number of people. Murdered a couple of men with his bare hands."

Philip looked up. "So he's liable to be vulnerable about that?"

"Philip—I've lived in Hong Kong," said Baden. "Murder, crimes—all part of everyday life in China. Especially in the forties and fifties, when all hell was breaking loose. Sung Lee won't be the least sensitive about any of it."

"The folder says he's superstitious. What does that mean?"

Dirk laughed dryly. "Like we said. He rose from the masses. The masses in China are incredibly superstitious. Demons and gods everywhere."

"Buddhist?"

"Hard to say," Baden answered. "Nearly all the temples are a mixture of Buddhism and Taoism and Confucianism. Plus whatever local deity is there."

Philip closed the folder. "That's my weakness. I'm stuffed with book-learning about China. The high culture. But I don't know beans about how people think and smell and pray to gods in China or Taiwan."

Baden and Dirk looked at each other, eyebrows raised. After a pause, they turned for the door, silent.

"A couple of more things," said Philip. "Sharon, I want you to handle the media. Everything. I don't want anything diverting my attention from my work. I'm off limits. You'll be the official point person for our mission, and leave me the independence to do things my own unconventional way, meet anyone anywhere at any hour, just like in New Delhi. Got it?"

A groan, as she nodded.

"And this. We're playing hardball here, aren't we? I assume there's groups in Taiwan and China that would kill to derail these talks from succeeding. Right?"

Another dry laugh from Dirk. "You need a scorecard to keep track of them all. Factions within the military in the People's Republic, plus the old Tien An Men Square hardliners—both fervently want China to obliterate Taiwan."

"And in Taiwan," said Baden, "the extreme wing of the Democratic People's Party, who are convinced any deal will lead to China calling all the shots."

"And in the U.S.?" asked Philip.

Baden and Dirk exchanged another glance. "Well, sure. The old Claire Lee Chennault folks: Commies are bad and we're good and it's Armageddon."

Philip thought of how he'd felt after the barest sip of his last champagne at the reception that night. It was weird, and reflecting on it had only made it more weird. He wished he'd seen the waiter who gave it to him, but he hadn't so much as glanced at him.

"Who knew I was going to be tabbed as the mediator before tonight? Say, a day or two ago?"

Dirk thought about it. "The only ones who could know for sure who was decided on, would be the deciders. The President and John Ravenhurst."

Philip decided maybe he was being paranoid.

"You seem a bit concerned," Dirk continued. "Any particular reason?"

Philip shrugged. "Like I said, we're playing hardball here. Just like in New Delhi last year. Remember that alleyway in the old quarter, Tom? Week two of the negotiations, coming back from drinking tea with the Pakistani delegation all night?"

Tom grunted.

"Two mujahadeen came after me, from roofs above us. Tom got both of them before they hit the ground, but the far guy managed to activate a grenade. Tom was on top of me before it exploded. I was OK, but Tom still has scars up and down his legs."

They all glanced at Tom. He looked up from the magazine.

"Well, hey, those fancy new Kevlar shrapnel vests can only cover so much of a guy's body, huh? Especially mine."

Dirk shook her head. "The mujahadeen are hard to stop."

Tom tossed the magazine to the side. "Incredibly brave, and dedicated. But not very sophisticated, in terms of weapons or tactics. It'll be different in Taiwan. The Chinese had bamboo books on advanced assassination tactics and weapons 2,500 years ago. Way beyond Sun Tsu. Real interesting reading. You can learn a lot from 'em."

Silence.

"I like having Tom along with me on these little pleasure jaunts to see the world," said Philip. "One last question for you two."

Baden and Dirk tore their eyes off Tom.

"In all these temples you mentioned. Who's the god of the sea?"

"Pardon?" said Dirk, with a quick, puzzled look at Baden.

"Sung Lee's superstitious. He's a shipper, makes his living hauling things over oceans. I bet he pays a lot of attention to the god of the sea. Who is it?"

Baden and Dirk shook their heads.

"Ask around. See if anyone knows any damn thing about Chinese folk religion."

They nodded, stiffly, and left, pulling a curtain behind them.

"Hey, Tom. Could I persuade you to get me some tea?" Philip said, picking up another folder.

"Sure thing. The usual?"

Philip nodded, already into an analysis of Taiwan's military. Morgan returned in a minute, and set the cup on the table beside Philip. Philip absently picked it up, and took a sip. The steaming hot tea burned his lips, and he set it down. And smiled, as he remembered another drink of tea from Tom Morgan that had burned his lips, nearly two decades ago. He had drunk it greedily, burning lips not mattering, then. Jesus, he had been cold. Never so cold in his life, before or after. Roped onto the side of a cliff in Vermont in October. After his grandpa had told him his mom had been killed in Bosnia.

"Thanks for the tea, Tom."

Tom looked up, and guessed what his friend had been thinking. He nodded, and didn't say anything.

Philip bent back to the green-jacketed folder. He had a lot to get into his head, and not much time to do it.

bent

Chapter Seven

Day Two. *Taipei, Taiwan*

He awoke with a start. Where was he? Ah, his own bedroom. A girl in bed to his left. He didn't remember anything about her. Faint light coming in the east-facing window to his right. It must be dawn. Dawn in his penthouse in Taipei's East District.

It came back to him, through the fog of jet lag. Barely catching the flight from D.C. The dog, the damn dog, spilling the beautiful box-jellyfish toxin he had delivered to his target. A shame to waste such a beautiful, untraceable substance. Not to mention the work to collect the animal and extract the poison. Damn. But there'll be another opportunity. He stretched.

Who was this girl, anyway? He turned toward her, pulled the sheet down, and stared at her body in the soft light coming through the window. Her breasts were small, but nicely pointed, the nipples a beautiful dark color, almost purple. It played off the purple tinting in her long black hair, a nice touch. Had she thought of that? Probably not. Few of them were that subtle. Everyone tinted their hair purple these days.

She lay with one arm resting on the pillow above her head, the other down over her hip. A thick smudge of dried semen ran along a thigh. He bent to her and smelled her odor, his nose in the little hollow above her collar bone. Ah, yes. A lovely suggestion of musk, unusual, mixed in with the usual oriental backdrop of fruit and the fresh sweetness of young women everywhere.

He finally looked at her face, and then he remembered. He had been angry about the failed attempt in D.C. Of course, when your methods are subtle, you will fail occasionally. And frustrated, at being literally at his mark's elbow, then not succeeding. He had gone straight to a fashionable bar after landing in Taipei, and been surprised to find her there. She was a friend of a friend. Many scotches later, everything begins to blur. He rolled off the bed and stood, waking the girl with his movement.

"Oh, Jimmy," she slurred. "You were so physical last night. You scared me."

He grunted, still not remembering a thing about the sex.

A giggle from the girl. "What did you call me, last night?" She made a rumbling sound in her throat. "Duckling!" she exclaimed. "You called me your Duckling!"

He froze. Yes, he could have called her that. Ironic—that had been his nickname for her friend, his first infatuation. College days, in Berkeley. The only woman he had ever wanted that he hadn't won. Or just taken. At the time, he actually imagined he was in love. A brief sadness welled up in him, which quickly transformed into the accustomed contempt and hatred. Some day he'd take her. Ignoring what the girl on the bed was saying to him, he walked out of the bedroom to his office in the next room.

He settled into the leather chair facing the big window, liking its feel against his bare skin where the incoming morning light had warmed it slightly. His eyes went to the wall of newspaper and magazine photographs to the left of his desk. Taipei's most beautiful women, each aglow on the arm of the wealthy socialite Jimmy Chan. He lingered on them, remembering the smell of each one. Their voices, their breasts, even their Golden Valleys blurred in his memory, but the smell of each remained strong and distinct. As this one would. He'd have to get a photo of this one, to add to the collection.

With a satisfied grunt, he reached over the chemistry journals on his desk, articles on phospholipases and mercuric oxides checked in red, and picked up the two dark blue folders. CIA colors. He had already studied them, before the trip to D.C., but the details had to stay sharp in his mind, to craft the next attack. He opened the top one. A photograph, Sung Lee. Not his target, but provided because Lee would be interacting with the target in Taipei. Below the photograph were details of Lee's personal life. Father unknown, raised by his mother working in an orphanage. Began his vast shipping fleet by ferrying clients in a rowboat to brothels in Fuzhou's harbor. Moved to Taiwan in 1949, married a wealthy Taiwanese. Four daughters by his wife, three others by his several concubines. Still no sons. Jimmy Chan laughed. Poor bastard. No father, no sons. Doomed to wander the netherworld forever as a Hungry Ghost after he died, no sons or even nephews to honor him in the afterlife.

He shivered at the horrible prospect, and decided to drop by the Lung Shan temple to pay his respects to the gods before the Hungry Ghost Festival next week. Should he marry soon, father sons now to keep his line alive? His eyes glazed as he contemplated it. He looked up at the photographs of women to his left. No. Not a chance. Plenty of time for marriage and family, later. Now it was the sweet life for him. He'd always diligently paid his respects to the gods, so an untimely death needn't be feared.

He opened the second folder. The target.

Another photograph, this one a Caucasian face. The one at the reception. Six foot two, strong. Yale, majored in China and India. Rock climber. He picked up the red pen on the desk and circled that. Fond of Scotch. Jimmy Chan circled that, also. Key man in last year's Kashmir Accords in New Delhi. Dating President Hayes' socialite granddaughter, Tiffany Hayes.

He stared out the window. He'd have to screw more blondes. The smell was usually too sweet for his taste, but still, it was quite an experience. He returned to the pages, studying them for another five minutes. He finally put the folder on his desk, open. Measuring the man. He had survived the first sally. A few others had. A few had even survived the second approach. But he had always succeeded, in the end. He looked at the wall to the right of his desk, also covered with photographs, but these males. More than a dozen men, all vigorous, strong leaders in their countries. All of them a challenge, testing his knowledge, his skill. All of them dead.

He heard high heels on the tile at the foyer, and ignored it, out of habit. Then he remembered that she was his first "duckling's" friend—perhaps it was time to teach her that no one spurned Jimmy Chan, not even a prominent newspaper reporter. He should cultivate the connection.

He rose from the leather chair, and picked up the Caucasian's photograph. He grabbed a tack, and with a smooth movement jabbed the photograph against the wall to the right at an angle, joining the other men he'd killed. Jimmy Chan smiled, liking the look of the photograph there with the others, askew. He turned and opened the door onto the foyer, still smiling. The young woman hesitated, her hand on the doorknob, as she saw Jimmy Chan emerge from the study, naked.

"Leaving so soon, duckling?"

"Jimmy, I've got a job. And I've got to go change my dress, at my apartment. You tore it last night."

He took her in his arms. "I'll miss you. You're something. Special."

"Really?" she squealed, unable to keep the delight from her voice.

"Really." Women were so easy. "I'll call you. I want to see you tonight."

"Oh, Jimmy." She kissed him long, and hard, and freed herself from his arms, whimpering a little to indicate reluctance, then was gone.

Shaking his head, he returned to his study and walked into the closet to the left of the women's photos. He opened a concealed door at the back of the closet, and a hidden room appeared before him. Scientific equipment lined lab benches on three walls. Beakers and glassware, precision analytical balances, a centrifuge. The fourth wall had a stock of chemicals in brown labeled bottles, some standard, some decidedly not.

He hummed a tune, the blonde, Lady Gaga, as he donned a lab coat and retrieved a plastic bag from the freezer compartment of the refrigerator, then dumped a small frozen octopus onto the lab bench. The head, smaller than his fist, stood above the tangled mass of tentacles. *Hapalochlaena lunulata*, the blue-ringed octopus. Among the world's smallest octopods, yet by far the most deadly of them, thanks to the maculotoxin the little beast produced in its two posterior salivary glands. He supposed he should learn about the creatures whose poisons he utilized, but it was so much easier just to pretend to being a researcher and order the beasts, or sometimes just their poisons from supply houses. Anyway, it wasn't the creatures he liked. It was their juices. Sort of like his women, eh?

He trimmed away the tentacles with pruning shears, until the beaklike mouth was visible. With concentration he cut the head into two pieces, splitting the oral cavity. He found himself humming another song. Madonna, he realized, an old tune. He thought briefly of the girl from last night, then switched to a Lady Gaga song. Yes, he'd have to begin seeing some blondes, soon.

He placed one of the half-heads onto the stage of a dissecting scope and clicked the 10 power lens into place as he picked up a scalpel. He focused, found the opening of the duct from the posterior salivary gland, clicked the 30 power lens into place, refocused, and dissected up the duct until he came to the darker, tightly packed cells of the gland itself. He cut away the gland and carried it on the scalpel blade to a mini-blender containing 25 ml of methanol. Turning to the other half of the head, he soon had the gland from it also, and added it to the mini-blender. Two pulses, of about 20 seconds on low, homogenized the tissue and freed the deadly maculotoxin molecules.

Still humming and thinking of blondes, he absently poured the mixture through a 3000 molecular weight exclusion filter to remove the cell membranes and large molecules, then through a silica gel column to isolate the small molecules he was interested in, the maculotoxin molecules being grabbed by the silica as everything else flowed past. Then he poured a solution of 50% chloroform in methanol down the column next, which pried the maculotoxin molecules from the silica and deposited them below in the tubes of the old Golden Retriever fraction collector he had purchased from surplus at Berkeley.

He stepped back from the dripping silica gel column and pictured the chemical bonds forming between the chloroform and the maculotoxin molecules, permitting the chloroform to wrest the poison from the silica and carry it down the column into the tubes rotating below. He liked electrons and the way they linked molecules together. Liked the clean, reliable way they operated. No emotions. No betrayals. No heartache. Once you understood how they worked, you could always be sure they would do what you wanted them to. That was satisfying. Better even than blondes. More dependable, certainly.

He removed the deadly tubes from the fraction collector, and poured their contents into a round-bottomed flask. The last step was getting rid of the chloroform and methanol which held his purified poison. He snapped the flask onto the attachment of a Buchi rotary evaporator and swung the arm down, immersing the flask into the warm water bath. Then he switched the evaporator on, and for the first time, relaxed his focus.

He smiled, as he thought of the purity and crystalline beauty of the white powder that would remain in the flask when first the chloroform and then the methanol slowly evaporated off. The beautiful white powder, heavy with the maculotoxin produced by the little beast in the freezer. His pinch of maculotoxin powder would kill a man ten minutes after he had taken it. In food. Or Scotch. Ten frightening minutes, as the toxin bound with sodium ions in the membranes of neurons leading to his victim's diaphragm, paralyzing the muscles. Respiratory failure. Not the worst way to die, he thought with another smile. Not nearly as exciting as the heart attack brought on by the box-jellyfish poison, all those sympathetic system neurons firing away uncontrollably in the flood of catelcholines in the poison. But just as deadly. And of course the maculotoxin, like the jellyfish poison, is complexed and eliminated rapidly in the victim, so that no trace of it remains for even the most dedicated pathologist. Just another one of the inexplicable tragedies of life that some are cursed with.

He stretched, and yawned. It had been a good morning. The girl. The little octopus in the freezer. He would celebrate as the powder was drying. A light breakfast. Catch up on his chemistry journals. Then perhaps the organizer of the symphony gala would be available later this morning. Wasn't today the day her husband spent at Kaohsiung on business? She wasn't a blonde, of course, but he remembered her subtle smell, and the way she shivered under him. Yes, he should celebrate this morning. Because this afternoon he would be at Chiang Kai Shek International, as the American mediator's plane landed. To study his man. For round two.

search

Chapter Eight

When Sung Lee emerged from the elevator doors on the eleventh floor at eight o'clock in the morning, the entire floor went instantly silent. The manager of the Information Processing Section was already bowing before him, and led the way to the left, emitting small squeaking noises as he went. After several turns they came to a small cubicle in the corner. There sat the young man Hsing Foong before a large computer screen, hunched over his keyboard, mouse in hand. He stood when he saw Lee approach, revealing a short, stocky fellow with bright gold-dyed hair.

Lee scowled. From the name, he had expected a normal Taiwanese boy, black hair, angular, deferential. Chinese. This boy, in addition to his shocking hair, had the not-quite-right look of a half-breed, although you could never be sure. Lee frowned on marriages between the races. The young man stared at the ground, waiting patiently for the boss to open the conversation. At least that showed proper Chinese respect. "You're an American-born Chinese," he said. "An ABC."

The young man looked up, a friendly smile on his face. "Afraid so, sir."

"They didn't tell me that when we hired you." He glanced over at the section manager, hovering nervously at the entrance to the cubicle.

Hsing Foong was actually staring him straight in the face. "I believe you hired me for my computer skills, Mr. Lee. Not my racial purity."

Lee stared stonily at him, wondering whether to fire him on the spot. "Well, let's see what you can do," he finally said.

The boy dragged a chair over beside his own, sweeping his foot across the floor to clear it of the coffee cups strewn haphazardly over it.

Lee winced at the mess. "What's your real name? Your American name," he asked.

The boy grinned at the screen. "Kevin, sir."

"Well, Kevin. You got the photo?"

Kevin clicked the mouse, and the photo instantly flashed onto the screen.

Lee gasped. The photo was now bright and clear, and in color yet. He stared rapt at his mother, here young and happy, smiling broadly. She had been a handsome woman, he realized with a start. Had he ever seen her happy?

"Made the usual assumptions, sir," Kevin was saying. "Taking into account damage of the print during aging. The blurred profile of the fellow required more assumptions to get him sharp and clear, but nothing unusual."

Lee said nothing, still trying to digest the very existence of this photo of his youthful mother and his—his father. Father, by the gods.

"Do I understand we want to learn more about the mystery man, Mr. Lee?"

A silent nod.

"Want to see what he looks like from a front view?"

"What? You can do that?"

Kevin circled the mystery man's face, made it a new file, and opened a tool box. "Hope you don't mind, but I sort of anticipated what you might want, and called a friend at the Taiwan National Security Office. He sent me their Facial Reconstruction Protocol, a present from the FBI."

As Kevin highlighted the profile and clicked in the tool box, Lee saw the skin and flesh dissolve off his father's image, revealing a side view of the skull bones.

"The program requires us to work with the bony structure in reconstructions, sir," Kevin explained. "Less likelihood of making a mistake if we're working from the basics of the facial structure. So now let's make a whole skull out of our side view, sir." A list of options appeared beside the skull in profile.

"Assume our mystery man is East Asian—that's easy." Another several clicks. "Now what kind of East Asian?" Kevin continued. He pulled down a list of options. North China, South China, Coastal China, Hakka, Korean, Japanese, Vietnamese, Malay, and Hmong.

"Try North China," Lee suggested.

"Build of body?"

"I was between medium and stocky, as a youth," he said.

The skull profile jumped and shifted while buzzing noises emanated from the computer. Then the profile began to turn, and slowly the skull swung around to the front. Flesh appeared on the skull, then finally the skin, ears, and eyebrows. A young oriental man stared out at them, face heavy-set, cheekbones high.

Eagerly Lee met the skull's stare, wanting to see the face of a father. But a stranger gazed at him from the monitor. He shook his head.

"No. That doesn't look a bit like me. Or like my father could have looked."

No reaction from Kevin to the word 'father.' "Care to try any other assumptions, Mr. Lee?" he asked, tentatively.

Lee slumped in his chair. He thought back to the little his mother had told him about his birth. Somewhere near Shanghai. The war years. He thought of his mother's aversion to speaking of his father, anything about his father. He caught his breath. Surely that was not possible. A bitter taste came to his mouth and his skin tingled as revulsion swept over him. Surely not. He suppressed a shiver.

"Try Japanese, Kevin," he whispered.

Kevin froze, glanced briefly at Lee, then clicked on the option list. Again the skull jumped and shimmied, swung around, and flesh and skin materialized on it.

Lee held his breath as the face appeared. He did not want it to look anything like him, or even vaguely familiar or possible. He stared intently at what the monitor showed him for nearly a minute, then exhaled in relief and slumped back again.

"No. Thank the gods. Not remotely right. Print up the frontal view of the North Chinese option, and we'll attach it as a possibility. Let's see the original again, Kevin."

Lee stared at the photograph. His mother and father—father!—were standing in front of what appeared to be a temple in the left background, with what appeared to be the ocean and a promontory of land in the far right background.

"This looks to be a temple, on the coast, does it not?" asked Lee.

Kevin nodded. "Shall we see what's inside the temple, sir?"

Lee looked over his mother's right shoulder. "Nothing there, is there?"

"Not much we can see now, sir. But let's see what we might pick up if the pixels are enlarged and enhanced."

He circled the black interior of the temple, made it a file, then applied enhancement to it. Where there was only darkness before was now a fuzzy image, various shades of gray. A seated figure, in a bulky robe. A headdress of small round objects arranged in several horizontal rows in the vicinity of what would be the forehead of the figure. But where the head should be, nothing but blackness.

"Peculiar, isn't it?" Kevin said. "The face is missing."

Lee's hair stood on end. "Not missing, Kevin. The face is black. The image in the temple is Ma Tsu, the black-faced goddess of the sea."

Kevin sat straight up, and excitedly peered in. "You're right, Mr. Lee. Look, you can just make out a darker blackness where her face would be."

"Where her face *is*," corrected Lee, his tone hushed. Ma Tsu, the goddess whose favor had given him his rowboat decades ago in Fuzhou harbor, and blessed him on the seas ever since. His mother and father were standing in front of a temple to Ma Tsu in this gift from the past. Surely this was an omen, that he was going to discover his father.

"But aren't Ma Tsu temples all up and down the south China coast?" asked Kevin.

Lee nodded. "Right. What is peculiar to this temple?"

Kevin brought the original photo back on the screen. Lee scanned it eagerly. The roofline was conventional. Two columns, one between his mother and father in the background, another to the right of his father, just beyond his profiled face.

"There. The right column. It looks—bumpy. Can we see it better?"

Kevin drew an oval around the column, pulled it out, and enhanced it.

"Yes!" said Lee, leaning forward. "Look at those—what? It almost looks like spines or something embedded in the column."

"Yeah. Connected to scalloped edges. Weird."

Something Kevin had said tugged at Lee's mind. "Scalloped edges. That's it! Kevin, could those be seashells of some sort, plastered into the column?"

Kevin peered in. "Beats the hell out of me, Mr. Lee." He caught himself as he realized what he'd said. "Sorry, Mr. Lee. About the language, sir."

"Kevin, say whatever you want, my boy," Lee answered. "Whatever."

A grin spread over Kevin's not-quite-right face.

Lee whipped out his cell phone. "Miss Ling. Get me the phone number of that crazy female reporter who takes a swim in the ocean every morning, and pokes around tidepools. She interviewed me last year. Bei? Soo? Something like that. She's a painter, too. Have her call me here in Kevin's office...Hsing Foong...Right."

Kevin returned the original to the screen. "Look at that promontory of land jutting into the ocean, Mr. Lee."

"Probably one side of a bay. So what?"

"Well, look at its profile, its shape. That's a profile every bit as distinct as the mystery man's profile."

"So what?"

Kevin leaned back, running a hand through his golden hair, which obediently sprang back to its spiked shape. "I've got another friend, Mr. Lee. In the computer section of Military Intelligence. He's told me that they've got satellite photographs of every foot of China's shoreline, from Canton to Tientsin."

Lee's phone rang. He clicked it on. "Yes. Thank you, Miss Ling. But first, what is her name? Oh yes. I remember. Put her on."

He cleared his throat, and sat up straight. "Yes, Miss Bei. Very good of you to talk to me, Miss Bei. I often remember our wonderful evening together, over dinner, after your interview." Sung Lee was a rough man, self-made, but quite capable of charm.

"Yes, yes. I quite agree. Now Miss Bei, I have a little problem for you. I remember your charming habit of swimming in the ocean every morning, and exploring tidepools." A short pause, as he listened. "Really! Just this minute returned from this morning's swim? Perfect, Miss Bei. I need you to identify a seashell for me."

Another pause. "Yes, we have an image of it. Hold on." He took a pen, wrote something down, and slid it to Kevin. "This is her e-mail address at the newspaper. She says you can make the image a file and e-mail it to her. Right now?"

"Sure," Kevin replied, as he typed. "You've been so generous in funding our section, Mr. Lee, that we have the fastest server on the market. Here... here it goes."

Lee fidgeted. "Ah! You have it already, Miss Bei? Do you recognize it?"

He was writing again. "Yes. Spider conch. Chiragra spider conch. Oh, even the Latin. *Lambis chiragra*. I am impressed, Miss Bei."

Lee leaned back into the chair, an excited grin on his face. "I knew I could rely on your knowledge, Miss Bei. I often think of our evening together, and how much I enjoyed your company. Perhaps we may meet again sometime... Yes. Thank you again."

He turned to Kevin. "So. We have a Ma Tsu temple on the coast, with spider conch shells embedded in the columns. That should narrow it down considerably."

"And if we give my friend in Intelligence the outline of your promontory here, their program can adjust for the angle and magnification and compare it with satellite views of the coast until it finds a match."

"But will they make their program available to us?"

"All I have to do is mention that the request comes directly from you, sir. It takes a ton of computer time, of course. Shall we restrict the search to a particular stretch?"

The chair creaked as Lee leaned back and stared at the ceiling. "Say Fuzhou north to Shanghai. And do whatever you can to hurry it along."

"Got it. We won't be able to carve out much time during the day, but I'll have it going all night. And squeeze in whatever we can during the day. We might have something by—say, tomorrow early evening?"

"If that's what it will take," Lee said, then picked up the phone again.

"Me again, Miss Ling. Call up that fellow who coordinates my support of Ma Tsu temples along the coast. Tell him we need an expert who can tell us which temples between Shanghai and Fuzhou have spider conch shells plastered into their columns. I'll want the answer by tomorrow morning."

souls

Chapter Nine

He tried to put aside his anger at the newspaper woman pestering his clan's conglomerate as he opened the ebony doors to the altar. Shen's ancient eyes swept over the wooden tablets containing the *hun* souls of five centuries of his ancestors. Indeed. What did she or anything matter, compared to all this? His sons would handle her, just as he had handled the problems getting the altar and the tablets and the incense burners to Taipei from Shanghai seventy-some years ago. Through the streaming refugees, the bandits, the chaos.

A wheezing sigh escaped his old frame as he examined the incense burners before the altar. All three shimmered, their golden curves gleaming with red and green highlights like stars in a night sky. He settled into the ritual that Shen family males had faithfully kept for five hundred years. Capture a new charcoal brick with the silver tongs, and push it under the ashes against the old piece, burning two days now. The new brick would take up the fire to keep the incense burning, and also keep the burner itself warm and shimmering with the same unearthly glow that it had shown five hundred years earlier when it had emerged warm from the furnace in the imperial workshops.

His ancestor in the Ming dynasty court had suggested to Emperor Hsuan Te that copper tribute from Burma and the ground rubies from Turkestan's tribute be combined with the lumps of gold remaining from the palace that had burned to the ground just days before. To create a series of bronze incense burners, unparalleled in richness. The Emperor had commanded it. When seven of the magical burners had emerged from the furnaces, warm and gleaming, the Emperor had immediately given three of them to Shen's ancestor in gratitude.

So it had gone for all those centuries, faithfully replacing the charcoal and keeping the burners alive with the warmth of their casting. Never for five hundred years had they been allowed to cool and take on the dull, brassy look of every other piece of bronze. They shimmered still, warm and radiant. Alive!

He laughed, the cackling laugh of a man nearly one hundred years old. What was this latest challenge, compared to all that? A nobody from a nothing family. Prying into his clan's affairs, dragging her newspaper's shallow notions of legality to the enterprise that had brought wealth to the Shen family for five hundred years. They and their wooden tablets and their three radiant incense burners had survived the brutal fall of the Ming nearly four centuries ago, the savagery of the Taiping Revolt two centuries later, then the chaos at the fall of the Ch'ing a hundred years ago. Compared to all that, who was this newspaper woman? A female, yet! She would not be bothering them much longer. Who would notice when she was gone? Who would care?

He laughed again. All was well. The three incense burners glowed in the dark of the room, gold and copper and rubies from another age, another world, warmly alive for five hundred years. The dynasties, the republics, this newspaper woman—all were transitory. Ephemeral. Only his ancestors and the three shimmering jewels before them persisted, their radiance gleaming through the rising smoke of incense.

*   *   *   *   *

Meiling sat before her computer in her office. She hated to admit it, but her new assignment intrigued her. How to make contact with the American negotiator? Dawson. She scrolled down the articles on her monitor, from the paper's archives. The rock-climbing was a possibility—she had not climbed seriously since her Berkeley days, only a couple of times here on Taiwan. But she knew something about it. She had briefly met his companion Tiffany Hayes several years ago, at a convocation in San Francisco of prominent world women. *Nyuquanren*, the Managing Editor had called her. She was proud of that, being included in Taipei's group of strong, independent, modern women. But she didn't know the Hayes woman at all, really.

She laughed aloud. Well, that narrows it down to my good looks, she thought. She grabbed the phone and punched her cousin's extension.

"Ping? Could you see me? We're going to work together on an assignment you'll like. I'll be here another five or ten minutes."

She punched another, outside number.

"Yes, Meiling Bei here. How are you? Listen, we're doing a story on the American mediator, and I need to know where he'll be staying. Yes, I can hold."

She swiveled her chair and stared at the haze of pollution outside. Before she had left for Berkeley twelve years ago, you could see the Yangmingshan hills from here on good days. There weren't any good days anymore.

"What? The Hilton? Oh, straight to the negotiations? Thanks so much, Hsiao Yun. How is your mother? Yes…Wonderful. Say hello for me. *Dzai jyan*, goodbye."

One more call before Ping arrived. Her friend at the morgue. "Yes, hello Jie-fu. Anything interesting on that fellow killed on Kungyuan Road yesterday? Yes, the headless one… Oh really? Sand particles on his hands? How strange. What does that mean?…No, me either. Well, thanks. Your father's health is still well? Good."

Why would a man have particles of sand imbedded in his hands? He certainly wasn't a construction laborer. But sand on his hands? It didn't make any sense. But it wasn't her problem, anymore. His death had frightened her. She was done with it.

Where was Ping? Dear Cousin Ping, her constant companion growing up. Her housemate, now, in their fashionable East District apartment. How could we be so different, Meiling wondered again, but with a smile. Ping the party girl, trying so hard to look and act American, seeking out the karaoke bars and parties she herself shunned. Ping with half the salary but twice the clothes as her. And twice the lovers, too, she thought with a wan smile. No. More like—what? Ten times the lovers? Since Tom Ling at Berkeley, there had been only one man. Rou-jing, an artist in love with life as much as her, one of the few males she knew faithful to a woman. Two glorious months together last year, after meeting him at her watercolor show at the Apollo Gallery. Then an unexpected death. Just like Tom, again. And Rou-jing only forty years old.

Her throat suddenly got tight, and Meiling fought back tears that rose into her eyes, scolding herself for letting all this into her mind again. The brush with the rip tide yesterday had really addled her. She was not cursed, she reminded herself. It was just a horrible coincidence. Two lovers, both suddenly dead, was a tragedy. Not a curse. She gratefully heard Ping laughing gaily in the corridor outside her office. Pulling a handkerchief from her desk, she dabbed at her eyes and blew her nose.

"So, hello cousin. What's the sudden mysterious assignment?" Ping breezed into her office and took a seat, as Meiling smiled at her happy outlook on life.

"I'm supposed to contact the American negotiator. Don't ask me how."

Ping's eyes widened. "Sounds more like something for me. He's young and handsome and single, I understand," she said with a laugh.

"Yes, he is. Unfortunately, though, I got the assignment. But you can help me, if you'd like."

"Sure. What's your plan?"

Meiling smiled ruefully. "No plan, yet. He'll arrive today, and stay at the Hilton. You and I will watch the place and follow him when he leaves. Maybe he'll—I don't know. Ask directions? We'll improvise as we go."

"Wow. You ace reporters sure are smart!"

They both laughed.

Meiling sat back, letting Ping's brash attitude wash over her. "Maybe I could run him over with a moped. Break his leg, say, and insist on helping him to the hospital."

"Perfect. I'll disguise myself as a nurse, and apply some loving care to his bruised Jade Stalk. I have nurse friends who say it happens all the time!"

Meiling rolled her eyes. Irrepressible Ping.

"What happened to your knees?" Ping blurted out. "They look horrible, Meiling."

Meiling bent forward to look at them. They were, in fact, black and blue from yesterday, and did look horrible.

"I crawled over some rocks yesterday. Looks worse than it feels," she lied. She looked closely at Ping. "You look a little worse for wear yourself, dear. Short night?"

Ping blushed. "Short, but glorious. I can hardly walk," she giggled, "if you know what I mean!"

Meiling looked at her soberly. "I don't, and I don't want to guess. But let's get down to business. The hours will be arbitrary. Can you spare time from your latest?"

Ping rolled her eyes. "I shouldn't. He's so dreamy. You know him! Your old boyfriend, Jimmy Chan."

"Jimmy? Hardly an old boyfriend. More like an old friend. High school together here, then both of us to Berkeley."

"He says you went out together."

"Well, coffee, movies. Maybe half a dozen times, at the most. That doesn't make him a boyfriend, Ping, even if he maybe had a crush on me. Listen, to work. The American, Dawson, will arrive this afternoon. He'll go straight to the Sun Yat Sen Memorial for an initial session with Sung Lee and the People's Republic negotiator, Zhu. From there he'll go to the Hilton, arriving about nine this evening. Let's meet in the foyer at 8:30, and one of us take the front entrance, to Chung Hsiao Road, and the other the side door."

Ping looked disappointed. "Oh, I was going to a party with Jimmy tonight."

"Well, those wonderful memories of last night will have to suffice. Eight-thirty at the Hilton, front foyer. All right?"

"Oh, all right." She left the office, momentarily subdued.

Meiling called up a photo of the American mediator on her monitor. Did the face appeal to her? The nose was too prominent, and arched. What did they call it? A Roman nose. Typical Caucasian face. Not movie-star handsome, true, but there was something likable about it. The face seemed open to life, enjoying life. Expressive lips. The light brown hair curly and tossled. The eyes—what color are they?—drew you in.

She laughed at herself. Get hold of yourself, woman. The poor man had an impossible task. Persuade Sung Lee and China's man Zhu to agree to a union. What a notion. Sung Lee. One of the richest men in Taiwan. Unknown father, only the memory of a mother to connect him with any past. And no sons to connect him to any future.

Her mind drifted to the evening she had spent with him, dinner at Taipei's most expensive Fujianese seafood restaurant, after interviewing him for a story. He had proposed to her that evening. Well, propositioned her, but very honorably. To be his mistress and produce children, hopefully sons, for him. She had been tempted, that evening. He was very manly, brilliant in a practical sort of way, and because his rugged face smiled so rarely, when he did smile it nearly overpowered you with happiness. But she had declined. She wanted more from life than what he offered. Poor man. He has everything in the world, except for the two things he wants most. A father, and a son.

It made her own situation seem less serious, to think of Sung Lee. She was alone, and unlucky in love. But she was young, had her future before her, and her devotions to the goddess Ma Tsu were frequent and sincere. So what if she had been unfortunate in boyfriends? Twice, yet. She lit incense daily to Ma Tsu, and swam in the goddess' abode every morning. Ma Tsu would look after her. Find her a decent mate, strong enough or fortunate enough to survive her love, to raise children with her. She wanted children, wanted to share with them the joy of being strong and alive. Why shouldn't she have all this? She wasn't cursed. Ma Tsu wouldn't allow it.

Would she?

mountain

Chapter Ten

Taipei, Sun Yat-sen Memorial

Steaming tea filled Philip's golden tea cup, red bats fluttering up its sides. He stared at the shapely arm of the woman pouring the tea, saw her gracefully lift the lip of the teapot as the tea neared the brim. During this first session's introductions he eyed his counterparts. Lee was tall and rough-hewn. As tough as he had anticipated, though he wore his black suit and silk tie well, as if he'd earned them. The Chinese head, Zhu, was the opposite of Lee. Plump and soft in his Italian suit, his round face expressive behind large glasses. Zhu had earned a Masters in international relations at Yale. Philip could size up Zhu easily. Lee was from another world.

Dirk finished introductions for their team. All eyes turned expectantly to Philip. Showtime, he thought. Wish me luck, Grandpa. He rose. Bowed slightly, from the waist.

"Mr. Lee and Mr. Zhu. The People's Republic and Taiwan have wrestled with your relationship for half a century. The United States is happy at this opportunity to help you resolve the issue. My grandfather came to China over 70 years ago as a missionary to help its people. I've long admired Chinese culture, so it's a pleasure for me to retrace his journey in part." Be warm, be positive, be personal, Philip reminded himself. Just like Grandpa. Just like New Delhi.

Soon the delegations were split into three working groups. Dirk, Baden, and most of the aides in all three camps moved to nearby rooms, leaving Philip and an interpreter from the Monterey Institute in the cavernous main hall with Lee and Zhu and half a dozen of their aides. She of the shapely arm refilled the tea cups.

"Gentlemen," began Philip with a warm smile. "We're charged with addressing military matters and the nature of the union. As your mediator, I appreciate your agreement to conduct the sessions in English, which I understand you both are conversant in—certainly better than my Chinese. Let's begin with the issue of disposition of armed forces. Mr. Zhu, where had your talks gotten to, on this subject?"

An aide handed Zhu a notebook, which he began to read from.

"Mr. Zhu. I've read your initial position papers. Please just speak plainly to me about the direction of your discussions on the subject with Mr. Lee."

Zhu raised his eyebrows, dropped the notebook, and leaned back in his chair. "Our Civil War was decided more than sixty years ago. We expect the Taiwanese military to be incorporated into the forces of the People's Republic of China. Just as the nationalist troops of the warlord Fu Tso-yi were at the fall of Beijing half a century ago."

"Nonsense!" came Lee's deep voice from the other table. "To demand that we unilaterally disarm ourselves is nonsense." He leaned back as his chief aide whispered in his ear. "And Mr. Zhu should remember that his own Deng Xiao-ping promised in the 1980's that Taiwan could in fact retain our military after reunification."

"That was three decades ago," snapped Zhu. "You refused to accept reunification then. This is now. You have since added a belligerent arsenal of weapons to what you had then. They cannot remain pointed at your brethren across the Taiwan Strait."

"Mr. Zhu, thank you for stating your position," Philip interjected. "I appreciate your points. Mr. Lee, what is your position on the issue?"

Lee's face had a hard, impassive look. "We must keep our military. And we cannot permit any armed forces of the People's Republic onto Taiwan," he said bluntly.

"Now that is the true nonsense," Zhu shouted, losing his composure.

"Every citizen of Taiwan has the image of July 1997 burned into his mind," Lee said slowly. "Armored personnel carriers swarming into Hong Kong, soldiers with rifle barrels gleaming in the dark rain. The same APC's we had seen in Tien An Men Square in 1989. No one on Taiwan can let those scenes from that long rainy night happen here. No one."

The great room became quiet at Lee's words. Zhu lit a cigarette, dragging on it several times. Finally he spoke, softly, no hint of argument in his voice.

"The APC's in Hong Kong were WZ523's. Newer than the ones in Tien

An Men Square in 1989. My son was in the Square, saw the old ones at very close range."

"Well," said Philip, attempting to keep his tone positive. Evidently there'd been precious little movement on disposition of armed forces. He guessed the same would be true for the next subject. He would start at the beginning, with the basics. "Let's consider the form and content of any possible union. Mr. Zhu. Let's be direct. Can you envision Taiwan as part of China, yet retaining features of independence?"

Zhu tossed his cigarette on the floor and leaned forward, his eyes now grim. "We cannot tolerate the use of the word 'independence', Mr. Dawson. It creates false and unattainable impressions. We are happy to speak of a Taiwan with its own legal, economic, and political systems. We will not speak of a Taiwan with independence."

"Also nonsense," Lee interrupted, his face grim. "The whole point is that our systems must be independent of China's."

"I do not hear—*ting-bu-dong*!—the word 'independence'!" Zhu shouted, bringing a closed fist onto the tabletop with each syllable.

The young aide beside Lee immediately began shouting "Independence!" at the top of his lungs. Zhu jumped to his feet shrieking "*Ting-bu-dong!*" back. In an instant the aides at each table joined in the shouting, chairs toppling every way, angry yells echoing through the room. Philip watched the spectacle for a moment, slumped in his chair, stunned by the vehemence. Finally, fearing fisticuffs, he moved between the two tables, arms outstretched.

"Gentlemen! Please. Let's all calm down." He strode back and forth several times. The shouting gradually died down, as the sides retreated to their seats. "Gentlemen," Philip said over the scraping of chairs being put aright. "Are we getting tangled up in semantics? I suggest we find a way to refer to systems within Taiwan with a phrase, rather than the word 'independent.' Would it work for you, Mr. Lee, to say that you require legal, economic, political, and cultural systems in a re-united Taiwan that are *different* and *free of influence* from the People's Republic?"

Lee's chief aide whispered in his ear, but Lee cut him off. "If it is perfectly clear what we mean by that—functional independence—then I have no problem with it."

"Wonderful," said Philip. His eyes found the tea lady, and motioned for more all around. She walked gingerly between the two tables, ready to bolt at the first hint of more hostilities. She filled cups right and left in long arcs streaming from the pot.

"Now, Mr. Lee," resumed Philip. "If Taiwan's systems were guaranteed to be different and free of influence from the People's Republic, could you entertain some notion of participation in a common national sovereignty with the People's Republic?"

The huge room became silent. Even Zhu's aides sat frozen by Philip's question.

Very slowly, Lee leaned forward. He wet his lips.

"The Republic of Taiwan could only consider participation in a common national sovereignty with the People's Republic if the ind—" He paused. "If the different and influence-free status of its systems were reflected and guaranteed in the very form of common sovereignty, and the title reflecting that form."

Philip took a long sip of steaming tea. The image of a frozen young boy on a Vermont cliff flitted across his mind. "Wonderful," he said, and turned to Zhu.

"Mr. Zhu. What form of union do you have in mind?"

"Taiwan has been a province of China for 300 years, far longer than the United States of America has existed," Zhu replied quickly. "We therefore—"

"No. No. No!" Lee said, his large hand hitting the table with each repetition. "We are not another province! No province is allowed the independence we demand."

"Mr. Lee," Philip interjected, before Zhu could respond. "Hong Kong is a Special Administrative Region. That certainly reflects something different. Could you contemplate a special administrative, or even a special political, region of Taiwan?"

Zhu began to protest, but Philip raised a hand to silence him.

"We are not Hong Kong, either," Lee continued, insistently. "Hong Kong has always been a colony, never been independent. We have in fact been independent for half a century, now. And we are twenty one million to Hong Kong's seven million."

"And we are one billion plus more than twenty one million!" Zhu yelled, his voice echoing. "How can twenty one million dictate to one billion and more?"

Lee's aide shouted back, and made to rise. Lee abruptly shoved him back with one arm, and the room went silent at the shock of the physical action.

Zhu glared at Lee, clutching his glasses tightly in one hand.

Philip spoke in a soft voice in the silence. "All right, gentlemen. Another format that has been suggested is a confederation of Chinese republics, the People's Republic of China on one side, and the Republic of Taiwan on the other."

Zhu angrily shook his head. "We are not two equal republics, joined in a confederation. Twenty one million is not equal to one billion!" he said, hitting the table and shattering the glasses in his fist. "The mainland, the homeland, must be accorded its due. Taiwan is part of China, not China and Taiwan equally part of something else!"

Lee did not restrain his chief aide this time, as the fellow again rose to his feet and shrieked at Zhu and his aides, who themselves rose and began shaking their fists at Lee and his aide. Philip thought of Dirk's comments on the plane. Like Mao Tse-tung yelling at Chiang Kai-shek, 1949. He sat silent, sipped his tea, and let the uproar die down. This was worse than he had anticipated, even. He needed some time to find a new angle.

"Gentlemen, I don't see that we're so far apart," said Philip, setting his teacup in its saucer. "Taiwan and the People's Republic in a common national sovereignty, with the different systems of Taiwan respected and guaranteed. Taiwan is more than a province or special region, but less than a republic equal to the People's Republic."

Lee leaned forward and began to object, but Philip raised his hand.

"Please, Mr. Lee. That summary seems fair to me, and I would like to let it stand as a rough guide for future sessions. I think we've made progress today. Shall we meet at ten o'clock tomorrow morning, when I will have some bridging proposals for us?"

Zhu, gathering broken pieces of his glasses off the table, gave Philip a curt nod. Lee threw Philip a skeptical look, then slowly nodded.

"One final request, gentlemen. May I ask Mr. Lee and Mr. Zhu, just yourselves, to join me outside for a moment?"

When Philip opened the door to the hallway outside, bright lights from a dozen flashbulbs greeted them. Philip led Zhu and Lee to the west side of the building and down stairs to a portico at ground level, beyond which several dozen children played in a grassy area that Philip had noticed when entering the building. Some of the white-and-blue-uniformed children swung badminton rackets with great shouts, while others dashed about after soccer balls, their cheeks glowing nearly as red as the bows in the girls' hair.

"This is the reason we're going to succeed, gentlemen," said Philip, gesturing to the children. "In spite of our initial difficulties today. The children of both your countries deserve to grow up and get jobs and get married and live out their lives."

Crossing his arms over his chest, he leaned against the balustrade, facing the others. "And it won't hurt to remind ourselves of what happens if we fail to reach an agreement, Mr. Lee. Mr. Zhu." He glared at them. "War, very likely. Instead of green parks full of laughing children, we have burning cities, with children's bodies blown apart and scattered among the blasted trees. Everything you've built up for decades, your parks and homes and water lines, shattered. In Taiwan, and in China also. And, if my country gets pulled into it, which I am authorized to say is quite possible, all this is poisoned by nuclear radioactivity, continuing the death and the sickness for centuries more."

The two men looked sharply at Philip, then glanced at each other. Philip let the silence hang. Lee and Zhu stood unmoving, faces of stone. The happy sounds of playing children floated to them from the park.

Zhu's stomach was roiling. He remembered his uncle, General Zhu, assuring the Politburo a month ago that America wouldn't risk a nuclear war over Taiwan. "They are preoccupied with their Arabian oil," he had declared confidently. "They have lost their courage, and will—what do they say?—they will 'blink' over Taiwan. I guarantee it." Uncle was always unaccountably confident in his judgments, Zhu thought bitterly. But he had won the Politburo over, and their course was set.

"Gentlemen," said Philip. "We are going to succeed. Because it is unthinkable, *unthinkable*, gentlemen, that we could fail and allow war to shatter the lives of these children, and those in China. Nuclear war, yet." Philip let it sink in. "Gentlemen? What do you think?"

A minute's silence. Zhu drew a deep breath, to calm his stomach. He forced his uncle out of his mind, and thought instead of his second son, and his son in turn. "My grandson is seven years. He draws, everything he sees he draws. I would not want him to draw scenes of war." A shudder of despair washed over him. "I am not so sure as you we can succeed. Not at all. We must get reunification. But I suppose it may be possible, to perhaps relinquish some things, in order to achieve our goal without war."

Lee's face was grim, impassive as he directed a long stare at Zhu. Finally, he spoke. "I am older than either of you. I have seen the face of war, as a child. The death, the destruction. I survived it, but I know what it does to people. To lives. So I am willing to explore giving up some things, also, to avoid war. But like Zhu, I have little hope we can succeed."

Philip knew they had a long way to go. But they had taken the first step. Flashbulbs began to pop again as they all three approached the stairs. Philip pulled a notepad and pen from his suit pocket.

"Mr. Lee. Might I ask a favor of you, sir?"

"What?" Lee asked gruffly.

"I'd like to visit a temple here, to ask a blessing on our endeavor. Could you write the name of one you're familiar with, so I could show it to folks for directions?"

Lee grunted his assent. "That would be Lung Shan Temple, in the old city."

Philip offered the pen to Lee's right hand, but the man pursed his lips and took it instead with his left, and wrote three bold characters on the paper with that hand.

"Thank you. We share a common misfortune, Mr. Lee. I'm also left-handed."

Lee pursed his lips again, and handed the pen back, directing an unfriendly stare into Philip's eyes. "Our fate is determined not by avoiding misfortune, but by coping with it, according to Confucius," he said in a hard voice.

媽祖

Ma Tsu

Chapter Eleven

Philip emerged from his shower, toweled dry, and rummaged through the chaos that was his suitcase. Tom Morgan was in the corner, poking an electronic sensor under the table where the television sat. The C.I.A. "cleaning crew" would have already thoroughly searched the Hilton room for bugs, but Tom knew the guys on the crew—drank with them—so he always double-checked.

Philip pulled on slacks and socks on the side of the bed, staring at the railway station across the street. The orange neon lights of half the four Chinese characters on its roof were on the fritz. About the same state as the negotiations, he reflected.

"Good first session?" came Tom's voice from under the table.

A laugh from Philip. "If you like professional wrestling, you'd have loved it."

"That bad, huh? Say, Phil, couldn't you choose a damn city less hot and humid to save the world in, next time? This is as bad as New Delhi." He disappeared into the bathroom, sensor in hand.

"In New Delhi I knew what the hell I was doing," Philip yelled into the bathroom. "Here, we're going to have to do some research. Jonathan Spense at Yale said I should visit a temple, when I called him for advice. And I got Sung Lee to recommend one. So I'm off, in the window I have while Baden and Dirk debrief their people and write up reports on their sessions this afternoon."

Tom hurried out of the bathroom. "Now, Phil. We can't dispense with standard security procedures."

Philip shrugged. "Can't be helped, Tom. I won't learn a thing if there's the usual dozen sun-glassed agents whispering into phones all over the place. I need to talk to folks here, learn about the god of the sea, get a feel for Chinese people and what makes 'em tick. You'll be there, but lay low and don't alarm everyone."

"I'll need backup, and a car for communications. I'll drive you there and back."

"Thanks, but I'll walk—I need to breathe some real air. You can follow in a car if you want. No one other than you in the temple, though."

"Goddamn it," Tom muttered. "When do you take off, Gunga Din?"

"Ten minutes, from that side entrance off the lobby."

Tom slammed the door as he left to arrange for a car.

*　　*　　*　　*　　*

Meiling, deep in a leather chair in an alcove at the Hilton's main entrance, glanced right to the far end of the lobby to see a tall figure lightly leap down the last two stairs there, and disappear toward the side door. She didn't see the face, but the way the man moved rang a bell. She bolted from her chair and hurried down the length of the lobby. With a curse she swept past Ping, asleep in a chair by the side door, and onto the street. Outside, she nearly bowled over the tall man, who was asking the porter a question.

"—to Lung Shan temple?" she heard him say, showing the man a piece of paper.

Meiling swerved to the side and kept on walking. It was Dawson all right. She dodged mopeds from every direction to cross the street and stepped into a CD shop until he passed her.

She felt a guilty pleasure spying on Dawson the thirty minutes it took to walk to the temple. He seemed amused at the parked motorbikes cluttering the sidewalks, the old men peeing on walls in side streets. He nodded pleasantly to people, and veered into shops along the way. Shopkeepers took to him, and sent for their children, who emerged from watching television in the back rooms to speak English with the tall American. Meiling found herself enjoying his company, even incognito and at a distance. Somehow she felt safer, from the conglomerate, with him nearby. Now that was strange.

She passed him and hurried into the temple, through its outer courtyard, and purchased a bundle of incense sticks at the counter on the right. Where to position myself? she thought. The shrine to Kuan Yin in front? Too busy. Ah yes. Ma Tsu's altar at the back. What if he didn't go back that far? But no. She could rely on Ma Tsu. And her man's curiosity. She felt like she already knew him, just from watching him on the street. He would explore, every corner. And Ma Tsu would make sure he noticed her.

*　　*　　*　　*　　*

Philip joined the throng passing under the bright red, green and gold gateway into the temple's huge open air courtyard. Water cascaded down a twenty-foot waterfall on his right. To his left was a smaller pool, beyond a long board with newspapers tacked upon it. A babble of voices came from dozens of old men crowded before the board, dissecting the events described with much gusto and dramatic gesticulations of scrawny arms. Around the courtyard, more old men and women sat in clusters, gossiping, in undershirts with pants rolled up over the knee.

Some temple, Philip thought. More like the Elks Lodge in Montpelier on a warm summer night. Except—what? Louder. Festive, almost. Old and young, families. When Tom sauntered into the courtyard, Philip joined the crowd of people streaming through a second gateway. On the other side, a bright red shrine appeared, fronted by tall incense burners with dragons writhing up their sides. He stood, rapt, senses overwhelmed by the pungent smell of incense, shimmering light from hundreds of candles, voices rising and falling in chants. People thronged past him to the incense burners and placed burning sticks into them, doing a peculiar little bow before and after, hands to their foreheads. Like a dance, almost.

Another flow of people passed this main shrine hall, down a corridor lined with rooms and shops. Curious at what was down there, he joined the movement, and soon was at a row of smaller altars stretching across the back of the temple, each altar fronted by a table and dull bronze incense burner, full of glowing sticks. People bowed in front of each altar, doing the little bobbing dance, stuck part of their handful of burning sticks into the urn, then moved on. He ambled down the row, peering in at the objects at the back of the altars. A scowling, red-faced statue in golden robes, sword in one hand. A serene Buddha-type. A black-faced matron with a fancy headdress in the next one, pearls hanging down her dark visage.

Suddenly Philip stumbled over something on the floor—a kneeling figure, he saw as he skipped to the side. A woman. She didn't move, and he mumbled an apology and backed away. She knelt there, still focused in prayer, for a long moment, then rose in a smooth, graceful motion. She was tall, for a Chinese woman, wearing a cream-colored business suit, with a blue blouse. As she put the last of her incense sticks in the vase fronting the altar and turned, Philip saw her face for the first time. Fine features, although nothing delicate about them. She carried herself proud and confident. For some reason, Philip thought of the hawks he had tended seven summers ago in India.

If he was looking for some answers, Philip decided, he could hardly do better than this. He hurried after her, and touched her arm lightly as he reached her.

"Pardon me, miss. I'd like to apologize for bumping into you back there."

She turned her head slightly, but didn't slow down. Regarded him with cool eyes for a moment, then nodded curtly and kept going.

Philip stopped, struck by her rudeness. She disappeared into the crowd. "Damn," he sighed. He wandered out to the front courtyard, gazing around at the knots of old people there, wondering if any of them would speak English.

A fine mist festooned the sun-lit courtyard with a hundred twinkling reflections, and his gaze followed the mist to the waterfall thundering into the pond. She was there, the lady in the cream suit, leaning against the ledge fronting the pond, her back to him. She was perfectly still, completely absorbed in the waterfall. Again, the hawks from India came to his mind, the way they sat graceful and contented on their perches, staring off into the distances, absorbed in something wild and beyond Philip's ken.

Round two, Philip thought, enjoying the pursuit. He sauntered over to the waterfall and leaned on the ledge beside her.

"It was clumsy of me to run into you back there. I apologize. Good evening."

He glanced over at her. She was staring straight ahead, no response. The roar of the water hitting the pool was considerable, but she had to have heard him. With an exasperated sigh he straightened up, turned, and walked away.

"New England, I think."

Her voice was rich, confident, like her walk. Four steps away, he stopped, a smile playing on his lips, his back turned to her.

"I've been stumbled over before," came the warm voice. "We get too many tourists here."

His smile evaporated. He turned, an edge of anger in his voice.

"I'm not a tourist. I'm here to get some questions answered."

She turned from the waterfall and faced him. Bright eyes regarded him coolly. They were jet black, set in intense white, the eyelids curving up into a long, thin point to the outside.

"Questions?"

"Yeah. Is there a god of the sea? What does he like? Dislike? How do you get on his good side? His bad side?"

She eyed him, coolly still. Mist drifted over her, leaving small droplets scattered in her jet black hair. She could be a goddess herself, Philip thought. She was like Venus in Botticelli's painting, rising from the waters. Except clothed, of course.

"How much do you know? About our culture?" she asked, mocking, challenging.

"A bit," he answered, keeping his distance from her. "Lots about dynasties and wars and Buddhism. Confucius and Lao Tse. Less about folk religion and all the gods."

A smile came to her lips, her eyes narrowed. "What gender is Heaven, dragons?"

"Male, of course. The yang side of things."

"So below Heaven, the earth and the sea, foxes and fish-creatures?"

He laughed. "Of course. Female, yin. So she's a goddess, of the sea?"

"And what would we decorate her with, this goddess of the sea?"

He liked this game. He liked the playfulness of this black-eyed Venus. He wanted to beat her at the game.

"You'd decorate her with precious objects from the sea. With—"

She raised an eyebrow as he paused, a smile playing on her lips.

"Seashells," he said quickly. "Iridescent seashells, with lustrous purple surfaces."

"Close," she breathed, huskily. "Be more concentrated, more costly."

Blood was surging into his head, and his groins. He struggled to stay focused. This was a demanding game. Concentrated and costly, associated with sea shells. He tore his gaze off her lips, down to her neck, strong and finely sculpted.

"Pearls!" he breathed. Then he knew. "The statue you were kneeling before. The lady with pearls hanging down her forehead. She's the goddess of the sea."

"You're good," she said, and a smile bloomed on her lips. "Her name is Ma Tsu."

"Tell me about her. All about her."

"Ma Tsu lived in the tenth century on Mei Zhou, an island off the coast of Fujian," she began, her dark eyes glowing. "She set fire to her house on the shore to guide sailors in from a taiphoon one night. Her *hun* souls left her body in a trance and pulled her brother's boat to safety in another storm." The dark Venus shook her head, and droplets of mist sparkled from her. "She's been worshipped for over a thousand years, and grown to be the Queen of Heaven, Tien Hou, and the patron saint of Taiwan."

The patron saint of the island, yet. Perfect, thought Philip. This Ma Tsu is my ticket to Sung Lee. Somehow, she's going to be important.

"Fascinating. And how do you get on Ma Tsu's right side?"

Another smile played on her lips. "Why are you so interested in Ma Tsu, Mr.–?"

He hesitated. "Uh, Morgan. Tom Morgan. I'm a businessman, a little of this, a little of that. Trying to get a deal with one of your shipping tycoons. I'm guessing he owes a lot to Ma Tsu, so I'd like to know more about her. Say, it's noisy here. Could we talk somewhere? Maybe eat?"

He watched her warily. Would she buy it? She glanced at him, then away. Her eyes were quick. Black islands in a sea of white, with a curving shore.

"I see. Good approach. To your shipping tycoon, I mean. It is noisy here, and I am hungry. There's a place near here they call Snake Alley, in the tourist books."

Chapter Twelve

Snake Alley, a long, covered street with vendors crammed on either side and lights strung overhead, was even more crowded than the temple. Philip and the black-eyed Venus joined the throng jostling down the lane, surrounded by laughing, exuberant conversations and more smells than he could hope to sort out. They passed tattoo parlors, food carts, music shops filled with CDs and youths, and small stands brimming with shelves of miniature statues.

"These must be for family altars," Philip guessed, pointing to the statues. "There's the Buddha, the laughing Buddha—and this is Kuan Yin?"

"Yes. Look, here's Ma Tsu." She pointed at a seated matron, the familiar pearls over her forehead.

"Wonderful. Let me have that one." He picked it up, and gave the shopkeeper a twenty dollar bill, which was promptly accepted, and change given in the Taiwanese currency with a broad grin.

"Who's that fellow?" Philip asked, pointing to a stout official on the top row of a shelf.

"The Jade Emperor, more of a god than a saint," she answered, moving away. They came to the restaurant section. Dozens of water tanks fronted the entrances, with live lobster, crab, and shrimp dancing in slow motion along the bottom as squid glided above them. Dozens of shellfish extended their siphons out of rough shells, the tubes swaying in the water.

"I hope you like seafood, Miss—?"

She hesitated, weighing it. To his surprise, she answered.

"Dao. Ping Dao."

"Ah, Miss Dao." He felt a twinge of guilt, at lying to her about his identity when she was so honest about hers. "But why do they call this Snake Alley?"

She glanced across the lane, at several shops with bamboo cages stacked in front of tables. As they strolled up and paused in the crowd, a young fellow pointed to a yellow snake in the top cage and said something in a boisterous tone. The vendor opened the side door to the cage, thrust a hooked metal rod into it, and dragged out the squirming reptile. Philip saw a hood flare just behind the head, and he stepped back as the cobra hissed. The vendor nabbed the cobra behind its neck in a firm grip.

Almost quicker than Philip could follow, the man attached a wire loop over the cobra's head, ran the rest of the wire down the snake's body, and pulled the squirming body taut along the wire. Then he hung the stretched cobra on a hook and in one long motion slit open its body from top to bottom with a small knife. He grabbed a glass of clear liquid from the table and pressed it against the middle of the cut with one hand, while he squeezed several greenish glands, squirting a green liquid into the glass. Nonchalantly he handed the glass to the boisterous customer, who loudly toasted his red-faced girlfriend and drank it in one long draught.

"One of the tonics for male potency, I take it?" Philip said to Miss Dao.

She turned laughing eyes to him and nodded. Philip leaned down and inspected the dozen bamboo cages, peering between the slats. More cobras. And a relatively short snake, with rough overlapping scales and a cross on its head.

"Hey! Some of these are saw-scale vipers, Miss Dao!"

She glanced at the cages. "I haven't heard of that one."

"It's from India. More dangerous than a cobra, by far. Aggressive. Kills thousands of people every year, an incredible venom."

"Well, the more poisonous the snake, the more potent the drink."

The vendor was collecting the dying cobra's blood in another jar, then he slapped the writhing snake onto the table and peeled the skin off, from tail to head, in one continuous pull. At the hood, he deftly cut the skin with the intact head off the body and tossed it to the side, the wire still attached.

"He's going to cut the meat off the body, for snake soup," explained Miss Dao.

"Another gift for weak-hearted men?"

"No. A general tonic. Good for everyone."

"Can we have some? I'm famished."

She hesitated, then laughed. "Sure. Have a seat."

They entered the small shop and sat at the lone table near the back. She said a few sharp words to the man, as Philip surveyed the scene, a grin on his face. The grin abruptly vanished as he noticed the high stack of cages at the front of the shop sway, then begin a slow fall to the floor. As the cages crashed, their doors sprung open and half a dozen cobras and vipers streamed towards them, their dark bodies scratching harshly on the pale linoleum floor.

Philip jumped out of his chair as screams filled the area. "Watch out!" he yelled, grabbing Miss Dao's arm. They staggered backward, slamming into the back wall of the shop. The snakes pressed on toward them, excited by the fall and the commotion at the front of the shop. Philip looked up—nothing to lift them off the floor, and snakes between them and their chairs. He kicked toward the lead snake, one of the saw-scale vipers. Several cobras were coiled up at their feet, hoods flared and about to strike. Their hissing and the harsh, sawing noise from viper scales rubbing together pounded in their ears. The musky smell was overpowering.

As Philip kicked out again at the pile of coiled snakes, Miss Dao knelt to the floor and pulled a canister from her purse. In a steady movement she aimed it point blank at the snakes. A reddish powder erupted from the canister. As it hit the snakes they flung themselves backwards, long writhing loops of snakes flying through the air away from them. She sprayed a ring around herself and Philip. The snakes streamed toward the crowd at the front of the shop, who stampeded madly amidst screams and shouts.

The vendor was grabbing the snakes in sure nabs, and had three already stuffed back into the cages and latches secured. Shrieks filled the air still, as people shoved to escape the remaining snakes.

"Good thinking, that pepper spray, Miss Dao," Philip said, helping her up, eyes watering. As she rose, he saw a cobra coiled in the corner behind her, hood flared, quivering. He jerked her away as it struck, barely missing her. The cobra slapped against the linoleum floor under their feet and with a scratching noise quickly coiled again, less than a yard away. Philip looked around for a weapon, anything. He leaned over to the front table and grabbed the skinned snake by its tail. He whipped it toward the coiled cobra. The headless top of the snake slapped against the quivering hood of the cobra and it veered away. Philip slapped the dead body at the cobra again, and it slithered to the front of the shop, where the vendor grabbed it by the neck and stuffed it into a cage. The man darted toward the last two snakes streaming down the lane, littered with packages and handbags abandoned in the crowd's headlong panic.

"Are you all right?" Philip asked Miss Dao, dropping the skinned snake body on the counter. To his surprise, she seemed relatively cool and steady, although a bit flushed, and breathing fast.

"I suppose. That's the first time I've ever used the pepper spray. I almost quit carrying it." She walked to a chair and collapsed on it.

The vendor returned with a squirming viper in each hand. Philip picked up the last two cages scattered on the floor, and the vendor shoved the snakes into them and latched the doors shut. Both men checked the stack of cages. Every one with a snake, doors latched shut.

Miss Dao confronted the vendor and exchanged several heated bursts of staccato words. People returned to the shop, and soon angry comments were flying between the crowd and the vendor. Finally Miss Dao turned to Philip.

"Several people claim they saw some men brush against the cages, almost like they were pushing them over. Others say no, it was an accident. No one can explain why the doors opened, every one of them. Some suggest the same men unlatched the doors, but no one saw it. The crowd is accusing him of having unsafe cages."

The vendor was arguing loudly with the crowd, particularly the young fellow who had just consumed the snake bile. He was in the vendor's face, the two of them nearly to blows. Suddenly the vendor turned and with a sweep of his skinny arm knocked the top two cages to the floor. They hit the floor with a scratching sound and skidded again toward Philip and Miss Dao. The doors stayed latched. The vendor bent down and picked up the cages and shoved them toward the young man, hitting the still-shut doors with his palm.

Philip looked at Miss Dao. Her eyes were agitated, and avoided his.

"Look, I've lost my appetite for snake soup," he admitted.

She nodded. "It's been a hard day for me, Mr., uh, Morgan. I really must be leaving. I apologize for the ...accident with the snakes."

"Accidents happen," he shrugged. "I still have a lot of questions about Ma Tsu. Do you come to the temple every night? Perhaps I could see you again."

She finally fixed her eyes on him. They were drawn and pained. "Perhaps," she echoed, and pushed into the crowd and was gone.

Tom pushed his way through the crowd to Philip. "What the hell happened here? I stopped to look at some statues, and the next thing I know a wall of people is pushing me the other way, shouting like all hell is breaking loose over here. I had a heck of a time getting to you."

"Some snake cages got knocked over. No big deal."

"Smells like pepper spray. Your eyes are watering." Tom peered into the cages, and jumped back. "Hey, those look like cobras."

Philip nodded. "And saw-scale vipers." He walked to a tank holding some lobsters and squid next door, and washed the snake-gore off his hands.

"Say, I'm starved. How long do we have before we meet with Baden and Dirk for the assessment of today's session?"

Tom looked at his watch. "Little over an hour."

"Wonderful. Let's get a table in here and order some fresh seafood. But stick close to me, Tom. Something about that snake business makes me nervous." He thought of his last champagne, at the Indian Embassy. Had that really been just yesterday? He was getting suspicious of food and drink. He laughed. Next it'll be women. The laugh died in his throat as he thought of the dark-eyed Venus.

Chapter Thirteen

Dirk and her team were the last to drag themselves into the conference room at the American Institute, looking even more dead-tired and drained than Baden and his team. Her session had lasted the longest, dragging on past midnight. They crumpled into chairs around the long table at the center of the room.

"OK. We're all tired and jet-lagged," Philip said in a flat tone. "Let's be concise. How did it go in your room, Baden?"

The familiar wide-eyed, enthusiastic look tried to compete with the weariness on Baden's face. "No serious problems, Philip. Everyone is tired of having to fly to Hong Kong to get to China. Of having their mail take three days to get across seventy miles of Strait. Some strained exchanges, but nothing too bad. We worked pretty steady until 11:30. All that's left is another session or two of grunt work, getting the protocols aligned."

"Wonderful. Dirk?"

She pulled herself together with an effort. Her face was lined, eyes puffy. "Like pulling teeth," she opened. "The Taiwanese want to avoid Hong Kong's problems. So they're insisting on a guarantee that mainland firms doing business here be subject to Taiwan's laws and regulations. The People's Republic wants nothing of it."

"Is it important enough to them to resist to the end, no matter?"

Dirk shrugged, and looked to Baden. He sighed and thought. "I don't think China will insist. They'll wait until the bitter end. But they can live with that."

"What else?"

"The economic stuff is pretty straightforward," Dirk said. "The People's Republic has already said Taiwan can keep all its own practices and procedures. Taiwan's demanding documented, specific guarantees of it all, which Beijing is balking at. It'll just be days of grinding out the wording. Word by word." She raised her hand to her temple and began rubbing it.

"And?"

"Like you suggested, we put off the political issues to the last. Really, each side just stated its position. Shouted its position, rather. China's very insistent on titles being changed, particularly at the higher levels. They're curiously hung up on names, words."

Philip grunted, and sat up in his chair. "I hear that. Same with me. All sorts of table-pounding about words and names, but they're not really too far apart on the basics. Although they evidently haven't moved a dime off their opening positions, in spite of—what has it been, three months of talks?"

"Really, Mr. Dawson?" said the interpreter from the Monterey Institute. "I got the impression they were miles apart and would rather die than yield an inch."

"Yeah. That's what they want to project," Philip answered. "But it's mainly show. You should have been in New Delhi last year, for some really stormy fights."

Dry laughter twittered around the room.

"Here's your assignment," he said to the interpreter. "Find me a word or phrase that describes a political entity that's above a province but below a republic."

"Six letters, begins with a 'k,' 14 across," Baden said, to more laughter.

"I need it by ten tomorrow morning. Better have several versions. There are people in the AIT, Taiwanese, who can help you." The American Institute in Taiwan functioned as a de facto embassy.

Philip turned to the others. "But the really stormy part was over the military. They turned into the snarling, spitting enemies that Dirk described on the flight over. The PRC wants Taiwan's military demobilized and the weapons turned over to them. Taiwan wants no PRC forces allowed on the island, period."

Several people gasped. Silence fell over the room.

"That could be a trifle difficult to reconcile," Dirk said, dryly.

"Yeah," Philip said. "So you tell me. How do we do that?"

More silence.

"I thought we might try to stage things," Philip said. "Jigger with the time element. Taiwan keeps its forces for five years. Then hands over certain elements in the next few years. PRC forces allowed on the island in ten years. Something like that."

"Those things very rarely impress either side," Dirk said, putting a hand to her temple again. "And for good reason—they so rarely end up happening. Something always comes up to wreck the timetable,"

"Yeah. Any other ideas?"

No one spoke. Dirk slumped back in her chair. "We could look at the spatial dimension," she rasped. "Have the bunker fortifications on Quemoy and Matsu dismantled within five years. Taiwanese forces withdraw completely two years later. In ten years, Taiwanese air bases in south Taiwan get abandoned. Work the way up the island."

Philip shoot a look at Baden. The thin man's eyes refused to light up. "Might work," he ventured, unconvincingly. "Won't hurt to try."

"We'll work on it," Philip said, without much enthusiasm. "Let's all keep thinking on this one. Talk to the AIT folks here about it. I'm worried that we haven't helped you out much, Dirk."

A groan, as Dirk shifted in her chair. "You know what, Philip? I get the feeling that if you can hammer out something on the big issues, the rest of it will fall into place. It's like everyone was looking over their shoulder, back toward the main room with you and Lee and Zhu, today."

"Yeah. Well, anything else?" Philip said, looking at his watch.

The dozen and a half people in the room were wearily pushing themselves up from their chairs when an AIT staffer came rushing in. "Something on the late news you'll want to see," she said, grabbing the remote off the table and pointing it at the big screen in the corner of the room.

The television blinked into footage of the two U.S. aircraft carrier groups stationed in Japan. The voiceover described how the President had just given the order for them to move out to the Taiwan Straits, two dozen warships in all plus several hundred airplanes on each of the two carriers themselves, setting off within hours.

A stunned silence enveloped the room.

"You," Philip said to the AIT staffer. "Get the President on the line for me. Now. Tom has the access code."

She stared wide-eyed at him. Tom emerged from the opposite corner and gave her a card. She stumbled to the phone on the long table, one of the round conference call models, wireless, and punched numbers in.

"Sir, do you want me to set up video teleconference connection?" she asked, looking back at Philip. "It'll take twenty minutes or so."

"We'll all be asleep by then," Philip growled. "Just set the phone volume so everyone can hear this." He stood up, and began pacing around the table.

Silence reigned for nearly half a minute while the call was routing through. Baden and Dirk, pale, alternated from watching the carriers on the television to watching Philip, pacing round the table.

"Ravenhurst here," erupted a voice from the telephone suddenly.

"Ravenhurst, this is Dawson, in Taipei. I'm trying to get hold of the President."

"President Hayes is unavailable. Meeting a group of schoolkids from Dubuque or some such place. I'm taking the important calls."

"Great. I just saw on the news that he's sending two carrier groups to the Straits, for Christsake. I want you to tell the President that I don't like learning about key developments from my television set, goddamn it. Nor do Baden and Dirk. And secondly, tell him that sending more American military presence into the Straits makes our job a hell of a lot tougher. Why didn't you consult us before making such a decision?"

Nothing from the phone for a long moment.

"The President felt it was important for the Communists to know that we are serious about assisting our friends in Taiwan," came Ravenhurst's voice finally, with a slight quaver. "To know the depth of our commitment. We assumed you've relayed that to them, and forcefully."

"They know of our concern, and of the possibility of our intervening in any conflict that might ensue. But don't you fellas know anything about human nature? People don't much care to negotiate when they're backed into a corner with two damn carrier groups being shoved down their throats. Don't you understand that?"

A silence, longer this time.

"All I can say is that the President felt a renewed show of force was advisable, looking at the larger picture."

"Christ." Philip grabbed the phone off the table into his hands and spoke slowly into it. "Look, Ravenhurst. Tell the President what I said. I'm sending a cable with the same points, to corroborate what I know will be a trustworthy account from you. I'll do what I can to keep the negotiations going, but it's sure as hell going to make a hard job even harder. Perhaps we'll be able to salvage some of the momentum from today. But don't take any more steps without putting me and Baden and Dirk in the loop. You heard what the President said about confidence in me, full support and all. I expect us to be in the loop, damn it."

"I will relay your concerns to the President," came the voice, very formal.

"Yeah, I know you will. Goodbye."

Philip clicked the phone off. He looked up at the television across the room, where airplanes were swarming off the flight decks and screaming into the skies overhead. He raised his arm, took a step toward the television, and threw the phone as hard as he could. It sailed across the room and shattered the television screen, which went instantly black with a loud pop.

A stunned silence. Everyone sat absolutely still.

"Nice throw," said Dirk.

Philip collapsed into his chair. "It's easy with the big screens."

Everyone laughed nervously, except the AIT staffer, who had stared wide-eyed throughout everything.

"I've got a bad feeling about those two new carrier groups," said Philip.

"Yeah, we noticed," Dirk drawled. "But you know what? I think you're right."

"What are the odds we've still got talks tomorrow, after Zhu sees that?" asked Philip in a hollow voice.

All eyes went to Dirk, then Baden.

Baden shrugged. "Fifty fifty?" he ventured.

Dirk considered it. "If we're lucky."

Everyone looked at Philip, who was slumped in his chair.

"Get some sleep, folks," he said. "We've got a meeting at ten tomorrow morning. This morning, I mean."

They filed silently out of the room, leaving Philip slumped in his chair, and Tom flipping through a magazine in the corner.

He pulled himself out of the chair. "Let's go home before anything else exciting happens today, huh Tom? I really need some sleep."

search

Chapter Fourteen

Day Three

Lee swept into the reception area of his fifth floor office in his usual assured gait. Miss Ling looked up from her mahogany desk with a professional smile and turned for the pot of tea that was halfway into its three minute brewing.

"Get me Admiral Feng, Miss Ling. I have to talk to him this morning about those two new aircraft carrier groups. And I assume old Liu has that schedule of departures of our big liners for me. And lock the door behind you when you come in, Miss Ling."

She raised her eyebrows and put the telephone on the one-ring message mode. Should she wait for the tea to brew?

He was sifting through the pile of messages from Taiwan's political and business elite when Miss Ling entered the room and locked the door behind her. When he looked up, she already had unpinned her hair and was reaching up to unbutton the pearl fasteners on her silk blouse. He leaned back in his chair and watched her undress. She was something like thirty-five years old, not strikingly attractive, but slim and pleasant to look at. Lee's view of secretaries was simple. They were here to help him. Mostly, it was organizing, keeping track of messages going out and coming in. They had to be good at that, and completely discrete. But part of helping him was attending to his requirements. Tea was one, sex was another. No attachments, but occasional sex when the need arose and his wife or mistresses hadn't met the need for one reason or another.

Miss Ling had been with him for, what, nine years, Lee thought as she carefully folded her blouse and skirt on the chair by the door. Her body was not so angular as nine years ago. The years had softened her, rounded her hips. Another year, and he would offer her the very comfortable retirement he had offered every personal secretary once they had served him for a decade. She would take it, as had the ones before her. And he would have several dozen of the secretaries in the business eagerly applying to be her replacement, fully aware of their responsibilities. Picking the successor was always a pleasant duty. The only requirement other than competence and discretion was that she had to be older than his oldest daughter. That was only decent, he felt.

She walked with an engaging lilt to his desk and took him by the hand, pulling him to the oversize couch under the window. He shook his head as she began to undo his tie, and after removing his jacket he took his shoes and pants off and they lay on the couch together. As he kissed her neck he felt her gently caressing his organ, which needed little coaxing. He progressed to her breasts, and spent some time kissing them, to bring her to her own readiness. He heard the soft sigh that signaled she was ready, and moved atop her and gently slid himself into her. As always, she received him easily.

They made love wordlessly and with a courteous regard for the other. She had always appeared to enjoy it, so far as he could tell. So had her predecessors. But of course, that was part of their job, and it didn't really matter to him. He was kind to them, and not demanding. As he moved in and out of her, he completely forgot about aircraft carriers, messages from the premier, getting his big ships out of port, and all the myriad things he was working on. That momentary forgetting, as well as satisfying the need, was what lovemaking was all about, to his mind. Only one thing intruded this morning.

"Any word back about the Ma Tsu temple?" he whispered lazily into her ear.

She took a while to respond, which he interpreted to mean that she had given herself up to the pleasure of it also, and the thought pleased him. He waited patiently for her reply, his rhythm increasing as he felt the old explosion stirring itself deep in his core.

She nodded, and uttered a soft, animal-like sound that meant yes.

"Oh, really!" he muttered. He increased his rhythm, and the explosion gathered speed and began to move down his axis and soon came rushing to his Jade Stalk and presented itself with a flourish to Miss Ling.

As his gasp trailed off, he felt her squeezing his organ, massaging it with the walls of her Golden Valley. He had never known a woman to do this better than Miss Ling, and it had been a pleasant surprise to him after he had chosen her.

But the temple! He pulled out of her. She handed him several tissues from the box on the adjacent table.

"When did they call?"

"An e-mail message. From the mainland authority on Ma Tsu temples in Fujian."

"You are a wonderful woman," he declared as he pulled on his pants.

She laughed as she wiped the last of him off her thighs and glided over to the chair and re-dressed herself. He complimented her often. It was the way he treated his trusted employees. She never complimented or thanked him, knowing that all she had to do was perform her job competently and pleasantly.

As she pulled her skirt on and fastened it, she picked up the notepad on the chair. "A Dr. Jin. From Fuzhou. Shall I get him first, or Admiral Feng?"

"Dr. Jin by all means! Hurry!"

As she unlocked the door and scurried out of the room, Lee picked up the list of departures that old Liu had prepared. Yes. Another six of the big ships today. Going all over the place. But at least away from Taiwan. And nothing coming in. That was good.

He drummed his fingers on the desk. All four of his daughters had executed their assigned duties the past two days in the search for the man in the old photo, with no results. It was a long shot, from the first, recognizing a face in a photograph seventy years old. But if he could pinpoint the temple, that would narrow the search considerably.

He jumped as the buzzer on his phone rang.

"Yes! Sung Lee here."

"This is Jin Feizhong from Fuzhou," replied the line. "An honor to speak to you."

"Good. I have a bizarre request. I have recently discovered an old photo of my mother, standing on the coast before a Ma Tsu temple with seashells embedded in the columns. Seashells of the Chiragra spider conch, I am told. I am very interested in learning where the photo was taken. Can you give me any leads?"

"Perhaps. Since Ma Tsu is of course the goddess of the sea, it is not unusual for her temples to have incorporated seashells in their material. Usually the shell is a scallop, occasionally the small clams. I know of only three temples to have used spider conches."

Lee's pulse quickened. "Indeed! And where might those be, Dr. Jin?"

"I have actually visited one in Quanzhou, some 200 kilometers south of Fuzhou here. It is a splendid temple, and still standing."

"That is unlikely to be it. It will be north of Fuzhou, perhaps near Shanghai."

"The other two I know only from photographs and descriptions. One is in Ningbo, a large temple complex recently rebuilt. You should visit it, it is very grand."

"Right. Ningbo. And the other?"

"A small village outside of Shanghai. A very modest temple. I doubt that it is still standing. The Red Guards in Shanghai were very zealous in the early seventies. What is that village called? Hold on while I check my files. It is not in Fujian, you understand, so I don't know so much about it. Hold, please."

Lee swiveled and looked out the window. He knew Ningbo. Had picked up some bamboo there, as a young man, before the Communists had taken the mainland. He tried to remember it. Failed. It had been over sixty years ago.

"Hello, still there?"

"Yes!" He swung around to the desk.

"I have it. A village called Jinhua. Jin-yuande jin, shwo-huade hua."

Lee scribbled the characters beside those for Ningbo.

"And where did you say Jinhua is located?"

"I don't know. Somewhere near Shanghai. Sorry."

"You have been an immense help. What institution are you with, Dr. Jin?"

"The Fujian Institute of the Study of Religion. But don't trouble yourself—"

"Nonsense. Expect a token of my appreciation. I'll reconnect you to my secretary. Please give her your address. Thank you and goodbye."

He punched Miss Ling's light.

"Get this fellow's address. And send a thousand dollars to him, personally, at his Institute. He can decide what to do with it. And get me that ABC in Information Processing. The one with the orange hair. Or purple? Whatever."

A minute later the buzzer sounded again. He picked up the phone. "Any luck with the satellite search yet, young man?"

"Kevin, sir. Plenty of luck. The computer has found four possible matches, and it's got another 100 kilometers to go."

"Four matches? What does that mean?"

"It means that out of a couple of thousand kilometers of coastline, sir, there's more than one place that looks a lot like the photograph. Don't worry. We'll call up those four, and whatever else it might find, and compare for ourselves."

"When will it finish up?"

"We need another couple of hours, which are tough to get during the day. Say by six o'clock this evening?"

"I'll be there." Lee put the phone down, and noticed that his hand was trembling. Well, why not? He was tracking down his father. It made him feel like a young man again. Energy surged through him. He thought of calling Miss Ling in again, and telling her to lock the door again. No, that would slow down the work she had to do. He opened his drawer and pulled out his copy of the old photograph. Thank the gods for that column of spider conches. He thought of the reporter, the woman who explored tidepools.

To his intercom again. "Miss Ling."

"Yes, Mr. Lee." He noted a touch of exasperation in her voice, and laughed. "Send flowers to that female reporter. The one that did the interview of me for the newspaper last year. Sign it for me. Thanks, best wishes, or something like that."

He could imagine Miss Ling rolling her eyes in the outer office.

"Very good, Mr. Lee. Roses?"

"Whatever, Miss Ling."

mountain

Chapter Fifteen

Philip walked to his table in the huge hall at the Sun Yat-sen Memorial, nodding to Lee and his aides at another table. As he took his seat between Baden and Dirk, he noticed Zhu, sitting alone at his table, no aides. His heart sank

"Mr. Zhu, I imagine you have something to say," he said, noticing the single sheet of paper on the table before him.

"Yes, I do, Mr. Dawson," replied Zhu, putting on his thick glasses and picking up the paper. "I have been instructed by my government to announce that the People's Republic of China regards the dispatch of two aircraft carrier groups of the United States military into the Strait of Taiwan as a provocative act. It clearly signals to us that the United States continues to interfere in the affairs of the people of China. That it has no understanding of our position on the question of Taiwan's reunification with the motherland. That in fact it is again reverting to the bellicose spirit first exhibited in 1949 and again in 2001 with your Navy spy planes harassing our coastline."

Zhu paused, adjusted his glasses, and read on. "To protest this new insult to the people of China, the People's Republic is hereby terminating negotiations on the issue of reunification. The deadline, now seven days from today, remains in effect. Reunification will occur then."

Zhu appeared not angry, but discouraged, in the long moment of silence that followed the announcement. He set the document on the table, stared at it for some moments, then removed his glasses and eyed Philip.

"I may add, Mr. Dawson, that I am thoroughly perplexed at your government's actions. In my view, a glimmer of hope shined in our session yesterday. No more than that, but at least that. I am disappointed." He gathered his papers, and stood to leave. Philip stood also, and met him at the door, offering his hand. Zhu took it. They walked together down the hallway toward the stairs, Philip's arm over Zhu's shoulder.

"Mr. Zhu. I appreciate your personal words at the end of your presentation. I must tell you that I was as surprised and disappointed at my government's action as you."

They were at the top of the stairs together now. Zhu stared at Philip for a brief moment, shook his head, then descended the stairs, the huge statue of Sun Yat-sen looming on his right. Philip watched him trudge down the steps.

"Bad timing, those aircraft carriers," Lee commented tersely when he arrived at the top of the stairs beside Philip. "We appreciate them, but a week earlier, or later—"

Philip nodded. "They surprised me as much as you, Mr. Lee."

"Really?" He strode to the stairs. "Goodbye, Mr. Dawson," he said.

*   *   *   *   *

Baden, Dirk and the rest of the team shuffled into the AIT conference room, faces downcast. A new television squatted in the corner, silent.

"Well, we got blindsided," Philip opened. "No fault of ours. But it looks like we're through, for now. I want everyone to stick around for a couple of days, in case we get surprised and something good happens."

A few faces looked up.

"Meanwhile, in case things do look up, I want thorough reports on the first session yesterday. What issues were covered, what each side said about them, what agreements were either made or seemed make-able. In detail. Tell me where you'd go and how you'd handle it, if talks ever get re-started. To me by this time tomorrow. Baden and Dirk, could you stick around a minute?"

The others shuffled out. Tom looked up from his magazine. "Shall I go, Phil?"

"No."

Philip fixed Baden and Dirk with a somber stare. "I've got a couple of things bothering me, that I wonder if you could throw any light on."

"Only a couple?" said Dirk, leaning back in her chair.

"To start with," said Philip. "Number one, why the hell didn't the President send Secretary of State Talbin here, with me? Or instead of me, for that matter?"

Silence, as Dirk and Baden avoided Philip's eyes.

"Well?"

Baden stared resolutely at Dirk, who shrugged. "Beats me, Philip. When we requested you, we expected Talbin to be here also. Did you ask the

President to head up the delegation yourself? Do better without Talbin over you?"

"Hell, no. It surprised me as much as—as these goddamn two carrier groups."

Shrugging again, Dirk remained silent.

"You know," Philip drawled. "I try not to be paranoid. The world's a complex place, and things are rarely simple. But I do wonder about the influence of John Ravenhurst on the President."

"Talbin hates him," Baden burst out.

Dirk nodded. "Yeah," she said slowly. "Talbin sometimes wonders if Ravenhurst doesn't really want—" She checked herself.

Philip waited. She'd already said more than he thought she would.

"Anything more on that subject?" he asked the two of them.

More silence.

"Number two. I'm going to approach Lee and Zhu about secret negotiations."

Baden's and Dirk's eyes jerked to Philip's.

"The president didn't authorize that, did he?" asked Dirk

Philip met her shocked gaze for a long moment, then shook his head.

"Why, then, you can't do it," she declared, a note of hysteria in her voice.

"I can and I will," Philip countered.

"Philip, it'll cost you your job, to begin with," Baden said.

"Not if it works. There's plenty of sentiment in the Senate, and lots in the business community, for this to happen. He won't dare nix a peace agreement."

Dirk was spluttering. It was the first time Philip had ever seen her speechless.

"But—but…" She finally got her tongue. "You can't make our foreign policy, Philip. That's not your job."

Philip glared back at her. "My job is to keep China and Taiwan—and the United States—out of a war. The president gave me that job. I accepted it, and I damn well intend to see it to the end." He stared unflinching into her frightened eyes.

Dirk slumped back in her chair. "Philip…you're on your own on this. I appreciate your, uh, your zeal for peace. But Baden and I can't go there with you. It would mean our heads. No doubt of it."

"I'm not asking you to. All I want you to do is stay put for a couple of days. Keep your teams here. If I get lucky and something happens, I'll want your advice. If we're really lucky, I'll need your people to finish up the details of an agreement."

"What will you tell the President about our staying here?"

"That the United States needs to show it's receptive to the resumption of talks. That's true enough. I just won't tell him, at this stage, that I'm pursuing them actively."

"Everyone was looking back at your room, yesterday," Baden said, the old light back in his eyes. "If you and Zhu and Lee can work something out on the big problems, then everything else will fall into place. I'm sure of it."

"What do you think my odds are?" Philip asked.

"Damn low," said Dirk. "How are you even going to contact them about this?"

Philip's turn to slump back in his chair. "Haven't a clue. Any suggestions?"

"I can tell you how it can't be done," said Dirk, staring out the window. "If it's done through normal, official channels, you won't be able to keep it a secret, and if it's not a complete secret, you don't have a snowball's chance in hell of it working. The opposing factions in both countries will jump all over it and squash it. Not to mention Ravenhurst, our friend behind those two carrier groups."

"Tom," Philip said, talking over his shoulder to the corner. "You've read the C.I.A. files on Lee and Zhu. How do we contact them, under cover?"

Tom tossed his magazine onto a table. "Zhu does Tai Chi or Qi Gong or whatever you call that stuff, every evening at five. At home, he does it in a courtyard of the Forbidden City, just across the street from the Jongnanhai complex where the elite live and work. The Plum Bower Courtyard, it's called. Here, he does it in the southern end of New Park, a couple of blocks behind the Hilton. Every evening, five o'clock."

Dirk and Baden whistled softly.

"I tell you, he's a handy man to have around," said Philip. "And Lee?" he asked in Tom's direction.

After a long moment, Tom shook his head. "Real tough. He holds court at his shipping headquarters in Keelung. Everyone goes there to see him. No way to sneak in there, secretly, that we know of. He goes to a couple of restaurants here in Taipei, depending on, uh, who he's eating with. But again—public places. Impossible to be covert. We don't know any phone numbers that don't go through at least one layer."

A long silence in the room.

"So we start with Zhu, and work on Lee," Philip said. "This evening."

"I don't like this, Philip," said Dirk, standing. "At what stage do you let the President know what you're doing?"

"When I've got something to report. Something firm enough that Ravenhurst can't squash it out of hand."

From the pained look in her eyes, that didn't help Dirk much.

"Well, good luck. I'll tell everyone we're staying put. Being 'open to the possibility of talks resuming.'" She wandered out of the room, followed by Baden, who gave Philip a thumbs up from the door.

Tom picked up his magazine again.

Chapter Sixteen

Philip signaled the driver to stop a block from New Park. He emerged from the big black limousine, followed by Tom and four other security men. Two of the men preceded him and Tom, two were behind. As they arrived at the north end of the park, the security men fell back. Philip and Tom walked alone the length of the park along Kungyuan Road, past a red pavilion surrounded by a moat of water. Not a soul was visible in the park.

"Where is everyone?" Philip snapped. The empty park bothered him. "This time of day, all sorts of people ought to be in there."

"Everyone's home," Tom said, his eyes flicking from the park to the street and back again. "Calling off the talks has people spooked. They're counting how many packets of instant ramen they've got in their cupboards."

As they neared the south end of the park, black-suited men appeared inside, large with impassive faces. Security men all look the same, Philip thought. Zhu's, mine, whoever's.

"Who's going to do the talking?" Philip asked.

"Me," said Tom flatly. "We'll have to get through security. My kind of folks."

"Yeah, I never could talk security-ese very well."

"That's the damn truth. By the way, don't make any sudden movements in front of these guys."

They turned into the shaded entrance and walked past the brick restrooms there. Half a dozen very large men in black suits materialized in the pathway ahead of them. Tom nodded curtly to the one in the middle.

"Mr. Dawson would like to speak with Mr. Zhu."

The man stared stonily at Tom for a moment, then jerked his head back up the path behind them.

"No," said Tom. "Mr. Dawson would like to speak with Mr. Zhu." He said it coolly, no heat in it.

The man put a large hand on Tom's chest, and exerted pressure to push him back.

Tom didn't budge.

" Tom," said Philip. "Maybe these guys don't speak English."

"I do the talking," Tom said, with some heat now. "And this guy does speak English." He said this without taking his eyes off the man with the hand on his chest.

The two of them stared at each other for a long moment. Then the man removed his hand, and very slowly, reached into the pocket of his suit. He pulled out a phone and hit a button. Turning away from them, he spoke something into it.

He put the phone away and glared at Tom. The men to either side closed in, making a tight half circle around them. Philip shifted his weight, half-expecting punches to be thrown. The men were awfully big. Dumpy, perhaps, but big.

"Stay where you are," Tom said quietly to Philip, all the while nose to nose with the man in the center.

Everyone stood rooted to their spots for nearly a minute.

Philip was about to tell Tom to back off and reconnoiter the situation, when a young man arrived from the interior of the park, also black-suited, but not nearly so large.

The ring of men parted, and the newcomer stepped up to Philip, ignoring Tom. "May I be of assistance?" he asked, his bearing not nearly so courteous as his words.

Philip glanced at Tom, who nodded.

"I would like to speak with Mr. Zhu, if he could spare a brief moment after his exercises," said Philip.

"Mr. Zhu is not here," the other stated.

"I believe Mr. Zhu is doing his exercises in the park at this moment," Philip said in a friendly manner. "Perhaps you overlooked him."

More unfriendly staring. "Does Mr. Zhu expect this visit?"

"No," answered Philip. "I am requesting an unscheduled brief time with Mr. Zhu. I believe that he would want to be aware of this."

The young man blinked several times as he absorbed and pondered it.

He suddenly spat out a torrent of Chinese to the security men and walked away.

The wall of men parted, and the one in the middle motioned Philip toward a bench behind them. With a look at Tom, Philip edged between them and sat on the shaded bench, which faced the interior of the park. Tom backed off several steps and stood surveying the scene, alert.

From the bench, Philip could see a dozen more of Zhu's security men fanned around a shaded opening in the park. They all looked as large and slow as the ones he and Tom had encountered. Not much good in a fast-moving situation, he judged.

Someone was moving about in the shaded area. But that can't be Zhu,

Philip thought, not wearing those baggy pants rolled up to the knees, and that sleeveless undershirt. Scraggly shrubs prevented his getting a good look. The man seemed medium height and stocky, his whole body the shape of a squat tube. He was doing something like t'ai chi, except the movements were too tight, too circumscribed. But there was a curious fluidity and intricacy to the moves.

After a minute Philip decided that in fact this was a powerful person. The skin was smooth and lustrous and stretched taut over considerable muscle bulk beneath. And those small, subtle kicks and punches flowed out from the body in such a way that the entire bulk of the body was contained in them. Just a twist of the body, really, but that hand was directly in line with the twist, and focused the body's bulk.

Philip sat up, intrigued. The man was now twirling about in a rapid series of blocks and kicks and punches, turning this way and that, but hardly moving from his spot, the axis of his body providing the focal point for the subtle but powerful strength directed now here, now there. Philip could plainly see several dozen ghostly attackers handled readily and lethally in the calm revolutions about that steady axis. Another twirl, both arms now doing a graceful checking to either side, and the man at last was still, bright eyes intently focused just beyond his nose, his breathing slow and deep. The pose was held for perhaps half a minute, then the man relaxed and walked over to a bench, where he picked up a bundle of things as the young security man approached him.

"Well I'll be damned," Philip muttered, as the man put his glasses and shirt on, transforming him into Zhu, the plump, owlish economist. He heard out the young man with no change in expression. For a long moment he stood staring back into the clearing he had just left. Then he turned and walked over to Philip and took a seat beside him on the bench. No greeting, as he rolled his pant legs down, then sat back comfortably on the bench, one arm resting on the back.

"Quite an exhibition, Mr. Zhu," Philip said.

Zhu directed an empty glance at him, then away. "Nothing special, Mr. Dawson. Just some simple exercise to get the ch'i focused. As you may have noticed yesterday, I tend to be rather mercurial. The exercises calm me down."

"Ah. Center you," Philip said.

"You sound like you're from California, rather than Vermont," Zhu said, a smile playing on his lips.

"I always thought of t'ai chi as more dramatic. Bigger movements."

The smile became tight, bookish. "Those styles seem most popular in the west."

"What style is yours, Mr. Zhu?"

"Shan-yu. The mountain's speech." He looked briefly at Philip. "You wanted to talk about—?"

"First, I want to apologize again for my government's actions in the two carrier groups. My government wants to assist you and Sung Lee to achieve success in your talks. But it also wants to express its support of Taiwan's position."

"You are one man, although very able, of course. The carrier groups are many men and weapons."

"True enough. And I can't fault your government for breaking off the talks. Certainly we must respect our governments. But I would like to broach with you the possibility that we could also explore the possibilities for peace—in private talks."

Zhu studiously directed his attention away from Philip, into the trees.

"Private talks? I have no instructions or authorization for such a course."

"I don't either, Mr. Zhu. But I do have a keen desire to avoid the catastrophe of war. No country wins a war, in my view. One side only loses somewhat less than the other. I am willing to explore in an informal way whether we can avoid a war. If we come up with a formula, our governments of course retain the authority to agree or not."

Zhu shifted on the bench, still looking into the center of the park. A girl in the familiar blue and white school uniform, red ribbon in her hair, dashed across a path.

Perfect, thought Philip, holding his breath for Zhu's response.

"Did you arrange for that twin to my granddaughter to appear, Mr. Dawson?" "There's children all over Taiwan, sir. And the People's Republic, also."

Zhu nodded soberly and finally directed his gaze to Philip. "Yes. So what harm could secret talks do? Other than getting me sent to the deserts of Xinjiang province to oversee date production, of course."

"Good clean air in Xinjiang province, Mr. Zhu."

A short, cynical laugh from Zhu. "Although somewhat contaminated with radioactivity from our nuclear tests there, I understand."

A pause.

"You understand, of course, that the deadline is inviolable," Zhu said, suddenly focused. "We have only one week. And the sessions cannot be here in Taipei. They must be in a private, remote spot. Absolutely secret. You, me, and Lee. No one else. No interpreters. One or two security men for each of us, no more."

Philip etched it into his memory. "Any other conditions, sir?"

A sharp look through thick glasses. "A week is only time for several sessions, Mr. Dawson. You'd best have some very original and compelling proposals for us."

"I've got them already, Mr. Zhu. You will be impressed." He was getting awfully good at lying, between Miss Dao and the negotiations.

"You asked us to think about points that were absolutely essential to us, at yesterday's conclusion," continued Zhu. "For the People's Republic, it is the dissolution of Taiwan's war machine. There must be no hostile forces facing us any longer. Regardless of what Deng Xiao-ping said decades ago. There is more, but that is the most difficult point, I think."

"Yes. Thank you for agreeing to further talks, Mr. Zhu. How will I contact you, for time and place?"

Zhu rose and took a card from his shirt pocket. "The number written on the back is my personal secretary. You can inform him."

Philip took the card and put it in his pocket.

"I will talk to Mr. Lee Soon—tonight if possible. Then, if he is agreeable, contact you early tomorrow."

Philip edged through the phalanx of black suits, rejoining Tom. He wondered if Mr. Zhu's dumpy security men also studied Mountain speech. And how he was going to contact Sung Lee.

Ma Tsu

Chapter Seventeen

Meiling turned into the temple courtyard just after seven, wearing a light, feminine dress in subdued golds. She had hooked him the night before, she felt sure. In spite of the business with the snakes. She could get a smashing story on his reaction to Beijing's boycott of the talks. As she stepped over the board to the inner courtyard, she saw him. He was holding a bundle of incense sticks, looking decidedly out of place.

"Hello there," he said, as she approached the altar, studiously not noticing him.

She feigned surprise, and allowed a bare glimmer of warmth.

"I wanted to thank you for telling me about Ma Tsu, last night. There's a lot more I need to know about her. Could I join you burning some incense to her?"

She'd never seen a caucasian burning incense at an altar. But the saints were tolerant of human foibles.

She lit his incense sticks in the gas flames by the courtyard. They glowed orange at the tips, small twirls of smoke trailing behind them as they silently walked to the back of the temple.

He stopped at the first altar there. "This fellow, with the red face. He's Lord Kung, isn't he? The betrayed general from the Romance of the Three Kingdoms?"

"You know your Chinese history."

"His martial spirit could help me in my, uh, my business dealings. Incense, please?"

She handed him two sticks, and watched as he held them to his forehead, bowed twice, and placed them in the burner. He caught onto things very quick.

At Ma Tsu's altar, she took a bottle of cooking oil from her purse and placed it on the table with flowers and fruits already there. She faced the black-faced icon and bowed twice with the incense sticks on her forehead. He did the same. Aware of his eyes on her, she knelt on the stone floor and closed her eyes.

Ma Tsu, Holy Mother of Heaven, she prayed. *Protector of women and children, and those who sail the seas. I celebrate your sea, and all the creatures who flourish in its embrace. Look upon me with benevolent eyes, my Mother. Keep me safe from the restless spirits of your world and the evil ones of mine. May my incense please you.*

She opened her eyes, and stared at the dark face on the altar. *Forgive me for this show. He is important to my career. Make him pliant. Easily deceived. And talkative.*

She was about to rise, when she suddenly shut her eyes again. *And Ma Tsu. Help me not to fall in love with him.* As she rose, she wondered why she had thought that.

The temple was crowded with worshippers of all ages. The lit ends of incense sticks bobbed through the night in every direction, the pungent scent filling the air. She pushed her way past the chanting crowd at the Kuan Yin altar in the front, and into the outer courtyard. He followed her closely. Shivers ran through her when he bumped into her.

"I've got more questions about Ma Tsu," he began at they reached the outer courtyard. "Could we talk somewhere more—more quiet?"

"Sure. Would you like to buy me a tea at the MacDonald's across the street?"

"At the—MacDonald's?" he said quizically. "Well, sure. Let's go."

Outside the temple they hit the traffic light as it turned green. Dodging several speeding cars that seemed to have missed the change in the light, they crossed the street and entered the fast food shop. She ordered tea for both of them, and they climbed narrow stairs to take seats near the second story window, overlooking the temple.

"This Ma Tsu," he began. "You mentioned she was a person, in the tenth century. Yet you call her a goddess. How did she become a goddess?"

She stirred her tea. "To our way of thinking, if you live a full life, have a family, go through many seasons and their festivals, you become an ancestor when you die. Your *hun* souls are cycled naturally into those of your family."

"But if you die young, then, without going through all that—it's different?"

"Exactly. Typically, you become a *ku hun*, an orphaned soul. The world is full of them, upset at their fate, resentful. They're part of the Hungry Ghosts.

They have their own festival—next week, in fact, where Taoist priests attempt to placate them."

"But Ma Tsu isn't an orphan soul?"

"No. She was full of power when she died, due to her extraordinary spirit. Being a virgin, also, her yin energy was formidable, dangerous even. Close to a demon."

"So her power made her a goddess. Not her virtue?"

"Virtue has nothing to do with it. Ma Tsu is a source of power. And she began as a saint. Saints are simply demons with unusual spiritual power, which you can tap into."

"Tap into? For what ends?"

"For what everyone wants," she answered, with an impatient wave of her hand. "Health. Happiness. Wealth. A large family."

A surprised look on his face. "That's it? No moral betterment? No afterlife?"

Poor caucasians, she thought. They're impossible. "It's this world we're living in, Mr. Morgan. We accept our frailties. We're not trying to be something we aren't."

He gazed down at the temple. "So someone who Ma Tsu has blessed with wealth and a long life—that man would need to be careful to stay on her good side. Right?"

"Of course. He would be in debt to Ma Tsu. So. Will all this about Ma Tsu help your business dealings here, Mr. Morgan from Vermont?"

"Oh yes, my business. Well, today was a tough day for business."

"Indeed? I'm sorry."

He sipped his tea. "Oh, all is not lost. Perhaps. Maybe Ma Tsu will help me save the—the deal, after all. I try to be positive, keep trying different angles." He suddenly stiffened, and shot a suspicious look at her.

Time to ease up, she thought. "What do you do for enjoyment, Mr. Morgan?"

His suspicion turned to surprise. "Well, I guess rock-climbing, Miss Dao."

"Rock climbing? That's very strange."

He laughed, throwing his head back. He has so much life in him, she found herself thinking. His neck was muscled, and smooth, leading to the clean lines of his jaw.

"Yeah, I suppose it is strange," he said, his eyes sparkling brown. "I don't suppose you know of any climbing spots close to Taipei?"

"Why, yes. There's a popular spot, close to where I go every morning, to…"

He nodded, encouraging her. "Every morning, you…?"

"Well. I swim every morning, in the ocean. And explore the tidepools. To start my day. On the coast northeast of here."

His green eyes glowed at her with—delight? She felt a warmth filling her core. The way his eyes seemed to change color with his mood intrigued her.

"Now that's—that's even stranger than rock-climbing, if I may say so, Miss Dao. Why in the world do you swim and—explore tidepools?—every morning?"

"I just love the sea," she said after a pause. "The smell, the noise. Using my muscles until I'm exhausted. I explore tidepools to see what strange and dangerous creatures I can find. Just this morning I found a cone shell, golden triangles on white, as gorgeous as it is deadly. And a shimmering green nudibranch."

A fascinated smile swept his face, his eyes golden now. Her heart leaped, and warmth spread over her body. She dropped her eyes as she felt the tingle. What are you doing, woman? Get a grip on yourself, she thought. This is a job, not a cheap movie.

When she trusted herself, she spoke. "I hope you have some success in your business venture. You'll have another chance to persuade your clients, tomorrow?"

He shook his head. "Maybe. I have to figure out a way to contact one, first."

"I know a lot of people. Could I help you?" She could hardly believe she had said it. But she had a job to do.

She could see his mind working as he stared at her, surprised by her offer. "Well," he finally said. "Why not? I need a way to get hold of a shipping tycoon. Fellow named Sung Lee. Ever hear of him?"

Oh my, she thought. Lying is so much harder than just saying the truth. "Why, yes. My, uh, store does business with him. In fact, I have a private number of his."

His eyes narrowed. "You—what?"

She began to get flustered. "I'm a, uh, fashion buyer for a department store. We do a lot of business with him. We sell a lot of clothing to his wife and daughters, I mean. Clothing, and accessories. So I have a private number. For his wife, plus also for him."

His face mixed confusion and suspicion, but finally he shrugged. "Hey. Would you have any problems giving it to me? I wouldn't use your name."

"You seem to be a very honest and reliable person, Mr. Morgan. I have no problem with it." She opened her purse, extracted her appointments book, and copied Sung Lee's private phone on a paper. She gave it to him.

"Do you have a phone I could use to call him, now?"

Better and better, she thought, and handed him the phone from her purse.

He punched in the number, rose, and walked away so Miss Dao couldn't hear.

"Sung Lee, please," he said. "Oh, Mr. Lee. This is Philip Dawson. I apologize for contacting you outside of official channels. But I wanted to set up a very brief meeting—just the two of us." A pause. "I want to explore the subject of some private sessions, Mr. Lee. Just you, me, and Mr. Zhu. Zhu has already agreed. I was hoping that I might be able to meet you sometime soon."

Philip paced beside the table. "Tonight? Of course. Give me directions, please." He gestured to Miss Dao, and she provided pen and paper from her purse.

"Yes. Past Keelung." He wrote, fast. "Coast road, yes."

Meiling was working hard to keep excitement off her face. A secret meeting with Sung Lee to restart negotiations—secret negotiations, yet! What a scoop!

"Yes sir. Two hours. See you then, Mr. Lee." His face glowed as he handed the phone back. "Miss Dao! You've saved my life, for the second night in a row."

Meiling was in shock. Good fortune was smiling on her, showering her. She was completely confused at how much of her happiness was from the looming coup as a journalist, and how much was personal, from the way he was beaming at her.

She stammered a reply. Not trusting her feelings or words, she abruptly stood.

"Happy I could help," she finally got out. "Glad you were able to contact Mr. Lee and set up your...your business meeting. I really must go."

She rushed to the stairs and descended to the first floor. As she stepped onto the sidewalk, he caught up with her, and laid a hand on her arm. The light was green.

"Miss Dao. Would there be any chance that you might show me that climbing spot some time? And perhaps your tidepool?" They stepped off the curb into the street.

"I really doubt it, Mr. Morgan." They reached the middle of the crosswalk. "But you never know, do you? I'll probably be here tomorrow night."

A lady in front of her screamed. With an effort she broke her concentration on Mr. Morgan. Tires squealed to her left. A huge black car, bearing down on them, its engine roaring. Its chrome grill flashed in the streetlight, malevolent, lethal. A parked blue sedan blocked the crosswalk in front of them. She leaped onto the hood of the sedan, anything to escape the tons of metal accelerating toward her. His hand pushed against her back as he also leaped. Her face slammed against the blue of the hood and the sedan jolted as the acrid smell of metal grinding metal assaulted her. A harsh grating sound wracked her ears as the sedan turned a half circle and shuddered to a halt. She flew off the hood and crumpled to the sidewalk beyond, a sharp pain erupting into her shoulder.

Chaos. People running up to her. Helping her up. Shouting questions. She was completely hemmed in, surrounded by the smells of sweat, metal, and tires. Suddenly his face appeared before her.

"Jesus! Are you all right?" His eyes close to hers were bright green now, shimmering like the green of the nudibranch in her tidepool this morning.

She tried to speak, but couldn't. She tried to move her shoulder. With relief she saw it move, with only a dull pain. Finally she found her tongue. "I guess so. You?"

"I'm OK," he said, his face still close, holding onto her arm, supporting her.

A large man arrived, shoving the crowd aside easily, shouting into a cell phone.

"Phil. You OK?"

"Yeah, more or less."

"Ask her the name of this street."

"Wan Da Road," she said.

The man shouted into the cell phone. "Going south on Wan Da Road, for a couple of blocks, then they turned right. See if you can pick them up."

The big man shoved the phone back into his pocket.

"Let's get out of here, Phil," he said, his eyes darting over the crowd.

"I'm sorry," he said to her. "This is my—bodyguard. He's right. This crowd—"

"I'm all right," she said. "Good luck, tonight. Your business deal."

"You sure?"

Her focus was wavering. The snakes last night. This, tonight. *Ma Tsu, what did it mean?*

"Well, I'll go then. Be careful, Miss Dao." The big man was pulling him away.

Shaking, she pushed her way out of the crowd, toward the temple and her cooking oil on the altar. Mr. Morgan—Dawson—turned back to look at her, then disappeared from her sight on the other side of the crowd.

What did it all mean, Ma Tsu?

search

Chapter Eighteen

Lee strode toward Kevin's corner of the computer floor shortly after six, the anxious Section Manager trailing behind. He was annoyed at the American mediator's unexpected phone call—on his private line, yet. More importantly, the shocking cancellation of the negotiations had sent scores of government and business leaders to his office this afternoon, hysterically demanding to know if the island would be in flames in a week. And he couldn't say much to assuage their fears. The Taiwan stock market had plunged seventy five percent in an hour, and stores all over the island were already swamped with panic buying.

So the American's proposal for secret negotiations should have made him feel better. It didn't. Aside from coming on his private line—how in the world had he obtained that number?—he had little hope that secret negotiations would fare any better than the public ones.

Well, the island may be in flames in a week, people may be panicking—rightfully so—but it cheered his heart to see so many of his employees still at their desks an hour after the end of the business day. And Kevin's bright gold hair reminded him that he was on the trail of his father. His father!

He waved the hovering section manager away as he entered Kevin's cubicle and took the open seat.

"So. Finished?"

Kevin looked up, his young face a bit puffy. He's been up all last night, Lee thought. Good.

"Yes, sir. We ended up with just those four matches that I mentioned earlier."

"Well, let's see them!" Lee could not remember being more impatient and excited. He hunched close to the screen, not even shying away from the young man's iridescent gold hair.

"So here's our promontory by the Ma Zu temple in the photo. I'll put it over here in a corner of the screen, to compare." Guided by his hand on the mouse, the cursor zoomed around the screen, windows opened and closed, then he leaned back. "Ready to travel, Mr. Lee?"

Lee nodded eagerly.

Kevin clicked the mouse, and on the screen appeared a portion of coastline, as if viewed from a low-flying airplane. Lee's eyes bored into the screen, watching the scenery pass. At the top of the screen a promontory appeared, and the image froze as it reached the middle of the screen.

"That's it!" Lee said, jabbing his finger on the image.

"Well, that's one of the possibilities," Kevin said.

"What's its name?"

"On the heading above the screen, sir. Nankoku. Central Fujian. We'll make a copy of it." He circled the promontory with his mouse, copied it, and labeled it. "There. We'll put it in another corner of our screen, and continue the ride."

Two other promontories scrolled up and were frozen in midscreen, Lee exclaiming for each that it was the perfect match. One was in northern Fujian, the other in central Zhejiang. Kevin copied them and put them in the remaining two corners of their screen.

"Last one, Mr. Lee. It's in southern Jiangsu province, not too far south of Shanghai."

The coastline scrolled by, a village, a temple. Finally the promontory loomed on the top of the screen, then rushed to the center and was frozen. Lee stared at this one in shock. He had thought the others were matches, but this one was even more perfect.

"Kevin," he said in a hushed voice. "Can you move our original down over this one?"

Kevin moved his cursor, and the two melded.

Two characters gleamed above the screen, red against the black background. Jinhua.

"Jinhua," Lee said in a cracked voice. Where the Ma Tsu temple with spider conches was. The hair rose on the back of his neck. He half-rose in his chair and pulled his cell phone from his pocket. With awkward, jabbing motions he hit his office number.

"Miss Ling," he whispered hoarsely. "Arrange for my helicopter to fly me and Kevin to Fuzhou, across the Strait, tomorrow. Yes, Miss Ling. Get me the governor of Fujian province on the phone, I'll clear it with him. Better get General Fou of our coastal defense, too. Then arrange for a private plane to Shanghai from Fuzhou. Then a helicopter at Shanghai—we're going to a little village south of there. Jinhua, Miss Ling. My birthplace."

"Jinhua," Lee repeated, putting the phone down. His birthplace, probably. Certainly where his mother and father had met. And stood for a photo in front of a Ma Tsu temple with spider conches in its columns.

"Can we look again, at the village and temple south of the promontory?" He ignored Kevin's intrigued look. The boy had doubtless grown up with a father. What could he know or understand about the prospect of discovering a father you'd never known?

Kevin reversed the direction, and the Jinhua promontory receded up to the top of the screen. A structure came into view, curved roofline, open courtyard fronting a small building, right on the coast.

"That's it! The temple!"

Kevin froze it. No details were discernible, but it clearly was a temple. Lee put his finger to the screen. "There. That's where the person stood, taking the photograph. Screen back more. Let's see what we can of the village."

The temple receded toward the top of the screen, and more structures came into view from the bottom. A dozen or so fishing vessels in the harbor. A factory-type building, rectangular. A large compound, surrounded by a wall and containing several smaller buildings fronting a large one in the rear.

"That will be the local gentry's mansion," Lee guessed.

Several dozen smaller structures, looking to Lee like homes and businesses. Only one road, paralleling the coast. Then the last of the structures disappeared beyond the top of the screen, and nothing but coastline presented itself.

Something bothered Lee. What was it? He had seen—something. "Scroll back up, Kevin."

The road. The smaller structures. The gentry's mansion. The factory. The harbor.

"That's it! Freeze it," he said.

The harbor with the fishing vessels filled the screen. Ten fishing vessels, the usual kind, sampans with patched sails, and long wooden rudders extending behind them. It was the eleventh vessel that had stuck out, that wasn't right. Nearly twice as large as the others, and clearly not a fishing vessel. Although it had a mast, it was a modern yacht, which would have a very large motor at the rear. An ocean-going vessel, whereas the sampans were strictly for plying up and down the coast.

"Curious," Lee said softly. "What's a modern, ocean-going yacht doing in a nothing harbor like this?"

He rose from the chair. "Well, no matter. The important thing is we've found the temple." He picked up the phone again.

"Yes, Miss Ling. Call my home. Tell Little Jade I want her to come with us, to Jinhua, tomorrow. One of my children should be with me when I find my father."

He stared out the window beside the computer. Huge white clouds scudded across the afternoon sky above the dark green sea. A wind kicked whitecaps up as far as the eye could see. Tomorrow, he thought. Tomorrow Kevin and Little Jade and I are going to my birthplace. A little village with a temple containing spider conches in its columns. *Thank you, Ma Tsu. Thank you. I will light incense to you there, Ma Tsu. And find my father.*

souls

Chapter Nineteen

Old Shen sat erect in the classical Ming dynasty chair, the brush straight vertical in his right hand. The inkstick rested on a jade block beside the jasper inkstone, the black ink in its depression glistening in the candlelight. He dipped the brush into the ink and moved it over the Korean paper. With precise, flowing strokes he wrote the first four characters, dipped into the ink again, and wrote more. *I met you often when you were visiting princes.* Dipped again, and wrote more. *And when you were playing the lute in noblemen's halls.* As the poem filled the paper, his soul expanded. He was reincarnating Tu Fu, taking part in the creation of the poem as one with the master poet of the T'ang dynasty, twelve hundred years ago. *Spring passes. Far down the river now, I find you alone under falling petals.*

As he finished the poem, he was breathing heavily. His body tingled. He could plainly hear the soft whish of plum blossom petals falling past his ears. His eyes wandered over the objects on the desk, caressing each one. The jasper inkstone, fashioned at the same time as Tu Fu had first written the poem, over a thousand years ago. The jade block, plucked from the Yurungkax riverbed five hundred years ago and fashioned to its simple, clean form in Nanjing when it was the capital of the Ming dynasty. The jade armrest upon which his arm now rested, also washed down from the Kunlun mountains, this fifteen hundred years ago, and fashioned to its form in Xian, soon to be the capital of the glorious T'ang dynasty.

His eyes ranged over the jade carvings on the front of the ebony desk, which was itself six hundred years old. The Song resting horse, the Qing winged unicorn, the Eastern Zhou pi disk, twenty five hundred years old, through which countless emperors had communed with Heaven. He closed his eyes and breathed deep. Breathed in two thousand five hundred years of refined men creating beautiful works of art. He surrounded himself with it, immersed himself in the harmonious flow of *ch'i* emanting from the art. Just as his ancestors had, stretching back five hundred years in unbroken succession. Five hundred years of tablets in the altar looming in the back of the room, beyond the three glowing incense burners. Five hundred years of his kind, steadfastly keeping the burners alive, building the family and its fortunes, collecting paintings and inkstones and calligraphy and jade, mainly jade, the stone of heaven washed down from the Kunlun mountains far to the west. The Shen family had accumulated strength and wisdom from five hundred years of immersing themselves in the company of jade.

A gentle knock interrupted his reverie. He sighed, put the brush down on the jade brushholder, and composed himself.

"Come in." A slight cloud hovered over his perfect world as his twin sons entered the room. A hint of disappointment intruded upon his serenity. Not at their homosexuality, really. It was not uncommon in their family, and really amounted to nothing, so long as they at some point planted their seed where it would grow, and produced sons to continue the family. Nor at their dissoluteness, either. Even though he had abandoned sex promptly upon producing his sons—so messy, so sweaty, and so intimate with those less cultured than you—he did not begrudge them their devotion to it. It was human.

No, what disappointed him in his sons was that they lacked culture. He looked at them in the glow of the several candles in the room. Their robust bodies and perfectly slicked back hair could not divert attention from their slack jaws, their porcine eyes, glazed yet too eager at the same time. Despite his resolve to not notice it, his eyes went to the bright green jadeite ring each of them wore. Burmese Jadeite! *Fei-cui yu*, the very stone that had turned their culture's attention away from the sacred "old" jade from Kunlun to the west. And hurt business, to boot.

"I've been thinking, my sons," he began in a dry voice. He was nearly one hundred years old. Why shouldn't his voice be dry?

"We have tried to be subtle. To remove this reporter before she reveals our family's secret, remove her in a way that appears accidental. The snakes. The car. We have failed."

He was being charitable. Of course it was his sons who had failed. But he knew it was not easy to discretely kill another human. It had been, what, sixty five years since he had killed, for the family, to protect their fortune?

"No more subtlety. No more failure. Take your pistols. Take some of the grenades." A sharp edge crept into his voice. Coarse, almost. "Blow her apart. Tomorrow."

The sons looked at each other, and smiled. There it was. The true man did not take pleasure in destroying another human. He might be forced to do it. Often, perhaps. But he took pleasure in calligraphy. Painting. Feasting his eyes on beautiful pieces of jade. On glowing bronze incense burners. He did not smile at the prospect of killing.

"Of course, you cannot be caught. That would stain the family. Can you accomplish it, or should we contract out for it?"

The one on the left shook his head. "She is lax. We can do it, father."

They seemed eager to go, to get started on the preparations. Sift through their guns, their grenades. He lifted his hand, and shooed them away. As the door closed behind them, he heaved himself out of his chair, grabbed his cane—it was pear wood, capped with a silver handle by an artisan at the Imperial workshop in Peking two hundred years ago—and hobbled on felt slippers to the family altar at the back of the room. The slippers made a tiny whishing noise against the wood floor. He had put a felt tip onto the cane, so it made only a dull rubbing sound as it came down on the floor.

Reaching over the narrow incense table, where the three bronze burners glowed like stars in a night sky, he opened the front of the altar. It was crafted of ebony, five feet tall, and three feet deep. Many dozen wooden tablets lined the six shelves side and back, each tablet tall as a skull but narrow, with the name of a male ancestor written in blood. For five hundred years Taoist priests had written the name of the deceased at the top of the tablet, then offered the brush to the eldest son, who breathed on it. His two sons would breathe on his tablet together, when he had died. Then the sacred brush would be dipped again in a small pool of their blood, and the priest would dot the tablet and pronounce the sacred formula. *I mark your eyes and your eyes see.* Dip in blood again. *I mark your heart and your heart beats.* By the end of the ritual, the tablet was not just a memorial. It possessed the living *hun* souls of the dead ancestor, and would for as long as the rites of respect were observed.

He bowed his head, keenly aware of the *hun* souls of five hundred years of ancestors hovering in the altar box. *My sons are coarse,* he acknowledged to the spirits. *But they are what we have. Guide them tomorrow. Give them your strength, the accumulated ch'i of all your hun souls. We are going through difficult times. Just as you went through so many difficult times. And war looms again, as it has so often. With luck, and your accumulated ch'i, we will persist for another five hundred years into the future. I honor your hun spirits. I honor your legacy.*

With trembling hands he lowered himself onto aching knees, and in infinite slowness bowed forward until his head bumped the floor just before the altar. Once. Twice. The third kowtow he held against the floor. Life was so rich. He was filled with beauty, with the sweetness of five hundred years of accumulated *ch'i*, his kind's efforts and wisdom and energy sustaining and uplifting him. Plum blossom petals sailed to the floor all around his ancient kneeling body.

jade

Chapter Twenty

_____

Near Keelung

"Damn headlights," Philip said to Tom, whose head was silhouetted in the light from the Secret Service car following closely behind on the road to Sung Lee's seaside mansion on the north coast of the island.

Tom sighed. They had already argued about the car of Secret Service men. "Two attempts on your life, buddy. Normal security doesn't seem excessive."

"Two possible attempts," Philip snapped. "The snakes were probably an accident."

"And that Mercedes tonight? You've found yourself quite a new girlfriend, Phil."

Philip was silent. He didn't shake easily, and the near rundown had shaken him. Plus he was edgy. It was the girl, Miss Dao. She had got him into contact with Sung Lee, true. But he had to face it—he was interested in her. A Chinese fashion buyer from Taipei, of all things. Even though Tom was right—every time he saw her he almost got killed. He knew guys who loved danger in a romance, who sought it. Many of them had ended up dead, killed by a husband or overdose of drugs or whatever. He had always thought it was stupid as hell. He'd never felt that urge—until now. He still thought it was stupid as hell. Jesus, get your head together, he thought, trying to concentrate on the dark shapes of trees flashing by outside the window. You're here trying to avoid a war. Keep focused. This is just like rock climbing. You stay focused and move deliberately and you accomplish something difficult. You don't and you get yourself killed.

Tom drove past the turnoff to Keelung and continued east along the coast road, climbing at a steady rate. He turned left into a long winding driveway, exchanged words with a guard at the stone gate, and came to a stop outside the two story stone mansion nestled among trees. As Philip emerged from the car, he saw large burnished doors open and Sung Lee appear in the doorway, wearing a crewneck sweater and slacks. The trailing car arrived and four Secret Service men piled out and fanned around the house.

"Good evening," Lee said curtly as Philip approached the doors, mahogany by their look. His eyes were following the Secret Service men fanning out around the house, not liking it. Philip decided not to say anything. Lee led him through a large tiled foyer with a waterfall cascading down the central wall. Koi fish, white, orange, and yellow, glided around the pool at its base, their colors bright against the jet black tile of the room.

A thick white carpet muffled their footsteps down a hallway. To their left opened a large, high-ceiling dining room. They turned right into a spacious study with the feel of wealth. Tasteful wealth. Large paintings adorned the walls, Chinese landscapes mostly, but a pair of running horses at the far end. Pieces of jade sat on mahogany tables, carved into fish, horses, discs, or landscape scenes, some abstract.

Philip joined Lee on a sofa fronting a window, moonlight glinting off the sea beyond. As he sat, Philip was startled by a young woman appearing out of nowhere. She glided noiselessly to a table and set a lacquer tray on it, bending effortlessly.

"Thank you, Hsiao Pang," Lee said, still curt. She stood there, patiently, evidently awaiting orders. She was nearly as attractive as Miss Dao. A lot like her, actually, Philip decided. Lean, strong. Beautiful, really. Her eyes moved around the room, checking out the corners, the window, the door. That reminded him of Tom.

"Would tea be acceptable to you with our snack, Mr. Dawson?"

"I'd love some."

"*Cha*," he said crisply, not looking at the woman. She glided out of the room.

"Help yourself, please," said Lee, pushing the tray toward Philip.

A dozen small shells were arranged in a curved row, with small forks, silver and exquisite, on either side. Philip loved new food, the more exotic the better. He picked one shell up, about the size of a half dollar, although oval, and used a fork to transfer the meat into his mouth.

"Delicious, Mr. Lee. I've never seen abalone this small."

Lee was helping himself to one. "Nine-hole abalone, Mr. Dawson. Fresh from the northeast shore, here. Hsiao Pang collects them every morning."

"My compliments to the cook."

The woman returned with a tray containing a teapot and two cups.

"Hsiao Pang prepares them, also." He looked at her as she set the new tray on the table, and very nearly smiled. "She is a woman of many talents."

He said something in Chinese to her, and a brief but brilliant smile flickered across her face, and was gone. She bowed her head to Philip. Her eyes were still roaming the room. Another word from Lee, and she disappeared.

Showtime, thought Philip, as he picked up another abalone and quickly swallowed the meat.

Lee picked up his teacup, gesturing to Philip to do the same. The cup was a thin celadon, with a fruit of some sort painted on the inside bottom. A peach?

"Sir, I met with Mr. Zhu earlier this evening. He agreed to pursue informal talks to come to an agreement, stipulating that they be closed and not publicized."

Lee had one of those faces which looked coldly angry when it wasn't making an effort to appear pleasant. It wasn't trying to appear pleasant now. Was Lee really angry?

"Did he say whether he had his government's permission to pursue these secret talks?" asked Lee. There was no pretense of courtesy in the sentence.

"He didn't say. For now, it doesn't matter, Mr. Lee."

Lee fixed Philip with a cold stare. "Although it will matter a great deal, should we come up with anything."

"True. Will you be joining us?"

Another long, fierce stare.

"And you, Mr. Dawson. Do you have permission for secret talks?"

Philip hesitated. It was always preferable to be honest in negotiations. "No, Mr. Lee. The President asked me to mediate. He did not stipulate that the sessions be public. In my mind I am merely continuing to do what he asked me to do."

A piercing stare from Lee, who finished his tea and set the cup on the table. "Do you feel, Mr. Dawson, that your President is fully supportive of your efforts to prevent a war between the People's Republic and us? I ask because I wonder whether any agreement we might reach would be acceptable to President Hayes. The fact that he didn't send Secretary Talbin bothers me."

It bothered Philip too. But he put down his cup and leaned forward toward Lee, his eyes hard. He spoke slowly but forcefully.

"Mr. Lee, I've had considerable experience and some success in negotiations of this sort. The more complicated they are, the more points of contention, the more fluidity there is. It is a mistake, sir—a mistake—to go into these negotiations looking over your shoulder and second guessing whether this government or that will find our agreement acceptable." He saw Lee stiffen at the word mistake, which was fine with him.

Philip leaned back, without taking his eyes from Lee's. "This is the way I do it, Mr. Lee. It has worked before. I am convinced it can work here and now, also. It doesn't really require President Hayes' involvement, except at the very end. Will you join Mr. Zhu and me in giving it a try?"

A long breath out from Lee. His face softened a very small degree. "Not many people speak to me like that any more, Mr. Dawson."

Was this going to backfire? Philip held his breath.

"But those that do, usually have something to teach me. So yes. I will join you and Mr. Zhu. After all, history will judge us harshly if we don't do everything we can to avoid the tragedy that looms before us, eh?"

Philip breathed a prayer of thanks. To Ma Tsu? Perhaps to Lord Kung. Perhaps to his Grandpa.

"Mr. Zhu stipulated a secluded location away from the eyes and ears of Taipei," Philip said quickly. "Absolute secrecy. Can you arrange it?"

Lee stared at the glint of moonlight off the water for a moment. "I don't imagine Zhu would approve of Chiang Kai Shek's old summer quarters on Lishan mountain."

He didn't laugh, but the ironic tone was enough to break the strained atmosphere as he turned back to the room and Philip. "There's a temple on the east coast, south of here, near a small town, Tali. It faces Turtle Island. Very scenic. Very isolated."

"How long to get there?"

"By car? Well over an hour. Twenty minutes, though, by my helicopter from the Sungshan domestic airport on the outskirts of Taipei. We could do it without notice."

"Could the temple be closed off for us?"

He nodded. "We'll say it's being cleaned for the Hungry Ghost Festival coming up next week. It would work. It's a very isolated temple, although large and grand."

"When could we have our first session there?"

"Well, it would take…arrangements. And I'm busy tomorrow, already. Possibly the day after tomorrow?"

"Good. Please do it. Say at one o'clock in the afternoon? I'll contact Mr. Zhu and have him meet us at the Sungshan airport at one."

Lee was staring at Philip, in an unsettling sort of way. Almost like he's trying to remember something about me, Philip thought.

"What is it, Mr. Lee?" he asked. He didn't like being examined.

Lee started, and actually looked embarrassed. "Oh, nothing. Nothing.

Well. Now that is settled, would you care for a drink before we part, Mr. Dawson?"

"That's not necessary, Mr. Lee. But thank you."

Lee actually smiled. "I have a good selection of western whiskies, Mr. Dawson. Surely you must already miss your American bourbons."

"Actually, I am a Scotch man, Mr. Lee."

"Indeed? Well, I have several Scotches. Shall I select one for us?"

This was a side of Lee that Philip had not seen before. It intrigued him.

"Whatever you wish, Mr. Lee."

Lee rose, and strode to the bar. Philip heard the clink of glass behind him as he admired the jade piece on the table. It was melon-sized, carved into a mountain scene. Rushing streams, trees, a small pavilion. It was whitish, hints of green in the trees, not painted but inherent in the rock.

Lee returned and handed him a glass of Scotch.

"A lovely piece of jade, Mr. Lee. Is it the older jade, called nephrite, I believe?"

"Yes. In Chinese, we in fact call it *lao yu*, old jade. All my jade is from China. Xinjiang province. Washed down from the Kunlun mountains in the spring floods, spotted by Uygur jade pickers, and fashioned into art by Chinese carvers. For thousands of years. Nothing in this room is less than twelve hundred years old."

Philip whistled, low. "And you have quite a lot of it."

"Plus another dozen pieces, in a vault in the next room. I circulate the pieces."

"You prove your culture's old belief, that jade brings health and good fortune."

Lee acknowledged the compliment with a bow of his head, and sipped his Scotch.

Philip swirled the ice cubes in his drink. "I put ice in my Scotch, too. Drives the British crazy."

"Everything drives the British crazy," agreed Lee. "They still haven't gotten used to not having their Empire any longer."

Philip brought the drink to his nose and breathed in. Ah, yes. The smokey, peaty aroma of an Islay island Scotch. He held the short glass up to the light. The distinctive dark hue of the islands. He took a sip. The expected strong flavor, and sharp, but not the least bit sweet. A hint of iodine.

"Lagavulin, I would guess," he commented to Lee. "Although depending on the age, I sometimes confuse it with Laphroaig, next door."

Lee grunted, showing that he was impressed. "For the talks, Mr. Dawson. The points we must have. Our functional, day to day independence in the conduct of our economy, our politics, is too ingrained in us to give up." He swirled the little Scotch still in his glass. "And we cannot accept mainland Chinese—People's Republic—troops on the island."

In spite of himself, Philip shook his head. "Well, I understand and respect that, Mr. Lee. That will certainly be a, uh, challenge. But that's my job, isn't it?"

Lee stared hard at him. Sizing him up, Philip thought.

"You've surprised me already, Mr. Dawson. Perhaps you'll surprise us again. By the way, what made you think it was Lagavulin, rather than Laphroaig?"

"No hint of sweetness, and a little grace note at the end, reminds me of iodine."

Lee took a long last sip. "Where did you pick up your taste for Scotch?"

A laugh from Philip. "My dad says I inherited it from my grandfather. I come from a long line of Scotch drinkers."

A laugh from Lee, also, but soft, and a little sad, thought Philip.

"And you, sir?"

Lee cleared his throat, almost like he had been choked up on something.

"Oh, I don't know. I just like the taste of it."

search

Chapter Twenty One

Day Four. *Jinhua, south of Shanghai*

Sung Lee's eyes eagerly found the Ma Tsu temple as the helicopter swept over the promontory north of the village, with the sea stretching endless to the east. His heart was pounding. This was his home village, where his mother and father had been.

He noticed Kevin pointing down, at a pattern of stones on the promontory. "Looks like an old foundation," he shouted above the noise. "We missed it on the satellite." Not important. He was here for the temple, and the old people in the village.

The helicopter hovered above the road. Lee looked at Little Jade, next to Kevin. Her eyes were wide, and widened more as the helicopter sank toward the land, and touched down with a slight bump. He reached out and squeezed her hand.

Kevin was first out, and reached back to give Little Jade a hand. He offered assistance to Lee, but Lee refused. A stocky man with close-cropped hair was waiting just in front of the factory. He rushed up to Lee, bowing, flustered. Lee was used to people being nervous with him.

"Mr. Lee. I am Lin Yu, the village headman here in Jinhua. Our provincial chief has directed me to afford you every hospitality. We are honored by your visit. Please come into my unworthy home for tea." He spoke in rough Mandarin.

"Your courtesy is impeccable," Lee answered, also in Mandarin. "But circumstances prevent us from staying as long as we would like. Could you please just give us a tour of your charming village, and let me speak with your oldest inhabitants." The headman bowed again, then indicated the large building behind them. "Our old factory. Many years ago, the Shen family owned it and produced foodstuffs here."

"The Shens were the local gentry?" Lee asked.

The headman stiffened. "In the days before Liberation, yes."

"Where are they now?"

"I believe they all moved to New York, or New Jersey, after Liberation. We have arranged for you to talk with One-eyed Liu. Our oldest inhabitant, as you requested."

Kevin was staring at the factory, his spiky golden hair glinting in the sunlight.

"What is it, Kevin?" asked Lee.

"Well, I'm puzzled. How long since the factory was in use?"

"Not since Liberation," said the headman, scratching his head energetically. "Without the Shens, there was no capital to do anything here."

"Doesn't that seem strange?" Kevin mused. "Unused for sixty-some years, and yet the building's still standing. Almost as though someone's taking care of it."

The headman's face was studiously blank.

"Show us the temple," Lee said, impatiently. He felt a current pulling him to the spot where his mother and father had stood eighty some years ago for a photograph. A five minute walk revealed the temple to be in excellent shape, red and green and gold paint bright, flagstone floors swept, altars in good repair, incense burning throughout. And Ma Tsu gazing benignly down from her seat at the back, her black face somber but beneficent beneath the rows of pearls. Real pearls, it almost looked to Lee's eyes.

Lee bought some incense at the little stall in front of the temple, lit it from the burning oil lamp, then stood before her image, incense held to his forehead. *Mighty Ma Tsu. My patron goddess. Thank you for my good fortune. Thank you for my family. Thank you for bringing me here, to your temple where my mother and father worshipped you eight decades ago. Help me find my father, Ma Tsu. Help me find him.*

He bowed twice, and stuck the incense in the fine gray powder of the burner.

"Little Jade, Kevin. Stand—over there. Kevin on the right." Lee backed up, looking at the pair of them in front of the columns, the sea and the promontory behind.

"A little more to the left, Little Jade. Kevin, farther this way." There. They stood, just as in the photo. Little Jade looked exactly like his mother. Kevin didn't look a bit like his father. Of course, Kevin had caucasian blood in him. But this was just as they had been standing. He took the photo out of his suit pocket, and held it in front of him. Perfect fit. He found his throat tightening up. He wiped tears from his eyes, and became aware of Little Jade, hugging him. He laughed, and gently pushed her away.

"I'm a foolish old man."

The headman coughed politely, and looked back to the village.

"Yes. Show us the rest of Jinhua," Lee said, his voice still strange.

They walked back beyond the factory, and wandered about the dozen or so homes. Everything looked surprisingly prosperous to Lee. The road had gaping potholes, there were no fields around the village, no chickens or pigs, certainly no industry. Yet the homes were all the square, modern type, with stucco walls, tile roofs, neat hedges all around, television antennas atop each one, even connecting sidewalks.

"I don't see any outhouses," Lee commented to the headman. "Your village doesn't have plumbing, surely?"

"It all goes straight into the harbor," the headman nodded proudly, missing Kevin and Little Jade's little gasps as he said it. "And running water in every home, too, from a village well with a modern, submerged pump."

Lee looked around. Clearly, there was nothing more than the temple, the empty old factory, and these homes. Plus the few sampans in the harbor.

"So, Mr. Yu. What accounts for the prosperity of your fine village?"

The headman's face went blank again. Too blank, Lee thought suddenly.

"We are very fortunate," the headman finally said.

"Indeed, you are fortunate," Lee said simply, dropping it. It was discourteous to press a host. "You said you had one of your old inhabitants to speak with us?"

The headman nodded his head vigorously, glad to be on another topic. He darted away, entered one of the homes, and came out the door with an old lady, tiny, bent over nearly double with age, wispy white hair spilling over her bowed head. She hobbled toward them, a cane raising swirls of dust rose every time it hit the ground.

Lee frowned at Kevin and Little Jade, who were trying not to laugh at the spectacle. Age must be respected. She finally arrived.

"Mr. Lee. This is One-eyed Liu. She has lived here for nearly one hundred years."

Lee bowed. "Good day, Miss Liu. You are very kind to talk to us."

She squinted up at him, her head resting on her hands atop her cane. Her one good eye, the one on the bottom, seemed clear and alert to Lee.

"What do you want?" she suddenly asked, in a cackling voice so strong that Lee jumped at the sound. She spoke in the coastal dialect.

Lee offered the photo to her.

"Honorable Mrs. Liu," he said, in the coastal dialect of his youth. "I am interested, keenly interested, in learning the identity of the man in this photograph."

She gazed at the photograph in his hand for some moments, then with an effort took one hand off the cane and snatched the photograph from him. She held it close to her good eye, examining it minutely, then handed it back.

"It is very old," she rasped, enunciating the words slowly but distinctly. "Back when the orphanage was here. You can see it in the background, on the promontory." She paused, as if to catch her breath. Lee leaned closer to her, to hear her next words.

"They worked at the orphanage. They aren't villagers. I don't know their names."

Lee's heart plummeted. He closed his eyes, to hide the disappointment from the others, and clinched his teeth. By the gods, he thought. I had hoped it might be easy. I had yearned for a light of recognition in old eyes, and a name coming easily to dry old lips. But no. No. He swallowed the bitterness in his throat.

"Mother." It was Little Jade, speaking Fukienese. "Mother, is there anyone else in the village who might know the name of the man?"

The headman began to translate, but the old woman waved him off.

"I understand the girl." She looked up at her with a shrewd eye. "She is the granddaughter of the girl in the photograph." A dry, rasping laugh came from her lips. Not a humorous laugh, nor a malevolent one. Something like a tired wonderment at the twisting ways of the world. She laughed some more, shifting her eye to Sung Lee, and nodding. Her eye wandered to Kevin, and suddenly widened. A new volley of laughter emerged from her, but this one pure astonishment, as she pointed a thin finger towards Kevin's hair, back to her own, then back to Kevin's.

All of them laughed with her now, Kevin included. Even the headman. Then silence. Lee's disappointment reasserted itself. "Mother," Lee said. "Are you sure that the man in the photograph is not a village person? One of the Shens, perhaps?"

She peered up at him for some moments. "You want it to be. But it isn't. He's not from Jinhua. Look at him! So strange a face. He's from nowhere near here."

A shocked silence. What in the world did she mean by that?

"Mother, where would he be from?" Little Jade asked.

The old woman was shaking her head above her cane, seemingly lost in remembrances. "The Shens," she finally said, in the cackling voice. "The Shens, they ran the factory. Made moon cakes, for Shanghai." Her voice went soft, abruptly. "Wonderful sweet filling. Crushed beans, melon seeds." She gazed at Little Jade. "The bloom of the cassia tree."

The old woman shook her head at the memory. Lee remembered his mother complaining, every Mid-Autumn Festival, that she couldn't find decent moon cakes.

"The Shens, they were arrogant," she whispered, looking out to the sea, now. "They took anything they wanted in the village." She glanced over at Little Jade, the shrewd look back in her eye, along with something like pride. "Would you believe, little one, that the young Shen took me, when I was the age of your grandmother in the photograph?" She cackled. "Oh, I was a ripe fruit, then. Prettier than your grandmother, probably." She laughed, a robust laugh with life still in it. She laughed long, ending in a fit of wheezing. No one said anything.

She studied her hands atop her cane. "He fled the Japanese, before he even knew I carried his seed. Not that it would have mattered to him. I raised my little boy alone." She squinted back up at Little Jade, the light in her eyes fading. "My boy died, some thirty years ago. But his son lives here, still. That house over there." Her head jerked toward the home she had emerged from, with the village's largest television antenna.

No one said anything. The old woman appeared to be falling asleep.

"Mother." Lee was startled to hear Kevin's voice. He was speaking Mandarin. "Mother. Tell us about the old orphanage."

For some moments she didn't move. Lee assumed she had fallen asleep, or didn't understand the Mandarin. But then, without moving her head or opening her eye, she spoke. "What is there to say? About a decade after the dynasty fell, foreign devils came. Missionaries. They wore black, but they weren't priests." Her eye flickered open, and Lee imagined that he saw it twinkle.

"No, these were missionaries who were permitted to use their Jade Stalks for something more than pissing." She cackled merrily for a short moment. Then fell silent, and closed her eye. "Built the orphanage on the promontory, beyond Ma Tsu. Oh, there were lots of orphans, then. They roamed the countryside. Starved to death on the roads. Sold their bodies, when they reached the age." Her eye flickered open, and stared unseeing towards Little Jade. "Oh, it was a bad time. A bad time. Not that there haven't been worse." Her eye closed again over her hands.

Silence. "And the orphanage?" Little Jade asked.

The old woman made a soft noise. "They were foreign devils, but they helped the orphans. For some ten years, I suppose. Twenty. Thirty. But when the Japanese came, they left. Did their best with the orphans, when they left, but mostly the little ones just went back into the countryside. Starving. Selling themselves. The orphans."

She seemed to fall asleep again, her old cheek resting on her hands on the cane on the dusty ground. Then she spoke softly, slurring the words as she drifted to sleep. "The Japanese killed them whenever they saw them. Shot them like they were stray dogs."

Little Jade and Kevin looked at Lee, wide-eyed, as the old woman finished. It was nothing new to Lee. His mother and he had been one step ahead of the same Japanese. He was only four at the time, but he remembered parts of it vividly. The waves of refugees, stumbling south ahead of the Japanese. Children abandoned beside the roads, too heavy to be carried, too young to keep up. Mothers being dragged away from their children, wailing. He remembered it. Remembered especially the wailing of the mothers. And so the old woman's words didn't affect him much. It was a hard world. You survived only if you were strong. Like his mother. She had borne him, fled the Japanese with him, and helped him survive and build a fortune. Then she had died, finally. And ten years later, she had given him her last gift. The photograph of her with his father.

And it had come to nothing. He knew his father's face. Half of his face. But not his name. Not where he had come from, nor where he had gone to. So he really had very little more than he had a week ago.

"Come on, Little Jade. Kevin. Let's go home," Lee sighed. He turned to the headman. "Thank you for your hospitality, Mr. Lu. Don't bother to escort us back to the helicopter. Help Mrs. Liu back to her grandson's home."

The headman gently took the old woman's elbow. "Actually, I myself am the unworthy grandson of Mrs. Liu," he stammered, his face flushing. "She sometimes doesn't recognize me. Or even which house is hers." He led her away.

As they approached the helicopter, Kevin grabbed Lee's arm. "Let's see what's inside that factory, Mr. Lee."

"What for?"

"Well, what strikes you as odd about this place, sir?"

"That's easy," Lee scowled. "They don't have any industry or agriculture, in the middle of nowhere, yet their temple is immaculate and newly painted, like their homes."

Kevin's gold-tipped head nodded energetically. "Exactly. Plus a factory that hasn't been used in sixty years but is still standing and kept up. Now, could one oddity have something to do with the other?"

They were at the helicopter, now. Lee looked back, and didn't see the headman.

"All right. See if you can get in it."

Kevin sprinted away. He tried the front door, to no avail, and disappeared around the far side of the building. Then the front door opened, from the inside. Kevin waved.

Lee hurried into the factory, Little Jade close behind. As their eyes adjusted to the dim light, they saw dozens of pillars resting on thick wooden beams some hundred feet across. Sunlight streamed through the few windows, highlighting swirls of dust in the air above the dirt floor. The building was completely empty.

"Nothing," Lee said, his voice echoing.

"What's that pile of things in the corner?" Little Jade asked.

Swirls of dust marked Kevin's path to the corner, where he picked up two bags from a much larger pile, and brought them back.

Lee examined them. They were burlap, rough. He turned one inside out. Several chips of rock fell to the floor, hitting the dirt with a soft thump. He picked them up.

"That's...very peculiar," he said at last, turning the chips over in his hand.

"What's peculiar?" Little Jade asked, looking around nervously.

Lee took the bags and the rocks to the half-opened front door. He held them to the light there, nodded, then gave the bags back to Kevin. "Take these back where you found them." He put the rock chips in his pocket. "Fasten the door from the inside again, then join us," he said to Kevin.

"What was all that about?" Little Jade asked, as they neared the helicopter, and Kevin came sprinting up.

The blades whirled above them, making great whumping sounds. Lee shouted toward Kevin and Little Jade. "The rock chips are the rind of jade pieces. Large jade pieces. The burlap bags are what the Uygur jade collectors in Xinjiang use to carry the raw jade they find."

They stared at him. "So what?" Kevin asked.

Lee paused at the opening into the helicopter. "So now we know what pays for all the prosperity in the village. They're smuggling jade. Top-quality nephrite jade from the Kunlun mountains. Someone is making a lot of money."

Chapter Twenty Two

Washington, D.C.

Tiffany Hayes sailed through the restaurant's dining room with Daisy in her arms, soaking up the greetings and attention she attracted. She had just been seated at the specially-reserved table, Daisy on the chair beside her, when John Ravenhurst arrived.

"Ah, the beauty and the beast!" He gave the dog a friendly pat on the head, to which it responded with a tiny yip. Tiffany inclined her head and offered him her cheek, which he dutifully kissed.

"Tiffany, you look lovely. Have you ordered yet?" he inquired.

"No, I just arrived, myself."

He absently raised his hand while beaming at her, and the waiter promptly appeared. "The usual for me, Henry. And for you, my dear?"

"The chef's salad. Vinaigrette on the side."

The waiter gravely inclined his head and disappeared.

"I was surprised at your call," she said, almost with a trace of coyness. "I mean, you and grandfather must be frightfully busy, what with the crisis in Taiwan now."

He relaxed. "Well, it's got to be handled very coolly, and just right," he admitted. "Is Philip having much luck?"

A circumspect frown. "Let's just say he's doing his best. As are the President and myself. It's a very dicey situation." He cleared his throat and dropped his voice. "The President and I have about decided to put our military in the Pacific on full alert."

"My goodness. A full military alert, today?"

"Probably not until day after tomorrow. Let things settle down from the Chinese canceling the talks, then let them know how seriously we're taking this."

"But a Pacific military alert—wouldn't that throw the island into a panic?"

"Tiffany, this is serious business, and we're giving it our undivided attention. But let's not spoil a lovely luncheon with a beautiful woman with this kind of talk." He gazed at her with undisguised admiration. "I wanted to talk with you about something more personal, and perhaps a bit further into the future."

She paused while the waiter brought their food and left.

"Well, John. Whatever do you mean?"

He ignored his own chef's salad and spoke earnestly. "May I be frank, Tiffany?"

"Of course," she laughed, picking up her fork and stabbing some greens.

"I've long admired your way with people. And your incisive mind. You are very sharp, Tiffany, and people respect and admire you."

She cocked her head, pleased.

"I believe you could go very far, Tiffany. Become a very important player on the contemporary political scene."

She stopped chewing her salad, then slowly resumed. "Would it surprise you, dear, to know that that is exactly what I am pursuing?" she said in a husky voice.

He responded quickly, eagerly. "Of course not. But I see you going about it a very strange way, Tiffany. For the past several years I've seen you attaching yourself to up-and-coming young men, as if to ride on their successes. Perhaps some day to marry one of these young rising stars, and share in their glory."

She stared at him, fork in mid-air. Daisy caught the moment, and yapped as she stared between the two humans.

"Quiet, Daisy, dear." She turned back to Ravenhurst.

"Since we're being frank, John, perhaps you could tell me what would be so bad about being the First Lady of the land some day?"

He coughed up a bite of his salad in his excitement. "That's exactly it, Tiffany! Exactly! I have seen you assiduously and skillfully positioning yourself to be the wife of a President. But I want you, my dear—"

Leaning across the table, he fixed her eyes in a bold stare. "I want to make you a President, Tiffany Hayes. Not a First Lady."

He said it in a dramatic whisper, and let it dangle while he beamed at her. She stared back at him, wide-eyed, a little frightened at first, then she struggled to keep a broad smile from erupting over her face.

"Why, John Ravenhurst," she said, the smile finally overtaking her. "Don't you think that's a little much?" She was blushing furiously now.

"Tiffany! You are beautiful, brilliant, and well-connected." He gave her a conspiratorial look. "And we both know you lust for power, you want it the way a man craves a woman."

She blushed again.

"I know a lot, Tiffany. I daresay no one in the world knows how to seek and capture power better than me. And this is my considered judgment, my dear. If you and I work together, I can help you become the first female President of these United States. Guaranteed."

Her wide-eyed look mixed fright and lust and joy. Daisy caught the excitement and began yapping furiously.

"Now, now, dear," she stammered absently to the dog, for once not paying much attention to it. "Quiet down, Daisy."

Tiffany was in a daze. She picked at her salad for a couple of seconds. "Do you really think—that I could?" she asked in a trembling voice.

"You? By yourself? No."

She dropped her fork, picked it up again, but let it hang in mid-air above her salad. "But you said—"

He leaned forward, smiling suavely. "I said *we*, Tiffany. My expertise, your charisma. It would take both of us. Working very closely together, Tiffany. Intimately close." He whispered the last words.

"John. I take it you mean—"

"Yes, Tiffany. I want to marry you."

She dropped her fork again. Ravenhurst reached across the table and solicitously put it on the side of her salad.

"But John, dear. I'm—involved with Philip Dawson. You know that, dear."

Ravenhurst nodded, stuffed more salad in his mouth, and swallowed it.

"And a wonderful boy he is, Tiffany. To some eyes, he is destined to rise very high. Not to mine. He doesn't have the ambition, Tiffany. He'd rather be climbing cliffs, for Christ sake, than pursuing power. Am I wrong?"

She sat there, looking quite vulnerable and forlorn for a brief moment. Then she sighed, and took a bite of the salad. "Well, I don't know. Yes, you may be right. Or maybe not. I had thought I might provide the inspiration, the ambition, for him."

"Never go into a marriage with the idea of changing your partner, Tiffany," he said, shaking his head. "I've tried it three times. It never works."

She stabbed at her salad. "Of course, there's the other minor point, John. I like him very much."

"Doubtless. He is appealing, in a very youthful way. But Tiffany, Tiffany—"

He leaned forward again, the picture of solicitous experience. "Tiffany. Marriages have got to be grounded in something more than 'appeal.' You know that, my dear. Oh yes, the physical attraction is important. But you've got to be united by something more stable, something you can work for together, a grand goal that the two of you feel passionately about!"

He had her undivided attention. "I want to marry you, Tiffany Hayes. Bed you, yes. Make passionate love to you, using all the considerable skills I have in that department. But more important, Tiffany Hayes, I want to devote my life to you. To making you the President of the United States. The President of the United States! Madame President!"

Her eyes were locked into his, her breath coming in ragged gasps. When she could finally speak, her voice was hoarse. "You are shameless, John Ravenhurst. You're appealing to my very lowest desires, aren't you?"

He took her hand, and stared at her over it. "I understand you, Tiffany. I understand you to your core. There is nothing about you that I don't know. And understand. And share."

"Oh my," she muttered, in a daze.

Daisy had seen enough of this. She began yapping, loudly and insistently.

The yapping broke the spell. Tiffany and Ravenhurst broke into a laugh, and Tiffany leaned over and scooped the dog into her arms and began energetically stroking its head, almost slapping it in her excitement and inattention. Daisy cringed.

"My, my, John. You do know how to get a girl's attention."

"Think it over, my dear," he replied expansively. "There's no rush, of course. I completely understand your infatuation with the Dawson boy. He has considerable boyish charm to him. But remember what I've said, and if ever you lose him—uh, tire of him, my dear, then think about what has passed between us today."

He put his hand atop her arm that was cradling Daisy. "It's been special, Tiffany. I've felt something very powerful, very enduring between us today."

Daisy leaned her head against his hand, and whimpered happily.

"But now, I've got to get back to the White House," he said smugly, checking his watch. "I'll leave you and Daisy here to think things over, if I may."

Tiffany nodded her assent, still dazed. Ravenhurst rose and left, giving her a jaunty wave as he reached the door, tucking his bright red and white tie into his coat.

She sat, absently stroking Daisy's head. When the waiter approached to clear the table, she gave him a tight little smile. When he had left, she pulled her cell phone from her purse and scrolled down her contacts.

"Sally. Tiffany here. I know this is sudden, my dear, but I've got to go to Taiwan. I'm in a complete dither, and I need to talk to my man about some things."

A short laugh.

"Yes, I know. It happens to all of us, doesn't it? What's the quickest flight you can get me on?"

She returned Daisy onto the adjacent chair, and impatiently tapped the table with her elegantly painted fingernails.

"Yes. Perfect. That will give me tomorrow to pack, but get me on my way early day after tomorrow. En route and all that, before any—announcements. What time does that get me to Taipei? What? God, I'll look a fright. But yes, make the reservation. My, won't I surprise our young diplomat?"

She laughed, more nervously than gaily.

landscape

Chapter Twenty Three

Lung Shan Temple, dusk

Philip sat in the temple's outer courtyard, keeping his eye on the ornate door to the inner courtyards, through which Meiling had passed some twenty minutes earlier. Tom was in the corner opposite him, and four other security men were outside. The incident with the speeding car yesterday had ended Philip's lax security.

She emerged from the inner courtyard, pulled a gold scarf from her purse and put it over her head. Philip caught up to her halfway to the street.

"Miss Dao."

A faint smile came to her lips as she saw him. She continued tying the scarf below her chin, and didn't say anything.

"How are you doing, from the accident last night?"

"Oh, a stiff shoulder. This." She pointed to a bruise on her right cheek. "But nothing serious. You?"

"No problem. I have more questions about Ma Tsu. If you think we can avoid any more accidents."

He said it with a laugh. She didn't laugh in return, but reddened a bit. He pulled a bag from his pocket. "And I bought some of these on the street. Maybe we could share them, here or somewhere else. Maybe someplace quieter."

She smiled as she opened the bag. "Litchis. A favorite of yours?"

"Never had them. Didn't even know they were covered with that red rind. Thought you might know what to do with them, while we talk about Ma Tsu."

"I do know a quiet spot," she said, putting the bag in her purse. "The Botanical Gardens. I go there myself, for peace and quiet. There's a curious little stone house there that might interest you, since you're a rock climber. We'll have to stop at MacDonald's and get a knife, though, for the litchis."

"No need. I always carry a pocket knife. My grandfather said it was the one indispensable tool. It's his old knife, in fact."

They turned left, to the east, from the temple, skirting a stand of motorbikes on the sidewalk. The air was still warm from the afternoon. She wore a light, sleeveless dress. Philip remembered how much he liked the way she moved, smooth and confidently. The skin of her bare arms was lustrous, contoured with long lean muscles.

He had spent all day with Baden and Dirk, prepping for tomorrow's first secret session with Lee and Zhu. Shuffling the pieces, trying out various combinations of stages and places and military forces. Gauging where Lee and Zhu would bend, where they wouldn't. The Taiwanese seemed to be the sticking point, and Ma Tsu was the island's and probably Lee's patron saint. Going deeper into the black-faced saint was a wild card, he knew. But he also knew that wild cards sometimes mattered.

"So, were you able to get together with Sung Lee after you called him last night?" she asked. It caught him by surprise.

"Oh. Yes. As a matter of fact, I did. Thanks for giving me his number."

"You're welcome. Did you see him today and have any luck?"

A silence. He couldn't be rude—he wanted to know more about Ma Tsu from her.

"Not today. Perhaps tomorrow, though. We'll see. Tell me more about Ma Tsu. Beside saving sailors from storms, are there other stories about her—her personality?"

"She learned medicine from a Taoist monk on Mei Zhou island, studied herbs, and became a noted healer. People came to her from all over, even the mainland."

Philip paused at a street stand, looking at the stacks of fruits, candies, cakes, toys, and cheap paintings. "I love Chinese landscapes. Do you like this one?"

She laughed, for the first time that evening. "Not a bit. But painters are notoriously critical of other paintings."

"Oh. You paint? Landscapes? *Shan-shuei*, mountains and water?"

"Sort of. Listen, Mr., uh, Morgan. You've got to understand something. It's fine you want to learn about Ma Tsu. But she's not a toy or strategy, to manipulate." Her dark eyes flashed into his. "She's a source of power, an energy concentration. She has her own whims. If you try to use her without respecting her, it could be dangerous."

Her warning surprised him. Confused him. She was close to him, staring him full in the face. The blue of her bruise looked lovely in the olive sheen of her skin. Abruptly she turned, and they walked in silence for several minutes.

"Ah. Here's the Botanical Gardens." She led him between two stone pillars into a broad dirt avenue with overarching cedars. Bird song drifted through the trees to them. They took a smaller walkway past a greenhouse in the last faint light of the day, then onto a path along a tree-lined stream, with less light yet. Over a bridge, and she turned aside to let him have the view.

He could barely make out a small rock house, with an open stone stairway winding around it to the flat top of the structure. It reminded Philip of the Hawk Tower that California poet Robinson Jeffers had built in Carmel. Together they climbed the winding open staircase and emerged onto a red-tiled platform roof, surrounded by a low stone wall that made them invisible from the ground fifteen feet below.

"I sit here, to enjoy the view," she said, indicating a stone bench. Gardens and tree tops floated beyond the low wall, dimly lit by the crescent moon setting to their right.

"Did you arrange the moon?" he said.

She untied her scarf, and put the litchis atop the golden scarf in her lap. "The moon, and mountains, and oceans, arrange people. Not the other way around."

It could be Robinson Jeffers saying that, thought Philip. A strange mood was coming over him. The place, the woman, the night. It was all perfect. A sense of rightness pervaded him, sitting atop a stone house on a rock bench in the moonlight with this woman who swam in the ocean every morning.

A sudden sense of danger swept him, and he stiffened. Was it too right? Engineered to lead him here? He glanced swiftly about. Nothing. And how could Miss Dao be involved in a plot? For Christsake, he was the one who had stumbled over her two nights ago, in a temple Sung Lee had mentioned. He relaxed a bit, although an undercurrent still persisted about the woman. Well, Tom wouldn't be far away, and the other trailing security men.

"Let me have your grandfather's knife. I'll peel the litchis."

He hesitated, then reached in his pocket and handed her the knife, its brown, furrowed sides dark in the dim light.

"A plain, honest knife," she said. She opened one of its two blades expertly. "I imagine your grandfather was the same." He nodded. She had described the knife and his grandpa just exactly right. With sure, curving strokes she carved the tough outer skin off a litchi, and handed it to him. "You know it has a hard seed?"

"No. I've never had these. The vendor said the name, and I recognized it."

Something like a grin swept her face. When he put the peeled fruit in his mouth, he understood why. The sharp taste was completely unlike anything he had ever had, sweet and melting and bold at the same time.

"I'm in heaven, Miss Dao. The moon, litchis. You."

She began carving a second litchi, for herself, avoiding his eyes.

"You said you 'sort of' paint *shan-shuei*, rocks and water. What did you mean by that?"

"I paint water, but only ocean. Rocks, but only headlands rising out of ocean."

"You paint what you love."

"Well, of course. And another reason. Chinese civilization has always been continental, interior-looking. The mountain, *shan* part of *shan-shuei* has dominated, and the *shuei* has always been fresh-water. But of course, fresh water is ephemeral, temporary. On its way back to the sea, inevitably. And now Chinese civilization is also moving to the sea. The ancient interior look is giving way, and the focus is shifting to the coastline."

She put a peeled litchi in her mouth, and closed her eyes as she savored the taste. "The ancient centers of power were far inland. Xian, Chengdu, Beijing. Now it's Shanghai, Canton, Shenzhen, Hong Kong. An extremely important shift in Chinese civilization. The *shan* is giving way to the *shuei*. To the ancient homeland of *shuei*, the oceans. I'm among the first painters to sense this shift, and depict it in art."

Interesting, thought Philip. Could he use it in the talks? It seemed important, but still elusive. Frustratingly elusive.

"You're—known, as an artist? A painter of oceans?" he asked her.

She glanced modestly away. "Five showings here in Taipei. Another one opening in Hong Kong, next month."

"I'd like to see your paintings. To see how you paint the flow of energy in the ocean, in clouds. What rules you have."

"No rules," she said quickly, still turned away from him. "There're no rules for the flow of *ch'i* energy. It's not rational."

He was surprised at her sudden earnestness. "Well, what is it like?"

She hesitated, then spoke softly. "It's like falling in love," she answered, still turned from him, her eyes cast down. The words hung in the moonlight, shimmering.

Philip leaned over to her. He took his grandfather's knife from her hand, wiped the blade on the scarf, and carefully folded it. He put the knife into his pocket. Then he reached up and gently turned her chin toward him. Her eyes were wide, jet black in a white sea with a gently curving shore. Slowly, he bent down to her, bringing his lips closer to hers. Her lips were warm, and wet, and pushed gently into his. He returned her gentle pressure, until she pulled away.

"Before—before we go on," she whispered hoarsely. "Tell me why you love rocks."

He was mystified. At what was happening between them. At her question. He tried to speak, but couldn't. He cleared his throat.

"Because they're there," he said with a weak laugh.

She stared up at him, her eyes hard, suddenly angry. "Tell me why you love rocks, or I will walk out of your life and never see you again."

The words swelled into the night, pressed against his gut. He could not lose her.

"Why I love rocks? Two reasons," he finally said, his voice flat and rough. "First, because they're the most real thing in the world."

"Real?" she whispered back, her breath cool on his lips.

"Solid. They don't care about you at all. They aren't aware of you at all. Real."

"Trees aren't aware of you. But you don't climb trees," she whispered, fiercely. She put her arms around his neck.

"But trees are alive," he answered, as she stroked the back of his neck. "They're like us. They shift in response to you. Not rocks. They don't shift or respond. You can pound a piece of steel in them and they couldn't care less."

"So?" She brought her lips close to his.

"So that makes them honest. Themselves. Real. Because they're not human, not even alive. They're the most basic, most enduring and trustworthy thing on the planet."

She pulled his head down until his lips met hers. They kissed deep and long. Their lips fit perfectly, and something strong began pushing them into an old current. He moved atop her, and slowly pushed her back onto the bench, and put his weight atop her.

"And the second reason?" she whispered from under him.

"The danger," he whispered into her ear. He kissed it. "No, more the concentration, because of the danger. There's no kidding around, two hundred feet up on a rock. Your mind can't wander, a bit."

"So?"

"So it makes me feel alive. Focused."

They kissed in a long silence. Her body was firm under his, but soft, and he could feel her breasts and hips and knees pressing against him through their clothing.

She broke the kiss, and breathed a long sigh. "The ocean wants the mountain."

He raised his head to look into her eyes, and they stared at each other for a long moment. He saw not only her beauty, but the rightness of the night, the swirling energy of the ocean, her acceptance of his love of rocks. And without hesitation or thought he gave himself to the rightness of it and let the current take them.

Soon his pants were off, her dress raised, and their underpants dropped on the tiles beside the bench. They gasped with pleasure as they joined. As he began to move within her, she responded with her own movements and soon they were dancing the ancient ritual of sea and rock, soft and hard. They pulsed with the energy of tides and moons and molten rock, following a nature and need far older than humans. Time evaporated and nothing existed except each other's smell and taste and feel as together they guided each other along the swirling course deeper and deeper into the core of things. The ancient, shattering explosion of pleasure gathered force and began winding its way to the surface.

There it was. An explosion, hurting his ear. But it came from the other side of the wall, followed immediately by the staccato chipping of hundreds of little blows on the outside face of the wall.

What the hell?

He opened his eyes wide, and smelled smoke. Her eyes were wide beneath him, and together they rolled off the bench in an instinctive movement toward the ground. As they hit the tile floor of the platform, still joined, a second explosion shattered the air. This one came from above the stone ledge. Pieces of steel bit deep into the bench above them and the stone floor beside them.

"You all right?" he yelled in her ear as they clung to each other.

"What's happening?" Her voice was tight and frightened.

"Phil!" Tom's voice, from the ground, strained.

"Yo!"

"Busy with one down here. One's coming up the stairs. Here's some heat coming your way, buddy."

Philip rolled off Miss Dao and crouched, looking into the dark sky. A small black shape floated over the stone wall, then plummeted onto the tile floor with a metallic clatter. As he dashed toward it, a much larger black shape emerged from the stairs. A sharp command in Chinese whose meaning was clear, reinforced by the distinct dull glow of a pistol in the black shape's hand. As Philip froze, and rose to face the shape, his foot found Tom's pistol.

The man pointed his pistol at Philip's chest, then paused. He was staring at Philip's manhood, which glistened in the moonlight. The man grunted, and smiled. In the pause, Philip saw Miss Dao sweep her arm along the tile floor, catch her underwear, and fling it up towards the man. He stepped back in surprise as the underwear slapped into his face. Philip knelt down and grabbed Tom's pistol, found the butt of it, and without consciously aiming fired three shots at the black shape. They exploded out of his hand, filling the platform with deafening noise and an acrid smell.

Silence. Then a gurgling sound from the shape. It fell in slow motion toward Philip, hitting the platform skull first with a distinct crack of bone against tile. It lay still.

More silence, broken by the confused slaps of running feet from below, and shouting. Lots of shouting. Beams of flashlights jerked around in the sky above them.

Miss Dao rose, then sat back abruptly onto the bench, her hand to her head.

"You all right?" Philip said, going to her. He saw something white on the floor by the dead man's feet. He stooped and picked it up.

"You're pretty good with these," he said, handing her the underpants.

She snatched them from his hand and slid her long legs into them.

"Dawson!" It wasn't Tom's voice.

"Up here. Where's Morgan? He all right?"

"We've got him. Hurt, but alive. You folks?"

He looked down at her on the bench. Her eyes were raised to his. Black in a sea of white, gently curving shore. "Never better, but there's a body up her. Come on up."

"Wouldn't want to intrude, Mr. Dawson." It wasn't Tom's voice, but it was the kind of smart-ass thing he'd say. Philip put his clothes on.

Miss Dao stood. She wobbled a little, and leaned on Philip. Got her balance, and pulled away from him.

"Turn the man over. I want to check his face."

Philip bent down to the body and rolled it over. "What're we going to do tomorrow night, Miss Dao, to top this?"

She didn't answer, pulled a flashlight from her purse, and shined it at his face.

"Yes," she said, sitting back against the bench. "Yes. That explains it."

"Explains what?"

"He's one of the sons of a prominent jade dealer who heads a Taipei conglomerate. Homosexual. Explains lots of things, including his fascination with your Jade Stalk just now."

"Well, if I get your meaning, my Jade Stalk saved our lives, Miss Dao."

"Didn't my underpants have something to do with it?" she spit out. She put her hand on his arm. "Listen. It accounts for something else, also. I need to talk to you, Mr., uh, Morgan. I've got a lot of explaining to do."

Suspicion swept over him. "To me? I know I've got some explaining for you. But what do you have, for me?" He remembered Tom's feeling about the woman. Now Tom was on the ground, hurt, and she was talking about explaining things to him.

"What do you have to tell me?" he repeated harshly, grabbing her by the arm.

She wrenched her arm free, with surprising strength. "Not here, you idiot. And put that gun down. You're making me nervous."

"What? Oh, yeah." He put Tom's pistol on the bench behind them.

"We both have a lot of explaining to do," she said. "What time is your, uh, meeting tomorrow?"

Another wave of suspicion, this one sharper, deeper. He didn't answer, but stared hard at her.

"Oh, come on. One? Two?"

Tom had been right all along, hadn't he?

"Mr. Dawson?" came a voice from below.

"Yeah."

"We've got Morgan stabilized and on his way out. He says there was a second man, who got away from him down here. We'd best get you out of here, Mr. Dawson. And your friend. Before the authorities arrive." Even as he spoke, a siren's wail filtered to them from far off, but heading in their direction.

"We're coming down." He turned to her, cold. "I can meet you at eleven."

She nodded. Sweat glinted just above the bruise on her cheek. "Fine. At the Galley Pub?"

How did she know he was at the Hilton?

"Yeah, then," coldly. He reclaimed Tom's pistol.

They both got up, stepped over the dead man, and threaded their way down the stairs.

Chapter Twenty Four

Day Five

As he put the phone down, a wave of hopelessness swept over him. He reached out for his pear-wood Ch'ing dynasty cane and clutched it tightly as his eyes caressed the *lao yu* pieces on the desk front. His son's death last night had been most unfortunate, a considerable blow to both the conglomerate and the assurance of continuing the ancestral line. His eyes moved to the ebony altar, the incense burners shining before it. He still had one son, he repeated to himself several times. A healthy, vital son, well able to sire sons himself, in spite of his aversion to females.

But now this, in addition! He struck the floor with the cane. The Jinhua transfer warehouse discovered, Uhgyur jade bags handled—by Sung Lee of all people! There had been several others through the years, minor customs agents that had stumbled onto the warehouse, some that had even seen the bags and the jade rinds in them. It had been no trouble to eliminate them, often on the spot if they were alone. But Sung Lee! In a helicopter. Did Sung Lee realize what it meant? He was no fool. Of course he did. But would he take the time and trouble to notify authorities? He was in the midst of momentous dealings. Perhaps he would pass over it.

It all hinged, of course, on whether the Shen family name had come up when Sung Lee had spoken with the headman. If not—and there was no reason it should have—then nothing need be done. But if so—that was a very different matter. He had asked their operative in Hong Kong to clear up the point.

The soft bell of the telephone again. He reached his gnarled hand out and picked it up.

"*Wai?*" He listened impassively, then returned the phone to its cradle.

So. Not that Sung Lee would necessarily connect the old Shens of Jinhua with the Shen family jade dealers of Taipei. And then it would take several connections more, still, for him to come to the realization of what they were doing, the realization that would threaten five hundred years of prosperity for his family. But the key to that first connection lay in Sung Lee's hand. So be it. He pushed the button beside the phone.

His son—his only living son—entered some moments later. He was puffy-eyed.

"You have made the arrangements for the funeral?"

The son nodded.

"Good. And I have handled the apologies to the newspaper, and all—" He dismissed it with a flick of his hand. "Something else has come up, my son. For some reason, Sung Lee helicoptered into Jinhua and poked around, yesterday. He got into the factory and handled some Uhgyur sacks and some of the rinds."

The son stumbled back and placed a hand on a camphor table to support himself.

"Careful. That's six hundred years old and none too strong," the old man rasped.

The son passed a hand over his forehead. "So—now Sung Lee has to be killed?"

"We can't risk his making the connection. He asked who the old gentry were. The headman mentioned our family name."

The son nodded, but seemed bewildered, stunned by it all. "But how?"

The old man picked up the phone again, consulted a book beside it, and punched in a number. "Shen Loo-ming, here. Is Mr. Lee available? Thank you." As he waited, he picked up the *lao yu* armrest and ran his fingers over it.

"Mr. Lee. An honor to speak with you, sir." A pause. "Thank you. It is a heavy loss. Without the beauty of jade, how could we bear the tragedies of life? Just this morning I have obtained a piece that made me think immediately of you. It is an unprecedented find. Song dynasty, a flying horse. One of the most exquisite *lao yu* pieces I have ever seen, whether it were a thousand years old or not. Only you could properly appreciate this piece, Mr. Lee. May I show it to you?"

He listened to the voice in the phone.

"No doubt, Mr. Lee. We can only imagine the burden you are carrying for all of us, sir. I regret to say, though, that I've already been contacted by several others desirous to obtain this piece—it really is an unprecedented center to any serious *lao yu* collection. I want it to be yours, Mr. Lee, but I cannot hold the others off long, you understand."

Another pause, as he listened to Lee's reply. "I quite understand. If not today, then, perhaps sometime tomorrow? My son and I could bring it to your

Keelung home in the afternoon." He nodded his head. "Very good, Mr. Lee. Two o'clock tomorrow. We will see you then."

He placed the phone in its cradle, and turned to his son. "He gave no evidence of having made the connection—yet. Listen carefully. Here is how we will do it."

*　*　*　*　*

Meiling clutched the brass handrail tightly as she climbed the polished wood stairs from the Hilton lobby. Her muscles were taut, her mind racing. She dreaded this meeting. At the top of the stairs she turned right. Taking a deep breath, she walked into the Galley Pub, past the Secret Service types to either side of the entrance. There. At a table against the wall, between two bad paintings of sailing ships. Her glance fell to the plush green carpet, but she forced herself to gaze up and stride bravely toward him.

"Miss Dao," he said, pulling out a chair. She allowed him to seat her. He returned to the couch against the wall.

They cast suspicious glances at each other.

"A drink?" he asked her.

"No. Yes." She didn't like feeling awkward. Wasn't used to it.

"I can't have any alcohol. A meeting in an hour or so." He gestured to a waiter in black pants and yellow tunic, who approached the table. "Ice tea for me. Miss Dao?"

"Two."

They sat in awkward silence.

"Mr. Morgan."

"Miss Dao."

He had spoken just as she had. They didn't laugh.

"Look, Miss Dao," he said quickly. "I'm awfully interested in hearing your side of whatever the hell has been happening to us for the last three evenings. But I need to clear something up, from my end, first."

His eyes were hard, and green, as he glared at her.

"I do need to learn about Ma Tsu. And it's because of a connection with Sung Lee. You've helped me on both those counts." He took a breath. "But that's about all that's been true. I'm not Mr. Morgan and I'm not a businessman. My name is Philip Dawson, and I'm here to mediate the negotiations with China."

"Mr. Dawson. I—"

"No, let me finish," he said, harshly. He waited until the waiter set the ice teas on the table and left. "The last three evenings, we've had a suspicious, a probable, and a damn-straight attempt on my life. They've been amateurish, even last night's, but they've been real. I've put you in danger, exposing you to these attempts. I apologize."

He looked at her, anger in his eyes. "Now I want to hear what you know about all this, Miss Dao."

She took a deep breath. No way to make this pretty, she thought.

"Mr. Dawson, I appreciate your confession, and your apology. I accept both. No hard feelings. Because I can top them."

He sat very still, and his eyes darkened, to gray, nearly.

"I'm not Miss Dao, either. My name is Meiling Bei. I'm a newspaper reporter. Assigned to find out your thoughts and feelings about being a mediator to the talks."

Shocked silence. He blinked. Tried to say something, but couldn't. Tried again.

"You…somehow…arranged–everything?"

"Not everything," she replied briskly. "Just meeting you. Or your meeting me, I suppose." Here comes the hard part, she thought. "The rest of it—the murder attempts. They were aimed at me. Not you. You just happened to be there."

A replay. Shocked silence. Try to talk. Fail. He leaned over the table, head tilted, not believing her. "How the hell do you know that?"

She was businesslike. "I had been working on an investigation of a conglomerate with shady dealings. They warned me off. I—I ignored their warnings."

"But how do you know—"

"The man last night. One of the sons of the leader of the conglomerate, an old dealer in antique jades. The sons are well-known strong-arm men, for the conglomerate."

No movement from him. His eyes still squinted, head cocked. Not a handsome pose. Suddenly he hit the table, hard, with his open palm, with a sharp "Damn!"

She stood.

"Sit down," he said.

"I'm not going to sit here and be cursed by you, Mr. Dawson."

"Oh, I'm not cursing you, Miss—what did you say your name is?"

"Bei."

"Miss Bei. I'm not cursing you. I'm cursing myself. For being such a fool. And for Tom Morgan being right, all along. I hate it, when he's right and I'm wrong."

He waved his hand at her. "And sit down, please. I have more to say to you."

She remained standing.

"I'll be polite, Miss Bei," he said irritably, with a bad imitation of sweetness. It seemed out of character, to her. She didn't really know him very well, did she?

He waved his hand again. "Have a seat."

This will be a mistake, she thought, as she slowly sank to the seat.

"What's your first name?" he asked, abruptly.

"Meiling."

"Huh. Pretty."

He hit the table again and exhaled sharply. "So. Did you get a good story out of me? Last night's must have been a doozy."

"I haven't written a word about—anything," she said coldly.

"Why not? Saving it all for the Sunday edition?"

With deliberate slowness she leaned toward him. "For a hot-shot negotiator, you sure don't know much about how to talk to people," she hissed.

He brought his head close to hers, until their noses were almost touching. "When I'm angry," he said, "I sometimes say exactly what's on my mind. Horrible habit, huh, Miss Bei?" His breath was hot on her face, his eyes cold gray, like a chunk of steel.

She sat back, studied the picture of the sailing ship—anything to avoid his eyes.

"I haven't written anything because I've been…confused. About where my personal feelings belong in all—all this."

She chanced a glance at him. His eyes were green again.

"And, not being sure, I decided not to—to do anything. I told my managing editor a few very general things. No story."

"What do you mean? Personal feelings?" he asked, his face still hard, angry.

"None of your business."

"Come on, Meiling. We've made love. Or most of it. None of my business?"

A feeling of despair rolled over her. How could she have felt that anything might come of all this? She felt the tears rushing up, and knew that she wouldn't be able to stop them. But she would not cry in front of him. Never. She stood, abruptly, and looked him in his eyes. Green.

"Goodbye, Philip Dawson."

She rushed out of the room, and managed to hold back the tears until the stairs.

妈祖

Ma Tsu

Chapter Twenty Five

Tien Gong Temple, Taiwan's East Coast

Philip gave up on the hospitality table producing any of that elusive sentiment. He stuffed another crab cake in his mouth and turned away from Zhu and Lee, who were studiously silent beside the mounded delicacies. Zhu was adjusting his tie and checking the orientation of his cufflinks for the third time. Lee stared at the temple, still as a stone.

Below this upper terrace was a lower one, with a gray-tiled temple and Lee's helicopter on the flagstone terrace. Beyond was the sea, a humped island rising some half mile offshore. The setting was tranquil, separated from Taipei by nearly a hundred miles of forested mountains. But Lee and Zhu had brought the tensions with them.

Taipei and Beijing had traded charges all yesterday and today. Panic buying of foodstuffs was sweeping over Taiwan, amid rumors that the U.S. President would declare a military alert in the Pacific soon. Every flight off the island was full. The deadline for an agreement was three days away, and the dull red glow of war loomed on the horizon.

"I believe there's a table for us inside the temple," Philip said with false heartiness. Lee and Zhu stiffly walked under the red and gold eaves of the upper temple, into the cool shade within. Philip stopped abruptly as he stepped inside. Behind the simple table were the temple's icons. In the middle, surrounded by flickering candles and vases of fresh flowers, sat the black-faced lady, pearls adorning her headdress.

Thank you, Ma Tsu, Philip prayed silently. *Let things go well, today.*

The next fifteen minutes battered Philip's optimism, and exhausted the formulations he'd come up with yesterday with Dirk and Baden. Lee rejected

"The Federated Autonomous Region of Taiwan within the People's Republic of China" in a breath, growling that Taiwan was not another Hong Kong or Sinjiang. "The Federated State of Taiwan Within..." had lasted a bit longer, before Lee objected that "federated" cramped the notion of "state" unacceptably.

"How about just 'The State of Taiwan within the People's Republic of China?'" ventured Philip.

"Absolutely not," Zhu said quickly. "Too much like two equal states joined in something larger." He drained the cold tea from his cup and sat it down, hard.

Philip slumped in his chair. "So we need some kind of a 'state' within the People's Republic, one that doesn't constrain or diminish it for Mr. Lee, yet one that doesn't imply equality for Mr. Zhu," he muttered, mainly to concentrate himself as his eyes strayed to the bright day outside the temple.

"It cannot be done," said Lee flatly. As he said it, his eyes flickered to Ma Tsu.

Philip's heart quickened as he saw a strange look flash across Lee's face. Was it guilt? Remorse? And did the quick glance at Ma Tsu bring it on?

"Next topic, gentlemen. Disposition of armed forces. A tough one. Mr. Lee, you are sure that you cannot be flexible on People's Republic troops on Taiwan?"

Soft light from the flickering candles played on the harsh lines of Lee's face, throwing shadows over his cheek and forehead. As he leaned forward and put his clasped hands on the table, the shadows shifted, but persisted.

"It was a nightmare, watching armed People's Republic soldiers truck into Hong Kong on that rainy July night in '97. The armored personnel carriers rumbling into Central. We would spontaneously rise up in rebellion if that happened here. I guarantee it. Students, executives, tradespeople. Everyone. Hand to hand fighting, all over the island."

No room for compromise there, Philip thought. Maybe Baden's geography ploy. "How about letting PRC troops occupy Quemoy and Matsu, perhaps bases here in the sparsely-populated east coast, also?"

"Not enough," Zhu interjected. "It is too much like partitioning the island. All of Taiwan must rejoin the motherland."

"How about a staged affair? Quemoy and Matsu now, Kaohsiung and Tainan in five years, the eastern half in ten, then Taipei and the north in twenty years?"

"No!" Both men said it at the same time, harshly.

"We must not trust to future good will. Or hope that things will work out," Zhu said grimly. "It must be settled, now."

"I agree," Lee added.

The three men sat in the shadowed temple for nearly five minutes in silence. They had run through the best ideas of Philip, Dirk, Baden, the Monterey Institute fellow, and the AIT staff in less than half an hour.

"Mr. Lee. You are quite sure that Taiwan must retain its own military?" Philip asked, again. "Even considering that full relations between Taiwan and the mainland will be in effect? Even when your world will be at peace?"

Lee cast another one of those mysterious glances at Ma Tsu, then shook his head. "When the world is at peace, a gentleman keeps his sword by his side."

"Ah, Sun Tsu," Philip said, reaching for the teapot and refilling all three cups. "Can his *Art of War* perhaps help us in our efforts?"

Zhu glared at Lee. "Mr. Lee is thinking also of chapter four. 'Invincibility lies in the defense.' Your country, Mr. Dawson, has helped them build up their defenses, so they become stubborn and unrealistic."

Lee's face grew even harder in the shadows. "And Mr. Zhu is thinking of chapter three. 'In war the best policy is to take a state intact. To capture the enemy's army is better than to destroy it.' Mr. Zhu covets our F-16s and missiles and submarines."

"You would do well to remember a later chapter, Mr. Lee," Zhu snapped back, placing his heavy arm on the table and leaning toward Lee. "'In war, numbers alone confer no advantage. Do not rely on sheer military power.' And the very first chapter, also. 'Give the enemy young boys and women to infatuate him, and jades and silks to excite his ambitions.'"

"You think our prosperity has made us weak?" Lee said contemptuously to Zhu. He half-rose from his seat and leaned toward Zhu, his face contorted. "You envy our prosperity. You could be prosperous, too, if you didn't veer off every decade into Great Leap Forwards and Cultural Revolutions and massacres of your youth."

Philip groaned. Spitting and snarling again. He was too tired and discouraged to call Lee off. "So what does Sun Tsu say that you both can agree on," he said, wearily.

Slowly, ominously, Zhu rose and thrust his face in Lee's, glaring. "His very first line. 'All warfare is based on deception.'" His hand swept his teacup off the table. The cup shattered as it hit the stone floor, sending shards into Ma Tsu's altar. "It is finished. There is nothing more to be gained here."

As Zhu disappeared into the sun's glare outside, Lee's gaze was on the broken cup in Ma Tsu's altar. With a grunt he slowly got to his knees and reached his handkerchief into the altar, flicking the broken teacup's pieces back with choppy movements. He dumped the shards on the table, used it as a crutch to laboriously raise himself from the stone floor, and followed Zhu into the sunshine. Philip stared dully at the broken cup. Ma Tsu sat imperturbed in her altar, with the equanimity of centuries. Philip opened his mouth to speak to her, but abruptly shut it.

"Christ," he muttered. "Talking to a statue." His body ached. With a groan he pushed himself up and shuffled alone from the temple and down the stone stairs to the first terrace. Zhu and Lee were studiously ignoring each other beside the helicopter. Philip pictured Ma Tsu at the back of the temple above them on the hill. And Lee's glances at her. Despite everything today, she was a good sign. She was his only hope. Would her presence nudge Lee, if he were given another opportunity?

"Give me tomorrow to work on the name issue," he said to the two at the helicopter. "And on the difficulties with the military forces. Let's meet at Sungshan airport day after tomorrow, same time, and fly here for another session."

Lee and Zhu both had angry, shocked looks on their faces, as if they were staring not at Philip but at war. There was a long silence. The blades of the helicopter began to turn, sluggishly at first, then faster. A roar engulfed them, and violent gusts whipped around them.

"What is the point of it, Mr. Dawson?" Zhu shouted over the helicopter's roar.

"The point of it is we're trying to avoid a *goddamn war*!" Philip shouted back, his face dark, contorted. "Surely that's worth one extra meeting?"

The three men glared at each other under the whirling blades, their hair and ties whipping about in the wind, their ears throbbing from the roar of the shuddering machine.

"Very well," Zhu shouted. "One more meeting. Day after tomorrow. You realize that is one day before the deadline?"

"Yes."

Lee stepped toward the helicopter, and shouted from the door. "I will return, if you insist. But let it be clear. You must have something new."

Silence reigned on the return to Taipei. Philip's body still ached. He needed a stiff Scotch. Or two. His stormy early lunch with the Chinese reporter had put him off his game. Assuming there was any game left. It had been a colossal mistake, coming here, hadn't it? Thinking he could pull together two countries that had been snarling at each other for half a century. And then making a fool of himself over a lying Chinese reporter. He was dating the granddaughter of the President, for Christ sake. Thank god it was over with Meiling or whatever her name was. Why didn't that make him feel better? All in all he felt like hell.

The dark green of pines and cedars flowed below the chopper, punctuated by golds and reds of a few early hardwoods anticipating winter. Yosemite would look the same, Philip thought. He could be there now, the hard granite of Half Dome under his palm, his fingers searching for the slightest roughness to pull himself up. No job, no responsibilities, nothing to do but something he was good at. Something where his efforts were rewarded. Without thinking of Lee and Zhu beside him, he pulled his wallet out and flipped to the two photos he kept there. Grandpa in China, his young face full of confidence and hope, surrounded by young Chinese, some smiling, some somber. Grandpa was why he was here, trying to do some good. He would fail, but maybe it was right to try, he decided. He flipped to the next photo, his mom laughing at the café table in Sarajevo with some other reporters, a week before she was killed.

Beside him, Lee's eyes flicked to the photo. Philip quickly snapped the wallet shut. He would turn to Baden and Dirk once more for help on the military question. Maybe the AIT would have some more ideas. But as the green mountains of eastern Taiwan rolled beneath them, he felt little confidence that anything could be salvaged. Perhaps it was a good thing that people were either stockpiling food or fleeing the doomed island.

mountain

Chapter Twenty Six

He materialized beside her as she was bowing before the main altar to Kuan Yin at the front of the temple. A hundred people surrounded them, chanting as orange-robed monks beat gongs and lit incense inside the altar.

"What are you doing here?" Meiling hissed, over the chants.

"More people here than I've seen before," Philip said. "What's going on?"

"You may have missed it, but there's a war coming," she snapped, putting the burning incense sticks up to her forehead and bowing, once, twice. She stepped forward and put the sticks into the bronze burner with the dragons writhing up its sides.

"Oh. A ceremony to avert war."

"No," she said, facing him. "A ceremony to save the temple from destruction in the war that is coming." She narrowed her eyes at him. "What are you doing here?" she repeated. She hadn't expected to see him again. Ever.

Incense swirled around them, blurring his face. Sonorous chanting of monks swept the courtyard, and everyone fell to their knees, hands clasped. Except the two of them. They towered above the kneeling crowd, oblivious to everything.

"Well?" she insisted.

The gongs rang out with renewed clamor. He waited until the noise passed.

"I'm not sure. You lied to me. Damn near got me killed. Three times." He took a deep breath of the incense, held it, then released it. "But I still wanted to come see you. Talk to you. Why is that?"

"I don't know," she snapped again. "You're confused. I've got to go pay my respects to Ma Tsu at the back." She stepped over several people, fighting back the tears that were burning her eyes.

He grabbed her arm, but gently, and forced her to face him again.

"I had a funny feeling, last night," he said. "Before the grenades, I mean. While we were just sitting there, talking. Eating litchis and watching the moon."

A long pause. The people around them joined the monks in chants, swaying on their knees.

"Yes?" she said, when she could trust her voice.

"Like everything was—right in the world," he said. His eyes were warm, and shimmered green with—what? Life? It was like looking into a tidepool.

"Like you and I fit together," he continued, nearly in a whisper. "It was comfortable, and exciting and—and right. And then, when we started to make love—"

She looked away, not trusting herself.

He pressed on. "More of that same feeling. Except stronger."

He grabbed her other arm, and made her look at him.

"What was that all about? Do you know?"

She averted her head, and shook it. "No. I don't know," she lied.

"Did you feel anything of it?" he pressed.

She finally allowed her eyes to meet his, frightened at what she felt. She nodded. Yes. She had felt it, too. Something pushing them together. Making the world right.

His eyes gleamed as he saw her nod. With aching slowness he took her face in his hands and brought his lips to hers. As they kissed, the feeling of rightness overwhelmed the chants, the incense, the gongs. The two of them floated above the kneeling crowd.

People all around rose to their feet, chanting an ancient chorus in full voice, while the monks lit more incense and beat on the bronze gongs with renewed strength. They broke their long kiss. The incense drifted to them, enveloped them, its pungent scent making their eyes water.

She swayed. "I need to sit," she said, grabbed his hand, and led him to a bench.

"Does this sort of thing happen often to you?" she asked.

He shook his head. "You?"

"No."

"Are you all right?" he asked, his hand on her forearm. His touch was gentle but strong. "I'm worried about you. You said last night that the old jade dealer had two sons."

"They won't go after me, again," she replied, surprised at the warm glow his concern brought her. "It would be too public. The police noticed me leaving the gardens. Connected me to the gunfire, although I didn't mention you. The family—the father and the remaining twin—issued a statement this morning. Apologizing for the inexplicable conduct of the wayward son. Pledging restitution to me and the paper. Bewilderment for what could have gotten into him. And so forth. They're out of the picture."

"Scott clean?"

"So far. We still can't figure out what's accounting for the huge unreported income to the conglomerate. That's what could land them in prison, and that's why they were trying to—" She fought back a tightening in her throat, and sat there in silence until she controlled it. "Trying to kill me. We think they're smuggling things in, processing them, then smuggling them out again and selling them abroad—probably some high-tech electronic stuff. I'm glad that I'm off their list—real glad. But I'd sure like to find out what it is they're making all their money off of."

"The head man deals in jade. Could that be it?"

She shook her head. "He specializes in nephrite, old-fashioned jade. There's hardly any market for that any more. Everyone buys jadeite, the flashier stuff. Anyway, the only jade that brings high prices is the antique pieces—certainly not the newly made pieces, even if it were nephrite rather than jadeite."

The ceremony at Kuan Yin's altar ended, and people streamed every which way, a blur of blues and browns and golds, the sharp smell of sweat mixed with the pungent incense underlying everything.

"And you?" Meiling said. "All this panic of war seeming inevitable—the secret talks are over, then? You've given up?"

A wary look flashed over his face. "It depends on who I'm talking to," he said. "Meiling Bei the person? Or Meiling Bei the newspaper woman?"

She looked down. "I've already thought about it. I'll tell the managing editor I can't be on the story any more. Too much has happened—happened between us."

"Will it get you fired?"

"Probably not," she said with a short laugh. "I'm a pretty famous reporter."

"Yeah, I can believe that," he said, with a slow nod. "I can't say much—to anyone. But things don't look good. Zhu and Lee and I are having one last try at it, day after tomorrow. I need something really good by then. Something different. Dirk and Baden and I are meeting at midnight tonight at the AIT. We'll be up most of the night thinking up new angles, talking with the AIT folks. We'll take a break tomorrow morning, to let things settle out in our minds. Then a last brainstorming session late tomorrow afternoon, then get some sleep for the meeting early the next day."

"That's only a day before the deadline, isn't it?"

"Yeah. And here's where you can help, Meiling. I don't think all this brainstorming with the experts is going to produce anything new. Do you know where I get my new ideas? My really offbeat new angles on things?"

"Probably the same place I get mine. Away from rooms and people. Swimming in the ocean. Poking around in tidepools."

"You're my girl. We've got a lot in common. For me, though, that's hanging a hundred feet up on a slab of rock. Same thing."

"So?"

"So tomorrow morning, while Dirk and Baden and all the rest of the team are taking a nap, I want you to take me to that climbing place you mentioned. Three hours on rock will do me more good than a day with the experts. And you're going to be my climbing partner."

"What? I haven't climbed for—four years or so, I guess. Maybe five. Use Tom."

"Tom's got an arm full of shrapnel from last night. Besides, I'd rather be with you. If you don't want to switch leads, I can lead all the way, you can second. Can you get me some equipment?"

"What do you need?"

"I brought a new rope and my harness with me. It's all I had in D.C." He shook his head. "That's how bloody bad it's been this past year. All my carabiners and slings and protection at my home in Vermont, and I haven't missed them. For a solid year!"

"So you've got rope and harness. Need the rest."

"Uh huh. Know where I can get it?"

She nodded. "An old school friend of mine is head of the Taiwan Alpiners, our climbing group. And he's dating my roommate, my cousin Ping."

"So get the slings and carabiners and protection from him. I'll want to inspect them all, real good, before I use them. No reflection on your friend. It's just the way we do it. He'll understand."

"Sure." She got her phone from her purse, scrolled down her contacts to Jimmy Chan, and called.

"Yes. Hello, Jimmy. It's Meiling. Yes, isn't it? Well, you won't believe this, but I need to borrow some climbing gear from you." A strange look came over Meiling's face. She hesitated. "Well, as a matter of fact, yes, it is for him." A pause. "Hold on, please, Jimmy."

She glanced over at Philip, and put her hand over the mouthpiece.

"He guessed it was you. He had heard, somewhere, that I was in contact with you. But how did he know you're a rock-climber? Well, he wants to meet you, as a social triumph. Wonders if you—we—would care to come over for drinks this evening, to pick up the gear."

"What does he do for a living?"

She tightened her hand over the mouthpiece. "Absolutely nothing. He's a playboy. Tons of inherited wealth. Lives for women and parties."

"Sounds like my kind of a guy," Philip said. Meiling scowled at him.

"Just kidding. Sure. He sounds harmless. I'll have to have my security man around. Outside the door or something."

"Jimmy. It's your lucky day," she said into the phone. "So long as you don't mind his security man hanging around outside, he's willing." Another pause. "Oh, I don't know. Say, in an hour?" A glance at Philip.

Philip consulted his watch, then agreed.

"Fine. See you at nine or so…No, not at all. We'd love to have Ping there. It will be a double date, won't it, Jimmy. Goodbye."

She returned the phone and notebook to her purse. "Got to get another pepper spray," she said, staring into the purse.

"Do that. It came in real handy. Where does your playboy friend live, from here?"

"The East District. Just fifteen minutes by car."

"Tom will take us. That'll give us time to go to MacDonald's for some tea. I get a really good, spiritual feeling from that place."

She laughed, feeling much better about life than she had half an hour ago. "Give me ten minutes to pay my respects to Ma Tsu."

"Oh, yeah. Absolutely. Take your time. I want to have that lady on my side, as well. Mind if I stick some incense in the burner, with you?"

bent

Chapter Twenty Seven

Jimmy Chan checked himself in the mirror of the foyer. The pile of climbing gear at the back of the foyer reflected in the mirror. He was as handsome as he'd ever been. He patted the side pocket of his dinner jacket, felt the little folded wax-paper envelope with the two grams of white powder from the salivary glands of the little octopus. Soon he'd demonstrate his skills. Soon Meiling would have another tragedy. He smiled.

The bell rang. He waited a few moments, then opened the door wide.

"Meiling! Come in, come in!" He graciously waved them in.

"Hello, Jimmy. This is Philip Dawson. Philip, Jimmy Chan."

"A pleasure to meet you, Philip." He flashed his brightest smile and shook hands energetically. The caucasian had a strong hand, and nodded affably to him. A pleasant, open face. He could like this fellow, Jimmy thought. A pity he would kill him tonight.

"I hope you don't mind, Jimmy. This is Tom Morgan, my security man. He'll have to check your rooms out quickly."

"I understand, Philip. It's the price I pay, for having Taipei's most talked-about celebrity in my home!" He played the dizzy socialite consummately, enjoying the role.

He wasn't worried about the security man. He had pulled the closet panel in front of the opening to his lab, and only methodical measurements would reveal that the living room wasn't large enough to account for the space off the study. The man walked through his rooms, then stationed himself in the hallway outside. Jimmy closed the door, checked himself in the mirror again, then joined the others in the living room. He rushed to the wet bar when he saw Ping fussing with bottles there.

"Ping, Ping, that's the role of the host, my dear. You sit yourself down with our guests, darling." He gave her a firm shove away from the wet bar.

"I appreciate the climbing gear, Jimmy," he heard the caucasian saying.

"Not at all. We rock climbers understand that when the urge hits, you just have to feel some cold rock on your hand, eh? Let me fix us some drinks before you run off with the climbing gear, Philip. What's your pleasure?" Don't act like you know too much, Jimmy reminded himself.

"Oh, a Scotch would be nice. Meiling?"

"Pick one for me, Philip."

"Do you have some single malts, Jimmy?"

"Several. Glenlivet, of course. An 18-year-old Macallan. Lagavulin."

An easy laugh from the caucasian, as he settled back on the sofa. "I haven't yet met a person here who didn't have a very respectable collection of Scotches. Macallan will do fine, for me."

"You will have it. But I think, for Meiling and my lovely Ping, a milder Scotch. Johnny Walker Red, wouldn't you agree?"

"I suspect Meiling could handle any drink you have, Jimmy." He smiled at her.

"Ping and I will be happy with the Johnny Walker, Jimmy." She returned the caucasian's smile, flushed at the compliment.

Oh yes. Well, he's evidently spent time in California, thought Jimmy. Every woman is liberated. Oh, America. So competent, yet so utterly foolish.

Turning to the bar, he reached into his pocket and extracted the small envelope. With steady hands he opened the flap and poured the white powder into the heavy glass. He dropped the empty packet and reached for the Macallan. The red cork came off the brown bottle with a slight pop, and he poured a generous draught. The powder instantly dissolved in the alcohol. He pictured chemical bonds forming between the ethanol and the maculotoxin, aided by the 3.8 pH of the Scotch. So clean, so dependable.

"Ice, Philip?" he asked suavely, turning with the deadly glass in his hand. He felt the old exhilaration surging through him, the exquisite pleasure of knowing you were about to kill someone, essentially for the fun of it. It was a pure, cerebral joy, far preferable to sex, which seemed coarse and repetitive by comparison.

"If it doesn't offend you, Jimmy," the caucasian answered.

A good answer. He liked this fellow, really. He had liked some of the others, too. This was a difficult business, sometimes. Still, the exhilaration was unmatched.

"No offense at all. And I will add it to the ladies' Johnny Walker, also." He poured the two other drinks in lighter glasses, and added ice into all three.

"Here we are! Excellent whiskey for excellent company!" He set the tray down on the table in the center of the sofa and chair set and handed the two ladies their drinks, then the Macallan to the caucasian, who accepted it, then set it down on the table.

"Aren't you drinking, Jimmy?" asked Ping.

"After I've taken care of my guests," Jimmy answered, putting an affectionate hand on the back of her neck. He bent down and kissed her. The perfect host.

He returned to the bar. "Glenlivet for me, I believe. It's been a trying day, and I don't believe I'm up to the robust demands of Philip's Macallan." He watched the scene behind him reflected in the mirror of the bar as he poured the Glenlivet.

"Remind me of the difference between our Johnny Walker and your Macallan, Philip," Meiling said, picking up her drink and taking a sip.

"Only one batch of fermenting barley hops for the single malt," the caucasian replied, his reflection settling comfortably back on the sofa. "Gives it a sharp edge."

Pick up the drink, you fool, Jimmy thought. Pick it up!

"The Johnny Walker is a blend . You lose the bite of the single malts."

"Well, this is smooth," Meiling said, setting her drink down after a sip. "Let me see what it's like with a bite." She reached over to the caucasian's drink on the table.

No! thought Jimmy, as he saw her take the heavy glass in her hand. Her reflection in the mirror was sharp and clear, and her face was glowing as she raised the deadly glass toward her smiling lips, eyes locked on the caucasian's. A hot flush engulfed him as Chan pushed himself away from the bar and turned to the room, stumbling over a chair. His legs would barely obey him, and moved as if struggling through water. He yelled as Meiling brought the deadly glass to her lips.

"No!" He finally reached her in a lunge and swiped at the glass with his outstretched hand. His fingers caught it, and he knocked the glass away from her lips. It bounced off the table and landed on the carpet with a thud, scattering Scotch and poison.

He saw them staring at him, wide-eyed. The caucasian had sat up. He was aware of his shin throbbing, where he had jammed it into the table. He peered at Meiling's lips. No gleam of liquid there. With an effort he pulled himself together. The shin hurt.

"How clumsy of me, Meiling. I, I wanted our guest to have...the first drink of his Scotch." Her eyes mixed anger and puzzlement as they shined up at him. Her look transfixed him, its intensity, its fierceness, all concentrated directly at him. It was the exact look he imagined from her if he was atop her, inside her. He never wanted to leave that look, that universe. He realized he was panting, and vaguely saw the caucasian shift on the sofa. Ping stood from her chair. With enormous reluctance he pulled himself back, to his own room, his guests, to his maculotoxin and Scotch spilled all over his table.

"You…you don't know how eccentric we Scotch drinkers can be, Meiling," he stammered. "A single malt, Macallan—why, it was a very special gift from me to our guest. Mr. Dawson. Aren't we particular, eccentric, Mr. Dawson, about our Scotch?"

He turned to the caucasian, saw his puzzled stare. Saw his raised eyebrows, and his shrug. "Scotch drinkers can be a bit strange, at times," he heard him say.

"There! Didn't I tell you." He reached out to Ping, who was still standing, and put a hand on her elbow. "Darling, please pour Philip another draught. The Macallan is on the top shelf, to the right. I'll get a towel to clean up the mess I made."

He stooped, picked up the glass, and walked unsteadily out of the room and into the foyer. He made it to the bathroom. As the door clicked shut behind him, he put the glass down and leaned against the counter. He looked up at his reflection. *My god, am I that distraught?* With an effort he breathed deep several times, and smoothed his hair. Calm down, you fool. Compose yourself. He grabbed a towel.

All right. Damn! He had wanted to see the caucasian suffocate, turn blue and die in front of him. But no. What now? Of course. The climbing gear. He had already thought about it, in case he had no opportunity for the maculotoxin. He opened the door and walked softly to the climbing gear. He found the ring of nuts. His hands were trembling. Damn. He unclipped the number five nut from the ring, and put it in his side pocket. Where the maculotoxin had been. He noisily returned to the living room.

"Here we are. Let me clean up that Scotch."

With quick circular movements of the towel he wiped off the table.

"Again, my apologies to all. Doubtless I overreacted to my honored guest's Scotch being diverted from him. Did Ping give you a new glass, Philip?"

The caucasian lifted the glass in a silent toast, and took a long sip.

Chan folded the towel neatly, and tossed it onto the bar. "So. Did Meiling tell me you wanted a suggestion for a climb, Philip?"

"Yes."

The caucasian was being taciturn. He didn't look like much, really. Could this really be the fellow who had won everyone's praise in New Delhi last year? Chan picked up a pamphlet on the side table, and tossed it to the caucasian. "Here's a description of several routes at our best climbing site, on the northeast coast between Lung Tung and Pitouchiao. You know the place, Meiling?"

"Of course."

"I'd suggest the second climb, the Sacred Soaring. It's challenging, three pitches, rated five-nine. Just the thing to invigorate you, get you back to basics."

"That's what I'm after," the caucasian said with a nod, swirling the Scotch. "What kind of rock is it?"

"Sandstone. Coarse sandstone."

"Well-cemented?"

"Quite. And well-featured, too. Very grippy."

The caucasian grunted as he studied the route in the pamphlet.

"The club has banned bolts from this particular climb—'sacred' rock, after all, so you're a bit thin on protection here and there, particularly near the top. A good crack meanders through the first two pitches of the climb, though, which takes nuts in several places; I have a ring of them, of course."

"What's the crux of the climb?"

Jimmy grinned. Perfect. "The last maneuver of the climb, on the third pitch. There's a four-foot headwall just below the top. Solid rock. Fortunately, there's a recess just below the headwall that will take protection—fortunate, because you're climbing the thirty five feet of the last pitch without protection until the headwall. You set an etrier ladder with stirrups in the recess, and spring up and through the headwall to the jug hold at the top. 'Soaring,' eh? Very satisfying."

His glass tilted back, the caucasian laughed, then took a long swig of his Scotch.

Jimmy paused, and kept his voice very casual. "Some of us, the thrill-seekers, decline to rope into the carabiner holding the stirrup, so we're without protection that last lunge up over the headwall. It's a real rush. But I'd advise you to play it safe."

"I can take the route map?" the caucasian asked.

"Of course. Just return it with the gear. And don't forget to check the gear."

"I noticed it in the hall. I won't need the rope or harness. Brought my own. But the protection, the gear rack, slings, carabiners—I'll need all those."

"Fine. It's all in good shape, but I insist on your checking it out carefully."

"Will do. Mind if I do that while you folks finish your drinks in here?"

"Of course not. Meiling, another drink? I'll be happy to fix you a Macallan."

"I'll just finish this one, Jimmy." There was still a wariness in her tone.

The caucasian finished his drink, coughed a little, then left the room. Out of the corner of his eye Chan watched as he squatted before the gear. The caucasian picked out a piece at a time, pulled at it, brought it close to his eyes to examine, turned it over, examined that side, pulled at it again, then set it aside on the floor. Very professional, very cautious. He was a good climber. Too bad he'd have an accident, on the third pitch. Three hundred feet up on the cliff.

Chapter Twenty Eight

Philip and Meiling were in her apartment, with Tom guarding the door, in the hallway outside. Hopefully, that meant no grenades or hit men. They undressed each other silently, slowly at first, then with increasing urgency, kissing deeply. Soon Meiling pulled him atop her, and Philip again had the feeling as he joined with her that they were drifting in an ancient current, molten rock flowing to the sea. She knew every move he would make, and responded to amplify his pleasure, and hers. He had never before felt so right with a woman, exploring deep into the core of her.

Meiling began to gasp in small bursts, and Philip let his own urgency assert itself, thrusting faster and deeper into her. They both began a long, low moan together, and clung desperately to each other as the spasms swept over them in wave after wave, obliterating time and space. At long last the shaking released them from its grip, and they lay, drenched in sweat, exhausted but profoundly filled.

He opened his eyes. So this is how the tide feels when it rolls in, he thought. How the moon feels, when it rises. He saw the smooth skin of her cheek, and beyond that the rough edge of a dark rock on her bedside stand. He made to rise off her.

She clutched him tight. "No! I want to feel you in me, longer." Her voice was rich, full. It cut deep into his soul and shimmered there.

He sank back, glowing with contentment. He focused on the rock. Igneous, with a swirl of light crystal imbedded in a black matrix. Yin and yang, he thought. He kissed her neck, very gently. He heard her whispering something very gently, to herself, it seemed. He moved his ear to her mouth, and listened.

"Come in the morning, you will see white gulls, weaving a dance over blue water," she whispered. "The wane of the moon their dance companion, a ghost walking by daylight, but wider and whiter than any bird in the world." She paused.

He put a finger on her lips, and finished the poem for her, his voice low and rough. "My ghost you needn't look for; it is probably here, but a dark one, deep in the granite, not dancing on wind with the mad wings and the day moon."

She laughed a deep, throaty laugh into his ear. "I should have known you could recite Robinson Jeffers back to me."

He made a contented sound, something between a sigh and a growl. "Where did you get that rock, on your bedstand?"

She lightly caressed his back. "In California. Years ago. Agate beach, the northern coast. For some reason I felt like putting it beside my bedstand, just yesterday." He grew small within her, and as he shifted position he left her. She made a throaty sound of disappointment.

"Amazing," he said. "We made love without any grenades or assassins interrupting us. Or snakes. Speeding cars."

"Well, I suppose it helps to have your private security guard outside. But I don't think Tom much likes me. Or at least, us. Being together."

He reached down and pinched her butt, lightly. She yelped, and slapped his hand. "It doesn't matter, he said." "Tom and I go way back. Rock climbed together, as kids."

A silence, as he caressed her, softly cupping her butt, then rubbing it.

She purred. "Tell me a rock-climbing story. About you and Tom."

He grunted. If he couldn't share that with this woman, then who would he ever share it with? "I was in high school. Fourteen years old. My mom was in Bosnia, covering the war there, a reporter. This was the early '90s. We had just gotten a letter from her, with a photo in it, her at a restaurant, laughing. Well, I came home from school, one day in October. Dad was at work, so grandpa took me into the backyard and told me that mom had been killed by mortar fire."

She gasped, and her caressing hand froze on his chest.

"He told me real straight, his hand on my shoulder, clean and simple. But still, it made me crazy, even coming from grandpa. I ran—bicycled, actually—to the only thing I knew that was as reliable as grandpa. A cliff, that Tom and I had climbed a couple of times the summer before. I free-climbed it at dusk with just a couple of slings. Stupid, but I was crazy, crying and everything. I got a hundred feet up it, found a piton that Tom and I had put there that summer on a narrow belay ledge, and roped myself onto the mountainside. Stayed there all night, just crying and thinking of mom."

His throat wouldn't let him go on. He stopped, cleared his throat, then resumed. "As luck would have it, an autumn storm hit that night. Rain, turning to snow by midnight. I got cold. Real cold. Couldn't get down, my hands were so numb. A long night. But a good one. Lots of thinking. About mom, and things. Anyway, dad and grandpa had called Tom when I didn't show up that night. Tom guessed where I was. They showed up at first light, and saw me up there."

He laughed. "Just a little ball covered with snow halfway up the cliff. While dad went to call the fire department, Tom persuaded grandpa to be his second. They were afraid I'd fall if they didn't get me down, quick. Jesus, grandpa must have been in his sixties. Anyway, Tom led, grandpa was second, and he climbed up to me, with ropes and protection and all. Tom brought up a thermos of hot tea. Best thing I ever tasted. I'll never forget that tea. He strapped me into a harness, me and my numb, frozen hands, and belayed me down the cliff before the fire department even arrived."

They lay together on the bed. She reached up and kissed him, gently, on the lips.

"Do you have a picture, of your mother?" she asked, as she nestled into him.

Philip reached around to her bedstand, and grabbed his wallet there. He flipped it open, past the picture of his grandfather, and gave it to her.

Meiling stared at the photo a long moment, then flipped back to the other photo.

"This must be your grandfather, while he was in China." She looked from the photo to Philip, then back to the photo. "Easy to see you're related," she commented. She rolled off Philip and grabbed a robe from the chair on the other side of the bed.

"How about some family history from you?" he asked, tracing lines on her bare back as he propped himself up on an elbow. "Your parents? Grandparents?"

"Parents are pretty normal—both professors of literature at Taiwan National University. Grandparents, though—a different story."

"Tell me."

"My grandfather was a police inspector in Beijing—there when the Communists took over in '49. But he moved—escaped, actually—here during the Cultural Revolution, in the '70's."

"With your grandmother?"

A pause. "No. She was the head of an old Taoist temple in the Western Hills outside of Beijing. The Purple Mountain temple. When the Red Guards tried to destroy the temple—part of the evil traditional culture of China—she was killed defending it. Losing her was the main reason grandfather left."

"Wow. Colorful."

Meiling pulled on the robe. "Oh, if you want color, you should know of my grandmother's grandmother. She was also the head of a temple, this one in Korea, during the 1890's. The Chyong Pong sa. And she was also the most famous *kisaeng*—courtesan—in Seoul. Quite a woman. Lady Han, she was called. She was part of the Tong-hak peasant rebellion, which the invading Japanese crushed, killing her husband in the decisive battle. She exiled herself to China, to the Purple Mountain temple, in fact."

"So strong females and trouble have a long history in your family, in other words. Why am I not surprised?" Philip reached into the pile of climbing gear against the wall on his side of the bed, and began inspecting the slings.

"I thought you checked those out."

He nodded. "Once. This is two. Maybe even once more, before I climb with it."

"You don't trust Jimmy Chan?"

He shrugged. "I check my own gear out before I climb. I'll sure check a stranger's gear out, at least two times, before I trust my life to it." A pause, then a chuckle, as he tossed one sling into a corner and reached for the stirrups of the nylon ladder piece. "But I will admit, that Chan fellow put on a pretty weird display tonight."

"I've never felt comfortable around him," she admitted. "Even though he's one of my oldest friends. But tonight—that was as bad as I've ever seen him. Did it really have to do with me drinking your Scotch?"

He tossed the ladder in the corner, and picked up another sling. "Well, I've never met a Scotch drinker who wasn't weird in some way. But that did stretch the limit, huh?"

Pushing the sling aside, he picked up the loop with the nuts on it. "Hey! The number five nut is missing off the loop here. The one you use the most, probably."

"Can you do without it?"

"Hell, no. The nuts have got to fit into the cracks just right. They're holding you up, maybe two hundred feet up on a cliff."

She picked up her cell phone and scrolled down the contacts.

"Jimmy. Meiling here. Say, Philip says there's a nut missing from your string. Number five." She listened to his reply. "All right. No, we'll probably be gone. We're at, uh, my apartment now." Another pause. "That would be fine. Yes. Thanks."

"He misplaced the original one on a climb down south," she said, tossing the phone onto the bed. "Picked up a new one last week, but hadn't clipped it on yet. When he brings Ping home later tonight, he'll add it to the loop."

She ran a brush through her hair, and noticed Philip staring at the wall.

"Would it help, to talk about the negotiations?" she asked, quietly.

"Climbing on a cliff tomorrow will be the best help," he replied, dropping the loop and leaning back on the bed. "We're not so far from a title for the union. I expect Dirk and Baden might come up with some possibilities tonight. I hope. But man, all hell broke loose this morning when Zhu and Lee started talking about the military."

He watched her brush her hair, liking the way her breasts under her robe lifted with each stroke.

"People always disagree about something," he mused. "You try to be positive. Divide the issue into pieces, and parcel the pieces out to the two sides. Tried that with the military. Give up Quemoy and Matsu, keep Taiwan. Start in the south, then later the North. The eastern coast first, then later the west. Nothing worked."

She stood and tightened the sash around her robe. "You wouldn't believe how many schoolmates of mine went into the military. Nearly a third, I'll bet. Most of them the Air Force. Pilots are very popular. A few the Navy. Hardly any to the Army."

"Yeah, the Army is mainly grunts—" He stopped. "What did you say?"

"Nothing," she said. "Just that most of my friends went into the Air Force."

He nodded. "Yeah. Air Force. Navy. Army. That might be one way to do it!" He stood suddenly, and stared at the wall. They're separate, he thought.

"You all right, Philip?" she asked, behind him.

He didn't hear her. His mind was racing. Divide up the military services, not the island. Taiwan keeps some branches of the military. China gets the others. Add some stages. I'll bet that would work, he thought. There was still the title, though. Some kind of 'state.'

"Thanks, Meiling. Hey, can I use your shower?"

"Help yourself. Towels in the cabinet on the left."

He wandered into her bathroom and absently pulled the door. Army, navy, air force. Keep some, let go of others, he thought. And find some damn kind of 'state'.

*   *   *   *   *

Ping swung the apartment door open and removed her key. "Hello? Anyone in?"

Silence. Meiling and the caucasian had left. Jimmy Chan pushed in after her, and closed the door behind them. He grabbed her by the waist and kissed her hard on the lips.

"Jimmy! No! You hurt me this afternoon. Jimmy!"

He shoved her back against the wall, hard, liking the jolt of her body as it hit. He tried to kiss her again, but she twisted away and staggered down the hallway to her room and slammed the door. He heard the click as she locked it. He breathed deep the smell of her frightened sweat as she had rushed down the hallway. It had a nice salty tint to it.

He turned to the living room, and noticed his reflection in a mirror as he flipped the lights. He stopped and admired himself, smoothing his hair down and tightening his necktie. Now to find the climbing gear. Not in the living room. He could hear Ping sobbing in her bedroom. Perhaps Meiling's bedroom? He moved down the hallway.

The light revealed the unmade bed. He looked at it, eyes hard. She had done it there, with him. He could smell their smells. A black, dizzying hatred welled up. It would be her last time, with Dawson. He squatted by the pile of gear and pulled a thin single-edge razor blade from his pocket. He found the nylon ladder, noted its position, and picked it up. It was four feet long, with five black stirrup-like steps between the two red sides. Each step was sewn onto the two sides with four lines of red thread. The red thread stood out against the black steps on the inside, but blended in with the red sides. He gently sliced the razor blade across all four lines of stitching on the outside of the bottom step, right side and left side. It was done so delicately that the stitches remained in place. Even if Dawson checked it again, he wouldn't see it. Then he carefully replaced the ladder precisely where it had been.

He took the number five nut from his pocket, located the loop containing the other nuts, and clicked the new one into place.

At Ping's door he paused, listening to the sobs and moans. He was tempted to hurt her more. But that would be pressing his luck. Consider it a good day's work. The maculotoxin and the Scotch had been wasted. A pity. But tomorrow, he would read in the evening papers how the caucasian had fallen, on the last, long pitch. Thirty five feet up from his last secure point, so a seventy foot fall altogether. How the inexperienced Meiling had been unable to arrest the fall, such was the force exerted on the rope by the heavy body plummeting down the cliff face. That would add another two hundred feet to the fall. It was even better than the maculotoxin. More natural. More destructive to the caucasian's body as a whole. He breathed deep, savoring the remnants of Ping's sweat in the hallway, and smiled in the darkness.

Chapter Twenty Nine

Day Six. *American Institute in Taiwan*

The shades levered up, revealing the pale light of dawn outside. The dozen people at the beat-up table in the AIT staffroom blinked in surprise, thinking it had gone from midnight to dawn awfully fast.

Philip walked to the window, tossing his coffee cup into the trash on the way. Can't drink any more of that stuff, he thought.

"What makes you think it won't work to let Taiwan keep its army, but give up its navy and air force?" he asked the senior AIT man.

"That's where all their expensive toys are," the big, overweight man said, his eyes bleary from the all-night session. "The high-tech weapons that would make an invasion by the People's Republic very difficult to pull off."

"There's more," piped up Baden, the only one in the room still looking fresh. "Their most reactionary military people head the Navy and Air Force. Can you imagine Admiral Reng and General Zhiao relinquishing their commands to mainland people?"

"Won't happen," the AIT man replied. He shook his head with finality.

"Look, we've got Sung Lee to lean on those people, if he buys into it," insisted Philip. "Not to mention the rest of the Taiwanese business elite, who don't much cotton to the idea of their island in flames. Business has already gone all to hell these past few days, just at the prospect of war. The military might buckle if the tycoons lean on them. It's important not to preclude any possibility beforehand."

"There's someone else that needs to buy into it," said Dirk, slumping in a chair at the end of the table. Her hair was awry and her skin was gray, with red blotches on her cheeks. "President Hayes. We need to run it by him."

"Nothing doing," Philip spat out.

All eyes turned to him.

"And why not?" countered Dirk, dragging herself up in the chair. "We could use some guidance at this stage. We've been up all night dreaming up different kinds of 'states' among ourselves. Federated State, Special State, Autonomous State, Roast Beef on Rye State–where the hell is the other half of that sandwich?"

Amid laughter around the table, she rummaged through piles of paper and nabbed the sandwich.

"It's premature to bring Washington in on these early, informal explorations," Philip stated.

"Philip, we could use some help on this," Dirk said, the captured sandwich halfway to her mouth.

"Look, we're all tired. We've been up all night. Let's take a break now, sleep and shower, then take this up at our two o'clock session this afternoon. And Dirk, could I talk to you for a moment over here?"

A dozen pairs of eyes glanced about the room, puzzled. But the people around the table were glad to finally rise and shuffle out of the room, Baden last, leaving Dirk and Philip alone.

Philip shoved a fresh cup of coffee in Dirk's direction. "Here. It'll take some help, getting that sandwich down."

She refused the offer. "Philip, this has gone beyond the pale. The President still thinks we're just biding time here, and he's doubtless so busy laying out wartime military scenarios with the Joint Chiefs that he hasn't thought of us for days. But Philip, you're actively negotiating important points. You can't do this solo."

"I can and I will, damn it."

"This is a major new twist, separating out the military, letting the People's Republic take over the Navy and Air Force but not Taiwan's army. You've got to run it by the President, whether it's in secret negotiations or not."

"He'll have trouble with it. He's already told me that Taiwan has to retain most or all of its military hardware, or some such words. But more important—"

"I know what you're going to say."

"Yeah, but it's still true. Ravenhurst will drive a stake through its heart the moment he hears about it. No way around it."

"But Philip, if it's going to get killed, why bother with it at all?" She gave in and took a large gulp of the coffee. Her face flushed as it went down, and she crammed some of the sandwich into her mouth after it.

"Why bother? Because it's the last damn thing between us and a war," Philip said, his voice rising. "Believe me, there's no other way to do it. Hayes will bend to Ravenhurst and kill it if it's just an idea, a proposal. But if it's the linchpin of a peace agreement, with war in the balance—"

"Ravenhurst will still kill it."

"He'll try, but there's a good chance Hayes would buck him, if it's clearly that, or war."

"Do you see what you're doing, Philip?" Dirk said, lurching to her feet, her chair toppling behind her. "It's bad enough you're conducting secret negotiations without explicit instructions from the President. Now you're making our foreign policy, Philip!" Her hair was pushing every which way, and the red blotches in her face were blooming. Her voice rose in pitch with every sentence.

"You can't play President! You can't make foreign policy!" she yelled in a shrill squeak.

"If we go to Hayes with this as merely a possible proposal, Ravenhurst will kill it and we'll have missiles slamming down all over this goddamn island and the coast of China. Including American missiles with nuclear warheads, Dirk! That'll thrill Ravenhurst, but do you want that on your conscience? Do you?"

With an anguished cry she fell back into the chair next to hers. "It's not your decision to make. Our mine," she whispered hoarsely.

"I'm making the decision," Philip said, bearing down on each word. "I was brought here to stop a war and I'm going to do it, and I don't give a damn if you like it or not."

He leaned very close to Dirk's gray and red face. "Don't say a word to Washington about this," he hissed. "And don't let it leak from the AIT folks, either."

"Philip!" she cried.

"Not a word!" he yelled, slamming the door behind him.

*   *   *   *   *

Meiling had never seen Philip so angry before. The moment she saw him leaving the AIT headquarters and heading for her car, she knew. He walked fast and hard over the red and gray concrete squares, barely shy of a run, but stiff. His face was set, and he didn't say a word as he slammed the car door behind him.

"Tough day at the office?"

He stared straight ahead.

"Boy, do you need a climb on some rock," she said, then put the red Miata into gear and set off, ignoring Tom Morgan in the security car trailing behind. The streets were nearly deserted, populated mainly by police guarding storefronts where owners in undershirts nailed plywood sheets over display windows, the glass shattered the night before by pillaging crowds desperate for food and supplies.

Meiling was glad to leave the disintegrating city behind and head for her sea and the cliffs.

153

jade

Chapter Thirty

Near Keelung, Northeast coast

Sung Lee pushed his lunch plate away, scowling at the images on the television screen. Crowds of people rioting outside supermarkets and stores, all over Taiwan. Hoarding had surged with the American President's announcement of the Pacific military alert two hours ago. The atmosphere, tense already, had skyrocketed during the morning, as war seemed certain. Those who could afford it jammed airplanes and ferries fleeing the doomed island for any destination.

Hsiao Pang appeared noiselessly at his side, as always, and put his empty plate on a tray.

"It is war, then," she said, more a statement than a question.

Sung Lee shrugged. She didn't know about the secret sessions with the American mediator. Not that it mattered. They had gone nowhere the first session, and he knew they would go nowhere tomorrow.

He watched her leave with the tray. He liked the way she walked, strong and sure. It was the way she made love, also. Competent, and sure, not the least worried about her performance. He wondered again about leaving her and his other mistress, Hsiao Loo, here on Taiwan, and his three daughters by them. He sighed. It was difficult. His wife and 'official' daughters knew of his mistresses, of course. And didn't resent them at all, apparently. But part of the reason for that acceptance was the distinction drawn and maintained. The official wife and family were primary. The others, secondary. It was the way these things were, and it worked.

So Hsiao Pang and her daughter would remain here. Even with war coming. To face the missiles, the chaos. With him. He grabbed the monitor and angrily switched off the riot scenes. He picked up the phone, punching in the preset number to his stevedore.

"Liu. The last ships leave tomorrow?" A pause. "Good. Remember that my youngest daughters are never ready on time. And start planning to have our people evacuated away from the port when the deadline arrives." Another pause. "Yes, yes. But I expect they'll hit Keelung as well, just because I'm still headquartered here. Just be sure our people are out of harm's way." He put the phone down as Hsiao Pang entered.

"Master Shen and his son are here," she announced, using the old honorific title.

Sung Lee nodded curtly, and made a mental note to have old Liu pack his most prized jade pieces tomorrow and send them to Hong Kong with his last two daughters.

The old man hobbled into the room on his antique pearwood cane, followed closely by his son carrying a package—his lone remaining son, Lee thought.

Lee stood respectfully. "Master Shen. Thank you for honoring my humble home." The old man was like an antique himself.

"You're too polite," the old man wheezed, using the standard Mandarin phrase. He indicated a spot on the table, and the son placed the felt package there gently.

Lee's eyes followed the package onto the table, more curious than he could admit about the special piece that brought the old jade dealer here. He noticed the son's immaculately manicured, soft hands with a touch of revulsion. He was not judgmental about the son's sexual orientation, but still he had to suppress the revulsion.

"Please accept a very inferior tea, Master Shen," he said as Hsiao Pang set the tray holding the Song Dynasty teapot and cups on the table. They were a bold blue and white dragonfly pattern, not the usual delicate Song style at all. The tea was a Bi Lo Chun from Zhejiang, renowned for its flavor. Shen would recognize and appreciate it.

"It is a joy to visit your beautiful home and be bathed in such richness of our ancient culture," the old man wheezed in his cracked voice. Lee knew that Shen genuinely meant the formulaic phrase, and it pleased him. Old Shen lived squarely in the ancient world, and anachronistic as that was, he enjoyed his company. Although Shen's conglomerate certainly knew how to keep up in the modern business world.

The old man sipped the tea, and sighed softly. His eyes wandered over the room at the *lao yu* pieces Lee had placed there from his collection in the vault in the next room, specially for Shen's visit. Shen was smiling blissfully. "Such a joy," he repeated.

The son stood bored, with a vacant look in his eyes.

The old man brought himself back with a jerk of his head, and brought the felt tip of his cane down on the floor with a soft thud. "But we are here to add to this superb collection, if it is your wish," he said in a brisk tone. "Show our host the piece, my son." The soft, manicured hands untied the felt covering and let it fall dramatically to the side. A 'flying horse' stood revealed on the table, caught in midstride, only one hoof touching the ground. The muscles rippled beautifully, the mane and tail trailing behind in the wind. It was light and full of speed, yet wonderfully substantial, a gleaming white jade with splotches of gold on the horse's haunches and muzzle.

Despite himself, Lee caught his breath. It was probably the most beautiful thing he had ever seen, full of strength and speed, a piece of jade whose peerless crafting clearly bespoke its great age. He knew in an instant that he must have it.

The old jade dealer was nodding, perfectly aware of the effect the piece was having on Sung Lee. After a long moment, he spoke. "What do you think, Mr. Lee?"

Lee collected himself. "Yes, nice indeed. But these are such uncertain times, I don't know that I'll be able to pay what you must feel it's worth," he replied. The bargaining had begun. "Where did it come from?" Lee asked, knowing what Shen would say, but wanting to put it out for the bargaining process.

The old man shook his head. "Ah, Mr. Lee. I am afraid that I cannot reveal my source," he said in a querulous tone. "It is delicate, very delicate, to deal in works of art of this caliber," he said. "All I can tell you is that the piece is genuine, that it is early Song dynasty from the imperial workshops, a thousand years old, and that you have my personal guarantee of its authenticity."

Lee nodded. He had heard all this before, from Shen. Virtually every valuable piece of Chinese art that surfaced was characterized by a 'delicate' situation. Stolen, or discovered and bought for a shamefully low price, or obtained by blackmail. It did not matter to Lee.

"Ah. Your guarantee, of course, is enough. But in these threatening times—I am afraid I will not be able to afford this piece. If I may ask, what do you feel is its worth?"

Shen rubbed his hands on the silver top to his cane and let the question hang for some moments. He finished his cup of tea, and remained silent as Hsiao Pang refilled it.

"Its worth, of course, cannot be calculated in dollars," he began. "Its worth is far beyond what you or I could possibly ask or pay," he said dreamily, staring at the piece. "It is an eternal flower of our civilization, a gift from thousands of years ago—"

The son shifted his weight and sighed. Lee was surprised at the discourtesy.

The old man paused, then continued. "A gift which has the magical power to lift us above the current uncertainties, to lift us to a place far more real and enduring."

He jabbed his cane against the floor. "So I cannot say what it is worth. All I can say is that my expenses and my risk require four million American dollars."

Lee sat back, eyes still on the flying horse. It was about the asking price he had expected, once he had seen the incredible beauty and learned of the age of the piece.

"Truly it would be worth such a large sum," he said. "I very much hope you are able to find a buyer for that price. For myself, unfortunately, I would not be able to give you more than two million American dollars for it."

The old man picked up his teacup and examined it, then sipped the tea from it. "Two million would hardly recompense me for my own expenses," he said softly. "But you are an old and valued friend. I want to be able to let you crown your collection with this piece. Would you be able to find the means for three and a quarter million?"

Lee finished his tea, and stared at the cup as Hsiao Pang promptly refilled it. "You are very kind to me, old friend. Perhaps I could stretch myself and find two and a half million. But I am afraid that would be the best I could do."

The old man rubbed his cane's silver handle for some moments in silence. Now that the bargaining was occurring, his son was all attention and stood still behind him.

"How long would it take you to obtain the two and a half million?" he said softly.

Lee exhaled. "I would have to draw on my accounts in Singapore and Hong Kong. I would wire instructions today. The funds would be transferred by tomorrow."

Shen nodded. "At any rate, before this silly 'deadline,' then?"

"Yes."

Shen stared at the piece. "I will miss it, very badly," he wheezed. "But let us agree, then. And please have the funds transferred to my Hong Kong account, not to my account here." He reached into the wide sleeve of his gown. "Here is the code."

Lee leaned over and accepted the card. "I am happy we were able to come to an agreement, Master Shen."

"As am I," the old man replied. "I have but one request. I would prefer to transfer possession of the piece to you immediately, given its value and the inherent dangers of transporting it here and there. May I have my son put it in your vault here, and ask you to keep the vault closed until the funds have been transferred?"

"Of course. That is very trusting of you."

"My friend, given that we installed the vault for you and are familiar with its capabilities, we are very confident that the piece will be safe."

He turned to his son. "Please rewrap the piece and take it to Mr. Lee's vault."

A beatific look was on his face as he addressed Lee again. "May we celebrate by enjoying the last of the tea in the sunshine on your terrace?"

"Why, of course, Master Shen," replied Lee, somewhat taken aback. The old man had never shown the least interest in his terrace before. But then again, he had never been paid two and a half million American dollars for a piece before, either.

"Hsiao Pang, please bring the tea to the terrace," Lee said, rising. He held the door open for the old man, who tottered out on his cane, as his son carried the flying horse through the door leading to Lee's vault beside his bedroom.

The old man hobbled to the ledge above the cliff at the edge of the terrace, turned, and sat on the stone with a brief wince of pain. He lifted the teacup that Hsiao Pang gave him.

"To a piece of exceptional beauty, which now belongs to a collector of exceptional taste," he said, grandly.

Lee accepted a cup from Hsiao Pang and lifted it in salute to the old man, the ocean glinting behind him. They drank together.

"I believe the Bi Lo Chun from southern Zhejiang is one of my favorite teas," Shen stated. "It is at the same time subtle and mysterious enough to be drunk alone, as now, but also robust and flavorful enough to be drunk after a meal, so long as the meal centers on seafoods rather than meats."

Lee inclined his head and smiled, amused at the old man's garrulous mood. The sun shining off the ocean behind the man seemed to surround him in a halo. He really is an antique himself, Lee thought. A relic from another age.

"Ah. I see my son heading for our car," said Shen, peering over Lee's shoulder. "I shall join him. No need to stand on courtesy, my friend. Enjoy the day with your lovely helper, here, while I take my leave. Good day."

He placed the cup on Hsiao Pang's tray, bowed formally with clasped hands for a long moment, and hobbled off the terrace, leaving Sung Lee and Hsiao Pang to exchange bemused glances.

mountain

Chapter Thirty One

Northeast Coast, between Lungtung and Pitouchiao

Philip reached up onto the narrow shelf and hoisted himself high enough to cock his left arm. With a grunt, he pressed out the mantle and twisted around. Roughly shoving his gear rack to the side, he leaned back against the rock. He was still angry, and he knew it was dangerous to climb when your attention was elsewhere.

The shelf which ended the first pitch was a hundred feet up the cliff face in this wild, uninhabited stretch of the island's northeast coast. The sea stretched to the horizon on the east, blue furthest out, aquamarine closer. The climb should have taken over by now, driving concerns from his mind. That was the whole point of being here, to back away from the stalled talks, the panicked crowds hoarding food. To get it all out of his mind so he could come at it from a different angle.

He couldn't ask for a better climb. Good, hard rock with plenty of handholds. Sea washing into the thin stretch of beach below with a roar. Raucous gulls swooping on wind laced with the smell of sea salt. Meiling looking up from the foot of the cliff, lovely and strong in her halter top and climbing pants. It should be working, but sure as hell wasn't.

Relax, he told himself. You're here, with all this. Stupid to ignore it and let the anger persist. His eye traced the sea's transition from aquamarine to blue, drifting out to the horizon. And there he saw them. The carrier, its deck gleaming silver with jet fighters, with a dozen destroyers and frigates scattered around it. The anger came rushing back.

"Goddamn it," he muttered, jerking his eyes away from the horizon.

"Yo" he called down to Meiling, loud against the wind. "Let me set an anchor." She nodded, and he squirmed around on the ledge, pulling a midsize nut from his gear sling. He shoved it in the widest part of the crack running up the rock face from the ledge, at a spot where the nut provided multidirectional protection. A bit too loose. He replaced the first nut and removed the next larger one from his gear sling. Perfect, a bombproof nut. He placed two more nuts along the crack, linked them all with a sling that spread the tension, clipped two carabiners to the sling, reversed, then clipped himself into the anchor with a sling from his harness to the two reversed 'biners. Finally he ran the rope through his belay device and clipped its loop into the anchor.

"I'm off belay," he called down to her. "Come on up!"

"Off belay," Meiling acknowledged. She dusted her hands with chalk from the bag on her harness, and called out, "Do you have me?"

Philip checked his connection to the anchor—just enough sling to lean over the edge to belay her. His eye traced the rope through his black belay device to the anchor.

"On belay," he called out.

"Climbing," Meiling yelled. She put her hand on the rock.

"Climb," Philip answered. He watched her over the top of the ledge as he took up the slack in the rope. She climbed slowly and cautiously at first. But by the time she was halfway to him, her moves were more fluid, more sure, and Philip grinned as he saw the natural climbing ability showing itself. He was glad to see her at home on rock. He continued pulling in the slack, letting the rope slide over the edge of the ledge as she progressed up the cliff face. He didn't reach out to help as she put a hand on the ledge fifteen minutes later, but let her perform the mantle herself. Sweat beaded along her lips as she finished the maneuver and sat beside him. She tied into the anchor with a sling.

"Belay off," Meiling said, a half-smile taking over her face.

"Off belay," he acknowledged, liking the ritual. "Nice climbing."

She breathed deep. "Been a while."

"You climb well," he said, simply. Watching her climb, the edge had gone off his anger. Together, they leaned back against the cliff, enjoying the warm sun on their faces, the cries of the gulls, the smell of the sea.

"I like my rock, Meiling. But I can understand why you like the sea," he said, watching the waves spray high into the air as they crashed against boulders up the coast.

"Nice to be in a spot where we can appreciate both, isn't it?"

"Yeah, it is," said Philip, savoring the sea of white in the curved coastline of her eyes. He ran his thumb along her bottom lip, leaving a trail of white chalk. She nipped at his finger, coughed on chalk, and they both laughed, and nestled back against the rock.

"It does kind of grab you. The sea, I mean," he said, liking the feel of the sun on his face. It was late morning, and it hit them from high in the sky. "Hard to believe that China ignored it thousands of years, kept its focus inward, continental, like you say."

"Well," she drawled, her eyes closed to concentrate the feel of the sun and the smell of the sea. "It's true the cultural focus was on the *shan*, the interior mountains. But all those thousands of years, we still had people sailing out into the sea—fishing, or settling new places. Taiwan among them, but other places, too. Southeast Asia."

"I guess. Your people are all over the place. Rich and influential, too. Indonesia, Vietnam, Malaysia."

"San Francisco, Vancouver," she continued with a smile, opening her eyes.

"Hell, a whole other country—the overseas Chinese."

"Yeah," she replied. "And they do have a lot of money. Much of which is reinvested back in the homeland. They're a force to be reckoned with. 'Maritime China,' it's called, that 'other country' of our people who sailed into the Pacific and settled around its rim. Unofficial, but powerful."

"Huh," he grunted, considering it. "Maritime China. Nice ring to it."

"Hey, we're here to climb, not to chat," she reminded him with a poke in the ribs.

"Oh yeah. Where's the next pitch go?" he asked, pulling the route map out of his shirt pocket. He looked from it to the rock above, several times. "Over to the right for awhile, then straight up, then veer left to catch this crack. Pretty straightforward. Let's get you tied in, kid. Here's the rope, and my belay device."

"Hey, you've got the same Super Eight as mine," she said as she took the rope and the black belay device. "Except mine's the purple one."

He glanced at her gear sling. "So I see. Black and purple, mountain and sea."

"Well, I'll use yours today," she said with a laugh. She looped the rope through the black belay device and clipped it onto the anchor. "This the pitch with the etrier stirrup?" she asked, noticing the red nylon ladder on his gear sling.

"Nope. That's the last pitch. The last maneuver of the last pitch. Way up there." He grinned at her as he jerked his head to the very top of the cliff two hundred feet above.

"Belay on," she said.

As Philip got to his feet on the narrow ledge, a flash far out to sea caught his eye. The aircraft carrier. He let the anger flare, then ebb. "Climbing," he said, and he slid his hands over the rock. He focused on the rock, on his outstretched arm, warily slipping into the concentration. But deep in his mind, below his conscious awareness, a phrase from their talk was bouncing from neuron to neuron.

* * * * *

"No, Mr. Dawson is not in," said the desk clerk at the Hilton. "And he has a restricted access designation, anyway."

Tiffany Hayes smiled a tight smile. "I am sure I will qualify." It was just as well Philip wasn't at the hotel. She had just arrived after a long flight, and needed to make herself presentable. "Please send a hairdresser to my room from your salon. And put a message in Mr. Dawson's box, that Miss Tiffany Hayes is here and would love to see him."

She enjoyed the way the fellow's eyes widened, and with a satisfied air turned to make her way to the elevators. Should she wear the pink cocktail dress when she met Philip tonight? Or the gauzy purple one that he liked so much? Of course, he liked it only because he could take it off her so easily. Yes, probably the purple one.

* * * * *

Lung Shan Temple

Sung Lee caught old Liu's eye and nodded. "Shall we pay our respects, daughter?" he said to Little Jade beside him.

Little Jade handed him incense, avoiding his eyes. They stepped up to the large dragon incense burner in front of Kuan Yin's altar, put the sticks to their foreheads and bowed twice, then stuck them into the sand. They stepped back and bowed again, just as old Liu reappeared with the huge roast pig on a platform carried by four priests. The sweating priests lowered the golden pig onto a massive table put in front of Kuan Yin's altar for today's Hungry Ghost festival, eyeing the pig greedily.

"At least the priests appreciate your offering, father," Little Jade said dryly.

Sung Lee sighed. Of all his daughters, Little Jade put the least stock in the old ways. And yet she was his favorite. Strange. The world was laced with strangeness.

"They rightfully have what is left when the Hungry Ghosts are full," he said. Which is plenty, he thought, since ghosts only take the spiritual aspect of the food heaped onto the table. Little Jade was filling in at the temple for her mother, who had flown to Hong Kong with the older daughters. Ordinarily, he'd be happy just to be with Little Jade. But today even she couldn't shake Sung Lee's black mood. Bad enough that war loomed in three days, with the negotiations cancelled publicly and going nowhere privately. But his own hopes of discovering his father were now ashes, crushed by the inability of the old lady at Jin Hua to recognize the man in the photo. What had she said? "He's from nowhere near here." The phrase haunted him. He had thought he might have a father this Hungry Ghost Festival. And with a past, perhaps a future somehow.

But no. He was doomed to be a Hungry Ghost himself, after all. He watched the priests striking bronze gongs, the gongs swinging toward the tables heaped with his pig and great bowls of fruit and candies, colorful paper palaces, and huge bags of rice. All there to satiate the Hungry Ghosts who wandered in the netherworld, victims of early or violent deaths, lives cut off before they could fulfill the cycle of existence and be accepted into the family *hun* souls. Or spirits who had no known family to be accepted into after death.

A stab of pain wracked his gut. With no father to honor, he had no family *hun* souls to be absorbed into. And he had no sons to mediate for him after he was dead, to placate the netherworld. Even a nephew would work, a son of a brother. But no. A black anger rose swiftly below the pain. He had been so close to gaining his father.

He felt Little Jade's hand on his arm. He glanced over at her anxious face. She knew what he was thinking. She wrapped her arm around his. Yes, he was damned. To be a hungry ghost. He felt a lone tear struggle down his cheek, and angrily brushed it off.

The priests were not through, but he pulled Little Jade away with him and stepped over the demon-stopping board into the large courtyard. The pungent incense smell vanished, replaced by fresh mist rising from the water plunging into the pool to their left.

"Father, stay in our family home here in Taipei tonight," Little Jade said.

Sung Lee patted her hand. "Thank you, Little Jade. But I have work at the dock, and several meetings in the cliffside home this evening, politicians and businessmen."

A pause. "How is Hsiao Pang?" Little Jade asked quietly, avoiding his eyes.

Sung Lee knew that Little Jade and Hsiao Pang had met on several occasions. They were rather fond of each other, he believed, although he couldn't understand why.

"She is fine, Little Jade." He lifted her chin in his large hands, but gently.

"I will join you and your mother and sisters in Hong Kong once all this is over. We will be together, in three days."

Tears brimmed in Little Jade's upturned eyes. "If there is anything left on this island, you mean," she said bitterly. "If you are alive in three days."

Sung Lee's rough hands dropped. His broad shoulders sagged.

"Yes. That is what I mean," he said.

He signaled old Liu, gave a brief kiss to Little Jade's forehead, and strode from the temple.

Chapter Thirty Two

Two hundred feet up the cliff face, Meiling played out another several feet of rope as she watched Philip climbing toward the headwall, a massive brow of sheer rock at the very top of the cliff. He was about eighty five feet above the second ledge, where she was belaying his ascent of the third and last pitch. Philip was smoothly flowing up the rockface with hardly a pause. Watching him climb was like watching waves wash ashore over the rocks. Unhurried, sure, graceful. Powerful. Like he made love to her.

"Hey," he called down. "I think I can approach the headwall from farther to the left, along that secondary crack over there. It's not the route on the map, but it would be fun."

She bit her lip. The climbing club had banned bolts from this pristine stretch of rock. He was thirty five feet beyond the last protection he had clipped his rope into.

"If I can get to the other crack, I can put some protection in there, before the crux at the overhang," he shouted down to her, as if reading her mind.

She liked the idea of another protection point to clip his rope into as he climbed toward the headwall, another ten feet above. "Here's some slack," she said, playing out another two feet. She hoped his anger early in the climb wasn't clouding his judgment.

He was resting on the smooth rock, all four points on reasonably good holds. His left hand lifted from its hold and swept the rock face to the left, toward the secondary crack, two circuits up and down, then found something it liked. His fingers dug into the rock—there must be something there I don't see, Meiling thought—and his right foot began exploring the rock to its left also. The toe of his climbing shoe caressed the rock, sweeping back and forth, paused, then wiggled into a spot, again invisible to Meiling's eyes.

He shifted his weight as the left hand and right foot settled onto their tenuous new holds, and brought his right hand to the hold his left had just vacated. He wavered there for a brief second, his body now angled to the upper left, before his left hand shot out, far, and lunged for the other crack running vertically up the cliff face. A gasp bubbled out of Meiling as she saw his footholds fail, and her brake hand bent the rope across her belay device, expecting a fall. But he hung there, his two handholds holding him up—he had reached the other crack, and his left fingers were jammed into it. His arms lifted his body up and to the side, and his right foot went straight to the foothold formerly home to his left foot, which now moved quickly to the crack.

"Piece of cake now, Meiling," he called down. "Follow the crack right to the headwall, hoist myself up with the etrier stirrup ladder."

"Did you mention something about protection in the crack, Philip?"

He laughed, and extracted a nut from his gear sling. He tried it in the crack, replaced it with a larger one, tested it, then clipped a carabiner into the loop coming off the nut. He then clipped his rope into the carabiner.

Meiling's shoulders relaxed. Getting to the crack had been sketchy. He shouldn't have tried it, really. But being roped into protection there made her feel much better.

Above her, Philip worked his way up the second crack for ten feet or so, as it angled sharp to the left below the headwall, away from the old route. He arrived at the headwall, where the crack died. Here was still the crux of the climb. With the sure, confident movement that she was recognizing as his trademark, Philip jammed one of the nuts in the crack below the overhang, about a foot above his head. He attached a carabiner into the nut's loop, then reached down to his gear sling. The red of the nylon stirrup ladder flashed as he unhooked it, brought it up, and secured it to the carabiner on the nut. He glanced up at the headwall, whose bottom margin was a foot above him, with four feet stretching sheer and smooth above that.

Meiling held her breath as she saw him pause. He would step up into the first black stirrup of the five comprising the etrier and spring up from that foothold, flying across the headwall with arm outstretched to grab the jug hold at the top of the cliff. The "Sacred Soaring." And he would do all this in one smooth move, any pause making it nearly impossible to pull off.

But Philip hadn't roped onto the protection that held the etrier at the very base of the headwall, Meiling noticed with a shiver of foreboding. She remembered Jimmy Chan saying that some, the thrill-seekers, didn't. Was Philip seeking that extra jolt, or had he overlooked it?

Before Meiling could say anything, Philip flexed his right knee with a grunt and shoved the foot into the bottom stirrup. A very slight pause, then he sprang up, his left hand reaching high for the headwall's lip, strong fingers stretched out, arched, ready to clamp down on the jug hold at the top. Sacred soaring. But the powerful spring died before he was halfway up the sheer headwall, as the black stirrup ripped off the ladder and Philip's right foot scraped down the rock. Philip's outstretched hand slapped against the flat middle of the headwall, hung there for a split second, then gravity asserted itself against his spring. He fell down the cliffside, arcing away from the rock.

Even as she screamed, Meiling bent the brake end of the rope down against the belay device, hard. The rope jumped as it bit into the protection in the new crack ten feet below the headwall, and Philip's plummeting body was abruptly jerked back to the cliff face. His head hit the rock with a sharp crack just as his full weight on the rope slammed Meiling up against the cliff face.

"Philip! Philip!" she screamed, pushing away from the cliff and craning her head up. Somehow she had hung onto the belay rope in spite of it pulling her into the cliff. She saw Philip dangling against the cliff above her, some seventy feet away.

"Philip!" again. No answer. He swayed against the rock, limp.

"No, no!" Meiling screamed. She could hear Tom below them, yelling something at her. She couldn't make it out, even if she had been listening.

"Got to get him down to my ledge," she told herself, wiping away the tears that were blurring her vision. She slowed her breathing, but felt her heart racing apace. Belaying out seventy feet of rope to lower a body heavier than her would be hard. But she had to get him down to her, in case there was bleeding to be stopped or—whatever.

"Help me, Ma Tsu," she gasped to herself. She braced against the cliff face and the anchor sling, and began to work the rope through the belay device, her right hand controlling the angle of the rope into the device and thus how much friction the device exerted against the passage of the rope. Slowly the body came down, bumping gently against the cliff as it descended, foot by foot. She glanced up from her braced position. Philip was only thirty feet above her, still limp.

Meiling closed her eyes. *Ma Tsu. Please. Please. Not again.*

Just as her forearms were beginning to tremble, Philip's body arrived. Meiling shoved him onto the ledge, tied a loop into the rope coming off his harness, and clipped the loop into the carabiner attached to the anchor. He was secure.

"Philip!" she screamed at him. "Philip! Be alive, damn it. Be alive!"

She looked closely at him. Yes, he was breathing. Unconscious, but breathing. That was a start. She ran her hands over his body. No wounds visible. No bones sticking out. Bad scrapes on his shoulder and knee, some bleeding. A very ugly bruise covering his forehead, swelling even as she watched. That would be the dangerous one.

He moaned. It was the sweetest sound she had ever heard. "Philip! Philip!"

His arms shot out, convulsively, stretching, grabbing. She pinned him to the ledge with her body over him, one hand tightly on the rope leading to the anchor.

"Be still! You're back on the ledge."

His eyes opened. Brilliant green. "What—"

"The stirrup gave way. You fell."

He grabbed her arm, hard. "That's it! Maritime!"

Oh no, she thought. "Relax, Philip."

"The Maritime State of the People's Republic! Sung Lee will buy it, Zhu too!"

Oh, Ma Tsu. He's delirious, she thought. The fall, that horrible crack of his head hitting the rock. He's delirious. "You'll be all right, Philip. Your head hit the rock."

"No, I'm fine," he protested. He gasped, and winced. "God, my head hurts."

"Yes, you hit the rock."

A wild look flashed into Philip's eyes, and he sat up and began to speak again.

"Philip!" Meiling shouted in his ear, shoving him back against the cliffside. "Philip, that's a great idea. Maritime whatever. But right now, I want to get you off this cliff. Do you understand? You're on the second belay ledge two hundred feet up on a very high cliff, Philip. You've just taken a nasty fall."

He looked around him, over to her, then up. "Oh, yeah."

"You fell—only about twenty feet, thanks to that new route you found and the protection you set in the crack up there. But still—we need to get you down. To get you to a hospital and check you out."

"Yeah. I—I guess you're right. My head hurts. And my shoulder, too, come to think of it. I feel pretty—spacey."

"Now how do we get you down?" she asked.

"Oh, I'll just rappel down from this point," he said.

"No. You are not rappelling down. You're in no shape for that. I'll lower you."

"I don't think so. What are we? Two hundred feet up? That's a lot of tough rope control. I weigh a hundred eighty, Meiling. That would be a stretch for Tom, even."

"Well, Tom isn't here. He's down there, yelling his head off."

They both peered over the ledge. Two hundred feet below, Tom jerked an extra rope from the pile of gear at the foot of the cliff, and took off at a dead run up the path leading to the top of the cliff.

"What's he doing?" Meiling asked.

Philip didn't answer. He leaned back, closing his eyes. "Jesus, my head hurts."

Meiling surveyed the two hundred feet. Yes, it would be a stretch, for anyone to belay Philip that far. She checked Philip's connection to the anchor, giving it a hard tug, then untied his rope from her own harness and began hauling it down, through the protection above them. The end of the rope slipped through the protection and fell toward them. She caught it and reeled it in until she had the free end in her hand. She stopped suddenly, and gasped, staring at its green braided sheen.

"Oh, damn! A hundred sixty five feet of rope. But I've got two hundred feet to lower him!" She slumped against the cliff face.

"Yo! Miss Bei!"

Her head jerked up. Tom's face peered over the headwall a hundred feet above.

"How is he?" The big man's voice was strained, and he was gasping for breath.

"No broken bones I can see," Meiling yelled up. "But he's got a bad bruise on his head, where he hit the rock. He's a bit spacey."

"I'm lowering the spare rope. Tie him in, and I'll haul him up."

The end of the spare rope traveled down the cliff toward them. Meiling looked at Philip. The large purple area on his forehead was pulsing, and still growing.

"No," she yelled up. "Yanking him up is too risky. He'll bang his head against the rock all the way up. I'll lower him, we can do that slowly, gently."

"No dice. I'm yanking him up," came Tom's angry voice as he played out rope.

"You are not yanking him up," Meiling screamed back at him. "It's too dangerous. And besides, you can't raise a hundred eighty pounds against gravity for a hundred feet without setting up an advantage pulley system, and you don't have that."

"Be quiet and tie him into this rope while I find a spot to secure the other end to, up here," Tom yelled, his voice hoarse. His head disappeared.

The end of Tom's rope reached her. It was blue, and not new, which bothered Meiling. She grabbed it, and felt it go slack as Tom searched for a tie-off spot above.

"Thank you, Ma Tsu," she whispered, and began jerking the rope toward her, furiously, arm over arm, as fast as she could. Tom would be holding the other end only loosely, she bet. Sure enough, she felt a soft tug, heard a startled cry, and soon the other end slithered over the headwall and plummeted down the cliff to her. A hoarse, bellowing scream erupted above.

Tom's face reappeared over the headwall. It was bright red.

"What the hell! You pulled the rope off the cliff. Goddamn it, you stupid bitch. What do you think—"

Meiling didn't say anything, as Tom ranted on, above her. She now had three hundred and thirty feet of rope. Plenty to lower Philip down to the ground. She put the ends of the green and blue ropes together and tied a trace figure eight. Then she rechecked that she was clipped into the anchor with a sling, and took the belay device off her harness. Through all this, Tom's curses were raining down on her. She knew a lot of English, but some of the things he was calling her were completely new to her. Tom seemed to have a very thorough knowledge of female anatomy.

"Tom," she yelled up. The string of curses abruptly stopped. "I'm going to start lowering Philip down, soon. Please—"

"No you're not!" Tom bellowed down. "I'm ordering you to—"

"I don't take orders!" she shrieked back at him. "Now get your big butt back down to the bottom of the cliff, because Philip is going to be there soon."

She heard an anguished roar from the big caucasian. A second's silence. Then a voice, appearing to come through clenched teeth, the words spit out slowly, one by one.

"Miss Bei. I'm not sure *I* could lower a hundred eighty pounds of dead weight down *two hundred feet!*" The last three words were screamed.

Meiling put the belay device next to the anchor, then looped the green rope coming from Philip's harness through the small opening in the belay device and then to the anchor. The direct stress would be on the anchor, not her. She checked the sling securing her to the anchor, once again. The secret to not getting her and Philip killed was to check everything twice.

"Have you called for a helicopter yet, to take Philip to a hospital?" she called up.

Another hoarse scream of rage floated down from the top of the cliff.

sea

Chapter Thirty Three

Meiling took a deep breath of the salty air rushing up the cliff. *Help me, Ma Tsu*, she prayed. *I'm already tired, my forearms are trembling, and two hundred feet is, indeed, a long way to lower a body. Don't let me drop this man two hundred feet, Ma Tsu.* She knew the trick would be to keep the rope angled into the belay device enough to create friction, but not so much to preclude movement. With nearly two hundred pounds hanging from the rope as it comes out of the device, yet.

She reached over and shook Philip by the shoulder. His hooked nose was covered with scrapes, and the bruise on his temple throbbed, a shade of purple she had never seen before. He moaned, and opened his eyes, staring straight ahead.

"Philip," she said. "Philip, look at me." He swung his head to her. "Listen," she said, capturing his attention with her urgency. "You've had a bad fall. I know it's hard to concentrate. I'm lowering you down to the ground. It will be smooth, and slow. You've got to make sure you don't let your head hit against the rock any more. Protect your head, with your hands and arms. Do you understand?"

He nodded, dully.

"Tell me what you're going to do," she said to him, shaking his shoulder.

He winced. But he looked into her eyes. "Protect," he said. "Protect my head."

She nodded. "Remember that. And try to stay awake."

She reached over and unclipped his tied loop of rope from the carabiners on the anchor. Now it was only the belay device going through the anchor that held the rope coming from Philip's harness. She stared hard at the belay device. It was a Black Diamond Super Eight, the black color. Two openings,

171

the larger for rappeling, the smaller for belaying. The green rope passed in and out through the smaller opening, and was looped into the carabiner attached to the anchor. Everything looked in order. She took up the slack between Philip and the belay device, then pushed him off the ledge.

"Watch your head," she reminded him, as he slid off and hung below the ledge.

He grimaced. "Thanks, Meiling."

She forced herself to appear confident. Then she half-turned on the ledge, came to one knee, braced herself, and began playing out the rope. Her hands, already raw from lowering him to the ledge, immediately became alive with pain. She grunted, and ignored it. With her left hand she steadied the belay device to keep it from twisting to an unworkable angle against the anchor. With her right hand she grabbed the rope some four feet behind the device, hard, and played with the angle of the rope so that it slid through the belay device, but didn't lose its friction. When her right hand on the rope reached the belay device, she secured the rope there in the lock angle with her left hand while her right hand quickly reached back for the next four feet of rope. In five minutes her right forearm began to shake. She had lowered Philip forty feet.

The fingers on her left hand were fighting the tension of Philip's weight twisting the Super Eight. Sharp pains stabbed through the fingers. The right side of her body was aching. She forced herself to concentrate. If she opened the angle on the rope with her right hand too much, she'd lose friction and the rope would race through the device, nothing able to stop it—and Philip falling with it. Time detached from her consciousness. All that existed was the stabbing pain in her hands.

She was drenched with sweat, and gasping with each breath. But she had lowered Philip past the first ledge, over a hundred feet, more than half way. Tom was pacing back and forth at the bottom. With a surge of fear she felt her forearms twitching, the muscles at the far edge of their capacity. A moan escaped her lips, and she shifted her posture.

A roar grew in her head. Was she about to faint? Then she felt the wind from the helicopter, floating down the side of the cliff, past her. As it touched down below, Tom shouted something to the pilot. Two men emerged, carrying a stretcher. All heads inclined up to Philip's body. Then to her.

She switched her gaze to Ma Tsu's sea. The aquamarine was soft on her eyes. Down Philip descended, bit by bit. Suddenly Meiling flinched and cried out—something had hit her right hand as she slid it back for the next length of rope. The green and blue knot between the two ropes. She had forgotten about the knot. That meant a hundred sixty five feet down—only thirty five feet to go!

She stared at the knot, then four feet to the left at the black belay device. No. The knot wouldn't go through the opening on the belay device. Not even close. A cold sweat of fear rushed over her body, and she felt dizzy. She dropped to both knees, keeping the rope angled toward the wall to brake it. How was she going to get around the knot to lower Philip the last thirty five feet? Could she? A wave of nausea swept her. She forced panic down.

"Got to be a way, Ma Tsu," she gasped. She looked again from the knot to the belay device. That's not going to happen, she said to herself. All right. What would work? Secure the rope on Philip's side of the belay device to the anchor, untie the knot, run the second, blue rope through the belay device, then retie the knot?

She reached her left hand to the rope running out of the belay device, with Philip's hundred eighty pounds on the other end of it. She tried to pull it up. It didn't budge. There was no way to pull a hundred eighty pounds back up the cliff the four feet or so she'd need in order to tie a loop in the rope and clip it into the anchor.

What else would work? She stared at the belay device. It was the black one of the Black Diamond Super Eight series. Hers, hanging on her gear sling, was the purple one. Mountain and sea, Philip had called them. Of course. Set up a new belay behind the knot, with her purple device, then switch to it, somehow. But she'd need both hands to do this. How to keep the rope angled in the brake position without her hand holding it there? Shifting her position, she stepped on the rope just above the black belay device and jammed her foot toward the device, securing it in the brake position. Able to use both hands now, she pulled her gear sling around and unclipped her purple Super Eight. She formed a loop in part of the blue rope, jammed it through the small opening—the belay opening—on the purple Super Eight, and then clipped the blue rope onto the anchor with a new carabiner from her rack.

With the new belay device set up and attached to the anchor separately, all she had to do was minimize the length of rope between it and the existing black device—that was how far Philip would drop when she switched from the old to the new device—and make the switch-over by unclipping the black device from the anchor. She kept the rope in the brake position going into the black device with her left hand again, loosened the angle, and let the rope feed through the black system until the knot jammed up against it. That effectively braked any movement through the black device, so she was able to use both hands to work the blue rope through the purple Super Eight until it jammed up against the other side of the knot. She checked to make sure that the loop through the purple Super Eight was attached to the anchor.

"Now for the fun part," Meiling mumbled to herself. To remove the black belay from the system, she'd have to open and wrench the anchor carabiner holding its loop of rope until the loop slid out of the open carabiner. Since the carabiners were designed specifically to prevent this from happening, it would be tough. She unscrewed the locking device and opened the spring clip on the side of the carabiner. All of Philip's one hundred eighty pounds were pulling on the loop of rope in the carabiner. She twisted the carabiner to nudge the loop toward the opening on the free side of the clip. It didn't move.

She sat down on the cliff and shook her aching fingers. She felt like crying, but banished the urge. She allowed herself to gaze out to the sea. Waves relentlessly pushed toward the shore and broke on the rocks there. Gulls rode the winds rushing up the cliff.

"*Ma Tsu. Grant me some of your energy,*" she said to the sea. "*I know there is plenty of energy there. Let me have some of it, Ma Tsu.*"

She wearily got back to one knee. "*And Ma Tsu—don't let me do something stupid and get Philip and me killed,*" she said aloud, to herself and the sea and the gulls. She stared at the knot jammed against the black belay device—it was still an effective brake. She studied the rope behind the knot, the blue loop going through the purple Super Eight, then through the other carabiner attached to the anchor. Fine. Everything was fine. All she needed was to get the loop from the black device off the carabiner attaching it to the anchor. Nothing more. Ma Tsu would help her do this.

She bent toward the carabiner, and flipped the clip open again. With both hands she grasped the carabiner, gauged which direction to twist it to get the loop to the opening, and let a growl build in her throat as her muscles quivered. With a sudden jerk and a scream she wrenched the carabiner around and the loop shot through the opening.

The rope jumped and knocked her backwards as Philip's weight shifted instantly to the purple Super Eight. She heard the zing of the rope passing through the purple Super Eight—she had forgotten to secure it in the brake angle. She twisted with a cry and jammed both hands against the rope, bending it back against the cliff and to the brake angle. The rope slid another foot then abruptly jerked to a stop.

Meiling sat gasping on the ledge. Blood ran from her hands where the racing rope had cut into it before stopping. But it had stopped. She judged that Philip had dropped perhaps five feet or so.

Wearily she got to one knee again and reached back for another four feet of rope behind the new purple Super Eight, and fed it up to the device. Again. Again. The blood on her hands made it difficult to keep her grip, but in five minutes she had lowered Philip the last thirty five feet, and saw Tom and the pilot catching hold of him. She opened the angle of the rope and let the next few feet out freely, the numbing, aching weight no longer pulling on the rope.

Below, Tom eased Philip onto the stretcher. "Good job, Meiling," he shouted up. "Can you rappel down?"

Rappel? What was rappel? Everything seemed to be in a dream. She hit her hand against the cliff. The searing pain brought everything back into sharp focus.

"Yes," she called down, her hand throbbing. "I'll be right there."

search

Chapter Thirty Four

Sung Lee and Hsiao Pang lay in each other's arms in the bedroom, their lovemaking that night more passionate than usual. As tension over the talks had risen, so had Sung Lee's need for sex. Partly it was simply a release from the stress. But Sung Lee knew that war would come to the island very soon, and he knew that in times of struggle you lose things you love. So he was devoting more attention to the thing he most loved in the world—Hsiao Pang.

She was the daughter of the captain of the sport-fishing boat he and old Liu chartered regularly. At first, she was a twelve-year-old whose bright intelligence and competence assisting her father caught his attention. As the years rolled by, she had blossomed into a stunningly beautiful young lady—as well as intelligent and competent. As the daughter of a fisherman, her future was limited. When Sung Lee had approached her father, the man had given his hearty approval. Hsiao Pang herself, though, had demanded an education for herself and a generous trust for any children the relationship produced, male or female. Sung Lee had agreed. On her eighteenth birthday Hsiao Pang had become his mistress, and in the six years since had presented him with a daughter.

Even though she had borne him only one offspring, to the two his other concubine Hsiao Loo had given him, Hsiao Pang's intelligence, beauty, and love of life had won Lee's heart. She was now the part of his life that made his heart leap with joy.

They lay on the bed, arms and legs entangled, in the faint glow from the night light down the hallway with the jade vault. Both were drifting off, thoroughly satiated and happy. The faint rustling of felt-soled shoes inside the vault was inaudible to them.

The ring of the phone shattered the dark quiet. Hsiao Pang's slender arm reached out from the sheet and picked it up after the second ring. "Wai?"

Inside the vault, the man froze in position, stiff muscles rebelling.

"One moment, please." She bent her lips to Lee's ear. "It is the reporter, Meiling Bei. She says it is important, about the negotiations."

Sung Lee uttered a disbelieving snort, and sat up. "Sung Lee here," he snapped.

"Mr. Lee. Meiling Bei here. I apologize for calling at your private number, and at this hour. But Philip Dawson asked me to contact you, and Zhu Liang."

Sung Lee scowled, and pushed a pillow behind his lower back, which was aching a bit from his recent exertions with Hsiao Pang.

"Mr. Dawson was in an accident this afternoon," the voice on the phone continued. "He's being held overnight at Cheng Keng Memorial Hospital."

"What kind of—accident?" The last word was emphasized.

"A climbing accident, sir. We're not sure if it is suspicious or not."

"How serious?"

"Again, we're not sure. He fell twenty feet, and hit his head. The tests don't indicate any serious damage or unacceptable swelling of the meninges, and Philip—Mr. Dawson—is conscious and lucid. But the hospital wants to keep him overnight."

"I'm sorry to hear this. Does it mean the session tomorrow is cancelled?"

"No. He insists on going ahead with your, uh, session. But he's wondering if it could be delayed, from ten to something like eleven or noon, instead."

"Of course. Tell him that noon will be fine. I will expect him at the Sungshan airport then." He paused. "You are aware, Miss Bei, that these sessions are not public?"

"Yes. My connection with Mr. Dawson is, ah, personal, rather than professional."

Sung Lee laughed. By the gods, life is strange.

Inside the vault, the man settled on his haunches with a soft groan, waiting. He carefully cradled the pistol, making sure the silencer didn't hit the metal grill on the door.

Sung Lee hung up the phone, and lay back down, his arm around Hsiao Pang. They tossed and turned, their post-coital relaxation jangled.

"Shall I get you something?" Hsiao Pang whispered into his ear after five minutes.

He grunted. "What do I need? I have you."

She snuggled against his shoulder, one arm over his chest. Slowly they relaxed, and drifted toward sleep.

Hsiao Pang was suddenly awake. What had wakened her? Was it a sound? She stared into the darkness over Sung Lee's sleeping form.

There. A muffled click, faint but definite, from the hallway leading to the bathroom beyond the vault. She stiffened against his body. A brief hesitation, then she reached over his chest and into the drawer of the bedside stand, drawing out a 9 mm handgun. When she had a secure grip on the pistol, she shoved the sleeping Sung Lee off his far side of the bed. As Lee's head banged into the wall there, Hsiao Pang turned, the pistol in one hand and the other pinning the struggling Sung Lee to the floor. A shadowed figure emerged from the hallway and metal gleamed darkly. She fired the pistol just as the soft thump of the silencer came from the dark figure's pistol.

A groggy Sung Lee felt Hsiao Pang's body jerk off the edge of the bed and slam into the wall above him. Her body slumped over his.

"No!" he yelled, struggling up and pulling Hsiao Pang into his arms. "Hsiao Pang! Hsiao Pang!" He sat on the edge of the bed, oblivious to the body sprawled across the other side of the bed, oblivious to the two security men who burst into the room in a crouch, pistols extended, and the lights blazing on. All Sung Lee knew was that his dear Hsiao Pang was lying limp in his arms, a hole in her chest oozing blood. He forced his hand down over the wound, but the horrible blood kept flowing out between his fingers.

"No! No!" he cried, looking desperately into her eyes. Her beautiful, quick eyes met his, and glowed unnaturally bright for a brief second. Then they lost their focus, then their glow. As he watched in agony, her eyes grew dimmer, and finally the last spark left them and they flickered out.

"Hsiao Pang. No!" he sobbed, hugging her to his chest. He began to rock back and forth on the edge of the bed as sobs wracked his body.

"Mr. Lee. Mr. Lee, sir."

He looked around, dazed.

"Mr. Lee, sir." It was his chief security man, Jiao-rung. There was a body, a bulky man, laying face down on the other side of the bed. A large pistol, forty-five caliber with a silencer jutting from its barrel, dangled from the still hand of the man. The hand was soft, and manicured. Shen's son.

Sung Lee pulled himself back from his despair. He had never been so close to giving up, to letting the black hammer blows of life knock him into dazed submission. Slowly, tenderly, he lay Hsiao Pang's dead body on the bed. He gently pushed her eyelids down over her sightless eyes. Pausing for a last look at her face, he pulled the sheet over her. Another sob rose, but he willed it down. Life was such an agony.

"What happened?" he croaked in a broken voice.

Jiao-rung, a heavy-set man who had guarded him for twenty years, pointed down the hallway leading to the bathroom. "The door of the vault is ajar, sir. He must have hidden there, waiting for you to fall asleep. We don't see anyone else."

A sudden rage rose in Sung Lee. He remembered Shen sending his son to put the flying horse in the vault, then leading him and Hsiao Pang—Hsiao Pang!—onto the terrace. His elaborate toast, forcing them to face the sea. Claiming to see his son leaving.

He looked at the dead man on the bed, and Hsiao Pang on the other side. "Get him off our bed!" he roared suddenly. He would not have Hsiao Pang's *hun* souls associating with the dead man, the twisted, murderous fag. "Now!"

Jiao-rung and the other security guard dragged the body onto the terrace. Sung Lee checked the sheets, saw no blood or tissue from the dead man on them. He walked through the open doors to the terrace. Dark clouds obscured the moon rising to the east. "Throw the body over the wall, into the sea," he said. The affair would be purely private. No publicity, no prying reporters, no messy court appearances.

Lee heard the heavy splash some seconds later. Then he put his hand on Jiao-rung's shoulder, and leaned close to him, staring intently into his eyes. "You, old Liu, and One-eyed Lu. Kill Shen, the jade dealer. Tonight. No torture, no destruction of his place. Just execute him, cleanly and simply. You know, as always, that I will take care of your family, should anything happen to you."

Not a trace of emotion flickered over the big man's face. He grunted once, reached for the cell phone in his pocket, and left the patio. Sung Lee had survived three attempts on his life during the years Jiao-rung had been with him, four counting tonight. Old Liu, One-eyed Lu, and Jiao-rung had avenged the first three with no fanfare. Lee was confident tonight would be no exception.

Sung Lee returned to the bedroom, leaving both doors to the terrace open, to air out the room. He walked over to the edge of the bed and sat down, placing a hand on Hsiao Pang's hip under the sheet. He thought a while, then dialed the phone on the bedside stand, one-handed.

"Liu. Jiao-rung has contacted you? Good. Before you leave, call the Lung Shan temple. Have them send a Taoist priest here immediately. A priest they can trust to be discreet. He will be saying death rites for Hsiao Pang. He should bring the necessary incense and altar elements with him. I want a full ritual, but only one priest."

He dialed another number, one hand still resting on Hsiao Pang's hip.

"Miss Ling. Are you awake?" A short pause. "All right. Hsiao Pang is dead." He waited impatiently during the response. "No, no. I am all right. Please do two tasks for me first thing this morning. Call Hsiao Pang's father, the fisherman. Ask him to call me, here at this number, at his first convenience. He is up early, five or so. Later, call the airlines and get an extra ticket to Hong Kong with my two daughters this afternoon. The name will be Syao Loo Pang...Yes, Hsiao Pang's daughter. Our daughter. Do whatever it takes to get the ticket. But get it. Thank you, Miss Ling."

As he put the phone down, he heard a murmur of voices at the doorway. A half dozen of the house staff were there, in various stages of dress, staring wide-eyed at the scene. Sung Lee rose slowly from the bed, and approached the group.

"An assassin has tried to kill me, but Hsiao Pang killed him, before losing her life. I want each of you to know this, but I do not want anyone else to know it. No one. Ever. Do you understand completely?"

They stared at him, blankly, in shock. A few of them mechanically nodded.

"Old Jao. Where is Hsiao Pang's daughter, Syao Loo?"

"Sleeping, sir," replied a stout old woman. "In the far wing of the house."

"When she wakes tomorrow morning, send her to me, first thing. Have no one else talk to her first. Do you understand?"

She covered her face with her hands and burst into tears.

"Go. A Taoist priest will be arriving, soon. Escort him here." The group left.

Sung Lee walked back to Hsiao Pang, and again placed his hand on her hip. He lifted the phone again and dialed.

"Little Jade. Are you awake? I have something important to tell you."

A pause.

"Listen closely. Hsiao Pang has been killed." Another pause. "No, I am fine. It was meant for me, but—" Sung Lee's voice choked. He waited, patiently, for a moment. "But she saved me. Now, Little Jade. I am sending Hsiao Pang's daughter—my daughter, my Syao Loo—to you at our family home, tomorrow morning. She is going to Hong Kong with you and your sister tomorrow. Miss Ling will get the extra ticket to you. I am adopting Syau Loo as an official offspring. Please tell your mother, when you join her in Hong Kong. I humbly ask you and your mother and your sisters to accept her, as a full daughter to me and your mother, a full sister to you."

Another pause. "Yes. Thank you, Little Jade. Syau Loo will be very sad, and very confused. I am counting on you to help her." He placed the phone on the cradle.

Hsiao Pang's hip under his hand was growing cold. He felt his throat tightening. Two days ago he had lost the identity of his father which he thought he would learn in Jinhua. Today he had lost Hsiao Pang. And two days from now he might well lose many more things that had taken a lifetime to build. He sat there, hard and unflinching. This was how life was. His mother knew it. He knew it, too. One had to be hard, to survive when you lost things you loved. Which you always did.

He reviewed the actions he had set in motion. He couldn't think of anything else he should do. He would wait here, with Hsiao Pang, until the Taoist priest arrived. He could not bear the thought of her being alone. Tomorrow he would have Miss Ling call the Lung Shan Temple, plus the Ma Tsu temple on Chengtu Street, to have memorial candles and incense lit for her.

For the first time, he wondered why old Shen had sent his son to kill him. Nothing came to him. He was completely baffled by it. The three previous attempts on his life, it had been clear. Business, then, had been the root of it. Competition over resources, or routes. That was understandable. Expected, really. But this—he could not even guess. He glanced down at Hsiao Psang's body on the bed. Not that it mattered. Clearly, old Shen had ordered it, and set it up. He would be avenged, and that would be it, regardless of Shen's motive. But still …

He picked up the phone again, and dialed. "Has Jiao-rung arrived yet? One further instruction, Liu: ask 'Why?' But proceed regardless whether he answers or not." He put the phone down. Hsiao Pang's body was now cold under his hand.

souls

Chapter Thirty Five

Philip was falling in slow motion, drifting down through a dark night sky whose clouds prevented the rising moon from throwing much illumination. He twisted around, reaching out for something to grab, but all he found was air. He was strangely calm, and wondered why he was so calm. Below, he saw the red tiles of a temple roof rising toward him. For some reason he fell right by the temple, as if it were on the side of a cliff. Two figures were coupling in a courtyard of the temple, not frantically but calmly, rhythmically. With a start he realized the man was his grandfather. The woman was staring over grandpa's back, watching Philip fall. Her face was serene, and dark. She detached herself from grandpa and soared out of the courtyard toward Philip. In a moment she had caught up with Philip, and took him by the hand. She and Philip sailed back to the temple, where they alighted on the stone floor.

Grandpa turned to Philip. He was young. He put his hand on Philip's shoulder. It felt very strong, and solid. The woman with the dark face stood behind grandpa. Over grandpa's shoulder, Philip could see that she wore pearls on her forehead, her face below them still serene and sober.

"Philip, your mom died," grandpa was saying. "She was caught in mortar fire in the countryside." His young eyes were full of pain. "I'm sorry, Philip. Are you all right?"

Philip was breathing hard, and sobbing. He looked past grandpa, to the black-faced woman. She looked sad, but accepting. How could she be so accepting of something so terrible?

"Philip, are you all right?"

A hand shook his shoulder gently.

'Philip, are you all right?"

He opened his eyes. In the darkness he could make out the dark face of the woman still.

"Philip, are you all right?" she said again.

Her face seemed more familiar now. He knew her.

"Meiling?"

"Yes, Philip. You're in the hospital, Philip. You had a fall on the cliff. Remember?"

He wasn't in the temple courtyard. But it was still dark, and he couldn't let go of the dream.

"Meiling. I don't like it when people die. I hate it when people die on me."

"Tell me about it."

"It was like it had just happened. Meiling, don't die on me. I won't let the conglomerate kill you."

"Well, thanks. I hope you're successful."

"Don't joke. It was real strong, in the dream. This feeling that people are going to die. Goddamn it."

"Well, that's why you're here, Philip. Right now it looks like you're the one person between a lot of people dying, or not. The person who might bring Sung Lee and Zhu together. You mentioned something on the cliff, after the fall. About a maritime state."

"Oh, yeah. That might fly. Give Sung Lee what he wants, and be something that Zhu can live with. And the idea of splitting up the military forces, that you gave me last night. But it's all such a long shot. A bloody crap shoot, in fact. I get discouraged."

"Really? Funny, I get the opposite impression. That you never get discouraged. That you have limitless courage, confidence in yourself, confidence in your getting things done. That's what I love—" Meiling stopped, and looked around the darkness, flustered. "I mean, that's what I like about you."

"Huh. Well, maybe it's just because I'm banged up. I don't like being discouraged, wondering what the hell I'm doing over here. Don't like this feeling that people are going to die. But you know what, Meiling? Ma Tsu helped me. In the dream. I was drifting, and she flew up and guided me. Back to grandpa. That's got to be a good sign, huh?"

Meiling, still flustered, just nodded. "You'd better get some sleep," she finally said. "You've got a big day tomorrow. Or later today, I guess. Both Sung Lee and Zhu said noon was fine."

"Good luck me getting back to sleep. That dream rattled me."

"Lie back. I'll get you relaxed. Ping tells me it happens all the time in hospitals. No wonder, with these short, flimsy gowns…"

*　　*　　*　　*　　*

Shen had opened the cabinets with the security monitors, wincing as he admitted the cold, modern technology into his study. But with each passing hour without word from his son—his last son—the dreadful, unthinkable possibility became more real. His remaining son had failed. And retaliation from Sung Lee would in all likelihood be quick. And lethal. It was the sort of man Sung Lee was.

His pulled his eyes from the *lao yu* mountain scene on his desk and looked at the monitors. Yes. There it was. The guard at the gate was now slumped over in his box. Fools! He had put them on alert, and still, still they failed him. First his two sons, now—he saw the second line of security, the man with the dog, come into view on another monitor. The dog was straining on the leash, leaping toward something on the south side grounds. Without watching to see what would happen, he picked up the phone and punched in the pre-set number. His eyes returned to the monitor as he waited for his Hong Kong operative to answer, just in time to see the guard and the dog crumple to the ground.

"Listen!" he hissed into the phone as the sleepy voice came on the line at the other end. "I cannot talk long. It is over, here. I will be dead in perhaps a minute. My last son is probably already dead. There is but one male issue left. In Jinhua, the grandson of the old hag." Even as he said it, an image of her, young and beautiful and ripe beneath him under the plum tree behind the mooncake factory, flooded his mind. He banished it, instantly. "Bring him here. You will have three days before the incense burners die. Three days! You will carry on the business, he will carry on the line, and the burners. Hurry!"

A noise echoed down the corridor leading to his study here. He dropped the phone, not bothering to return it to the cradle, and grabbed the pearwood cane. He stumbled over to the altar and swung the doors open. Dropping to his knees, he grabbed the package of charcoal bricks and spilled three onto the table fronting the altar.

"Damn, damn these fumbling hands!" he said as he dropped the first of the small bricks from the silver tongs. He breathed, deeply, and picked up the brick more deliberately, then slid it into the ashes and against the old charcoal in the first burner, its golden curves glimmering with red and green from the rubies and copper. Quickly he picked up the second brick and shoved it into the second burner, feeling it bump against the old one.

The door to the room burst open and three men rushed in, crouching, pistols extended with both hands. He ignored them, and picked up the last brick of charcoal in the tongs. His hands were steady now.

The cold barrel of a pistol came to rest on his left temple. He looked up.

It was old Liu, the steward. He knew of three men the steward had killed through the years. Probably there were more.

"Why?" Liu's voice was soft, almost gentle. He was cultured. That was good to know, that he would die at the hands of a cultured man.

He slid the last piece of charcoal into the burner, the third one. Its shining bronze, the rubies like red stars scattered over it, seemed to fill his eyes. He breathed deep, and sighed. He had given his ancestors three more days. Would the grandson of the young girl get here by then? Would this one be as faithful as the five hundred years of Shen males before him?

"Why?" Liu asked again, his voice harder now.

It would not be much longer, the old man knew. Sung Lee has not made the connection, then. Perhaps he won't, and the business can continue. Another five hundred years?

He dropped the silver tongs, and stared into the altar. Forgive me, he said silently to the *hun* souls there. My abilities were meager. My sons have utterly failed. Perhaps my youthful passion will bring another to you, to keep the bronze burners alive and glowing for you. If not—if not…A wave of despair washed over him, just as the sound of old Liu's pistol exploded into his temple. Five hundred years of *hun* souls, cut loose, adrift, howled through his last conscious moment.

Chapter Thirty Six

Day Seven

"What do you mean, he didn't return?" Tiffany said to the clerk at the Hilton's front desk. Her voice was loud and hard, implying that the young Chinese man didn't understand what he was saying.

The clerk's eyes flared angrily, but he knew this was the granddaughter of the President of the United States. The clerk melted away, relieved, as his supervisor approached.

"Miss Hayes. Good morning," the supervisor said with a tight smile. She was nearly as tall as Tiffany, dressed in a black suit outfit.

"I was just inquiring whether Mr. Dawson had picked up the message I left last night," Tiffany said. "There must be a misunderstanding. Your clerk said he had not returned to the hotel last night."

"That is correct, Miss Hayes. Mr. Dawson did not return," the supervisor said, eyeing Tiffany's elaborate hairdo and perfect makeup.

Tiffany shook her head in disbelief, her hair bouncing just the right amount, then springing back to its crafted shape.

"What—what does that mean?" Tiffany asked.

"He apparently spent the night elsewhere, Miss Hayes. What with all the security he has, we would be quite aware if he were here."

Tiffany stared into the supervisor's face, not noticing anything about her. She was just another black-haired, olive-skinned Chinese woman. In a daze, she made her way to the alcove off the front entrance, across from the desk, and sank into a leather chair beside the sofa there.

"Well!" she muttered to herself, a look of disbelief mixed with annoyance sweeping her perfect face. "I'll just wait here until my young man shows up, then." She settled back into the chair, and reached for one of the fashion magazines on the side table.

The glass doors beside the alcove swung open, and Philip and Meiling entered the lobby from Chunghsiao street, with Tom several steps behind.

"No, I'm all right," Philip was saying. "A bit stiff in the neck, but the session today is important and I'm up to it. I feel worse about making you miss your swim this morning." He had his arm around Meiling's shoulders, more for the good feeling it gave him than for support. His left temple area was badly bruised and slightly swollen.

"Well, pace yourself. You need to be on your game today for the negotiations, my rock climber."

"Yeah. Some rock climber. Taking a fall," Philip muttered.

"I told you. The stirrup just ripped. Not your fault or anybody's."

They arrived at the front desk. The supervisor had a shocked look on her face, and her eyes kept switching from Philip to something behind him. He followed her gaze the next time it swung, to the chair in the alcove.

"Wrong. Meiling, I'm not all right. I'm having delusions." He put a hand to his forehead, rubbing his temple gingerly.

"What?"

"I'm having delusions," Philip repeated. "I know this is crazy, but I actually think I see Tiffany Hayes sitting behind us there."

Meiling's eyes widened as she looked at the alcove. "You mean, as in a beautiful blonde, blue suit, long legs crossed elegantly? The one smiling in a cold sort of way and getting up right now?"

"Tiffany?" Philip said in a strangled voice as the apparition approached.

Tiffany's face was wreathed in a broad but very tight smile.

"Well, hello, Philip. So good to see you, dear." Her voice was hearty, but just like her face—forced, and more than a bit threatening.

"What the hell are you doing here, Tiffany?"

"Oh, I just got lonely for my man," she said with wide eyes. "Wanted to see him." Her eyes narrowed, to slits. "And I see that you've been lonely, too, darling."

"Huh?" Philip grunted. He saw Tiffany's eyes swing to Meiling, coldly furious. "Oh. Uh, this is a…friend. Meiling. Meiling Bei. This is Tiffany Hayes."

Tiffany shot out her hand, which Meiling took after some hesitation.

"Meiling! What a gorgeous name. And what a beautiful young lady you are," she beamed malevolently.

Meiling cleared her throat, and withdrew her hand from Tiffany's too firm grasp.

"Philip and I were rock-climbing together yesterday, Miss Hayes. He had an accident, and spent the night in Cheng Keng hospital. I'm just returning him to the hotel."

"Oh, how wonderful," Tiffany exclaimed, shaking her head just enough to make her hair swirl and bounce back to shape. "It's so nice when people share hobbies, isn't it?"

Her eyes became hard as they swung to Philip. "Darling, I think we need to have a nice long talk. Could you please escort me to my room?"

Philip was speechless.

"Miss Hayes," said Meiling in the silence. "Philip is a bit busy right now. Perhaps later?"

Tiffany's eyes didn't leave Philip, ignoring Meiling. "What could possibly be more important than you and I, and our relationship, darling?"

Philip regained his tongue. "Well, there's this little thing about an impending war, Tiffany. I've got a pretty important meeting with the folks involved in just about—" He checked his watch. "In twenty minutes, to see if we can do something about it."

"A meeting?" Tiffany said. "I thought the talks had been cancelled."

"I agree with Miss Hayes," interjected Meiling. "We do need to talk about—things. May I suggest we all get together after Philip's session this afternoon. Perhaps for dinner?"

Philip put his hand to his forehead again.

"Well!" said Tiffany. "If dinner is the best I can do, I'll take it. I do agree completely with Miss ... Miss Wong, was that it?"

Now Meiling's eyes hardened. "Bei," she said curtly.

"Of course. Could you recommend a place for dinner, my dear? You being the native here in this terribly exotic place?"

"I'd be happy to," Meiling said. "The Golden Phoenix has private rooms, and is quite nice. No interruptions. I'll make the reservation."

"Wonderful, darling." She beamed a tight smile toward Philip. "I'll see you this evening, Philip. Right here, at seven?" With an inclination of her head, she pivoted and swept through the glass doors onto Chunghsiao street.

"I don't believe this," Philip muttered. His head was beginning to throb again.

"Deal with it later," Meiling said firmly. "You've got some papers to get from your room, and I've got to get you to the Sungshan airport in fifteen minutes. You'll concentrate on the negotiations for the afternoon. It's more important than any of this. Now go."

Chapter Thirty Seven

Tien Gong Temple, on the east coast

"You said you would have something new," Lee said bluntly, his big hands clasped on the table fronting the altars. Three cups of tea sat untouched on the table, steam rising in the dim light. They were the first words that had been spoken since climbing into the helicopter back in Taipei.

Zhu stopped his fidgeting abruptly, and glanced sharply at Philip, his glasses reflecting the candles burning on the altars. He was as restless as Lee was stolid, constantly shifting in his chair. Until now.

Philip's eyes flickered to the black-faced icon on the altar. By some miracle, perhaps of Ma Tsu's doing, Dirk had not exposed his proposal on Taiwan's military to the White House. He could put it on the table and see where it went.

"I do have something new. It speaks to your special concerns. Mr. Lee, could you repeat for me the most objectionable aspect of People's Republic forces coming onto Taiwan?"

"I've not hidden it," Lee replied harshly. "People's Republic troops and APC's rumbling into Taipei would provoke an uprising. The images from Hong Kong in July of '97 made us cringe. It cannot happen here, whether the night is rainy or not."

"And you, Mr. Zhu. The single aspect of Taiwan's military you cannot tolerate?"

"Also not hidden," said Zhu, but smoothly. "In a united motherland, no particular region can have its own missiles and destroyers and submarines and fighter planes, threatening to unleash destruction on the motherland. These must be eliminated."

"Exactly," agreed Philip. "You have each pinpointed what you need, and I can give it to each of you."

Wary looks from Lee and Zhu.

"We've been talking about the armed forces as if they were one unit. Of course, they're not. I propose that Mr. Lee keep Taiwan's army units, to provide highly-visible inviolable ground-level protection and security on the island. No People's Republic army troops allowed on the island, ever. And I propose that Taiwan's air force and navy units be transferred to Mr. Zhu's People's Republic command, so that they no longer threaten the mainland."

A shocked silence swept the table. Even Zhu sat still, his eyes blinking behind his owlish glasses. A full minute of silence, then Zhu leaned back, and crossed his legs.

"Very ingenious, Mr. Dawson. Indeed. Possibilities. But sometimes the command structure of the missile-containing attack helicopters, the anti-missile missiles, and the radar systems we object to, are complicated, coming under army control."

"Yes. The agreement would of course spell it out. Where necessary, we would transfer the objectionable units to the air force, so they would come under People's Republic control. But most importantly, we would specify that the Stinger, Maverick, and Javelin missiles, the F-16 and Mirage fighter planes, the submarines and Knox-class frigates, the Kidd-class destroyers, the antisubmarine missiles, and the Pave Paws long-range radar system—all would come under People's Republic command, to disperse, destroy, reorient—whatever."

Zhu stared at the roof of the temple, gauging, calculating.

"Mr. Lee?" Philip asked. Lee was sitting just as he had from the beginning, hands clasped on the table. His face was impassive, but a purple bruise on his temple pulsed, the smaller echo to the bruise on Philip's forehead.

"The Super Cobra attack helicopters," he said suddenly. "They would be included in the arsenal that we gave up?"

"Yes," answered Philip. "Every weapon that can reach the mainland from here would be transferred. The agreements would be specific, and written by our teams, under our overall direction. Will it work, gentlemen?"

A long silence. The three icons in the dark recesses of the temple gazed soberly at the three newly arrived figures in the shadowed front. Security men with machine guns prowled the sunlit terrace beyond.

A long, growling exhalation came from Lee. He took in a long breath. "Interesting," he admitted, his voice rough.

"Would it work, do you think?" pressed Philip.

"For some, it would work," Lee said in a voice devoid of enthusiasm. "It works for me, frankly." He unclasped his hands. "For others—it will be very difficult. General Zhao and Admiral Reng of the air force and navy—I cannot imagine them relinquishing their commands. They are very old and very stubborn men. Not susceptible to pressure from anyone. And General Zhao is very fond of his Cobra attack helicopters."

"General Zhao's sister is married to my wife's brother," said Zhu. "I hear that the General is very fond of teas. And his sister's business enterprises on the mainland."

"So?" asked Philip.

"So we have many government villas along the shore of West Lake by Hangzhou," Zhu said, casually twirling the pencil on the table with his fingers.

"A prime tea-growing region, Hangzhou," said Philip, glancing at Lee. "The very center for Longjin tea. And I hear the lakeside villas are very comfortable."

"Yes, that could appeal to the General," Lee admitted. "But his family's business enterprises are equally important to him."

"I was speaking to my son last week," Zhu said, still twirling the pencil between his fingers. "He has jurisdiction over the Forbidden City's shops. General Zhao's sister has the Kentucky Fried Chicken franchise for Beijing, I believe?"

"You have been doing some homework, Mr. Zhu," Lee growled.

"It's well known. I believe my son could insure that the sister could locate a franchise in the Forbidden City."

"Ironic," commented Philip. "Your son has gone from facing APCs in Tien An-men Square to running the concessions within the Forbidden City behind it."

The pencil in Zhu's hand abruptly stopped. "This is son number two," he said softly. "Son number one, who was in Tien An-men, has not spoken to me—nor anyone—since that night in the square. Two decades plus of staring out the window in our villa."

"Oh. I'm sorry," mumbled Philip.

The pencil dropped to the table. "Yes. The closer you look at what happened in the Square, the more mixed it becomes. There was no nobility, on either side. Only people doing what people do. Some are strong, and survive. Some are weak, and don't."

"Well. It is always like that, isn't it?" Lee interrupted brusquely. "May we move on? All this talk of West Lake villas and Forbidden City concessions mean nothing if we can't solve the second impasse. The name of the union."

"Of course," said Philip. "We had agreed tentatively on some sort of 'state.' Mr. Zhu needs a qualifying term, so that it doesn't compete with the People's Republic. Mr. Lee doesn't want to detract from the 'state.' How about a descriptive term that captures Taiwan's special status—an island, a center of trade, of shipping? How about 'The Maritime State of Taiwan in The People's Republic of China'?"

He let it hang in the temple's pungent air, glancing from Zhu to Lee. There was not a sound in the darkened temple. Zhu and Lee, dim in the shadows, stared at him as unmoving as the three icons in the back of the temple. Outside, the soft noises of insects and the waves washing ashore on the coast below wafted into the temple.

Lee's impassive face relaxed in the shadows, and Philip was astonished to see a hint of excitement, flared nostrils, burning eyes. Lee whispered a phrase in Chinese.

Zhu was sitting bolt upright in his chair, eyes glittering behind his glasses, the pencil frozen in his hand. Zhu repeated Lee's phrase, shook his head, then answered with another. Lee pondered that phrase, shook his head, and softly formulated yet another version, the words shimmering in the silence of the temple. Both men stared beyond Philip at the three icons in the back for a long moment.

"So?" Philip asked.

Lee broke the silence, his face becoming sober again. He spoke carefully. "I cannot myself approve anything, of course. But there is some possibility that such a title, or some variant, might be acceptable to enough factions to make it work."

"I would say much the same," said Zhu, his face alive with excitement.

Philip shivered with relief.

"And of course," Lee said quietly, directing himself to Zhu. "It raises other possibilities. Other 'Maritime States' associated in the same way with the People's Republic. Hong Kong might prefer this status. Macau."

Zhu nodded, struggling to keep a smile from his face. "Singapore," he whispered. "Perhaps—Penang?"

"Whatever," Philip interrupted. "Let's concentrate on just one state for now—Taiwan. Do I sense that these two proposals are hopeful—worth working on?"

"Nothing is assured, Mr. Dawson," said Lee sharply. "You cannot imagine the number of people and factions I have to run this by. Whether it is the new name, or the division of the military, all factions will have their particular reactions and demands. It's still very much a long shot. In a way, I envy Mr. Zhu's more direct task."

"Yes," Zhu said, with a slight smile. "Unlike Mr. Lee, I have to gauge only the reaction of one or two men, most importantly, although they will inquire of another dozen men's opinions. There are disadvantages to a strongly centralized government, but there are some advantages, also."

Philip leaned forward, his heart racing. "Gentlemen. We are very close, aren't we? Finally we have something to work on, something that has promise. The deadline is day after tomorrow. Approach your various constituencies today. Begin the gauging of whether this or something like it will work. And let's meet again, tomorrow, ten o'clock in the morning. For a final decision on how we might change this formulation, to make it work better. Alert your teams, as I will mine, to be ready to begin marathon sessions at the Sun Yat-sen Memorial immediately tomorrow after our session, to tie down the details and get everything written down and spelled out for the day after."

"Yes, yes," Lee said impatiently. He rose, and shouted toward the sunlit terrace. "Jiao-rung. My phone."

"By the way," said Zhu as they all walked onto the terrace. "I was sorry to hear of your climbing accident, Mr. Dawson. Does your head feel as bad as it looks?"

"Not quite. I had a rough night. Dreams and stuff. But I think I'm coming around. I had some help, from a friend."

"And Mr. Lee," continued Zhu. "Your forehead looks nearly as bad as Philip's. Not a climbing accident also, I trust?"

"No accident," said Lee gruffly, as Jiao-rung approached with a cell phone in his hand. "There was an attempt on my life last night." He turned to the large security man. "Get me the premier."

"It wasn't business-related," he said to Philip and Zhu. "I'm not sure what brought it on. But you two should know. Alert your own security people. And if you have questions or want advice, feel free to call me."

He accepted the phone from Jiao-rung. "OK. Let's get to the helicopter. I have a lot of meetings to arrange, fast."

bent

Chapter Thirty Eight

Meiling, the climbing gear in her arms, watched Jimmy Chan's face carefully as he answered his door.

"Why—Meiling," he said, the trace of a wary look flitting over his eyes. "How did the climb go?" he asked heartily. But again, something wary in his eyes, she thought.

"The climb was fine. But your stirrup gave way at the crux, Jimmy."

"Why, that's terrible. Awful. I can't imagine it," he said, palms raised. "Why, I've been using that stirrup for, what? Two years? Three?" He stepped back, so she could enter, and took the sling and other gear from her arms.

"But, Philip. How is he?" he asked in a strange voice.

"Luckily, only some scrapes and a knock on the forehead that's not too serious."

"Oh? A seventy foot fall, and only a knock on the forehead?" His eyes were cold, and the puzzle in them seemed genuine now.

"Well, he found a new line towards the end, on the third pitch. Went over to a secondary crack to the left, and roped into some protection there before doing the headwall."

"Ah." It seemed to take a while for this to sink in.

"Well. What a relief," Jimmy finally said, now completely himself again. "But still most embarrassing for me. Do you have the stirrup?"

She gazed at him for a moment, liking the way he hung on her response. And a bit puzzled by it.

"Afraid not, Jimmy. We left it on the cliff yesterday, and today Philip's security man insisted on retrieving it, to send it to a lab. It's his job, to check for—sabotage."

She watched him closely as she said it. Even though she had treated the accident as just that, a part of her was suspicious. There had been too many accidents lately.

"Why, that's…that's ridiculous," Jimmy said, smoothly. "Do you mean I'm under suspicion?" He asked it fluidly, with no real concern evident.

Meiling shook her head. "It's just routine. All the same—did you make any changes or adjustments to the stirrup?"

"Of course not," he snapped.

"Could someone else have tampered with it? Was it available to anyone else?"

He pondered her question. "Well, it's a standard part of my gear sling. I take it on all my climbs. Any number of people in the Alpine Club would have seen it, had access to it before and after our climbs. Anyone. But really—we're all just climbers, Meiling. You know the crowd."

"Well, accidents happen. I don't imagine it's the first stirrup that has worn out."

"All the same, I feel terrible about it," replied Jimmy. "I insist on apologizing to Philip personally. May I see him, today?"

Meiling shook her head. "He's very busy in meetings this afternoon. And dinner is looking a bit, uh, complicated."

"He's having dinner with you?"

"Well, yes. And others. It's something—complicated. He'll want his privacy."

"Then I'd recommend one of the rooms at the Golden Phoenix."

"As a matter of fact, I've already made the reservation," she said, with a laugh.

"The 'Scented Bower' room would be perfect for you.'"

"If it were just Philip and myself. We'll have another person, so I got the 'Islands in the Sea' room."

He retrieved a Blackberry from his pocket, and fiddled with it. "Oh, damn. Even if I could convince you to let me drop by, I won't be able to. I have our monthly Alpiners Club executive officers meeting tonight. On the other side of town, at the Korean restaurant by the Lung Shan temple." He glanced up, a vexed look on his face. "Our meeting is at seven. If you're eating early, I could perhaps make it before the meeting."

"We're also meeting at seven, so it won't work. I'll convey your apology to him. And return your stirrup, when we get it back."

He extended his hand. "Again. I'm shocked, embarrassed, and awfully sorry."

She took his hand, nearly feeling sorry for him, were it not for the strange looks she'd seen in his eyes earlier.

"Can I offer you a drink?" he added, as an afterthought.

"It's barely past noon, Jimmy. Too early for this working girl to begin drinking."

"Of course. Goodbye, then."

*   *   *   *   *

Jimmy Chan leaned against the closed door until he heard the elevator door close behind Meiling.

"Damn, damn, damn!" he raged, throwing the climbing gear onto the floor and giving it a good kick.

Never had he failed in three attempts. One, plenty of times. Two occasionally. But three! And this of all times.

At the bar he reached high for the Macallan's, pulling the red cork stopper viciously. He poured two shots into a heavy glass and slugged it down in one swallow, not even stopping to add ice.

That was it, he told himself as he flushed at the whiskey. The flush calmed him. That was it. The more subtle your methods, the more likely to be considered an accident, the lower the odds for success. He had been subtle, very subtle. The jellyfish poison in D.C. The octopus toxin two days ago. The stirrup, yesterday. Brilliant, each of them. Textbook brilliant.

He threw the empty glass into the hallway, where it skidded across the floor and shattered against the far wall.

So much for subtlety. Tonight he'd resort to his old standby, when all else failed. He stalked to his study, glancing angrily at Dawson's photo on the wall, still askew. Still waiting to be properly added to the gallery. He jerked open the closet door, slammed the false wall aside, and strode past the microscope and the Buchi Evaporator, the part of the lab where all the subtle biological agents were prepared. Screw them. A crude wooden bench fronting a plywood work surface sat at the far end of the lab. He reached into the cabinet above the bench and pulled down the bottle of plastics components, with a glance toward the explosives in the adjacent cabinet. He exhaled as the odor of plastics assaulted his nostrils. He hated the smell of plastics. But it was effective. The Golden Phoenix, Sea above the Clouds room, seven tonight. Seated and enjoying things by seven thirty. Plenty of time.

*   *   *   *   *

Meiling was sitting very still in the front seat of her red Miata in the parking lot of the *United Daily Journal*, staring at the center of her steering wheel. Something had been gnawing at her during the drive from Jimmy Chan's place in the East District. It was only as she had turned the key to stop her engine here that she had realized what it was.

Something wasn't right. With Jimmy Chan. She'd been surprised when he'd begun seeing Ping. Ping wasn't nearly rich enough for Jimmy. Then the bizarre incident with the Scotch at his apartment two nights ago. Then his defective stirrup, giving way at the highest point on a climb he had recommended. And that wary look in his eyes as he had met her at his door just now.

Something...something not right. Not just one thing, but a whole series of things. She had no idea what it meant. But she couldn't ignore it. And that meant going right to the center of it. But in her own way.

She picked up the cell phone, got Philip's card from her purse, and called his number at the Hilton. She waited for the voice mail message, then spoke into the phone, softly despite herself.

"Philip. Meiling here. I—I have something important to do, this evening. It has to be at seven. It will take about an hour or so. I'll explain later. I'll join you and Tiffany at the restaurant before eight. Until then, I'll have Ping substitute for me. She'll meet you at the Hilton lobby at seven, as we arranged, and take you to the Golden Phoenix, stay with you in the room I've reserved until I get there. She'll keep you and Tiffany from tearing into each other, at least until I get there. Bye."

She clicked the phone off, then scrolled down her contacts.

"Ping. Yes, it's me. I need a huge favor. Ever had dinner with a granddaughter of a U.S. President before?"

Chapter Thirty Nine

Meiling felt the welcome click as the lock yielded before her. Thank goodness Jimmy Chan's condo was one of the large ones. That meant older, and that meant a regular keyed lock, rather than the fancy new electronic locks. That series on detectives was really coming in handy, she thought, as she pocketed the ring of picklocks.

"Hello? Jimmy? Jimmy? Your door was open."

No answer. She checked her watch. A few minutes after seven. So far, so good. Jimmy should be on the other side of town. She glanced right. That would be his bedroom. Then left—the front room. Straight ahead would be the study. Her first step crunched down on something. Broken glass. She carefully stepped around it.

The study was spacious, large windows in front, a teak desk with journals scattered over it. He keeps up on his chemistry, Meiling thought, surprised. To the left of the desk, a bank of pictures, cut from newspapers and magazines. Jimmy Chan and most of the available beauties of Taipei, at least the ones with money and social position. All of them beaming beside his dazzling smile. Easy enough to guess why those photos were there, and what all those beautiful young things had in common.

More photos to the right of the desk. But these, men. Not newspaper or magazine photos, and not with Jimmy in them. Single photos, all. Here was a puzzle. What did these men have in common, to get them here on Jimmy Chan's wall? She loved puzzles. It was why she had gone into the newspaper business, really. Her job gave her warrant to poke into puzzles. She settled into the leather chair and studied them.

Sixteen photos in all, she counted. Five rows of three each, with one below, at an angle. Her eye locked on the bottom one, and her breath froze. It was Philip. She didn't like that. What was Philip's photo doing here?

Her eyes moved to the top row. Left photo. Handsome, Latin type. Unknown to her. Top middle. An Asian. Not the least bit handsome. Ugly, almost. But a powerful look to him. Wasn't that—? The Indonesian. Head of that industrial group. She had heard something about him, years ago. A fatal accident? Fell off a cliff or something?

Top right. Another Asian. The Thai Minister of Resources, his promising young career cut short by a heart attack last year, to everyone's surprise.

Second row. Left side. This was easy. Riady Pemby, also Indonesian. He had toured their newsroom, two years ago. Maybe three. Just before his assassination, back in Indonesia. His killer was never caught.

She sat up straighter, and her eyes moved more quickly.

Second row middle, unknown. Second row right, also unknown.

Third row. To the left, another Asian. Was that—yes. The young politician from India. Up and coming cabinet minister, suddenly ill, quickly died from leukemia. One of those long Indian names, Kumaramangalam or something like that. Four, maybe five years ago, prompting outrage in India, that a member of the ruling elite could be so poorly served by the health care system as to have such a serious disease overlooked.

The other two in the third row were unknown to her. In the fourth row, the middle photo caught her eye. Another Latin type, very handsome. The vice president of one of the Latin American countries that recognized Taiwan. He also had toured their newsroom. And been killed several months later. By what? Was it a bomb blast?

In the fifth row, the two photos on the left were unknown. But the right photo she knew very well. The up-and-coming DPP politician from the southern part of the island. Died just six months ago, in a boating incident off Kaohsiung.

She sat and tried to think calmly over her racing heart. The ones she recognized, at least, were all prominent men, holding important government or business posts. All dead, having died under suspicious or violent circumstances. Her eye drifted down to Philip's photo. He hadn't died, under suspicious or violent circumstances.

Yet.

She gasped, as the short hair on her neck stood on end and her heart went from racing to pounding. Jimmy knew. He had extracted it from her, where Philip was eating tonight. The restaurant. The room. The time. So smoothly she hadn't even noticed he'd done it. She glanced up at the photos. All dead. Except Philip. Philip wasn't dead.

Yet.

She bolted out of the chair, remembering the Golden Phoenix wouldn't even allow cell phones past the front desk. And refused to even take messages for their guests under any circumstances. She dashed out of the study, slammed Jimmy Chan's apartment door behind her, and took the stairs two at a time down to her Miata on the curb.

*   *   *   *   *

199

Philip was miserable. He sat in the reserved room with a coldly furious Tiffany Hayes and Meiling's gushy, chattering roommate Ping. With nothing but a vague, mysterious explanation from Meiling on his voice mail. He glanced over at Tiffany. Still icy, staring straight ahead. Behind her, the ornate yellow brocade walls and red columns of their private room. They'd need all the privacy they could get, when Meiling got here and they'd start to talk "relationships." He groaned.

"—just like imperial China," Ping was chirping. "The columns, the décor. Even the food is all authentic imperial cuisine." Her eyes were shining, and she hadn't stopped smiling since the lobby of the Hilton, apparently oblivious to Tiffany's mood. "That's why they took our cell phones when we got to the restaurant. Can't have phones ringing in the private rooms, shattering the ambience, can we?" She laughed gaily. "Don't worry. You'll get them back when we leave. But for now, for the next enchanted hour, there'll be no interruptions of the twentieth century. Oh! Here's our waiter! Meiling asked me to order for us."

While Ping and the waiter conferred, Philip risked a look at Tiffany. She was staring at him pointedly.

"Miss Wong's friend is so attractive," she commented icily. "And vastly entertaining."

Philip sighed. "Bei," he said. "Meiling Bei. Look, Tiffany, let's just—"

She held up her hand, rings gleaming in the soft lighting. "No, Philip. Miss Wong deserves to be here when we get into all this. She did say she'd be here soon?"

"Eight or so," Philip answered. He checked his watch. Seven twenty five. Could he endure another half hour or so?

Ping's chatter began anew as the waiter left. Philip glanced at his watch again. He discovered himself clicking his fingers against the table, which was about six feet in diameter, one of those rotating serving trays in its center. It seemed to be very sturdy.

*   *   *   *   *

The Miata flew over the curb and screeched to a halt on the red carpet. The valet stared in astonishment as Meiling ran by him and through the restaurant's lobby.

"I beg your pardon, miss—" the hostess stammered as she flew by her into the first of the two main rooms.

"Philip!" she screamed, even two rooms away. "Philip! Get out of the room!"

The pleasant hubbub of conversation went silent in the large room. She crashed into a table, sending two men and their chairs flying. Angry shouts rose behind her.

"Philip! Get out of the room!"

She rounded the corner into the second large room, from which the private alcoves radiated out. She saw Tom staring at her as she careened off another table. "Get Philip out of the room! Now!" she yelled to him. Tom turned and burst into the alcove, and a second later barreled out shoving Philip ahead of him, with Tiffany in tow behind him. Ping appeared in the doorway, a quizzical look on her face.

A flash of light erupted behind them, followed by a deafening roar. Philip and Tom came flying straight toward Meiling, as if a giant hand had pushed them, hard. A flash of heat warmed Meiling's face. After the explosion, there was utter silence for a second or two, then screams and cries rose from all sides.

Meiling caught Philip and stopped his momentum. Their eyes met. Behind them, Tom was struggling to his feet, shakily. Tiffany was not, nor Ping.

Philip put his hand on her shoulder, hugged her close, then turned. "Tiffany! Are you all right?" He rushed back and knelt beside her. She was lying on her side, her hair flattened against her bloody forehead, black soot covering her torn dress. It was the purple one he liked so much. He shoved a table aside and grabbed her shoulders.

"Don't move her, buddy," Tom said, close to his ear.

"Is she—?" he asked Tom.

Tom was feeling her pulse. "Hard to say, Phil. But doesn't look mortal."

Tiffany groaned. Her eyes fluttered, as sirens screamed outside. Opened, and tried to focus on Philip. "Philip?" she asked, weakly.

Meiling pushed by Philip and tried to find Ping in the scattered debris.

"Stand back, folks," Tom was saying to the crowd of people around Philip and Tiffany. "Let the medics through." He began clearing a corridor, shoving people aside.

Meiling looked around, not seeing Ping. She forced herself to look into the demolished alcove. Red columns were blackened and shattered into odd angles. A body was crumpled beside the opening.

"Ping!" Meiling rushed to the body. It was blackened and covered in blood, limp. As she put her hand on the shoulder, though, the body jerked, and a groan bubbled up from it. Meiling began to tremble, and tears filled her eyes.

Tom appeared at her elbow. "Best let the medics in here, Miss Bei. Phil and I will be in the ambulance with Miss Hayes and your friend. Meet you at the hospital?"

Meiling stared blankly at him.

"Meet you at the hospital, OK?" he said again.

She nodded, and staggered up as medics arrived.

Ma Tsu

Chapter Forty

Meiling rushed down the hospital hallway. Light glinted off the white tiles and walls. The smell of antiseptics and soap hung in the air.

"Philip!" she screamed. What had the nurse said? Third door on the left? Fifth? There. The one with the security guards.

"Philip!"

He appeared in the doorway, between the guards. Hair even more disheveled than usual. Brown stains down his shirt—blood. His face haggard, drawn, squinting against the harsh light in the hallway.

"Philip." She ran into his arms, sending him staggering back into the room as he folded them around her, tight. She was crying. Her face was in his chest, her nose buried in the blood stains. It smelled sweet, and pungent.

"I'm all right Meiling," he said, stroking her short hair. "I'm all right. Thanks to you."

A loud, impatient cough came from behind him.

Meiling jumped a bit, and pulled away from Philip. Over his shoulder she saw Tiffany Hayes, sitting up in a bed, white pillows stuffed under her torso. Her hair wasn't close to perfect, sticking out in every direction, although it looked as if it had been subjected to a brush recently. Her face was puffy, especially under her eyes. There was a large bruise on her chin, blue and purple.

She looked a lot different than in the Hilton lobby that morning. But she still looked angry.

"Oh, I—I mean, I didn't know—"

"Evidently," in arched tones.

"Well—I'm sorry you got hurt. But I'm glad you're—alive."

"So considerate of you. You arranged such an unexpected greeting to my arrival in your exotic little world here. And what a lovely restaurant you recommended for our little dinner."

"What? You're the one who came barging in unexpected over here. And I didn't plant the bomb. Very much the opposite. I—"

This is what she really looks like, thought Meiling, as she stifled her rising anger. Tiffany's face bloomed swollen and red as she glared up from her bed at Meiling. This is what Tiffany Hayes really looks like without all the makeup and the perfect hairdo. Ugly.

"I've had some time to think," Tiffany resumed. "Not just about you two. But about our little meeting at the Hilton this morning. I hope I didn't make you late for your important meeting with the two negotiators, Philip."

"Huh? No. I made it."

"Strange. I haven't heard anything about further meetings since the Chinese canceled the sessions."

"Oh." Philip's face flushed. "We're, uh, pursuing some—some informal contacts." He glanced to the side, avoiding her eyes.

"Ah," Tiffany said slowly. "And Miss Wong. I'm so sorry about your enchanting friend. Ting, or Bing. Whatever."

"Ping!" Meiling cried out, grabbing Philip's arm. "How is Ping? Where is she?"

"Down the hall," Philip said, after a hesitation that made Meiling's heart jump. "I'll take you there."

"And on the way, my dear, ask one of those handsome guards outside to bring me a phone so I can have the Hilton send a hairdresser," said Tiffany.

Meiling dragged Philip into the hallway by the hand.

"You, uh, heard Miss Hayes?" he mumbled to one of the guards. The man nodded and flipped a cell phone from his suit pocket.

"Which way?" Meiling demanded.

"Down this hall," said Philip, heading for a darker corridor. Meiling hurried beside him.

Inside her room, Tiffany held out her hand for the guard's phone.

"Find me the international calling code for Washington, D.C. from here," she snapped to the man, grabbing the cell phone from his hand.

Meiling followed Philip through dim hospital corridors. "What is all—this?" she asked, eyeing the stacks of boxes lining both sides of the already narrow halls.

"Plasma. Saline solution. Syringes," Philip said. "They're expecting a lot of wounded people here in two days. The deadline."

The air changed. Damp now, and stale. The corridor got even darker.

"Not the VIP wing, is it?" Meiling said. She hated Tiffany and her hairdresser from the Hilton, her fresh linens.

Philip led her into a small room. Three beds were crowded into it, but only one was occupied. A small figure lay flat, shrunken and fragile in the poor light. An IV bottle stood on the far side of the bed, the line trailing down toward the figure.

Meiling stopped, shocked at the scene. She took two steps toward the bed.

"Ping? Ping?"

The figure barely made a mound under the sheets. The face was white, and so swollen that she looked twice before deciding it was really Ping. Ping, but so different, so still and quiet.

Eyelids fluttered on the figure. Ping opened her eyes, and tried to focus. She gave up, and looked blankly up.

"Meiling?" The voice was small but pure and beautiful, surprising Meiling. A voice that didn't belong with the battered body.

"Ping, it's me," she said, bending down to put her face close to Ping's. "I'm here."

Ping smiled a small smile. She blinked, trying hard to focus, but still not succeeding.

"We were happy, weren't we? When we were little girls," Ping said in the voice that didn't fit with her body.

"Yes, Ping. We had a really good time, as little girls. And as big girls, too." She swallowed hard.

Ping lay still. She moved her head very slightly from side to side, once.

"Better as little girls, I think. Things got so complicated when I grew up."

Meiling wanted to touch Ping, but she looked so white, so frail. Very gently she put the back of her hand against Ping's cheek, and rubbed.

"Well, I love it whenever I'm with you," Meiling said. "You made me happy, no matter who your boyfriend was or how things were going."

"Really?" came the small voice. Her lips weren't moving much, and the words began to slur. "I'm glad. But I wasn't really happy, Meiling. I was much happier, as a little girl, with you."

Meiling didn't know what to say. Her throat was tightening, and tears began their slow roll from her eyes, gathering speed on her cheek, then falling to the white linens.

"Remember?" Ping said softly. "How we played with each other's hair, when we were little girls?" She slurred the last words, badly. The pure voice was weakening, cracking into pieces.

Meiling bent down again, and put her wet face right next to Ping's.

"Yes. I loved putting your beautiful hair into pigtails, remember? And you were so good with my ponytail, Ping."

Ping made a weak small grunt. Her eyelids fluttered shut.

"We were happy. As little girls," she whispered, the words coming out soft over her dried lips. She made a slight whistling sound in her throat, then lay still.

Meiling put her hand, then her head, onto Ping's chest, and tried to think of her as a little girl with pigtails, tried to will happiness back into Ping's body one more time. It wouldn't come. She hugged Ping, her tears wetting the linens.

"Yes, we were happy. As little girls," Meiling tried to whisper, but the words wouldn't come out right; they fell out rough and broken.

Ping's chest wasn't moving. It felt foreign under Meiling's cheek, cold and inert. Meiling jerked her head up with a cry, and stared hard into Ping's face. It was gray and dull and like clay.

Meiling collapsed onto Ping's body, shaking with silent sobs.

She felt Philip's hand touch her back, and rest there, as she wept on the bed atop Ping's cold body.

*   *   *   *   *

Candles flickered in front of Ma Tsu's altar, the small flames wavering in the nighttime breeze. Meiling and Philip stood silent before the black-faced figure. They were in the Chengtu Street temple, whose gates did not close until late. Meiling had just lit the memorial candles for Ping, and placed them on the table fronting Ma Tsu's somber, beaded figure. The large cones of electric candles to either side of the altar cast a golden glow on Ma Tsu's green robe. She was flanked by two large vases filled with flowers of every color, with the whirling lines of sculpted magical mushrooms sprouting at her feet.

Strange, Philip thought. How many colors, how much of life, there was around this altar to a young woman that had been dead for a thousand years.

Meiling stepped back, and knelt on her knees. Philip followed suit, feeling awkward, but wanting to be part of what Meiling was doing.

"*Ma Tsu, protector of women and children, goddess of the sea,*" Meiling whispered in a soft, intimate voice, gazing directly at the black-faced figure with rows of pearls hanging over her forehead. "*I give Ping to your care. She died young and childless, a frightened child, herself. She was denied the years to become part of the natural cycle of family and old age. I will burn incense for her every day, this I vow, for the remainder of my life. I pray for your assistance to ease her passage back into our family hun souls.*"

Philip stood with Meiling, and had turned to leave when he heard her add another prayer to Ma Tsu, her voice tinged with anger, now.

"*And Ma Tsu. Help me punish the evil spirit who did this to Ping.*" She was looking fiercely up at the icon, the glow of the candles washing golden over her face, the glint of tears sparkling on her cheeks.

Meiling took Philip's arm as they walked back from the main altar, past a long table piled high with fruits and fish and cooking oil and more flowers, masses of flowers, the dark table top a riot of colors and smells. They stepped around three huge hundred-pound bags of rice, also left to be blessed, and down half a dozen stairs to the small open-air entry. Life-size statues of a tiger and leopard flanked more stairs to the left, with a lion beside the temple entrance, and a pool to their far right filled with koi fish and more statues, cranes life-size and a five-foot elephant spouting water from its raised trunk.

Meiling guided them to two cheap folding chairs beside the lion, and wearily sank into one, motioning Philip to the other. They sat silent for some moments.

"I'm glad," Philip said. "That you're taking care of Meiling's spirit."

Meiling stared at the stone flooring. "That's what family's for, Philip," she said, not looking up.

It sounded strange to Philip. It reminded him of something. What did it remind him of? A memory of sitting around the kitchen table in Vermont flashed through his mind, him and grandpa and his mom. The image hit him hard, filled him with yearning for—for what?

"By all the gods, though, I hate not knowing things!" Meiling burst out, stamping her foot and driving the image from Philip's mind.

"Not knowing who killed Ping, you mean?" said Philip, pulling himself back to the present.

"Oh, I know who killed her, damn him. But why? How does it fit in? And there's a whole boatload of other things I don't know." She leapt to her feet, and paced the stone floor between the tiger and the leopard. "The old man who's the head of the conglomerate I was investigating—he was found with a bullet in his head this morning, or what was left of his head. No clues, nothing. And his last son—the one who tossed the grenades up to the roof of that rock house in the Botanical Garden—has vanished."

"Meaning?"

"I don't know," she snapped, gazing at the pond and stamping her foot again. "All I do know is this. Jimmy Chan has photos of fifteen men in his study. The half or so I recognized were all prominent, public men, who died—violently or suspiciously."

A wild, desperate look flashed over her face. "And your photograph is on the wall, too."

"What? A photo of me, on Jimmy Chan's wall?"

"Yeah. And you came damn close to having something in common with all those other men, tonight."

"He's just interested in men who've done something with their lives," Philip said. "A morbid interest."

"Maybe. But he managed to trick me into saying where and when you'd be tonight. And a bomb went off right there, Philip. And it killed Ping—who was there instead of me."

"Christ." Philip slumped back in the rickety chair. "Hard to believe—Jimmy Chan? Why? And was the bomb meant for you or for me, anyway?"

"That's what I don't know. With the conglomerate head being killed, and his son missing—maybe a power struggle in the conglomerate, and they're tying up loose ends—like me." She paced across the entry, to the pond, then headed back for the tiger. "I just hate having so many things I don't know. Hate it."

Philip liked the way she moved in the light from the candles. Like a big cat, herself. It was what had first attracted her to him, so long ago in the Lung Shan temple. Why did it seem so right, to be here with her in a temple in Taipei festooned with lions and tigers and elephants and black goddesses with pearls on her forehead? It was weird, impossible, yet it seemed to be just where he belonged. He sat, entranced with her pacing, with the golden glow of candlelight on her face, with—

Her cell phone erupted. Meiling looked at him, their eyes locking, and they stared at each other for two cycles of rings, hearing nothing, lost in the worlds swirling before them. She finally reached into her purse.

"Wai." She shook her head to clear it.

"Mr. Lee. Yes. We're all right. Thank you. Oh, on the television? Yes. But Ping—" She burst into tears, and handed the phone to Philip.

"Yes, sir. No, we're at the Ma Tsu temple on Chengtu street. We lost Ping, so Meiling is lighting candles for her here. It's open later than the Lung Shan temple. Look, Mr. Lee. Meiling and I were just talking. There's a lot we don't understand, about what went on tonight, as well as other stuff. And it's pretty important that we figure it out. Today, at the negotiations, you said if we needed some help, we could talk to you. Could we possibly come over, tonight, and run some things by you?"

A pause. "Thanks, sir. We'll leave right now, and get to your place in—" He looked at Meiling.

"Within an hour," Meiling said, wiping tears from her eyes.

"Within an hour," Philip relayed to the phone. "Not possible, sir? Well, that's what Meiling says she can do it in. And I wouldn't want to bet against her, Mr. Lee." Philip laughed at something from the other end, then handed the phone back to Meiling.

"He's expecting us. Within an hour."

jade

Chapter Forty One

"Some Lagavulin for you, Philip. You look as though you need it," said Sung Lee, holding a short glass out for Philip as the security man Jiao-rung escorted him and Meiling into the study. Sung Lee was wearing a turtleneck, an off-white color, much like the pieces of jade throughout the room.

"A soda for you, Miss Bei?"

"I'll have a Scotch, too," said Meiling, noticing the ugly welt on Lee's forehead. "It's been a rough evening."

Lee raised his eyebrows, but poured her one. "I'm sorry about your cousin, Miss Bei," he said, handing her the drink.

A warm feeling rushed over Meiling with the first sip. She felt calmer. And better.

"You know Jimmy Chan, Mr. Lee?" she asked.

"Not well. But yes."

"Well, listen to what's on the wall of his study." Meiling described what she had seen there this evening, and what her suspicions were. Lee listened gravely, sipping his own Scotch frequently.

"Interesting, Miss Bei. But really. The Jimmy Chan I know is completely superficial. There's nothing there, under the charm. Nothing."

"I know, I know," Meiling said. "It's so damn complicated. Mr. Lee, Philip said someone tried to kill you recently. Any possible connection between that, and what happened tonight to us?"

Lee swirled the ice in the little Scotch that remained in his glass. "Not that I can see, but who knows? We know for sure who was behind the attempt on my life. It was Shen, the old jade dealer."

Meiling jerked to her feet with a cry. The heavy glass dropped from her hand and hit the thick white carpet.

"The head of the conglomerate?" she asked, ignoring the glass.

"Yes. Do you know him?"

"I was doing an investigative piece about the conglomerate. He sent his sons to try to silence me—kill me—several times."

"Then you and I have something in common, Miss Bei," said Lee, staring hard at Meiling. "He sent his remaining son to kill me last night."

"Ah. That would explain Shen's sudden…demise this morning. And his son's disappearance, too?"

Lee finished his Scotch, and didn't answer the question.

"I don't suppose it was a bomb, with you?" Philip asked.

"No," Lee said. "It was most ingenious. He told me he had a special jade piece for me, wanted to bring it out to see. He and his son came yesterday afternoon. A really fine piece, Sung dynasty flying horse. Old Shen lured me out to the terrace, while his son took the piece to my vault, beside the bedroom. He claimed he saw his son leaving, and took his own leave of us also. But evidently the son hid himself in the vault, and came out shortly after your phone call last night, Miss Bei. You probably saved my life. Hsiao Pang was still awake, heard the noise of the vault opening, and—" Here Lee broke off, lost his voice, and stared at the floor for some moments.

"Not Miss Pang?" Meiling said in a whisper. "Not—"

Again he didn't answer, but set his empty glass clumsily on the bar and covered his eyes with his hand.

Meiling sat heavily on the sofa, and picked up her glass from the floor. She searched for the ice, and put it in the glass. "Damn it. I'm losing too many people I like—to whatever the devil is going on here." She took a handkerchief from her purse, and blew into it.

"Mr. Lee. Again," said Philip. "Could there be any connection between what happened here last night, and what happened to us tonight?"

"I don't know," Lee answered wearily. "I myself have no idea what was behind the attempt here. I have absolutely nothing to do with Shen other than purchasing *lao yu* pieces from him."

Meiling gazed at the half dozen jade pieces about the room. "They are lovely. And all quite old, I believe?"

"Nothing but Tang and Sung dynasty pieces. The one he was showing me was stunning—the flying horse."

"Perhaps the attempt had something to do with that piece—it was very valuable?" asked Meiling

Lee laughed bitterly. "Yes. All these pieces are worth—well, millions of U.S. dollars."

"May I see the last piece, the flying horse?" asked Meiling.

Lee shook his head. "I returned it to the conglomerate today. And stopped payment on my check. I want nothing to do with that piece. It was involved in Hsiao Pang's death, so I could never enjoy it. It is unlucky."

"The only connection was jade," Meiling mused. "Has anything else out of the ordinary happened, Mr. Lee? Anything concerned with jade, or with Shen?"

"Absolutely nothing. Well, nothing relevant."

"Something … not relevant?" Meiling asked.

"It's nothing. I was on the mainland two days ago. Three days ago. Personal business. A small village south of Shanghai. We were looking around an old factory there, and discovered some burlap bags, the type Uygur jade hunters use, in Sinjiang. With some chunks of jade rinds in the bags, still."

"What in the world does all that mean?" asked Philip, eyeing the jade piece on the table in front of him, a disc with a hole in the middle.

"Smuggling is what it means," Lee snapped. "I've seen a photo of an ocean-going yacht anchored in the village's bay. Someone is smuggling chunks of raw jade from the Kunlun mountains out of China."

Meiling jumped to her feet again, quivering. Her mind raced. She glanced wildly around the room, at the jade pieces. The sightless eyes of a severed head flashed into her mind, lying on the sidewalk beside New Park, the hair sticking out in all directions. The man who had sand particles on his fingers. Shen's conglomerate man.

"Shen," she stammered. "Shen sells you these pieces—*lao yu*—for millions of dollars?"

Lee glanced sharply at her. "Somewhat less for some, more for others. What business is that of yours, Miss Bei?"

Meiling quivered. Something in her mind wanted to be connected, she could feel it. Two items in different worlds that wanted to somehow come together. She groaned at the effort.

"That's it!" she shrieked. "Sand! Sand is how they carved the old *lao yu* pieces. Sand is how they carved new jade to make it look like *lao yu*! Don't you see? You and I both ran afoul of Shen's conglomerate, Mr. Lee!" She beamed wildly at Philip and Lee.

"Run that by us, once more?" asked Philip. "And a little more slowly, please?"

Meiling picked up the *lao yu* piece in front of Philip.

"Mr. Lee. How do you know this is a Tang dynasty *pi* disc? Worth a million U.S. dollars?"

Lee stiffened. "I'm not a fool, Miss Bei. Shen is a recognized expert on *lao yu*. He attested to its authenticity."

"I'm not accusing you of being a fool, Mr. Lee. But really—what if Shen was lying?"

"I make a study of *lao yu*, Miss Bei," Lee said, anger in his voice. "I know what old jade looks like. It's carved differently than pieces these days. Perhaps that's what you were rambling on about just now—sand is the abrasive. No one carves with sand anymore. Plus the mottled, weathered look. *Lao yu* from a thousand years ago is very distinctive."

"All no doubt true, Mr. Lee. But did Shen tell you where he got his pieces? And did you check his story?"

"Miss Bei. Pieces of this caliber have murky pasts. No doubt many unpleasant and—what did Shen always say?—'delicate circumstances' are associated with every transfer of ownership. Shen would never tell me how he got the pieces. No dealer of pieces of this caliber will."

Meiling's paced around the room, a smile on her beaming face. "No doubt all that is true, Mr. Lee. Now let me tell you what I know. I know that Shen's conglomerate was hiding millions of U.S. dollars of profit every year. I know they were smuggling something into Taiwan—and out of it, I thought. And I know that they hired people who worked with sand, Mr. Lee. People who got killed when they talked, and had sand particles in the valleys between the ridges of their fingers."

Meiling stopped in front of Lee, and stood there twirling the old *pi* disc in her hands. Lee had a nervous look on his face as the jade piece whirled around.

"Now, put together what you know and what I know," she continued, oblivious to his discomfort. "I'll bet that old Shen was smuggling Kunlun jade into Taiwan, carving it the old way, probably soaking it in acid or something to help make it look old, then selling it to you and to others as Sung dynasty *lao yu*. Buying the pieces for hundreds, selling them for millions. Illegal, and highly profitable. You accidentally discovered where they were smuggling the jade out of China, while you were on some other business south of Shanghai. So you had to be eliminated, to protect the conglomerate."

Lee stared, dumbstruck, at Meiling. He glanced around at all his jade pieces, and swallowed, hard. "Of course. The gentry, who had the villa at Jinhua, before 1949. The headman said they were Shens. The old lady. She had a son, by one of the Shens. I never connected the name. There are hundreds, thousands of Shens. But now—of course. Old Shen would have been convinced that I knew what he was doing, or would soon figure it out."

Lee collapsed back into the sofa with a groan.

"Mr. Lee. I wouldn't assume that all these pieces are forgeries," Meiling said. "May I take a sampling of them? I know a mineralogist at National Taiwan University, a specialist in jade. He has friends in chemistry. They will be able to age these pieces for us, I'm sure."

Lee waved his hand toward the pieces, listlessly. "Take them. Take them all, if you wish."

"Now just a second," Philip said. "If I follow all this, it means that the several attempts on Meiling's life, and the attempt on your life last night, Mr. Lee, all had the same source. The conglomerate that Meiling has been investigating. So where does that leave tonight's attempt—Meiling or me? Jimmy Chan or the conglomerate?"

Meiling poured herself another Scotch at the bar.

"Get one for me, too," said Lee. "And your young man here, too."

The scotch rose in two more glasses.

"Ice in the bucket to your left," Lee suggested.

Meiling liked the sound the ice made as it dropped in the glass, the gentle slurp.

"So, where are we, on what happened tonight?" she said, walking their Scotches over to Lee and Philip.

"Well, old Shen and his two sons are dead," said Lee after a long sip. "The conglomerate is headless. Out of the picture. But I still can't believe Jimmy Chan is an assassin. I can't believe he has the steel in him to kill someone. Not to mention the intelligence. In my experience, it takes both steel and intelligence to kill successful people."

"Well, as for intelligence, he's not as shallow as he puts on," Meiling said. "I was at Berkeley with him, in the nineties. He majored in chemistry. Did fairly well at it. You can't major in a science at Cal and be stupid."

She began to pace the room, her mind racing again, a smile playing on her face. She did love puzzles. How to test her theory, that Jimmy was an assassin? She stopped, abruptly.

"Got a computer here, Mr. Lee?" she asked.

Lee looked up from his drink, his face old, and tired.

"I think so. Over there, on the corner desk. I had the people in my Information Processing section put it in. Told them to put everything on it. I rarely use it, myself."

Meiling sat herself and her Scotch down at the desk. She flicked some switches, and soon the monitor glowed.

"Philip, bring me my purse, would you?"

She extracted her cell phone, scrolled down her contacts, and called one.

"Little Poong! How are you? This is Meiling Bei." A pause. "Yes, I know it's late. But I need a favor. You book Jimmy Chan's trips abroad, I believe?" A longer pause. "Yes, I know. I am doing a piece on travel habits of the rich and famous. I need access to the records of his trips. I can get to your web site—I do it to order my own tickets through you—but I will need the access code to get into your records, Little Poong."

She tapped her fingernails impatiently on the desktop as she listened to the reply.

"Yes, I understand that, Little Poong. But my editor wants the story. And he's also been pressuring me to get more data about the alleged kickbacks in the travel agency business, in addition. I believe you and I talked about that, a year ago? Those irregularities in your books, Little Poong? You remember that, don't you?" A shorter pause this time.

"Yes. Well, I don't want to bring your agency into the story. You are an old friend. But I really don't know how much longer I can keep you out of it, Little Poong. Although I want to, I really do."

She sat back in the chair, and glanced briefly at Philip and Lee.

"Remind me not to get on Miss Bei's bad side," Lee said to Philip.

"Oh, that's wonderful, Little Poong. I do appreciate this," Meiling was saying. She scribbled some words down in her address book. "No, you can rest easy. I'll do my very best to keep you out of the other story. Thanks so much."

She clicked the mouse at the computer for several minutes.

"We'll get the dates for the deaths of the men on Jimmy's wall, first. From our archives at the newspaper."

Philip groaned and slumped on the sofa. "Got any food handy, Mr. Lee? I'm famished. Those nine-hole abalone were sure delicious, the other night."

"Those were Hsiao Pang's specialty. She gathered them, prepared them—everything." After a long moment staring at the floor, he signaled the gray-haired old lady in the apron hovering just beyond the doorway. "Food, Miss Jao."

Meiling clicked the mouse for ten more minutes at the computer, writing occasionally on a notepad. Philip and Lee were finishing a plate of cheese and crackers when she turned to them from the desk.

"So. The two Indonesians I recognized in Jimmy Chan's photos. One died in a fall off a cliff on Bali, April of three years ago. And Riady Pemby was killed by an assassin two years ago, November. The young Indian cabinet member, Kumaramangalam, died mysteriously in August of 2000. And the prime minister of Nicaragua, just last year, January, from a bomb blast. In a private room at his favorite restaurant in Managua."

She glanced up at Philip, then back to her list. "This year, March. Chien, the DPP dynamo, in a boating accident off the coast near Kaohsiung. And I made some guesses on another Latin American whose picture is there. Turns out he was the vice president of Paraguay. Also a bomb explosion in a restaurant, last December."

"Now let's see where Jimmy Chan has been vacationing lately, courtesy of the agreeable Little Poong." She manipulated the mouse for the next five minutes.

"Jakarta, April of three years ago and November of two years ago," she suddenly said, a note of triumph coloring her voice. "That's the cliff fall, and Pemby. India, July of 2000—a month before Kumaramangalam's death. Nicaragua and Paraguay, January and December of last year. Perfect fits, five for five. Plus half a dozen other trips, split between Thailand and South America. The other men on the wall, no doubt." She swirled around on the chair and fixed Philip and Lee with a fierce look. "Any bets whether Jimmy was boating off Kaohsiung last March?"

Meiling flipped her pencil back onto the desk. "Jimmy Chan, Jimmy Chan. An assassin for hire. Deadly, under all that charm." Her skin was tingling, the room was spinning. Her oldest friend, outside of Ping, was a killer. Jimmy Chan had killed Ping with a bomb meant for—her mind veered away from it, refused to think it.

"I was the target tonight, then," Philip said in the hush gripping the room. "To stop the peace talks from succeeding, no doubt."

The images were piling up in Meiling's mind. Ping cold and white on the bed. The brown blood on Philip's shirt still. Tom Ling in the morgue at Berkeley. Rou-jing slumped against the wall of his studio. She shut her eyes tight, but the images wouldn't go away. A cry bubbled out of her mouth. A hand around her shoulders. Philip's voice, low and concerned.

"You all right, kid?"

The images vanished with his voice. She nodded, shakily.

"Sure?"

Another nod, and a deep breath.

"But who hired Jimmy Chan?" Philip said, his hand trailing off her shoulder. "Who would want the peace talks to fail, bad enough to hire an assassin?"

Lee laughed bitterly. "I can think of three or four groups here on Taiwan. More in the People's Republic. And you can probably do as well, for the United States."

"There's the problem," Philip said. "We can't just go to the authorities, make a complaint. The orders could be coming from anywhere in any of the three governments, right up to the highest level."

"Indeed," Sung Lee sighed. "To the highest levels."

"I'm going to get even for Ping's death," Meiling said stubbornly. "And you two are somehow going to help me, not just to get Jimmy Chan, but to get whoever hired him for this."

Philip drained his drink. "Well, we can't go to our governments for help. That means we go to Jimmy Chan."

"We can't do that directly," said Meiling. "He's not stupid, and he's not easily intimidated."

"No, but he's arrogant. He thinks he's got everyone charmed. Let's invite him to a social occasion he can't decline. Dinner, here at your place, Mr. Lee. We'll get him here, corner him, and force it out of the bastard."

"And what's to keep him from bringing a gun and finishing his job at dinner, Philip?" Meiling asked.

"I've got metal detectors in the doors," Lee said in a soft voice. "He won't get in carrying a weapon. I think Philip's right. Let's get him here, then pressure him."

"When?" asked Philip. "The sooner the better, to my mind."

"Tomorrow night," answered Lee. "We'll all breath better—and we'll have a better chance to avoid this war—the sooner we beat him down and find out who's paying him."

Sung Lee's face had lost its tired look. The face was as hard as Meiling had ever seen it. She was glad he was on their side. They all stood, and Meiling retrieved her purse from the desk as Philip and Sung Lee carried their scotch glasses to the bar.

"Seven thirty tomorrow night, then?" said Philip. "You'll arrange for the meal, sir?"

"Fine," said Lee, glancing up at Philip from the bar.

"And you'll invite Jimmy Chan, Meiling?" Philip asked, looking over to her.

"I suppose," Meiling answered. "But it'll be hard."

Philip turned back to Lee. "Well, that's—"

He stopped. Lee was staring at him, dumbstruck, a frightened look in his eyes. Lee staggered back a step as he reached for the bar to steady himself.

"Are you all right, Mr. Lee?" Meiling asked, hurrying to the bar and putting a hand on Lee's elbow.

"I—I, uh," Lee stammered, still staring wildly at Philip. "Yes. All right." He couldn't tear his frightened eyes off Philip's face.

"Are you sure?" Meiling persisted. The man looked as though he'd seen a ghost. But he was staring at Philip, not a ghost.

"Yes. Dinner. Seven thirty tomorrow night," Lee said in a strangled voice.

"Well, we'll be off, then, Mr. Lee," said Meiling, releasing Lee's arm and taking Philip's. "Let us know if anything else comes up."

They left Lee supporting himself on the bar. A large security man and the old housekeeper with the apron were at the front door.

"Mr. Lee appears to be ill," Meiling said to the two. "Please check on him. Let us know if it's anything serious." She extracted a card from her purse and handed it to the security man.

*   *   *   *   *

Sung Lee's world was reeling. He clutched the edge of the bar to keep himself from toppling over. His breath came in short, fast gulps. When Philip had turned to Meiling, Lee had seen his father's turning face in the photograph with his mother. Same lines, same bones, same play of shadows, same profile. The same turning face. How could that be?

He knew the answer, but he refused to acknowledge it. Dawson's grandfather had been in China. It couldn't be.

Old Jao appeared in the doorway. She was smoothing her white apron with jerky movements of her hands, and she looked at him sideways.

"Are you all right, Mr. Lee?"

"Scotch," Lee croaked, pointing to the bottle of Lagavulin. "Ice," he croaked again. He held out his hand. It was shaking.

She put the drink in his hand, and closed his fingers around it. The security man, Jiao-rung, appeared beside her, with the same sideways look at him.

"Open the door to the terrace," Lee said, his voice closer to normal, now.

Lee staggered to the ledge overlooking the ocean. A quarter moon glinted on the sea below. He put the drink on the stone ledge, and leaned heavily on it.

He was trembling.

I have seen a ghost, he thought to himself. I have seen the ghost of my dead father. Come back to haunt me after seventy years. To haunt me? Or—

He picked up the drink, and poured half of it down his throat. It didn't help.

"Ma Tsu!" he screamed over the ledge to the sea. "What have you done?" The wind rising up the cliff took his voice and carried it away. A hundred feet below, huge waves crashed against the rock wall, sending great cascades of water into the moonlit air.

He put a hand to his head, and gingerly rubbed his bruised temple. It had been a hard day. Perhaps he'd just imagined it. Surely he had just imagined it. How could he tell?

He drank the rest of the scotch, and put the glass on the ledge.

216

"Get Miss Ling on the phone," he barked to Jiao-rung, anxiously watching from the doorway.

In a moment, Jiao-rung approached with a cell phone, which looked very small in his large hand.

"Miss Ling. Get hold of young Kevin, the gold-haired one from the sixth floor. Try his office first. He works long hours. Have him call me here at home." He handed the phone back to Jiao-rung, and turned back to the ledge. He brought the glass to his lips again, but discovered it was empty.

"More scotch," he growled, holding the glass behind him. Jiao-rung refilled it, a generous amount. Sung Lee took a long sip, staring at the glint of the moon on the ocean. It formed a long line, uneven, broken by Ma Tsu's waves for a mile or more out to sea, but pointed straight to him. Ma Tsu was telling him something.

The phone rang behind him. He held out his hand, and Jiao-rung slapped it into his palm. "Kevin? Good. You're in your office? Good. Bring up the program, the facial reconstruction program. Hurry."

Scotch in one hand, phone in the other, he strode to the computer in the study, its monitor still glowing.

"I want you to type in a new racial profile on the program that reconstructs the face from the skull. Kevin—try—" His voice shrunk to a whisper. "Try northern European." It brought a bad taste to his mouth as he said the words, and a shiver ran down his body.

"Yes, that's what I said. Put it in, damn it. Can you send me the image, on my computer here at home?"

He sat and clicked the mouse as he listened to Kevin's instructions. "Yes. All right. Yes. Fine. All right." When the link was established, he stared at the screen, saw the skull revolving, then stop, facing him. Flesh appeared on the skull, built up layer by layer, the muscles surrounding the eyes first, then the forehead, finally the large cheek muscles and those surrounding the mouth.

The computer hummed, and skin appeared on the flesh.

Lee saw the face leap out at him, confront him. Stun him. Philip Dawson was staring at him from his computer.

Not exactly Philip, but so close as to be his brother.

Or his father.

Or his grandfather.

Philip Dawson's grandfather. The—caucasian. The foreign devil. And his mother, had, had—. He veered away from thinking of it, feeling bile rise in his throat.

"Sir?" he heard Jiao-rung say, next to his ear.

Sung Lee stared at the screen. His world was reeling. He grabbed the top of the desk to keep from toppling over.

"Sir?"

Eyes still on the image on the screen, Sung Lee spoke. "Take a chair out to the terrace. Then help me there, Jiao-rung. And bring the bottle of Lagavulin—no, make it Macallan, the brown one with the red cork—and put it beside me, on the terrace."

Jiao-rung disappeared. In a few moments he returned, helped Sung Lee to his feet, and guided him onto the terrace. He placed him in the chair, facing the ocean. His glass was on the ledge in front of him, with the bottle of Macallan's beside it. The Macallan's was directly in line with the moonshine on the ocean coming straight to Sung Lee.

"Thank you, my friend," Sung Lee whispered. "Now go. I will be some time here." He bent over to his glass, and filled it, to the brim, before turning back to Ma Tsu's domain. The moon shone down, soft and bright, offering a benediction on the new world that stretched to the dark cloud-shaded horizon before Sung Lee.

mountain

Chapter Forty Two

Day Eight

Philip sat unmoving at the AIT conference table. The morning's diplomatic pouch lay on the table, dark blue with the eagle, vivid against the table's dull brown. He didn't stir when Dirk and Baden entered the room.

"You wanted to see us?"

He indicated seats across the table with his hand.

Dirk and Baden exchanged glances, and sat.

"First thing. Both Lee and Zhu were intrigued with my proposals at our session yesterday. Dividing up the military. Maritime State of Taiwan. They thought there was a chance they could make it fly, and spent yesterday and this morning trying to do that."

Audible sighs from both Dirk and Baden, whose eyes brightened.

"Second thing. Some interesting documents in the pouch this morning. A message from John Ravenhurst, telling me that President Hayes has heard I'm conducting unauthorized secret negotiations with Zhu and Lee. Instructing me to break off the talks and come back to D.C. with the rest of the team."

The silence in the room was immediately as heavy and dark as the mood that had gripped Philip when he had read the message himself earlier that morning. He cast an ominous look toward the two opposite him.

"You folks know anything about this?"

"Philip," Dirk began, folding her hands in front of her on the table. Her hair was newly coiffed, and she looked a lot better than the last time he had seen her, at the all-night brain-storming session two days ago.

"I won't say 'I told you so,' but it didn't come from us. Nor, I think, from the teams or the AIT staff. Everyone here assumes you've had authorization for the secret talks."

"Huh. Well, I believe you. I think it came from Tiffany Hayes. I let slip to her that I had a meeting, when she surprised me at the Hilton yesterday morning. So it's my fault."

He shoved the pouch toward them. "There are letters for you, too, from Ravenhurst. I can imagine the contents."

Dirk and Baden opened them, glanced down the pages, and put them down.

"So what are you going to do?" asked Baden.

Philip fixed his eyes on the eagle glaring up from the diplomatic pouch. He liked its fierce look.

"I don't know. Part of me wants to go back to D.C. and clean out my desk and go rock-climbing for a year. Did you know I was planning to resign a week ago, when Hayes gave me this assignment?"

"My God. No," spluttered Dirk.

"But there's another part of me," continued Philip, taking his letter in his left hand. "The part of me that likes kids playing in parks. Sort of likes some of the people I've met here. Even Sung Lee. Even Zhu, in a way."

He crumpled the letter in his hand, squeezing until it was a small, compact ball. "That part of me wants to say 'Screw you' to Ravenhurst, even to the President, go to today's secret session, and find out whether Lee and Zhu have gotten anywhere with this latest proposal.

"If we've gotten someplace, to spend all night with you folks and our teams, nailing down the details, and seeing if we can't put something together to avoid a war here. To spring it on the President tomorrow morning. See if we can't persuade him that it's a good idea to be flexible, bend a bit, to keep a war from happening."

With a flip of his wrist, the ball sailed toward the wastepaper basket in the corner. It bounced off one wall, careened around the lip of the basket, and disappeared. "What do you folks think?"

Dirk and Baden were staring at the basket. Dirk sighed, deep.

"How would you persuade the President to hear you out, tomorrow morning? How would you persuade him to take an agreement different than the one he wants?"

"No idea," Philip answered. "Particularly if Ravenhurst is at his elbow. I'll deal with all that when the time comes. Make something up. Keep trying 'til I find something that works."

Another sigh from Dirk, who shook her head.

"Whether it worked or not, it would mean your job. Your career," Dirk said. "I'm OK with that. Your life. But for Baden and me—if we've read these letters from Ravenhurst, and help you out—it's our careers. I'm not ready for that. Sorry."

Silence.

"You know," Philip drawled. "I'm a really sneaky guy. Devious. What if I never showed you those letters? Destroyed them before you saw them. How long do you figure before someone would notice, and send a follow-up letter, or try to get hold of you?"

A longer silence.

"About twenty-four hours, I'd judge," said Dirk in a quiet voice. "Maybe longer. I'm sure the President, and Ravenhurst too, are incredibly busy charting different military scenarios with the Joint Chiefs for tomorrow, consulting with allies, briefing congressmen." She glanced to her side. "What do you figure, Matt?"

Baden was giving close scrutiny to his hands on the tabletop. "This is a peculiar setup over here," he finally said. "No embassy proper. Diplomatic pouches that go to the highest-ranking official for distribution of contents. Who happens to be Dawson here, right now. It could be a day, before more instructions arrive. Before Sharon and I found out that you had deceived us, you dirty bastard."

A grin lit his face as he looked up. "But then, the deadline is ten o'clock tomorrow morning, anyway, isn't it?"

Philip had always liked Baden. The fellow's fresh, grinning face was the best thing he'd seen in days. He swung his gaze to Dirk.

"Sharon?"

She met his gaze. Not grinning, not a bit. Her face flushed. She reached out slowly and pushed the two letters back across the table. "I haven't seen a thing. Nor read a thing. But you need to know, Philip. The odds are long as hell against you. And if you fail, it could very well mean something more than losing your job. Destroying official diplomatic correspondence, disobeying a President—that's treason, Philip. There's a death penalty for treason, you know."

Baden gasped. Philip returned Dirk's somber stare for a moment, then reached out and put the two letters back into the pouch and took it under his arm. He stood and walked to the windows, where he pulled the blinds open. Sunlight streamed into the room.

"Yeah, I thought of that," he said. "On the other hand, war is sort of grisly, too, isn't it? Lots of people eating a death penalty in a war, right?"

Dirk slowly nodded. "You know, this is the reason we asked for you. Everyone knew this whole thing could fail, blow up right in our faces. No one else had the courage to take it on. To see it through, no matter how rough it got. We knew you would. Didn't think it would come to a treason charge, though. Good luck. Matt and I will assemble the team, ready to work if you get that far."

*   *   *   *   *

Lung Shan Temple

Meiling lit the memorial candles for Ping at Ma Tsu's altar in the back. The table fronting the altar was piled high with fruits and flowers and cooking oil. There was much need for blessings from Ma Tsu, with the deadline and war tomorrow morning. A photograph of Ping sat in the midst of the flowers. She was laughing, as always. Nearly always, reflected Meiling. It was a photograph of her as a little girl. Back when she was truly happy.

Tying a gold scarf around her head, Meiling brushed through crowds to the front of the temple, past the scores of people praying to Kwan Yin there, where thick wreathes of incense rose in the air and masses of monks chanted. As she stepped over the devil-stopping board into the front courtyard, her eyes drifted to the left, where she and Philip had talked. Had it only been a week that he had been in her life? So much had happened. Good things. Bad things. Things whose outcome could go either way.

She stopped abruptly. There, before the large waterfall, stood Tiffany Hayes, looking directly at her. She seemed a beautiful doll, blonde in a light blue suit, heels, heavily made up. They stared at each other for some moments, then Meiling warily walked to her. At the waterfall, she leaned on the railing, and breathed deep the air filled with mist.

"Philip's security man, from Vermont," Tiffany said. "He told me I could probably find you here." She seemed very stiff. Uncomfortable.

"And?" Meiling turned, and bore into the unnatural blue eyes.

Tiffany returned her stare, unflinching. "I need to know why you stole him from me. And how. I—I've never lost a man before, to someone else. It stunned me, really. Puzzled me. Why? How?"

The blueness of Tiffany's eyes unnerved Meiling. They didn't seem right, didn't seem human. Like she was a robot. A doll.

"I didn't steal him from you. I was assigned to cover him for a story, so I set up a chance meeting. And it just happened. No one steals anyone from someone else. People meet. Energy currents spring forth between them. They get pulled together. Plotting and scheming doesn't help. Doesn't work, really. I never do it."

"Really? I do it all the time. It works for me."

She was inhuman, after all. Ignorant of how humans work. How energy flows between creatures.

"And how do you know that this mysterious energy flow between you and Philip won't reverse current sometime?" Tiffany continued. "Push you apart as easily as it pulled you together?"

"It wasn't easy. We both fought it. I don't know where we are with it, to be honest. There are things you can do to cultivate it, to help it last. But sure—it could push us apart. Maybe it will."

"And would you be angry? Hurt? Like me?"

"Like you? I doubt it. I would survive it. Get over it. So long as he wasn't killed."

"How gruesome. Why do you say such a horrible thing?"

The mist rising from the waterfall hitting the pond sent flashes of sunlight glinting in every direction. Do I want to even talk with this inhuman doll, this barbarian, Meiling wondered? She remembered that Tiffany was important in Washington, D.C. That Philip would likely need a lot of help, and that Tiffany might be useful.

"Why say such a thing? Only because the two men I've lost weren't to another woman, but to death. One a mugging. One a heart attack."

"How awful." For the first time, a human spark briefly glowed in her strange eyes. "It must be hard. Twice? Do you think you're cursed, by some of these weird gods in the temple here?"

A breeze from the waterfall flapped the ends of her scarf against her neck. Meiling tucked them into the knot under her chin.

"It has occurred to me," she admitted with a weak laugh.

"So—no plot? No strategy, to get Philip away from me?"

"No. It just happened. Does that make it easier for you?"

"No. Probably harder. It makes it harder for me to hate you. To do something painful to you, to get even."

"It won't take much. Just wait twenty four hours. We'll have hundreds of missiles exploding around us, burying temples like this and people like me all over Taiwan. There'll be plenty of pain and misery."

"But we'll protect you."

"Oh yes. How wonderful. The defenses you've sold us will intercept maybe a third of the missiles. The rest will land and explode. Then you'll send your own missiles all over the coast of China." Meiling was spitting the words out, harsh. "How does that protect us? It just adds more death and exports some of it. You'll get revenge for us. That doesn't protect us. It doesn't bring anyone back to life."

Tiffany stepped back until she bumped against the waterfall's railing, recoiling at the force of the words. Her unnatural blue eyes widened. She absorbed it, tried to make sense of it.

"Well, perhaps we'll help you stop it."

"Philip is the only one of you trying to stop it. He's trying very hard, but he's getting precious little support from you or your grandfather, from what I understand. He's trying to stop a war all by himself. *All by himself, damn it!*"

Tiffany seemed dazed by Meiling's outburst. She gazed around the courtyard, at the families, the children, the old people.

"I'm not inclined to shower attention and assistance on Philip at the moment."

How could she be so ignorant? Meiling thought.

"Miss Hayes. Philip Dawson is your best friend in the world. Still."

"What? That's ridiculous."

Meiling shook her head contemptuously. "Whatever. I've got to go. Goodbye." She stalked to the temple entrance, brushed through the people pouring in, and disappeared onto the sidewalk.

Tiffany Hayes slumped against the railing. The encounter had drained her of what little strength she had. She dragged herself over to the benches against the courtyard wall, sat between two old women, and watched the people flowing past her, into the inner courtyard. There were a lot of children, she noticed. Laughing and joking. Though their parents were silent and grim.

Ma Tsu

Chapter Forty Three

Tien Gong Temple, East Coast

The helicopter blades whumped through the air on the lower terrace as the three men hurried away. Zhu and Philip took the stairs to the upper terrace two at a time, eager to begin. Sung Lee lagged behind, a bitter taste in his mouth about the impending session, and dreading the questions he had to ask Dawson before they began. He spat onto the shrubs edging the terrace and hurried up the stairs until he was at Dawson's side.

"I believe you said you had a grandfather who spent time in China, Mr. Dawson?" He tried to say it casually, even though his pulse quickened as he spoke the words.

"A long time ago, sir," Dawson said with a surprised glance.

"Did he ever tell you much?" Lee said, trying hard to keep his face impassive. "Where he was, what he was doing here?"

"Not really. For some reason he didn't talk much about it. He was a missionary. He worked at an orphanage, I do know that. Just before the second world war."

The ocean spread before them, more green than blue today, as they turned onto the upper terrace. The sky was shot with white exhaust plumes of jet fighters streaking by high above. A table laden with food fronted the ledge, as before.

"Ah," Lee commented. "Where was the orphanage?"

"Just outside Shanghai. South, I believe I remember my grandfather saying."

Lee stopped, although his heart raced. Yes, he thought. We have important other business today. But by all the gods—

225

"Gentlemen. Let's get right to business, shall we?" Dawson said, motioning at the small table inside the temple entrance. "Tom, bring some of those snacks to the inner table."

Lee shuffled into the dim interior, still dazed. For some reason Dawson insisted on the chair closest to the altars, and gestured for Lee to sit in the chair facing away from the terrace, toward the temple's interior. Lee couldn't tear his eyes from Dawson as he sat. My blood is in his veins, he thought. He is part me.

Dawson poured tea for all, filling the cups higher than was proper. Dishes appeared on the table. No one touched the food, or the tea, which steamed in the three cups.

"So," Dawson began, after a deep breath. "The President warned your country last night, Mr. Zhu, against precipitous action tomorrow, your deadline. Our two carrier groups arrived in the Straits yesterday. On the helicopter ride here, it looked like every jet fighter in Mr. Lee's Air Force was in the air. And doubtless your twelve hundred missiles in Fujian are all loaded and primed, Mr. Zhu."

With an effort Lee focused. Yes. All that was true. War loomed, big and ugly and seemingly inevitable.

"Yesterday I put a proposal on the table," continued Philip. "What reaction have you folks gotten to that proposal?"

The bad taste returned to Lee's mouth. He leaned aside to spit, but remembered where he was. His rough hands closed around the teacup, and he took a long sip. The tea was bitter, but bracing. Honest. Like his words would be.

A long pause. Dawson was fidgeting. Finally Zhu cleared his throat. He lounged comfortably in his chair, as always, but his posture seemed tense. Certainly his eyes were different, darting from one to the other of them.

"Many details remain to be worked out, of course," Zhu began. "The subjects we began to discuss early in the negotiations would have to be taken up again, and concluded."

More darting of his eyes, from Philip to Lee. "But the government of the People's Republic of China has authorized me to say that Mr. Dawson's proposal of yesterday, regarding the title of the union and the disposition of the armed forces of Taiwan, is acceptable to us."

Dawson's hand hit the table, once. He let out a triumphant snort. His eyes joined Zhu's looking at Lee across the table.

Lee steeled himself. It is just another hard thing in life, he reminded himself. A quick glance at Ma Tsu over Dawson's shoulder, somber and steady on her altar. *Help me, Ma Tsu. Help me strike the right balance.*

"I have contacted several dozen of Taiwan's leaders. In government, military, and industry," Lee began. "Mr. Dawson's proposal for the title of the union is acceptable to most elements. Provided that we can abbreviate it to 'The Taiwan Maritime State' on our correspondence and our flag. It would be the short, every-day title."

"It would not be construed as negating or replacing the full title? You would officially be The Maritime State of Taiwan in the People's Republic of China?" Zhu said.

Lee nodded.

"I will have to check that with my people," Zhu said.

"It seems not to be a large point, to me," offered Dawson.

"There is more," Lee said. He avoided Zhu's eyes. "Taiwan can agree to the main points of Mr. Dawson's proposal for our armed forces," he said, speaking very slowly. It had to be just right. Another glance to Ma Tsu.

"We keep our Army units. We transfer the bulk of our Air Force, all the F-16s, and all our anti-aircraft and anti-missile missiles, to the command structure of the People's Republic. But—" He finally raised his eyes to Zhu's, which were narrow and suspicious. "But our Navy must remain in our control. We must keep our 60 Mirage jet fighters and our 21 Super Cobra attack helicopters, also. And we must receive full compensation for the material that we lose—the $5 billion we paid for the F-16s, the $885 million we paid for the Stinger ground-to-air missiles, and the $656 million we paid for the antisubmarine missiles, the long range radar, and the electronic pods enhancing the F-16s. A total of $6.54 billion U.S. dollars."

A shocked silence gripped the table. Dawson's eyes blinked nonstop as he absorbed it. Across the table, Zhu did not blink. He stood abruptly, sending his chair flying onto the flagstone floor with a metallic clunk that echoed through the temple.

"You have chosen your fate, Lee," he hissed, his contorted face thrust close to Lee's. He wheeled about and made for the terrace.

As Lee watched Zhu's receding back, he heard a jet fighter roar by outside, and his mind instantly flooded with his oldest memory, of the ground shaking as bombs exploded, the sweetish smell of burning flesh, the high wailing of mothers being dragged from their children too large to carry, too small to keep up. He was four years old and fleeing the Japanese. The temple began to swim before his eyes, and he broke out in a cold sweat at the old wailing of the mothers.

"Mr. Zhu, Mr. Zhu!" Dawson grabbed onto Zhu's arm, and was dragged halfway to the terrace. "Please, sir. Do not leave just yet. Hear me out, sir."

Zhu made to shrug Dawson's hand off his arm, but hesitated.

"Please, sir. Let me ask a few questions of Mr. Lee. Let me clarify what he said, what he wants," Dawson implored, tugging Zhu back toward the table.

Without removing his hand from Zhu's arm, Dawson circled behind him and picked up the fallen chair.

"Please. Have a seat."

Zhu reluctantly returned to the table and sat, very stiffly now, glowering at Lee. "So, Mr. Lee," began Dawson. He noticed Lee's empty cup, and poured more tea into it, again filling it higher than was proper. "You have accepted a large chunk of what I proposed, yesterday. The name of the union. Loss of most of your Air Force and missiles. That is a big step, I realize." Dawson glanced at Zhu, nodding his head, asking for agreement.

Zhu sat still and silent.

"But tell us why do you feel you can't relinquish your Navy?" Dawson finished.

Lee exhaled, and shook his head to dislodge the wailing of the mothers. "Understand—this is not me. Mr. Zhu can work with one man. I have to work with dozens of men. Politicians, soldiers, businessmen."

Zhu refused to soften his own glowering face.

"The Air Force and Navy generals are the most difficult, of course," Lee continued. "You are asking them to terminate their careers. General Zhao of the Air Force was willing to compromise. So long as we leave him a semblance of an Air Force—the 60 French Mirage fighters—he can live with it. So long also as his sister's business on the mainland flourishes, as we discussed. But Admiral Reng—he has so far refused to even contemplate the loss of anything. He says the ships are our indispensable line of defense against betrayal."

"And this—this compensation demand?" asked Philip.

"Yes. The military believes that if we are losing weapons and systems that we paid dearly for, we should be recompensed for that loss. Many others agree. I agree."

"Six and a half billion U.S. dollars!" Zhu muttered, shaking his head. But he did lean back in his chair, and cross his legs. Ready to listen, evidently.

"OK. OK," Dawson said. "We knew this wasn't going to be easy. The Air Force general has indicated he will accept what is really a small remnant of his present forces, losing all the rest. Let's make the same deal for the Admiral. Not insist on his losing every bit of his Navy. Let's give him—what, Mr. Zhu? Give him those three Knox-class frigates he got from Clinton in '98? They're probably very comfortable, and in fact rather old and outdated. But you will get, Mr. Zhu, the arsenal that really matters. All the other surface vessels, including the Kidd-class destroyers from the second Bush. The diesel submarines. The antisubmarine missiles and launchers. The dozen P-3 Orion submarine hunters. That really would satisfy what in fact are your fears, your desires, would it not, Mr. Zhu?"

Zhu remained impassive. But he didn't contradict the assertion.

Dawson pressed on. "And surely, the 21 Super Cobra attack helicopters aren't going to threaten the mainland, are they?"

"They are very heavily armed, including their own system missiles, with a large range," Zhu said, biting off the words.

"Yes, yes. But really—they do not threaten the mainland, do they?" said Dawson. "Taiwan is giving up all its missiles and all 150 of its F-16s. Right?"

"We will not pay six and a half billion U.S. dollars in compensation," Zhu spit out, angrily. "It will not happen."

"It would now be ten and a half billion dollars," Lee said quietly, staring into his tea. "We paid four billion for the Kidd-class destroyers, the submarines, the P-3s which Mr. Dawson proposes we also give up."

Dawson grabbed a crab cake and paced around the table in silence. He took his seat again, and gulped some tea.

"Mr. Lee. When you buy a car, its worth plummets by at least 50 percent when you drive it off the lot. Now, F-16s are not Chevrolets. But the principle is the same. Full purchase value for that hardware seems excessive. If they cost—what did you say, new?"

"Ten and a half billion U.S. dollars," Lee said. He took a crab cake also, and quickly grabbed the teapot that Dawson was reaching for. He poured a proper amount of tea into his cup.

"Ten and a half billion, then. To me it seems very reasonable to ask for something between a half and a quarter of their purchase price. Let's call it a third. Thirty three percent." Dawson whipped out a notebook and a pen, and did the math. He turned to Zhu. "A compensation of three and half billion dollars to Taiwan, Mr. Zhu. Not a lot of money, for a country the size of the People's Republic."

Zhu snorted and shook his head. But he reached for his teacup, and drained the cold tea in one swallow. Lee refilled his cup.

"So here's what seems fair to me, gentlemen," Dawson said, his hands spread on the table, palm down. "I propose that Taiwan keeps its Army, including the twenty one Super Cobra helicopters. But Taiwan gives up virtually all its Air Force and missile defenses, retaining only the symbolic 60 Mirage jets from France. They give up virtually all their Navy, retaining only a symbolic three Knox-class frigates. They receive a partial compensation for what they are transferring to the People's Republic. Three and a half billion dollars, U.S. Certainly both sides can live with this, to achieve reunification and peace."

Dawson rotated his palms upward, and stretched them to Lee and Zhu. "That seems to be a fair compromise to me. Mr. Zhu? Mr. Lee? Is this preferable to war? Is it preferable to destruction of Taiwan, to American nuclear weapons unleashed on the Chinese mainland?"

In the silence Dawson reached his outstretched arms to Lee and Zhu. "What do you say, gentlemen?" he pressed.

With a heavy sigh, Zhu pulled his cufflinked sleeve away from his suit cuff. "Perhaps. There is some chance that it may be acceptable."

Lee grunted. "The same for me."

"No!" Dawson shouted, hitting the table with his palm, hard, the sharp sound echoing around the temple.

Lee and Zhu jumped, as the tea sloshed in the cups.

"Perhaps, perhaps—perhaps is not good enough, gentlemen," Dawson said angrily. "We are trying to prevent a war, Mr. Lee, Mr. Zhu. The deadline is tomorrow. Ten o'clock tomorrow morning! It's down to the three of us, gentlemen. The three of us, here, now. Perhaps is not good enough, not close to good enough!" Dawson's angry eyes bored into Lee and Zhu.

The eyes of a barbarian, Lee thought. Their color is ambiguous, shifting. But my eyes share the blood in those eyes, through my father. Incredible. Those eyes and what they demand cannot be rejected out of hand.

"Gentlemen, we have to decide to *make* this work," Dawson continued, jabbing his index finger against the table as he spoke. "We are not passively relaying decisions made by others. We must commit *ourselves* to doing *whatever* it takes to make our countries accept this. This is it, gentlemen. A fair compromise that will avoid the destruction of war tomorrow. I want you to agree to make this happen, so that I can convene the rest of our teams from a week ago, have them work through the night to hammer out their respective agreements in their areas, and have it all written out for you and me to sign at ten o'clock tomorrow morning at a public ceremony at the Taiwan National University soccer stadium. To *sign* at ten o'clock tomorrow."

Dawson leaned forward on the table, swinging his face from Lee to Zhu, nearly nose to nose with each in turn, his barbarian eyes allowing no escape, no equivocation.

"Tell me that this is how it will work, how we each will *make* it work, damn it."

Silence gripped the temple. Outside, cicadas buzzed, security guards shifted machine guns from shoulder to shoulder, waves washed ashore. A jet screamed down the coastline. But inside the temple, not a sound broke the silence. Dawson glared at Lee, then at Zhu, then back at Lee. The silence lengthened, from one minute, to two. Then to three.

"I am with you, Mr. Dawson," Zhu finally said, in a hoarse voice. "It may cost me dearly, but I believe I can make it work."

Their hard, desperate eyes turned to Lee. To avoid their intense gaze, Lee stared over Dawson's shoulder into the depths of the temple. He found Ma Tsu, her black face barely visible in the dim light. She was staring back at him. Her orange robe glimmered. The pearls on her forehead glowed dully. Lee glanced at Philip's face, then up to Ma Tsu's. It was the photograph of his mother and his father, from a thousand miles and eighty years away. The same two faces, peering at him.

Ma Tsu, what are you telling me? Lee wailed inside. His face was impassive, but inside his head a cacophony of sounds burst. The waves pushing the old rowboat into the cove in Fuzhou harbor, the rowboat that Ma Tsu had given him to begin his drive to prosperity. The cackling laughter of the old woman in Jinhua, telling him that his father was "from nowhere near here." The waves beating against his cliff last night as he sat in the moonlight, wrestling with the realization that the father he had found was a father he didn't want to find.

Lee wasn't sure he could make Philip's modified proposal fly. In fact, it seemed unlikely that Admiral Reng would ever agree to it, and that would undermine the support of the hawkish newspaper publisher Juli, and both would make it difficult for the DPP to convince the left wing of their party to tolerate it. For Lee to agree to push for this new proposal would mean staking his whole reputation and fortune on the outcome, with defeat somewhere between likely and probable.

Ma Tsu's face bore into his eyes. The old rowboat she had brought to him in the cove off Fuzhou harbor washed again into his mind. All the lucky breaks he had gotten, building his empire. His competitors' poor decisions. All the times he had guessed right, about cargoes, about materials suddenly precious to the world. Ma Tsu pulled the admission from him. *Yes! My fortune, my reputation, my family come from you, Ma Tsu. Are you calling the debt in, today?* No sign could be stronger than the grandson of my father making the demand. No sign stronger than you peering over his very shoulder, reminding me of what I owe you.

Lee shut his eyes. Everything he had worked for the past eighty years was being put in jeopardy. His family would suffer along with him if he staked his reputation, his fortune on this proposal, and it failed. Did he owe Ma Tsu that much? Did he owe this strange, new, unsettling father and nephew that much? He tried to twist away from the choice, from Ma Tsu's black face, from the sound of the waves washing the old rowboat ashore, from the wailing of the mothers leaving their children behind.

He found himself opening his mouth, and heard himself speaking.

"Yes. I will do it."

The noises instantly vanished inside his head. There was a clear, beautiful silence. There was Philip Dawson's joyous face, beaming below Ma Tsu's somber black face above the orange robes.

Philip grabbed him by the arm, and held Zhu's arm in his other hand. His barbarian eyes were misting over. He doesn't realize how much is at stake, Lee thought. He doesn't realize how unlikely it is that I can pull it off.

"Jiao-rung," Lee yelled, holding out his left hand. "Get me Miss Ling."

Jiao-rung put the submachine gun on his shoulder, and hurried over, fiddling with a cell phone. He slapped the phone in Lee's hand.

"Miss Ling. Call our negotiating team, and send them to the Sun Yat-sen Memorial, immediately. Have Jing-lu contact me for instructions when he gets there. Meanwhile, put me in contact with—let me think. The easiest ones first, building up to the hard ones. President Ma, the Kuomintang party head, General Jiao, in that order. Then the DPP chief, the head of Taiwan plastics, and General Woo. Have them all contacted, and when I'm through with one, put the next on directly. When I'm through with them all, then publisher Juli. Admiral Reng, last."

He kept the phone to his ear, and spoke to Philip and Zhu as he waited for the Taiwanese president to come on the line. "I'll stay here. This has to be done immediately, and the helicopter's noise will not permit it if I ride back with you. Send the pilot back here when you arrive at Sungshan." His eyes flicked to Jiao-rung, who nodded.

"You can get your own negotiating teams to the Sun Yat-sen Memorial. Immediately?" he asked, his eye moving from Philip to Zhu. "You can get things going, there?"

"Can do," Dawson said crisply. Dawson glanced at Zhu, who replied by taking his own cell phone out of his pocket.

"Tom," Philip called, extending his hand for a cell phone as he had seen Lee do it. "Get me Dirk and Baden at the AIT."

Ma Tsu, somber, poised, unblinking, gazed at the three men and their aides talking so urgently into their plastic and metal devices at the front of her temple. Beyond them, rays from the sun illuminated the stone courtyard. A myriad of insects buzzed, their droning calls bringing lizards and birds to prey. Palm trees made sugars in the bright sunshine, the green in their leaves shuttling electrons from protein to protein. Waves washed up onto the shore, grinding stones into sand. Everything was as it should be in the cosmos.

bent

Chapter Forty Four

Jimmy Chan's gold convertible pulled up to Sung Lee's mansion just as Meiling and Philip were getting out of their car. Only Meiling caught how Jimmy's exuberant cheerfulness was forced, his movements subtly exaggerated. He plans to kill someone tonight, she thought. This is how he motivates himself to do it.

Jimmy was boisterous even with Jiao-rung as he opened the mansion's door for them, clapping a hand upon the big man's shoulders while he gripped his hand in a handshake.

"Good evening, Philip, Meiling. And Jimmy—good to see you again," said Sung Lee, advancing up the hallway from the dining room in back.

Jimmy again shook hands effusively and draped an arm around Sung Lee in the hallway. As they passed through the doorway into the dining room, a loud ring erupted from the ceiling.

Jimmy Chan stopped abruptly.

"How ingenious! A metal detector!" He whirled around and reached into his pocket. Jiao-rung was suddenly at his side, his fingers on Jimmy's hand as it emerged from his pocket.

Meiling caught her breath as she saw a metallic glint.

"My keys!" Jimmy said with a grin, his teeth gleaming white. "I carry a full set of keys for each of my cars, everywhere." He handed the keys to Jiao-rung, who dropped them, and leaned down slowly to retrieve them from the carpeted floor.

Jimmy backed up, then passed through the doorframe again.

Not a sound.

The metal detector did not protest as Sung Lee, Philip and Meiling joined

Jimmy in the dining room, where light flooded in along the wall of windows. Meiling noticed the large ebony table was gone.

"Jiao-rung and I moved the table out to the terrace," Sung Lee said, noticing Meiling's inquisitive look. "This may be the last sunny day before the rains resume, after all. It will be pleasant to eat out there."

The party strolled onto the terrace, and Old Jao brought drinks for all, Macallan's with a single cube of ice. A lacquer tray of sushi and crab cakes sat on the rock ledge, the pinks and golds of the food bright against the red of the tray, and the gray rock below that. The ebony table was set formally perpendicular to the ledge, a white linen cloth covering it and dark blue porcelain plates at each setting, along with silver and wine glasses that caught the sunlight and scattered it along the table.

Meiling sipped her Scotch in silence, as Jimmy Chan dominated the conversation, bouncing from topic to topic. Philip ate crab cakes, avoiding the sushi.

Soon, Old Jao carried a dark hardwood carving block onto the patio, and set it down in the middle of the table. A roasted duck sat on the block, its golden skin glinting in the waning rays of the sun.

"Ah, our main course," Sung Lee declared with relief. "Let's be seated."

"I'll sit next to you, Jimmy," Meiling said to the beaming Chan. Jimmy gallantly helped her to her chair, across the table from Philip and Sung Lee.

"Where's Jiao-rung, to carve the duck?" Sung Lee asked Old Jao, who was hovering behind his chair.

"Jiao-rung isn't feeling well," the old woman said. "He asked me to carve."

Sung Lee grunted, then moved his chair aside to permit her to get to the large block. She picked up the heavy cleaver beside the golden fowl. Everyone's eyes watched as the cleaver rose and fell with jarring thuds. She was a skilled and energetic carver, and soon the duck was reduced to the customary pieces, which were arranged in neat rows along the cutting block. She added some sprigs of garnish from a bowl and stepped back.

"Thank you, Lao Jao. That will be all," Sung Lee said. "May I serve you, Jimmy?" He picked up the large fork beside the carving block and reached out his hand for Jimmy's plate.

Jimmy, who had been watching the old lady disappear into the dining room doors, turned to Sung Lee with a strange smile on his face.

"Before we begin, Mr. Lee, I have a surprise for everyone, if I may?"

Before anyone could say anything, Jimmy rose from the table and stepped a few paces over to the ledge. He looked over the ledge, down the face of the cliff, moved down another step, then leaned far out and reached down with a grunt. He pulled up a large burlap bag, set it on the ledge, and slipped his hand into the bag.

"What the—?" said Philip, standing up.

Before anyone could move, they found themselves staring into the black metal of a long silencer extending from a pistol in Jimmy Chan's hand.

"No one moves or says a thing," Chan said, the broad smile still on his face. He pulled a length of rope and a climbing harness out of the bag and set them on the ledge. Then he strolled over to the table and sat on its edge, crossing his legs elegantly and keeping the pistol trained somewhere just between Sung Lee and Philip.

Sung Lee had half risen from his chair. As he slowly sat again, his eyes flickered toward the doors to the dining room.

"No, Mr. Lee, I'm afraid you'll be getting no help from your man. Poor Jiao-rung is quite dead by now. I injected a moderate dose of cobra venom into his trapezoid muscle when I entered, a rather simple palm-held syringe, very thin needle, the tiniest of pricking sensations."

Sung Lee rose, his face glaring. "I'll see you dead for that," he said in a menacing voice.

Jimmy Chan laughed. "Oh, I'm afraid not," he said gaily. "Your internal security man is gone. The doddering old woman won't be back for some time. And even though young Mr. Dawson here is my target, I'm quite afraid that I'm going to have to kill you and my dear friend Meiling also. I need time to rappel down the cliff and make my escape in the motorized dinghy I left moored to the cliff face."

Meiling was nearly numb with shock, her hands tingling on the tabletop. Somehow she made her lips move. "So you do—kill people, for money," she said.

His eyes darted to her, then back to Philip and Sung Lee. "Oh yes, my dear. Although more for fun than for money. I thought you might have suspected, and that it might have been behind the invitation to this splendid dinner party. That's why I scaled Mr. Lee's cliff before dawn and planted my weapon—and my escape gear—out of sight but within reach. And everything is working so splendidly, isn't it? Jiao-rung out of the way, you three about to join him, and I'll putter away in my dinghy to the nearby mooring, drive straight to Chiang Kai Shek International, and be on my way in—" He checked his watch, his eyes returning to Philip. "Be on my way to Buenos Aires in a little over an hour."

He turned his smile onto Meiling just as her hands, still tingling, were inching toward the large fork sitting beside the slices of duck.

"Keep your hands under the table, my dear," he said tightly. "That goes for you gentlemen, too. Hands below the table, if you want to earn another minute of life."

Meiling's hand froze, and went to her lap. She glared at Jimmy, who sat on the edge of the table on the end next to the ledge, his pistol leveled at Philip and Sung Lee, his other hand resting against his thigh. He looked like a caricature from an early James Bond movie, perched elegantly in his tuxedo and black tie on the end of the table against the backdrop of the rock ledge and, beyond that, the sea.

Meiling clutched the linen table cloth in her lap in her helpless anger. She forced her hands to drop the bunch of linen she had gathered. What could she do?

"I'm your target," Philip said, his eyes hard on Chan. "There's no need to kill Meiling or Sung Lee. Tie them up or something to give you time for your escape. But let them live."

Jimmy glared back at Philip, his gaiety evaporating. "Don't tell me how to do my job, caucasian," he hissed. "I'm very good at what I do. And part of it is not leaving any loose ends."

He glanced over at Meiling, still serious, all pretense dropped. "Although I do regret Meiling getting caught up in this. I'd prefer not to involve her. I don't mind killing her dear friends, her pitiful lovers, but I'd like to let her live if I could. It's just that I can't."

Meiling's hands were again clutching at the table cloth in her lap. Something Jimmy said penetrated the shock, stabbed past the dread feeling that she would be dead soon. What had he said?

"At least tell me who hired you to kill me," Philip said.

Jimmy Chan leaned forward toward him. "You're just putting off your own death, barbarian," he said angrily. "I'm not stupid. I'm quite smart, in fact. I've killed well over a dozen men, most of them in ways that appeared accidental. I'm an expert in biological poisons—a much better killer than you are a negotiator."

He leaned back. "And I don't ever reveal my clients. It's a rule, in this business."

"Yes, but I'll be dead soon enough. What harm is there?"

Jimmy Chan laughed, throwing back his head, and wobbled a bit on the edge of the table.

Meiling's mind was a chaotic churning. Something Jimmy had said was still reverberating, demanding to be dwelt on. Had he said something about her lovers? What did that mean? And then something else was demanding attention. The way Jimmy had wobbled a bit on the edge of the table as he had laughed. It wanted to be considered. It reminded her of something. What was it? She sat there, her mind reeling, trying to concentrate, her hands wringing the overflow linen under the table.

Jimmy Chan's laughter stopped. "I love to see you beg, Mr. Dawson. You've begged so well, I'll tell you. You are one of the few victims that I've had two clients engage me to kill. Congratulations."

He bowed his head in mock salute.

"One from Taiwan, a Chinese, and one from your country." His dark eyes flickered from Philip to Sung Lee. "Mr. Lee, you should be able to guess the person from here."

Sung Lee refused to guess.

"Come now. I'll let you and Mr. Dawson and Meiling live a minute longer if you guess, Mr. Lee," said Chan, gay again. He glanced from Lee to Philip, sitting side by side, both staring hard and angry at him, both in dark tuxedoes that nearly gleamed against the white of the linen table cloth.

"My, you two look a lot like each other!" Chan commented. "Have you ever noticed that, Meiling? How strange. But come now—guess or die, Mr. Lee."

"All right," said Lee. "I would guess either Admiral Reng or the publisher Juli."

"Wonderful!" crowed Chan. "It's the publisher, of course. Meiling should have guessed that. Her publisher assigned her to pursue Mr. Dawson, so that she could lead me to him. I thought of having Ping reconnect me to Meiling. And didn't it all work well!"

Beaming, he lifted a glass and took a sip of wine. "I'm afraid I don't know the name of your countryman, Mr. Dawson. Although I've done work for him before. Before, he was very high in the CIA. Several months ago, though, he moved to the White House. Some sort of a high advisor, I would guess."

"Ravenhurst," Philip breathed.

At that moment, it dawned on Meiling clearly and completely. A magic show she had seen at the Lai Lai Hilton two years ago. A table, set fancy like this one, with a linen cloth covering the table. She glanced down at her hands. Her hands had known already, had been trying to tell her. She wrapped another length of the linen cloth around her left hand, and braced her right hand against her left wrist. She glanced up at Jimmy Chan, saw him sitting on the edge of the table still. She had to act before he got up.

"And now, caucasian, it's time for me to blow your brains out," Chan was saying, his voice thick as he glared at Philip. He shifted position on the edge of the table, ready to step down to the floor.

"Now, Philip!" shouted Meiling as she sprang up, dragging the table cloth hard toward her, jerking it from under the sitting Jimmy Chan with as much strength and speed as her arms and legs could muster.

A small pop erupted from the gun in Chan's hand as he toppled back against the ledge, his arms flying up. Meiling felt a rush of air as the bullet passed over her. Philip sprang over the table and grappled with Chan atop the ledge. Philip was on top, and slammed Chan's gun hand against the sea edge of the ledge. Chan was bellowing with pain. The gun slipped from his bloody hand and clattered down the cliff face.

As he lost the gun, Chan twisted around and pulled Philip toward the ledge, then leveraged himself on top of Philip with a hoarse scream. He jammed his bloody fist into Philip's throat, then grabbed Philip's head in both hands and slammed it against the ledge.

Meiling disentangled herself from the table cloth and stumbled over her chair, lunging for the ledge. Sung Lee was almost there also, reaching out to grab Chan by the shoulders, when Philip's knee shot up and caught Chan in the stomach, pushing upward with all the force Philip could apply. Chan's body flew up and toward the sea, disappearing over the ledge.

Chan caught his good hand on the edge of the ledge, and joined the bloody one there quickly, the fingers in a good cling grip. He was hanging on the sea side of the ledge, dangling down the cliff. As Meiling helped Philip off the ledge, Chan tried to hoist himself up, but Philip threw a forearm against his face as it appeared, and knocked him down.

"If you come up again, I'll knock you off the damn ledge altogether," growled Philip, rubbing the back of his head, the hand smearing with blood.

"It doesn't matter," came Sung Lee's voice beside Philip and Meiling, as all three stared down at Jimmy Chan hanging on the edge of the cliff. "He has indeed killed Jiao-rung. For that, he'll die. Here. Tonight."

Meiling saw the old housekeeper over Lee's shoulder, sobbing in the doorway.

Jimmy was no longer laughing. His eyes were wild as he glanced below him, at the hundred foot drop to the sea. The waves dashed against rocks, his yellow dinghy bobbing twenty feet to the side.

"Low tide, Jimmy," said Philip in a quiet voice. "Lots of rock exposed down there. Ever had a friend drop a hundred feet onto rock, Jimmy?"

Sung Lee stepped up to the ledge and laid a hand on Jimmy's fingers gripping the ledge.

"Sir. Are you sure you want to do this?" said Philip. "He's confessed, in front of Meiling and me. Could we rely on the courts?"

Sung Lee didn't take his eyes off Chan's wild face looking up from the cliff face. "Not for a second would I trust our legal system, Mr. Dawson. I feel completely right about this."

Lee braced himself to shove Chan's fingers off the ledge. Meiling put her hand on Lee's.

"One moment. I have a question for Jimmy." She peered over the ledge. Jimmy's eyes were bulging up at her.

"What did you mean, Jimmy, when you said you didn't mind killing my friends, my lovers? What do you know or care about any of my lovers, Jimmy?"

The bulging eyes jerked up with a gleam of hope in them suddenly. "You are my duckling, Meiling. The only woman I've ever cared for. I couldn't share you with the others. I couldn't."

"Jimmy!" Meiling screamed, her face twisted with pain, her hair blowing straight back in the sea breeze rushing up the cliff. She leaned down at him. "You didn't kill Tom Ling! Tell me you didn't!" she screamed, her eyes ablaze.

"But I did!" Jimmy yelled back at her, tears coming to his eyes. "He didn't deserve you, Meiling. He was my first kill, and it was clumsy, but I did it."

"And Rou-jing?" she whispered, dread in her voice.

"Yes, your weak artist friend also. But with him, one of my poisons. Very subtle. Very subtle, Meiling."

She stared down at him, aghast. Her short hair fluttered in the breeze. Her arm muscles rippled with the effort of leaning over the wall. She felt Philip's hand on her hip, steadying her.

Meiling slowly straightened up. She stared past Jimmy's fingertips on the ledge, at the sea, waves glinting white against the dark blue.

Tears streamed down her face. "He's been killing my men," she said, in a choked voice. "Killing Tom. Killing Rou-jing. Trying to kill you, Philip."

She leaned back over the ledge, and took two deep breaths. When she finally spoke, her voice was soft, but rich, full. Menacing.

"You're twisted, Jimmy. Poor Jimmy. You're sick and evil and twisted. And you are one of my oldest friends."

Chan couldn't bear to look up at her, and dropped his face to the cliffside. His arms began to tremble, and he changed his grip, from the cling to the open grip, fingers extended onto the top of the ledge.

Meiling stared past Jimmy again, at the sea below, the waves dashing up against the rocks showing above the surface. The waves beating against the cliff face seemed hungry to her, seemed to be wanting something.

Meiling understood, as clearly as if the goddess had spoken the words in her ear. "Jimmy. This is your lucky day. You're going to be made whole, Jimmy. I am going to give you to Ma Tsu, Jimmy. She will cleanse you. It may take her five hundred years, but she will wash all the darkness out of you, Jimmy, and make you balanced. Whole."

Sung Lee stepped up to the ledge beside Meiling.

"Perfect," he said. "It will be our gift to Ma Tsu, Meiling. We'll give him to her, to punish him and to restore him to balance."

Sung Lee put his hand against the fingers gripping the ledge.

"No!" Meiling said, a harsh strength to her voice that made Sung Lee stop. "Don't touch him. He's unclean. And he's hurt me more than you. He has been my curse. It is mine, to give him to Ma Tsu."

Meiling glanced around. She picked up the cleaver beside the butchered duck.

"Are you sure?" Philip moved close to her, and put his hand on her hip again.

Her face was set, as though made of stone. She raised the cleaver, and brought it down hard on one set of fingers. The blade cut into the stone with a clang.

"Duckling!" Jimmy yelled as the stump of hand fell away from the ledge. "My duckling! You're the only women I ever—"

Meiling raised her arm and brought the cleaver down on the fingers of the other hand, hard again, with another clang of steel against stone.

Jimmy Chan dropped down the cliff, screaming.

They all watched him bounce off the cliff face halfway down, then crash into the rocks showing above the surface of the water. His body lay completely still for a second. It washed up onto the rock limply as the first wave hit it. The second wave knocked the body off the rock into the surrounding water, where it slowly sank out of sight.

Six cut fingers sat on the ledge. Meiling put the edge of the cleaver against the ledge and flicked them off, into the sea below. She stared at the bloody cleaver for a moment, then pitched it into the sea also.

"Oh, Philip. I'm not cursed any more." She burst into tears, and collapsed into his open arms, sobbing. Philip held her close. Below them, waves crashed against the cliff face, and Jimmy Chan's fingerless body was being pulled out to sea by a riptide.

search

Chapter Forty Five

Sung Lee dropped ice into his Scotch at the bar and swirled the drink in his hand. Meiling slumped on the study's sofa, drained, her face white. Dawson was pacing about the room, still agitated after his fight with Chan. And the shock of Chan's death. The first half dozen people to die in front of you did rattle you, Lee supposed. He had trouble remembering back that far.

His own nerves seemed stretched, taut. Hsiao Pang had said he wasn't capable of feeling nervous. Was that what this was? Watching Jimmy Chan fall to the rocks had been easy. Calling Jiao-rung's family had been hard. His external security men and Dawson's guard—Tom, was it?—were taking Jiao-rung's body to his family, then disposing of Chan's convertible.

No, he wasn't nervous about death, his own or anyone's, any more. He was nervous about life. About confronting the awful truth he had stumbled upon last night. Could he be wrong? His eyes followed Dawson about the room. He took a large swallow of Scotch.

"Looks strange, without the jade here," Dawson said. He was just talking to talk, Lee judged, too keyed up to tolerate silence. Unlike Meiling Bei, small and still on the sofa.

"Yes. Even before this evening, this house has been feeling less and less comfortable to me."

"I called Baden and Dirk while you were contacting Jiao-rung's family. They say that things are going good between all three teams. Slow but steady. How are you doing with the military questions, sir?"

Lee swirled his drink again, and took another large sip. "Before Jimmy Chan arrived, things looked bleak. The small people have been no problem. I convinced them, just on my own acceptance of the proposal. But many of the large people are stalling, waiting to see if I can persuade two of the most powerful obstacles. And the two obstacles were not budging."

He smiled a small, malicious smile, and brought his glass to his mouth, finishing off the drink. "Until tonight. One of the obstacles was the publisher Juli. Based on what Jimmy Chan told us, I believe I will be able to convince him to see the merit in the proposals."

Meiling stirred on the sofa, the mention of her publisher bringing an angry light to her hollow eyes.

"Based on Juli coming around, some of those presently wavering will also come around. But there is still the second obstacle. Admiral Reng. I have not yet found a way to persuade him. But I will keep trying."

Tom appeared in the doorway, inclined his head slightly to Philip, then left.

"Well," began Philip, holding his hand out to Meiling on the sofa. "Tom is back, Mr. Lee. We'll be off."

Sung Lee held his arm out, to forestall Philip's movement.

"Just a moment, Mr. Dawson. Philip. I—I have something more to say, to say to you."

"Sir?"

Sung Lee willed himself not to pour another Scotch. He had to have a clear head for this. He flirted with not saying any more. But no. *I have searched for this my whole life,* he thought. Doubts assailed him suddenly. He wasn't used to doubts. He reached into his pocket and pulled out the photograph that Little Jade had given him.

"Would you please look at this, Mr. Dawson. Tell me if you recognize the man."

Philip cast a puzzled glance at Meiling. He stepped slowly up to Lee, wary, and took the photograph.

"Why—sure." He glanced into Lee's face. "But how in the world did you get a photo of my grandfather, when he was a young man in China? And who's the girl?"

Lee put a hand against the bar to steady himself. His face, usually so hard and impassive, was making small movements, as if about to reconfigure itself.

Meiling appeared beside the two men. She glanced at the photo, then quickly up to Lee. "That's your—your mother, beside the man, isn't it, Mr. Lee?"

Willing his face not to break apart, Lee inclined his head.

"Philip," began Meiling, the color back to her face, her eyes alive again. "Show Mr. Lee the photo in your wallet. Of your grandfather."

Philip pulled out his wallet and flipped to the first photo.

"Show it to Mr. Lee."

Lee raised his hand, and put a large finger on the second person to the left of the young man in the photo. A girl, somber, her dark eyes looking out suspiciously. Even then, afraid of what the future might hold. Knowing that she was about to set herself against her culture, her family, the whole world as she knew it.

"That," he began. His voice cracked. He tried again. "That is my mother," he finished. His finger was trembling on the photo. Had he ever known his fingers to tremble? His voice to crack?

"Would someone please tell me what is going on here?" Philip said, looking from Meiling to Lee.

"That can't be," Meiling whispered, tears brimming in her eyes. "It can't be—but it is. Oh, Ma Tsu."

"Damn it, would someone please tell me what the devil is going on here?" Dawson repeated, his voice rising.

Sung Lee looked to Meiling, imploring her to say it. She stared back, wide-eyed, and shook her head. It would have to be him, he realized. A tear trickled down his cheek. He brushed it away, brusquely, with his large, gnarled hand.

"Son—I mean, Philip. Mr. Dawson. Sit down, please," he said.

"No thank you, Mr. Lee. Whatever this is, I'll take it standing up," Dawson answered.

"It's a long story," Lee began. He glanced to Meiling for help again, and saw that none was coming. "Growing up, I never knew my father. My mother fled the Japanese army when they pushed south from Shanghai, with just me. She wouldn't even talk about my father. Ever. A week ago, I came into possession of this photo, willed to me by my mother. On the back of it—she identifies the man." He looked Dawson in the eye. "Identifies him as my father."

Dawson's face was blank. Shocked. Slowly, comprehension grew. He laughed, stopped abruptly. Looked to Meiling. Then back to Lee.

"Why, that's ridiculous," he said. "That would make you—make you my, my uncle."

Tears were streaming down Sung Lee's face. He couldn't remember ever crying, even as a boy. "Yes, it would," he said, his voice cracking. "And that would make you my nephew, Philip. And the male heir of my family." His gnarled hand brushed tears from his cheek. More promptly flowed down. "At long last, someone to honor me and my own father, when I'm gone."

In his mind, Lee clearly saw his own wooden tablet on the family altar, red dots of blood for his eyes, his heart. Next to it was a tablet for his father, and another for his father's second son, who had produced Philip. He saw hands for generations into the future, rough male hands, placing their fathers' and uncles' tablets reverently onto the altar. He smelled the incense that would burn there for centuries. He groaned, and felt eight decades of despair slough off.

Lee abruptly poured himself another scotch, and belted it down. He let the scotch steady him.

"I think I'll take another scotch, too, Mr. Lee," Philip said in a shaky voice. "And I think I'll sit down, after all." He wobbled over to the chair by the sofa and collapsed into it.

"Christ. My uncle," Philip said, taking the drink from Meiling and downing all of it. He coughed. "No wonder grandpa never talked much about China. He wasn't married when he went to China—hadn't even met my grandma. But being a missionary and all—" He looked up at Lee suddenly. "Not that it makes any difference, of course, Mr. Lee."

Lee had recomposed his face. But it seemed softer. It felt different.

"You'll have to start calling me Uncle Sung, Philip," he said, a small smile breaking over his different face. He liked the sound of it. Uncle Sung. "And yes, it was a love outside the bounds—even more so here in China, where foreign devils—I mean caucasians—were deeply distrusted, even hated, in those days."

Lee stared into the empty glass in his hand. "It must have been hard on my mother. Knowing that he would never be part of her life. Or mine." He banged the glass on the bar firmly.

"Nephew. You will accompany me to our family tomb tomorrow evening. We will put your new photo on the altar, and we will together light incense and honor my father, your grandfather. My father, by the gods! And introduce you properly to the *hun* souls of our family."

"Welcome to the traditional Chinese family, Philip," Meiling said dryly when he shot a quizzical glance at her.

"The evening is getting late," Lee continued. "I have a personal visit to pay to Meiling's employer, the publisher Juli. Then another visit to Admiral Reng. And phone calls to several dozens after that. You had best go."

"Mr. Lee. Uncle Sung," began Philip. He stopped abruptly. "That's going to be hard to get used to." He shook his head, then tried again. "Uncle Sung. The signing ceremony is set for ten tomorrow morning. Shall we try to push it back?"

"No!" Lee said decisively. "It would make The People's Republic nervous if we did that. For all I know, they have already programmed their missiles for shortly after that hour. Let us meet as scheduled. And pray that all the pieces have fallen into place by then." His face resumed its accustomed hard, brutal mien.

"Dirk and Baden report that the teams are working hard, on the routine points. I'll go straight to the Sun Yat-sen Hall and try to push things along."

Meiling offered Philip her hand, and helped him up from the sofa. They limped out of the study. Philip paused at the doorway, looked back at Lee in wonderment, then disappeared.

Lee shook his head, in wonderment like his nephew Philip at the ways of the world. He started to call for Jiao-rung to bring him his phone, then caught himself. Hsiao Pang gone, two days ago. Now Jiao-rung. He felt his throat tighten. Such losses. But no! It is the way of life. Precious gifts are taken from you. Even as others are given. He finally had a father. And beyond that, a nephew. No longer cursed to be a Hungry Ghost. He made a note to call Liu to arrange for the trip to the family altar tomorrow evening. He would buy a thousand dollars worth of flowers. Assuming that there were no missiles raining down on the island.

A grim smile. He was looking forward to his visit with Juli. And sometime between now and the morning, he had to think of something to convince Admiral Reng. He had all of twelve hours to do it. His father's *hun* souls would help him.

Chapter Forty Six

Day Nine. *Nine o'clock am*

The hazy morning light filtered through the garden beside the AIT compound. Philip sat on a bench along the side path, flowers and green grass on three sides. It was the only well-tended park in Taipei, he reflected. Grass fertilized, watered, and cut regularly. Flowers rotated, always blooming. Very American. Very un-Chinese.

His stomach was in knots. The deadline was only an hour away. The detailed agreement documents had just been wrapped up among the teams at the Sun Yat-sen Memorial, and were now being copied by AIT staff inside. It looked like Zhu was going to get final approval. Probably. Sung Lee was a different matter altogether. He hadn't made much headway overnight with Admiral Reng. And the Taiwan President and power structure had made it very clear. If General Zhao and Admiral Reng didn't both sign on, the deal couldn't fly.

Tiffany Hayes materialized in the weak light at the far end of the path. She was easy to spot, in a bright pink pants outfit, her hair glowing yellow. She took several steps toward him, tentatively, as he rose.

"Tiffany. Thanks for coming. You doing all right?"

A long pause. "I'm getting over it. It hit me hard."

"Yeah." He looked down. "I'm sorry."

She sat on the bench, looking tired. Philip sat on the other end of the bench.

"To tell you the truth, you weren't the only one wavering. That's why I flew over here. To see where we were. Because I wasn't sure, from my end either."

"Ah."

"Could it have worked out? Between us?"

"Long-term? I don't think so, Tiffany. We enjoy each other's company, and have a lot of fun together. But gosh—we're real different. In ways that are pretty important."

"Yes. You're not much into politics and scheming, are you?"

"No. Not at all. I'd honestly rather be outdoors. Climbing a rock cliff. Anything but power politics."

"Still. A couple doesn't have to have exactly the same interests."

"Maybe not. But there's more. I want to have a family. A big family. Teach my kids to rock climb. Have family the focus of my life. That—that doesn't sound like you."

A weak laugh. Then a stronger laugh. "No. And I guess that's important."

He shifted on the bench. Was it time to get to the bottom line yet? He opened his mouth.

"Philip, I saw Meiling yesterday," Tiffany said, cutting him off. "She said a strange thing. That you were the best friend I'd ever have. I thought it was ridiculous, and said so. She just left. But I thought about it. And I remembered something. When I opened my eyes, after the explosion. You were there." A tear streamed down her cheek, leaving a gully in the makeup. Another tear brimmed on her eyelid. "You really are a good friend, still, aren't you?"

Philip leaned over and patted her shoulder. "You bet."

She pulled a handkerchief from her purse and dabbed at her streaked makeup.

"I must look terrible," she said with a weak laugh. "Meiling also said you might need some help. This morning. What can I do?"

Praise the lord, thought Philip.

"You can get me through to your grandfather. Right now. He took me off the negotiations yesterday, but I went ahead anyway. He won't want to talk to me. You can change his mind, if you want."

"Will he be awake? It must be—some other time in D.C."

"It's a bit after noon there. We're less than an hour from the deadline. He'll be huddled with his advisers and the Joint Chiefs in his office, watching things. Let's go. The AIT folks have got the video teleconference hooked up. You can stop in the restroom to fix your makeup."

*　　*　　*　　*　　*

The AIT conference room was still chilly from the past night. Tom and a technician were finishing the video teleconference hookup beside the big television screen when Philip and Tiffany entered the room.

"All set?" Philip asked, checking his watch. Nine-fifteen.

"Yep," Tom said. "It's satellite feed, rather than Codec. So you're on real time. We dial the number. Tell them we're on video. They choose whether to talk, and whether to watch. Good morning, Miss Hayes."

"Tom. You know my grandfather's number? Philip says he'll be in—what, the Oval Office?"

"More likely the side office," Philip said. "Dial us up, Tom."

"You want me to stick around, Phil?"

He considered it. "Probably not. It could be touchy, at first. Stay close, outside the door, huh?"

"Got it. You're on," he said after dialing, and clicking the conference call button on the table setup. He left the room, behind the technician.

One ring.

"The White House. Ravenhurst here," from the speaker.

"John. This is Tiffany."

"Tiffany, my dear. What a surprise. How are you?"

"Fine. John, I want to talk with grandfather."

"Tiffany, the President's very busy. We're right in the middle of the China crisis. War is on the—"

"I know, dear. I'm calling about that. I'm in Taipei. It's important. Please connect me to him."

Muffled voices from the other end.

"Tiffany?"

"Grandfather. I'm here at the AIT with Philip Dawson. We need to talk with you, tell you where things are."

"Philip is no longer involved, Tiffany."

"No, grandfather. He's got important developments to report. You will want to hear them. We're set up for video teleconference over here. I understand you can connect up with us at your end. Please do."

"Tiffany—"

"Grandfather. You're the President. You need to know everything you can from this end. It's not good policy to ignore intelligence, particularly when war hangs in the balance. Please hear Philip out."

More muffled exchanges, some of it intense. Suddenly, the television screen bloomed and President Hayes filled it beside his desk, still messy, with Ravenhurst looking angry and anxious at his elbow. Several men in uniform could be seen leaving the room in the background.

"Philip. I understand you have something to say," said the President stiffly, his ruddy face solemn. Ravenhurst glared at Philip.

"Yes sir," said Philip, gripping the arm of his chair tightly. He hadn't had time to rehearse a speech. He figured he had maybe a minute before he was cut off.

"You sent me here to mediate between China and Taiwan to avoid a war.

In spite of the aircraft carriers, we were making progress in private talks when you sent instructions for me to desist. I felt that our own national self-interest would benefit from a peaceful resolution to the crisis. So I forged ahead with the secret negotiations. And I can report—"

"You admit disobeying a Presidential directive?" said Ravenhurst in his metallic voice, leaning into the screen with a tight smile on his lips.

"Yes, but—"

"And Dirk and Baden claim they never saw their messages from the President. Do you know anything about that?"

"Yes. I destroyed their messages. They didn't know our efforts had been called off."

"Philip!" whispered Tiffany, putting her hand over her mouth.

"Mr. Dawson, are you aware of the penalty for treason?" hissed Ravenhurst, his face alight with triumph.

"I felt it was important for me to give President Hayes as many options as possible this morning," said Philip evenly. "And I'd like to report on my progress."

Ravenhurst's bulging eyes filled the screen. "I don't think the President—"

"Relax, John," came the President's voice. He gently crowded Ravenhurst out of the screen. "Before we quite hang Philip from the nearest banyan tree out there, let's hear what he has to say. Tiffany's right. We should hear him out."

"Thank you, sir." He glanced at his watch. Nine-twenty. Forty minutes from the deadline.

"We have an agreement formulated, sir. The minor points are approved by all parties. Commerce, transportation, and such. The major points are close. The People's Republic of China will probably sign on. Taiwan is another story. It could fly or not. There's one person we need that's holding firm against it. We may not know until very close to ten o'clock. The deadline."

"What are the terms of the major points?" the President asked.

"Taiwan has complete autonomy in virtually all areas of its national life," Philip said quickly. "They are incorporated into the Chinese nation as 'The Maritime State of Taiwan in the People's Republic of China.'"

"Names, names," snapped the President. "What about their military hardware?"

"Yes. That's the only sticking point, from either side. The Taiwanese get to keep their Army, including all the Super Cobra attack helicopters. They keep the Mirage jets and the Knox-class frigates of their Air Force and Navy. No mainland infantry troops ever allowed on the island. But the bulk of the offensive weapons in Taiwan's Navy and Air Force that could hit the mainland—the F-16s, the destroyers, the submarines—as well as the antimissile defenses and the radar systems, are sold and transferred to the People's Republic."

"What?" yelled Ravenhurst. "That's outside, well outside the boundaries that the President set for you."

"It's the best deal we could get," Philip shot back. "And if the Taiwanese agree to it, then we should respect their judgment."

"The Taiwanese are not the only side in this dispute," Ravenhurst said angrily. "The United States is a Pacific power. We are in fact *the* Pacific Power. *We* have to agree to it."

"No!" Philip shouted back. "It's the Taiwanese and the Chinese that will have the missiles exploding on their people. It's *their* decision, not ours. If they agree, then we've got to respect that agreement and support it."

"Tiffany." The President's voice cut through the shouts, and imposed a silence. "Tiffany. What's your perspective on all this?"

Tiffany sat up very straight in her chair. "My perspective?" she stammered. She looked quickly at Philip, then back to the President on the screen, who waited calmly as Ravenhurst's head bobbed beside him, eyes bulging.

"Well, when I arrived here, I probably would have agreed with John," she began, slowly. "This is power politics, and I'm not averse to wielding power."

She took a deep breath.

"But I had a few surprises in store for me here. I've talked with some of the natives—the people here. I sat in a temple yesterday and watched them. I think Philip has a point. We're a long way from D.C. here. These are the people who will go through a war, not us. If they can come to an agreement to avert it—why, it would be horrible of us to force it on them."

President Hayes stared at Tiffany. "Huh," he said.

"Sir, if I may," came Ravenhurst, leaning close to the President. "These are wonderful sentiments. But this is a geopolitical decision. This is about maintaining the United States as the Pacific power. This is—"

"Ever been to Taiwan, Ravenhurst?" cut in Philip. "Ever strolled the streets here, watched Taiwanese children play?"

"No," Ravenhust replied archly, his big eyes glaring at Philip. "But I have written two books about the nuances of power in the Pacific. I am an expert on wielding power, and on the role of war as an instrument of policy—"

"No!" shouted Philip, erupting from his chair and pointing a finger at Ravenhurst. "War is *not* an instrument of policy. War is a *failure* of policy! A failure that gets people killed—

real mothers and fathers and kids *killed*, damn it!"

Ravenhurst shrank back, behind the President. He looked around the

President's massive figure. "But wars are sometimes necessary, and—and happen, and people—why, they move on," he spluttered.

"But it should be *their* decision to go to war, not someone else's sitting in an air-conditioned office five thousand miles away!" thundered Philip.

"Ok, fellas, OK," said the President, his voice still calm. "Settle down. I've heard all I want from each of you."

"And what do you think, grandfather?" said Tiffany quietly.

"I don't know," said the President after a heavy sigh. "I agree with both of them." He put a large hand on his forehead, and stared at his desk.

Philip sat slowly, his face intent upon the President's.

"No more argument from me, Mr. President," he said quietly. "But I do have one further important item of information, that may influence who you listen to last."

"It had better be quick. How far are we from the deadline?"

"Thirty-five minutes, sir. Briefly, I've had several attempts on my life in the week I've been here. Tom can confirm that. We figured out who the assassin was. We cornered him, just last night. In front of a respected journalist, and the Taiwanese negotiator Sung Lee, he confessed that he had been hired by an American to kill me. A former head of the CIA who now advises the President of the United States."

A strangled cry came from Ravenhurst. He glanced around wildly as Hayes slowly turned to him.

"John? What the hell—"

"Nothing can be traced, sir! There's no way he can prove it."

"Look at his face, Mr. President," said Philip. "Just look at his face."

"John!" screamed Tiffany, jumping to her feet. "You nearly got me killed in that restaurant explosion. Why, you—you…" She grabbed the phone from the table and raised it above her head, taking a step toward Ravenhurst's frightened face on the screen.

"Easy, Tiffany," Philip said, taking the phone from her before she could throw it.

"Wow. We had more in common than I thought."

"John," rumbled the President. His voice was soft, but ominous. "You son of a bitch. You could get me impeached! You could cost me my re-election!"

"But they can't prove it!" protested Ravenhurst, his bulging eyes darting wildly around the room.

"These witnesses," the president asked Philip. "They're reliable? Respected?"

"Yes sir. In spades. They are willing to keep it confidential, providing that Ravenhurst is banned from the United States government forever."

"Sir, sir—" spluttered Ravenhurst.

"Quiet!" the President roared. He sat stone still, only his eyes dancing about as he made a thousand political calculations.

"John, is this video being recorded?" he said quietly.

"No, sir. Only you can activate the record mode, sir. It's off. Sir."

"Your end?" the President said, looking at Philip.

"Tom!" Philip yelled.

Tom opened the door and looked in.

"Is this being recorded?"

"Nope. The AIT doesn't have recording capabilities yet for the video teleconferences."

"No, sir. Not recorded at this end, either," said Philip to the President.

The massive head was unmoving again under the mane of silver hair. Finally he grunted.

"John. You've betrayed my trust. Exposed me to—hell, to criminal proceedings. Not to mention nearly getting my granddaughter killed. I know I can rely on you to keep this quiet, since you'll spend the rest of your life behind bars if it gets out. John, get out of here. You have thirty minutes to clean out your office. And clean it out real good, because you're never going to have a position in Washington, D.C. again."

"But, sir!" croaked Ravenhurst.

"Get out!" roared the President.

Ravenhurst's figure could be seen staggering to the door.

"Now, Philip. Do I understand correctly that none of Taiwan's weapons to be transferred to the Communists contain our current generation of electronic systems?"

"That is correct, sir. They're all either one or two generations old."

"The agreement doesn't involve any of our own military forces? There's nothing in it that I'd have to get through the Senate?"

"Correct again. It's not an American treaty, it's an agreement between the People's Republic and Taiwan. We have merely facilitated it. Our signature will be as witness to the agreement, nothing more."

"And as I understand it, this agreement of yours in fact may or may not come through and fly in the next half hour, right?" said the President, his hazel eyes boring into Philip.

"Right. It could go down to the last second before we know. Twenty-eight minutes from now."

"OK. Here's how it's going to be. Listen carefully."

"Just a second, sir. Tom!"

The door opened again.

"Get in here and listen to this, Tom," said Philip.

Tom entered the room and stood beside the table, hands clasped in front.

"I agree with the fine agreement that Philip has brokered, with my guidance and support," began the President. "If China and Taiwan agree by the deadline, then we're all happy and can have a party. Tiffany, you witness the agreement for us. Remember, give your left face to the camera if you can. Don't smile too wide. You'll probably earn a Senate seat this morning, because half the world will be watching."

Tiffany nodded, a stunned look on her face.

"On the other hand, if China and Taiwan don't agree by the deadline, then we've got a war on our hands, and it doesn't matter what kind of pretty speeches Philip makes about war or not. Here's where you need to keep some things in mind. Our information is that the Chinese will wait until ten-fifteen your time to fire up their missiles. That's the real, definitive deadline. It doesn't matter how close you are to an agreement or any damn thing. If they don't see a signed and sealed agreement by ten-fifteen—they launch."

The President stopped, fished a handkerchief out of his pocket, and rubbed his brow, which was red and pouring sweat.

"Philip—and Tom—if the agreement falls through, your job is to get my granddaughter off that fucking island—pardon my French, Tiffany—before ten twenty-five. That's when their missiles have crossed the Strait and begin coming down on Taipei, ten minutes after launch. That means by ten twenty-five you have to be with Tiffany on Air Force Two and the plane has to be airborne and headed due east. Understand? Do you goddamn well understand this completely?"

"Positive on that, sir," said Tom crisply. "We're going to be a bit busy here, sir. Can you have someone at your end communicate with Air Force Two, have them expecting us and the engines warmed up and the runway cleared?"

"Positive on that, Tom," said the President. He turned to Philip and Tiffany.

"Good luck, kids. Just make sure I see you again, whichever way it goes."

"Thank you, Mr. President," said Philip, rising. "Come on, Tiffany. Tom, pick up the copies of the agreement from the AIT people. And call Sung Lee. He promised us his helicopter to take us to the soccer stadium where we're signing things. Have them pick us up here in five minutes. And don't forget some pens for the signing."

mountain

Chapter Forty Seven

Nine forty-five am

The helicopter approached the Taiwan National University soccer stadium from the east. The stadium was packed, with only a narrow open space around the platform on the field where the dignitaries sat, hopefully for a signing ceremony. Sung Lee's pilot spoke into his microphone, and a phalanx of security men began beating the crowd back to the east of the platform.

"Bring us down as close to the platform as you can," Philip said. "We may need to get to Chiang Kai Shek International in a big hurry." The pilot glanced over at Philip, and the craft veered closer to the platform to begin its descent.

"Whose is that?" Tiffany asked, pointing to another helicopter hovering above the stadium to their left.

"People's Republic," Tom said. "That'll be for Zhu. He's making sure he can get out of here fast, too."

Their chopper set down twenty feet from the platform, nearly crushing a dozen spectators who resisted the security guards' efforts to push them back.

"Stand by," Philip said to the pilot. "How long from here to Chiang Kai Shek International?"

"In a hurry? Not worrying about landing instructions?" answered the pilot, a young Chinese with a British accent. "Ten minutes, maybe a bit less."

"All right. The same ten minutes it takes the missiles to get here. If we leave by ten-fifteen, we're at Air Force Two and airborne at ten twenty-five when the missiles hit. Radio them and make sure you know where they are—they'll be cleared for takeoff on one of the runways."

"Roger that," said the pilot.

"You hear that, Tom?"

"Affirmative. We're off the platform by ten-fifteen."

Tom opened the helicopter door and helped Tiffany, Dirk, and Baden out. When Philip joined them, clutching the three copies of the peace agreement to his chest, Tom and five of the security guards formed a ring around the group. They were instantly engulfed by a shouting crowd. Tom and the other guards shoved and slugged their way through the crowd. Tiffany grabbed Philip's arm and stumbled after him as he tried to keep up with Tom. Dirk and Baden cowered along behind them in the ring. It took almost a minute to fight their way through the crowd to the raised platform, where the signing would take place—if it took place. Wild-eyed people were shrieking in Chinese at them from every side. Philip guessed they were demanding to know if war would come today. It was a good question. Philip didn't know the answer.

Ahead of him, Tom shoved through the last of the crowd and stepped onto stairs. He and the other security men held the crowd back while Philip, Tiffany, Dirk and Baden hurried up the seven steps and emerged onto the platform.

"Pens," Philip yelled at Tom as he passed. "Bring them up to the center table."

Straight ahead, at the center table, Zhu and his key advisers sat on the left, with the rest of the team behind them. All looked exhausted, their faces and shoulders sagging. Zhu was speaking rapidly on a cell phone, nodding as he spoke. When he saw Philip climb onto the platform, he raised a hand, and motioned towards himself.

Philip glanced to the right end of the table, where Lee's principle advisers sat. Lee was not in sight. That can't be a good sign, Philip thought, setting the bulky accords in the center of the table.

Taiwanese officials, some in uniform, most not, sat in six rows of chairs fronting the table. Philip recognized the Taiwanese president. The others were unknown to him, cabinet members and business leaders, he guessed. In the very back row, Meiling sat next to one of the dozen television cameras, all with blinking red lights, recording the scene. He made his way toward her with Tiffany, and stumbled over a figure bending low over a seated man. It was Lee. The seated man wore a naval uniform, and an angry, stubborn face. They were talking fast, in urgent tones. More like arguing. Philip said nothing as he passed.

"Meiling. Keep Tiffany out of trouble here. I'll signal to you if and when we need her up front. That's Admiral Reng, the one Zhu is talking to?"

Meiling nodded, apprehension in her eyes.

"If this doesn't pull together, then it's your job to get Tiffany to me at the stairs as Tom and I exit. We'll be in a rush, not a second to lose to get to the helicopter. Do you understand?"

Meiling locked into Philip's eyes. "Yes."

"But Meiling will come with us, won't she?" asked Tiffany.

"No," Meiling said. "My home is here."

Philip put his hand behind Meiling's neck. It was wet. From the humidity, he wondered? Or had she just gotten back from her morning swim? He smiled into her eyes. She kissed his lips, then pushed him away. "You've got work to do, Philip. Hurry."

"Everything OK?" Dirk asked as Philip arrived at the front table.

"Evidently not quite," Philip said. He glanced at Lee's empty seat, then to Lee, who was dragging the Admiral down the line of dignitaries in the front row, making short remarks to each. The Admiral was stone-faced.

"That's the lone holdout. But he's important," he said to Dirk as he checked his watch. Ten minutes before ten.

"Looks like Lee is putting some heat on him," Dirk remarked. "Showing him everyone else who's fallen in line." Red blotches were scattered over her ashen face, and red lines crisscrossed her eyes. She showed every sign of having been up all night, working hard. "Is this going to fly?" Dirk asked, a glint of panic in her bloodshot eyes. Philip didn't have the vaguest idea whether it was going to work or not. From the attention Lee was giving the Admiral, it wasn't flying yet.

Zhu's gesture came to mind, and he jerked to his feet. "Zhu has something to say to me," he said to Dirk. Alarm complemented the hint of panic already in her eyes.

He edged sideways down the table to where Zhu was seated. The two of them turned away from the table, facing out over the sea of spectators in the soccer stadium. The noise from the crowd rendered their words private.

"I have the Chairman on the phone," said Zhu. "He insists on one small change. We are willing to pay the three and a half billion U.S. dollars for the transferred arsenal. But the money must go to schools, hospitals, and social programs. He cannot permit the funds to go to the Taiwan military men."

A groan escaped Philip's lips.

"I know. But he insists. Mr. Lee has his problems with his military people," Zhu spat out, jerking his head toward Lee and the Admiral. "Well, my Chairman has generals he must placate, also. They will not countenance that amount of money going straight to the Taiwanese generals."

"Well, it's for the remnant of their military forces, not the generals themselves," Philip said.

"Don't be foolish, Mr. Dawson. Let me assure you, as Mr. Lee will, that nearly all the funds will go straight to the Generals' pockets."

Of course. Philip knew he was right.

"Why don't you and Mr. Lee and I meet, behind the front table here, for a moment," Philip suggested, in a coldly polite tone that belied the anger rushing up in him.

Lee was making his way to the front table finally. Philip motioned him to a small space between two steel poles thrusting lights into the sky behind the platform. Banks of electrical equipment blocked the three men from the table.

"How have you made out with the Admiral?" Philip asked Lee.

Lee's face was drawn. He looked very much the oldest member of the trio. Sweat trickled down his temples, and beaded above his lip.

"The son of a bitch was holding out for money. It's one of the two passions of his filthy life," he hissed, surprising Philip with the language and the intensity. "My apologies, but it will take four billion dollars for the agreement to work, not the three and a half we agreed to among ourselves."

"Impossible!" Zhu snorted.

"And Mr. Zhu has a new stipulation too," said Philip. "Seems his Chairman is insisting that the money be given not to the military, but to schools and hospitals—social agencies."

Lee stared at Philip for a second, then his face fell in utter defeat. He slumped against the steel pole beside him. His eyes suddenly jerked skyward, and he searched the horizon to the west. Toward the coast of Fujian. Where the missiles were coming from.

"No!" Philip insisted, clamping a steel grip on both men's arms. "We're too close to lose it now. Let's see. Let's see." He thought furiously. Keep it simple. Don't complicate things. Deal with the issues on the table. When all else fails—and that's where we're at—try splitting the differences.

"OK. If the People's Republic can afford three and a half billion, they can afford four, to get their reunification. Of that four billion, let's give the majority to schools and hospitals. Say two and a half billion. The People's Republic will like that. But Mr. Lee needs money for his admirals and generals. We'll give the remaining one and a half billion to the Taiwan military. That's still a lot of money."

Anguished groans from Zhu and Lee, and angry shaking of their heads.

"No! Don't shake your heads," Philip shouted to them. "Make it work, damn it. Somehow make it work."

Zhu flicked a cell phone out of his pocket and angrily jabbed some buttons. He turned his back to them, and spoke furiously.

Philip checked his watch. Four minutes before ten.

"Mr. Lee—Uncle Sung—can you make one and a half billion work for the military, if Taiwan is getting another two and a half billion for schools and hospitals?"

Lee was still slumped against the pole. He shook his head, then raised his eyes again to the west, searching the sky with anguished eyes.

"Uncle Sung—does the military have schools and hospitals?" Philip asked.

"Of course," Lee said dully, his eyes glazing over.

"So you'll decommission them, make them officially civilian, and give most of the two and a half billion to them. Would that help?"

"A bit. But it won't be enough." His face was twitching, and tears brimmed in his eyes. "Philip. Nephew. Take my helicopter. Get off the island. Now."

"Uncle Sung" said Philip, reaching out and touching his arm. "I'm not leaving. I'll get Tiffany Hayes and Tom to your chopper, but I'm not joining them. I'm coming back here."

"What?" said Lee, a wild look in his eyes.

"Uncle Sung. You're going to need help. It will be horrible here. I have to stay. It's a family obligation. Nephew to Uncle."

Lee's eyes shifted from wild to disbelieving, then returned to a wild, intense look. "Ma Tsu has blessed me," he muttered in a cracked voice. "Even as my island is wracked by flames and death."

"No!" Philip said. "We're not there yet. I'll think of something."

Zhu was shouting into his cell phone now, and jabbing the air with his free hand.

Philip kicked the steel pole. Think! he ordered himself. He kicked the pole again, hard. What else is on the table? Admiral Reng is the sticker. What else would he like to have?

"Uncle Sung!" he blurted out to Lee, grabbing his arm again and pulling him away from the pole, forcing his eyes off the sky. "Didn't you say Admiral Reng had two passions in his life? Money is one. What is the other?"

"Young women," Lee said, sagging in Philip's grip. "Beautiful, compliant, energetic young women." He slumped back against the pole. His bruised temple banged against the steel, and he winced. But then he jerked up, standing straight again, his eyes suddenly alive.

"By the gods," he muttered. He looked straight into Philip's eyes. "Maybe." He disappeared around the bank of electrical equipment.

Zhu snapped his phone off just as Lee disappeared.

"All right," he said angrily. "Four billion, if the majority goes to schools and hospitals. But that must be absolutely the last change. If anything else comes up—anything—then I'm catching that helicopter to get off this cursed island."

"It'll be tough to land that thing, if the crowds get any more panicky," said Philip, looking around them.

"It won't need to land. I'll go up to it," Zhu said, unbuttoning his coat and revealing a harness underneath, with a hook at chest level.

"They'll lower a line for you?"

Zhu nodded. "Philip. We have until ten minutes after ten for this to work. Everything signed. If it's not done by then—no matter how close we are—the missiles get launched. You should know that."

"Ten-ten? We were told ten-fifteen." Philip checked his watch. Ten o'clock exactly. A sudden hush swept the stadium.

The deadline had arrived. Thousands of eyes searched the sky to the west.

"I should know," insisted Zhu, glancing up from his wrist. "The missiles are launched at ten-ten. Ten minutes from now. I will be airborne by then, racing due west back to a very deep shelter north of Fuzhou." He buttoned his coat and looked around. "I may even get there before your own missiles hit our coast. Where's Lee?"

"Off to work on Admiral Reng again, I think," said Philip.

Philip and Zhu made their way back to the front table. Lee was with the Taiwanese President and Admiral Reng, off to the side of the stage. All three were whispering urgently, and chopping the air with their hands. The sudden silence that had gripped the stadium at ten was giving way to a nervous roar welling up from the crowd. All eyes were on the western horizon. It was two minutes after ten. Philip bent down to Dirk and Baden, and told them to enter the financial changes into the documents. An AIT staffer followed suit in the two Chinese versions. Philip closed his eyes to concentrate, and shouted the amendments to the agreement over the bedlam erupting on all sides, as Dirk and Baden and the staffer wrote furiously.

A noise came from a distance, low and jarring, rocking the platform. Philip looked over his shoulder, past the light poles. Bank after bank of jet fighters appeared on the gray horizon. Zhu was also staring at the planes, a look of horror on his face. A shocked silence again enveloped the stadium, and five thousand people froze. In the midst of it all, oblivious to the planes and everything else, Dirk, Baden and the AIT staffer scribbled the last changes into the agreements, while Lee and the admiral and the president whispered and gesticulated at the edge of the stage. The planes roared toward the stadium. Screams broke out in the crowd, which surged in every direction.

"Whose planes are those?" Philip yelled over the chaos.

Zhu was peering up at the first of the planes roaring overhead. "The F-16s," he said grimly. "They're airborne, awaiting our F-8s coming on the heels of the missiles."

Philip motioned Tom over.

"The launch time isn't ten-fifteen. It's ten-ten." He checked his watch. "Three minutes from now. Go get Tiffany." Tom sprinted off.

The roar of the crowd increased. A ring of security men around the platform kicked at hands reaching onto the stage, and threw people off as they clambered up. Philip glanced down the stage. Tiffany was wild-eyed beside Meiling, who had her hand on Tiffany's arm. Tom arrived and grabbed Tiffany.

Philip glanced to the only three people ignoring the planes now. The Taiwanese President disengaged from Lee and Admiral Reng, and walked woodenly to his seat, trying to keep despair off his twitching face. As he sat, he raised his wrist and stared at his watch. He looked quickly up into the sky. Tears streamed down his face as he gazed to the west.

Philip checked his watch. Eight minutes after. The downdraft of Zhu's Chinese helicopter washed over the stage as it positioned itself directly above them. The roar of the stadium crowd shook the platform. A white line dropped from the chopper and began to snake its way down. Zhu stood and unbuttoned his coat, flipping the ring out from the harness. His security men formed a circle around him, reaching up for the line.

Four other security men converged on the front table as Tom got there with the horrified Tiffany, her eyes wide and bulging. Tom drew his gun from his shoulder holster, and the other men followed suit. Dirk and Baden stood.

"This could get messy," Tom shouted above the gathering tumult. "We'll try to keep you in a ring, but some of us might not make it. Head for the chopper. Fight your way there, no matter what. Philip, Miss Hayes—don't wait for anyone who's fallen."

Tom reached out and grabbed Philip's arm.

Philip jerked his arm away and looked at his watch. Ten-o-nine.

"We've got another minute," he shouted at Tom.

"It'll take a minute or more to get to the chopper, no matter how many people we kill on the way," Tom shouted back. "Let's go. Now!"

Philip looked to the right edge of the stage as Tom dragged Tiffany to the steps and Dirk and Baden scrambled over the table behind them. At the edge of the stage, Lee draped his arm over Admiral Reng's stocky figure. He whispered something in the Admiral's ear. The Admiral looked sharply up at Lee, stared for a long moment, then looked out over the screaming crowd. The backwash from Zhu's helicopter waved Reng's and Lee's hair about wildly. Philip heard a metallic snap, and turned to see Zhu snap the chopper line into his harness ring. His eyes met Philip's—they were not frightened, but sad.

Philip turned back desperately to Lee and the Admiral. He saw the Admiral nod into Lee's face.

Tom grabbed Philip, rough, and began to drag him to the stairs, where Tiffany was halfway down, the guards hitting people to either side with the butts of their pistols.

"No! Tom! Lee's got it!"

Lee was shouting at the top of his lungs, his wild face grim as he dragged the Admiral to the table. Lee shoved a pen into the Admiral's hand, and forced it to the front page of the agreement. The Admiral scribbled his signature, then threw the pen down. Lee picked it up and quickly scrawled his own signature.

Philip looked to Zhu. He was on his tiptoes, the line from the helicopter attached and taut. Zhu whipped out his cell phone, jabbed it, and yelled into it as his toes barely lifted off the platform. Tom stopped dead in his tracks, and joined Philip and Lee and everyone else on the platform in staring at Zhu, dangling from the line.

Had the missiles been launched?

Zhu yelled again into the phone. He put his free hand to his ear, and listened. Yelled again. He looked straight at Philip, eyes shining. He raised his hand. Thumb up. Tears streamed down his face as he unsnapped the line from his harness and dropped back to the platform.

"Get Tiffany up here!" Philip screamed at Tom. Tom let go of Philip's jacket and sprinted to the stairs.

Philip put his face next to Lee's and shouted into his ear. "What did you give him, to make him come around?"

Hoarse, cracked words tumbled from Lee's trembling lips. "I gave him my other mistress, Hsiao Loo. And my seaside mansion to enjoy her in."

Philip froze.

"No."

"Yes." Lee stood ramrod straight, but his body swayed slightly. "I am too old for mistresses. My official family, in Taipei, has a new family member— Hsiao Pang's little girl. Too many ghosts haunt the seaside mansion."

A lone tear trickled down his cheek. He made no move to brush it away.

Tiffany was gingerly making her way back up the stairs amid the tumult, a disbelieving look on her face.

Zhu arrived at the agreements, picked up a pen, and signed them.

"Tiffany, we made it!" Philip yelled above the roaring crowd as she arrived at the table. "The cameras are over there. Remember—left side of your face. Take your time and sign it good, kid."

The dazed look on Tiffany's face was slowly replaced by a smile, which grew as she accepted a pen from Philip. Smiling much too broadly, she raised the pen above her head, to cheers from ten thousand throats. She waved it a time or two, tempered the smile on her face, and bent down to the agreements. With a flourish she signed, then grabbed the hands of the reluctant Zhu and Sung Lee and paraded to the side of the stage. The tumult from the stadium crowd engulfed them. She led the two men around the platform, hands raised high in triumph, greeting every segment of the roaring, chanting, weeping crowd. The fleet of F-16s began its second sweep over the stadium, completing the pandemonium.

Tiffany gestured to Philip to join them. Philip paused, then shook his head. He looked beyond the trio, to the back of the platform. Meiling stood on a chair between two television cameras. She was laughing, her eyes dancing in the morning light. Philip had to have her in his arms. In his life. He maneuvered toward her, brushing aside chairs and dignitaries. She watched Philip approach, her eyes now calm, steady. Islands of black in a sea of white, curving shore.

Acknowledgments

I gratefully acknowledge the kind assistance tendered me from all quarters in my several visits to Taiwan through the years. Dr. James C. Y. Chu, former Minister for Overseas Chinese Affairs of the Republic of China and former colleague at California State University, Chico, opened many doors for me. Newspaper practices in Taiwan were illustrated by gracious hosts at the venerable *Central Daily News*: then-Publisher Hwei-chen Huang, columnist Janice J. Yu, and reporter Diana Meng. C. T. Su, former Deputy Director General of the Tourism Bureau of the Republic of China, arranged for visits to the rock-climbing coastal region of northeastern Taiwan. Robert Egan of *The Placemakers* was very helpful with introductions and encouragement. For all this assistance I am grateful.

Much of the material on jade and jade-carving was garnered from the excellent permanent jade exhibits in the British Museum in London and the Asian Art Museum in San Francisco. I thank exchange student Frank Wu of Ningpo for kindly assembling the Chinese characters used in chapter headings.

Practical and direct rock-climbing experience was generously provided in Yosemite National Park by my Valley Oaks Village friends Richard Perrelli and Bill Travers, who also critiqued my description of Philip and Meiling's adventure on the cliffs of northeastern Taiwan. My geologist colleague Ann Bykerk-Kauffman enlightened me on Taiwan's geology. My biologist colleague John Mahoney of the Department of Biological Sciences at California State University, Chico kindly demonstrated procedures for the isolation of proteins from biological agents for my edification. Genial explorations into the art of drinking scotch were provided by my Valley Oaks Village comrades Cal McCarthy, Michael Cross, Scott Gunderson, Jay Goldberg, Richard Perrelli, and Bill Travers.

About the Author

Raymond Barnett studied Chinese history and language at Yale University, where he graduated Magna cum Laude. After serving in the U.S. Army in Vietnam, he earned his Ph.D. in biology from Duke University and taught biology at California State University, Chico for three decades. He was instrumental in the founding of the Gateway Science Museum there, for which he was named "The Father of the Museum" by the museum Board.

Barnett cultivated his interest in the Far East during his biology career, traveling extensively in China, Taiwan, Japan, and Korea, and writing the historical novel *Jade and Fire* (published by Random House) and the Taoism primer *Relax, You're Already Home: everyday Taoist habits for a richer life* (published by Penguin/Putnam). Since his retirement in 2003, Barnett has written *The China Ultimatum*, a thriller set in the near future, *The Death of Mycroft*, a Sherlock Holmes pastiche, and *The Return to Treasure Island*, a young adult novel set in 18th century Cuba (published by iUniverse).

For relaxation, Barnett enjoys backpacking in the Sierra Nevada high country, snorkeling in Hawaii, and bicycling in Chico. Further information and slides of his travels can be found on his website, www.raymondbarnett.com.